The
DECISION

The DECISION

PRAIRIE STATE FRIENDS *Book One*

WANDA *E.* BRUNSTETTER

BARBOUR BOOKS
An Imprint of Barbour Publishing, Inc.

Cover design: Faceout Studio, www.faceoutstudio.com

For more information about Wanda E. Brunstetter, please visit her website at www.wandabrunstetter.com

Published by Barbour Books, an imprint of Barbour Publishing, Inc., 1810 Barbour Drive, Uhrichsville, Ohio 44683, www.barbourbooks.com

Our mission is to inspire the world with the life-changing message of the Bible.

ecpa Member of the
Evangelical Christian
Publishers Association

Printed in the United States of America.

To caregivers everywhere,
who selflessly give to others.

Blessed are the merciful:
for they shall obtain mercy.
MATTHEW 5:7

PROLOGUE

laine Schrock shivered and pulled her woolen shawl tightly around her shoulders as she stepped out of the house Saturday evening. The air was cold and windy, like it had been most of the winter, yet it was two weeks into spring. They ought to be having warmer weather by now, but winter didn't seem to want to give in just yet. Last week, the temperatures rose into the upper seventies, and everyone caught spring fever. Neighbors and friends began preparing their gardens, and fields had already been plowed and were ready to be planted. Green shoots from flowers were coming up, and buds on the maples had turned red. Unfortunately, this time of year it wasn't unusual for the weather to tease people into thinking winter was finally gone. The calendar might say it was April, but Mother Nature said otherwise.

Heading toward the barn, where her grandfather had gone to check on the horses, Elaine hurried her footsteps. The wind howled noisily. She glanced toward the darkening sky and shivered. It almost felt like it could snow.

Elaine entered the barn and headed for the horses' stalls. "Grandpa," she called, seeing no sign of him in the first stall where Grandma's horse, Misty, had bedded down for the night.

She stopped to listen, but there was no response.

Moving on to the stall where her own horse, Daisy, was kept, Elaine still saw no sign of Grandpa. When she reached across the gate to stroke the mare's head, she heard a low moan coming from the next stall.

Hurrying over, Elaine gasped. Grandpa lay in the straw a few feet from his horse, Dusty. "Grandpa, what happened? Did you slip and fall?" she asked, opening the gate and quickly entering the stall.

Grandpa's eyelids fluttered, and he clutched his chest. "Lainie," he murmured, using the nickname he'd given her when she was a girl.

"I'm here, Grandpa," she said, dropping to her knees beside him. "Please, tell me what's wrong."

"I—I am *katzodemich*," he mumbled.

"You're short of breath?" Elaine's heart pounded when he gave a feeble nod. Although she tried to remain calm, she couldn't help noticing Grandpa's pale skin and the bluish tint to his fingers and lips.

"Lie still, Grandpa," she murmured. "I'll run out to the phone shanty and call for help."

"No, wait," he said, clasping her hand. "There's something I need to ask you."

"What is it?" Elaine leaned closer to him, barely able to make out his words.

"If I don't make it—will you promise me something?" Grandpa's voice seemed to be growing weaker.

"Of course, Grandpa. What is it?"

"Look after your grandma for me. She—she'll need someone to care for her now. C–can you promise me that?"

Tears welled in Elaine's eyes as she held his cold hand. "I promise that I'll always be there for Grandma, no matter what." She gave his fingers a reassuring squeeze. "Help will be here soon, Grandpa. Don't worry, you're going to be fine."

Elaine rose to her feet and dashed out of the barn. It had begun to rain hard, and the bleakness of her mood matched that of the foreboding sky. Tension mounted in her chest as she raced on shaky legs toward the phone shanty. The cold, wet drops made it hard to hurry as she slipped along, trying not to lose her footing. "Dear Lord," she prayed out loud, "please let my grandpa be okay. Grandma needs him, and so do I."

CHAPTER 1

$\mathcal{T}$ears coursed down Elaine's cheeks and dripped onto the front of her black mourning dress. The mourners had arrived at the cemetery a few minutes ago, ready to put Grandpa Schrock's body to rest in the ground. He'd died of an apparent heart attack just moments after the paramedics arrived Saturday evening. This morning, because Grandma wanted it that way, Grandpa's funeral service had been held in a large tent outside their home, rather than in the Otto Center, where some local Amish funerals took place.

During the service, one of the ministers quoted Matthew 5:7: "Blessed are the merciful: for they shall obtain mercy." Grandpa had always been merciful to others, and so had Grandma. When Elaine was five years old and her parents had been killed in a buggy accident, her father's parents had taken her in. They'd been wonderful substitute parents, teaching, loving, and nurturing Elaine, yet asking so little in return. She only hoped she could live a life that would be pleasing not only to Grandma, but also to God.

If I'd only found Grandpa sooner, could he have been saved? Elaine wondered. *Oh Grandpa, I already miss you so much.*

Elaine glanced over at her grandmother, standing to her left with hands folded, as though praying. Her eyes brimmed with tears. Grandma Schrock was a strong woman, but the grief she felt over losing her husband of forty-five years was evident on her face. And why wouldn't it be? Elaine's grandparents always had a deep, abiding love for each other, and it showed in everything they said and did as a couple. Elaine hoped to experience that kind of love when she got married someday.

Taking Grandma's hand, Elaine's throat constricted as Grandpa's simply crafted wooden coffin was placed inside a rough pine box that had already been set in the opening of the grave. Death for the earthly body was final, yet she was confident that Grandpa's soul lived on and that he now resided in a much better place. Grandpa had lived the Christian life in every sense of the word, and he'd told Elaine many times that he loved the Lord with all his heart, soul, and mind. Yes, Elaine felt certain that Grandpa was in heaven with Jesus right now and perhaps even looking down on them with a smile. Did Grandma feel it too? Quite possibly she did, for she gave Elaine's fingers a gentle squeeze as she turned her face toward the blue sky. *Thank You, Lord, for giving us a sunny day to say our goodbyes,* Elaine prayed.

A slight chill hung in the air, but at least it wasn't raining, and only a gentle breeze whispered among the many headstones surrounding them. A bird chirped from a tree outside the fenced-in graveyard, as though offering comfort and a hope for the future.

A group of men from their church district began to sing while the grave was filled in by the pallbearers. Elaine winced. Although she had been quite young when her parents died, she still remembered standing in the cemetery during the burial, holding her grandparents' hands. Elaine's maternal grandparents, who had since died, had been living in Oklahoma back then. They had decided not to uproot Elaine from the only home she'd known, and she was grateful that Grandma and Grandpa Schrock had been more than willing to take her in. As the last shovelful of dirt was placed over the coffin, Elaine remembered her final words with Grandpa and her promise to take care of Grandma. *And I will,* Elaine reminded herself. *For as long as Grandma needs me, I will be there for her.*

Bishop Levi Kauffman asked the congregation to pray the Lord's Prayer silently, which concluded the graveside service. It was time to start back to the house for the funeral meal their friends and neighbors had prepared, but Elaine had no appetite. She'd be going through the motions and doing what was expected of her. Grandma would no doubt do the same.

Scanning the faces of close friends and church members, Elaine saw that the heartache she and Grandma felt today was shared by all. Although nothing had been said during the funeral service earlier this morning about Grandpa's attributes, everyone knew that Lloyd Schrock was a kind, caring man. Having farmed in this community from the time he'd married Grandma until his recent retirement, Grandpa had proved his strong work ethic and commitment to the community. How many times had Elaine witnessed him getting up at the crack of dawn to head out to the fields without a word of complaint? Grandma always got up with him and made sure he ate a hearty breakfast before beginning another busy day. She'd done the same for Elaine throughout her school days.

Elaine would miss their shared meals, as well as Grandpa's smile and the stories he often told. On cold winter evenings, they would sit by the fire, enjoying apple cider and some of Grandma's delicious pumpkin or apple pie. All the wonderful times the three of them had together would be cherished memories.

As folks turned from the grave site and began walking back to their buggies, Elaine's friends Priscilla Herschberger and Leah Mast approached Elaine and her grandmother and hugged them warmly. No words were necessary. These two young women had been Elaine's best friends since they were children, and even though at twenty-two Elaine was the youngest of the three, they'd always gotten along well.

"Are you coming over to our house for the meal?" Elaine asked.

Priscilla and Leah both nodded.

"We'll do whatever we can to help out today so you and your grandma can relax and visit with those who attend." Leah, whose hair was golden brown like a chestnut, gave Elaine's arm a tender squeeze.

"You can count on us, not just for today, but in the days ahead as you and your grandma strive to adjust." Priscilla's dark eyes, matching the color of her hair, revealed the depth of her love.

"*Danki*, I appreciate you both so much." Given a choice, Elaine would prefer to keep busy, but she'd be expected to visit with the guests, so she wouldn't think of turning down her friends' offers of help.

"I am grateful for you too," Grandma said, her voice trembling a bit. "I value all of our friends in this community."

As Elaine and Grandma moved slowly toward their buggy, Elaine caught sight of Jonah Miller heading her way. For nearly a year, she and Jonah had been courting, and Elaine was fairly certain it was just a matter of time before he proposed marriage. A week ago, she would have eagerly agreed to marry Jonah if he'd asked. But with Grandpa dying, she needed to be there for Grandma. Perhaps later, once Grandma had recovered sufficiently, Elaine would be ready for marriage. But she would continue to look after Grandma, making sure that all of her needs were met.

"I'm sorry for your loss," Jonah said, his coffee-colored eyes showing the depth of his concern as he looked first at Grandma and then Elaine. "If there's anything I can do for either of you, please let me know," he added, pulling his fingers through the back of his thick, curly black hair, sticking out from under the brim of his black dress hat.

"We will," Grandma murmured. "Danki."

All Elaine could manage was a brief nod. If she spoke to Jonah, her tears would flow, and she might not be able to stop them. There would be time for her and Jonah to talk—perhaps later this afternoon or evening if he stayed around after the meal that long. Jonah had a business to run, and he might need to get back to work this afternoon.

As though reading her thoughts, Jonah touched Elaine's arm and said, "I'll see you back at your house." Nodding in Grandma's direction, he sprinted for his horse and buggy.

⟡

As Jonah stepped into his buggy and picked up the reins, he thought about Elaine and her grandmother and wondered what they would do now that Lloyd was gone. Would they continue to offer sit-down dinners in their home for curious tourists, or would Elaine find some other employment in order to help out financially? Although Lloyd had retired from farming, he'd continued to earn money by selling a good deal of the produce they raised to a local store where many Amish, as well as some English, shopped. He wondered if Elaine would end up taking over that responsibility.

I could ask Elaine to marry me now. That would solve any financial worries she and her grandma might have. Jonah smiled. *It would also make me a happy man.*

Jonah had been unlucky in love—at least when he'd lived in Pennsylvania. He had fallen in love with Meredith, a beautiful young woman whom he'd met several years before while visiting Florida. Meredith had believed that her husband was killed in a tragic bus accident, and after a suitable time of courting, Jonah and Meredith made plans to be married. But on the eve of their wedding, Meredith's husband, Luke, showed up. It turned out that he hadn't been on that bus after all, but had suffered from amnesia because of a beating he'd received at the Philadelphia bus station. For over a year, Meredith had grieved for Luke, until she'd finally given her heart to Jonah. When Luke showed up, claiming his wife and child, Jonah's whole world had turned upside down. Knowing he needed to get away from Lancaster County and begin again, a year and a half ago Jonah had moved to Arthur, Illinois, where his twin sister, Jean, lived with her family. Jean had also suffered a great loss when her first husband, Silas, was killed in a tragic accident. But since then, she had remarried. Jean had two children, Rebecca and Stephen by her first husband, and now she and Nathan had a baby boy named Ezekiel.

Jonah's bishop from childhood used to say, *"Everything happens for a reason. God can take the tragedies in our lives and use them for something good."* That was true in his sister's life, for she seemed happy and content. Jonah had also found happiness and love again when he'd met Elaine. He looked forward to the future and hoped to make the pretty blond his wife someday. But while she and her grandma were recovering from this great loss, he wouldn't bring up the subject of marriage. Instead, he'd be there for her, offering support in every way. When the time was right, he'd propose.

Thinking about the others who had been at the

cemetery, Jonah reflected on how Sara Stutzman had looked as though she might break down at any moment. Sara's husband, Harley, had been killed by a falling tree ten months ago. Attending Lloyd's funeral and going to the graveside service must have been difficult for her, especially given that Harley's grave wasn't more than ten feet from where Lloyd was buried.

It was hard for Jonah too, because he and Harley had been good friends. Since Jonah was courting Elaine, he had to be careful not to offer Sara too much support. But he, as well as several other men from their community, had gone over to Sara's several times to help out with chores. Jonah still dropped by occasionally to check on Sara and her two-year-old son, Mark. Usually Jonah's sister, Jean, was with him, as she and Sara were good friends. He wondered if Sara would get married again, since it would be better for Mark if he had a father.

But that's really none of my business, Jonah told himself. *If it's meant for Sara to marry again, she'll choose the right man when the time comes.*

❧

Back at the house, Elaine visited a bit and then headed for her bedroom to retrieve a gift she'd purchased the week before for Leah. As she walked down the hall, each step was a struggle. Walking into her room on the main floor, Elaine quietly closed the door. The voices from those who had gathered in the yard, as well as from inside the house, became muffled.

She stood by the bedroom window, her head leaning against the cool glass. Gazing outside at the people who were visiting in the yard, she was overwhelmed by how many friends Grandpa had made over the years. Elaine watched with blurry vision as Priscilla and Leah and a few other women dashed around, making sure food and drinks were readily available for everyone. It was nice to see Grandma receiving so much support on such a difficult day. For Elaine, it was like losing her father all over again, only worse because she'd been with Grandpa a lot longer. Grandma's heart was aching too. It would take some time to work through all of this, and they would need to rely on God.

Away from well-meaning people, the tears Elaine had held in for most of the morning pushed quickly to the surface. Quietly, she let them fall, covering her mouth to stifle the cries. Grandpa was gone, yet it seemed as though he were still here. His presence would be felt in this house for a long time. Grandpa's voice seemed to whisper in Elaine's ear: *"Make each day count, Lainie, no matter what. Things happen for a reason, and although we may not understand it, in time, you'll find the answers you seek."*

Grandma used to remind Elaine of similar things, often saying, *"The Lord knows what is best for each of His children."*

God, is all of this really what's best for me? Elaine's jaw clenched. *First, You took my parents, and now You've taken Grandpa, whom we need so much. I feel like I'm in a dark tunnel without any light to guide me out.*

She could stand in her bedroom and sob all day, but she had to get ahold of herself. It was time for her to support Grandma, just as she and Grandpa had always been there for her.

Elaine wiped away the tears with her apron and went to her closet to get Leah's gift, a bag of daffodil bulbs from the market. Leah's favorite color was yellow, and Elaine thought her friend would enjoy planting them and seeing them bloom every spring. She had enough bulbs to give half to Priscilla. She hadn't planned it this way, but it would be her way of saying thank you for all they were doing to make things easier on her and Grandma. She would ask them to plant the flowers in memory of Grandpa.

Elaine hesitated, wishing she could stay in her room a little longer. She took a deep breath, squeezing her eyes tightly shut. Grandma must want to be alone in her grief too, and yet throughout the funeral, graveside service, and now here for the meal, she had put on a brave face in the presence of others.

How can one go on after losing their soul mate and partner for life? Elaine wondered. *How does a wife begin each new day, knowing her husband is gone and won't be coming back?* First Grandma had lost her only son, and now her husband was gone. *Oh Lord,* Elaine prayed, *help me to be there for her in every way, offering all of the comfort and care she will need in order to get through each day.*

Elaine thought of Jonah and wondered what it would be like if she'd never met him. She cared deeply for Jonah and hoped to have a future with him, but how fair would it be for him to have to help her care for Grandma? The most difficult part of today was behind her, but now the real work would begin. It was time to pick up the pieces of their lives and try to move on.

CHAPTER 2

That evening after all the food was cleared away and everyone had gone home, Elaine went out to the barn to feed the horses. The sound of her steady stride had apparently alerted the animals of feeding time and sent the buggy horses into whinnying and kicking at their stalls. Patches and two of their other barn cats seemed excited to see Elaine, as they skittered across the lawn and pawed at the hem of her dress. "Not now, you three. I'm too busy to play right now."

When Elaine stepped inside, she was greeted by familiar smells—grain, hay, dust, and the strong odor of horseflesh and urine from the horses' stalls. They really needed to be cleaned, but that could wait for another day. She was too tired to lift a pitchfork, and it would be all she could manage just to feed the horses this evening.

As Elaine approached the stall where Grandpa's horse was kept, she bit back a huge sob. This was the last place she'd seen her grandfather alive, when he'd asked her to look out for Grandma. Grandpa had obviously known he was dying.

"I will be here to help Grandma through her grief," Elaine murmured. "And she'll be here for me."

A rustling noise behind Elaine caused her to jump. "*Ach*, Jonah! I thought you had gone home," she said as he moved toward her.

"I left to make sure my sister got home safely," Jonah explained. "Her horse was acting up, and since Nathan had to work and couldn't be with her today, I decided to follow Jean and her *kinner* home. Then I came back to check on you and your grandma and see if you needed my help with anything." He walked over to an open bale of hay and removed a few chunks to give Elaine's horse.

"Danki, Jonah." She stepped closer to him, feeling comforted and choked up by his consideration.

A look of concern showed clearly on Jonah's face, and it brought Elaine to tears. "Oh Jonah," she sobbed, "I came out here to feed the horses, and all I could think about was how just a few days ago, I found Grandpa dying in his horse's stall."

Jonah drew Elaine into his arms and gently patted her back. "Losing a loved one is never easy, but God will give you the strength to endure it, for He understands your grief."

She nodded, pulling slowly back and gazing up at his tender expression. "As much as I hurt right now, I know that Grandma is hurting even more."

"Jah," Jonah agreed, "and she will need to deal with the pain of losing Lloyd in her own way, in a time frame we can't control."

"Are you saying there's nothing I can do to help her get through this terrible loss?" Elaine could hardly believe Jonah would hint at such a thing.

"I'm not saying that at all," he said with a shake of his head. "I just meant that Edna will have to deal with Lloyd's passing in her own way."

"I know, but I made a promise to Grandpa that I would be here for Grandma, and I plan to keep that commitment."

Jonah nodded as though he understood and reached for her hand. "Why don't you go back to the house and let me take care of the horses? You've had a long day, and I'm sure you're exhausted."

"You're right about that," she agreed with a weary sigh. "And if you're sure you don't mind, I think I will go inside and make sure that Grandma's okay. I'll fix some chamomile tea, which will hopefully help us both get to sleep."

Jonah bent and kissed Elaine on the cheek. "I'll be back sometime tomorrow to see how you're both doing."

"Danki, that means a lot." As Elaine left the barn, she thanked God for bringing Jonah into her life. He was such a kind, compassionate man. She hoped that he wouldn't ask her to marry him anytime soon, for if he did, her answer would have to be no. For however long it took, Elaine's first obligation was to Grandma, which meant her own needs and wants must be put on hold.

✍

Sara Stutzman stood in front of her bedroom window, staring at the inky blackness of the night sky. Attending Lloyd Schrock's funeral today had been hard on her, as it brought back memories of when she'd had to watch her own husband's body being buried. She and Harley had been married a little over two years when his life was snuffed out by a falling tree, leaving Sara to raise their son, Mark, by herself. Life could be hard, and disasters could occur when least expected. But life continued, and Sara had a reason to live lying right there in his crib across the hall.

Her precious dark-haired little boy would never know his father, but she would make sure to tell him what a wonderful, loving man his dad had been. At moments like this, Sara wished she had a picture of Harley so she could share it with Mark when he got older. But posing for a photo was frowned upon in her church district, so she would do her best to describe to her son what his father looked like.

Biting her lip to keep tears from flowing, Sara wondered if it was right to continue living in Illinois or if it would be better to return to Goshen, Indiana, where her parents and siblings lived.

Sara had met Harley when he'd gone to Goshen to work for his uncle Abner one summer. They'd quickly fallen in love, and when Harley went back to Illinois, they kept in touch through letters and phone calls. He came back to Goshen to visit several times, and a year later, Harley had asked Sara to marry him. They'd lived in Indiana for six months before moving to his hometown, where he'd started a new business making windows. Sara liked Illinois, and she'd made many friends in the area, including Jean Mast, whom she considered to be her closest friend. If Sara went back to Indiana, where she'd been born and raised, it would be hard to say goodbye to those she'd become close to here. Still, was it fair to Mark to live so far from his mother's parents, whom he would never know as well as his father's parents?

So many decisions to make, Sara thought. *But I don't want to make any permanent changes just yet.* Like Harley's mother had said a few weeks after his death, *"It's best not to make any quick decisions about the future until you have had sufficient time to grieve."*

Betty was right. She still grieved the loss of her eldest son, just as Harley's father and younger siblings did. It had not been an easy time for any of them, but Sara was thankful they had each other's support, for without Harley's family, she wouldn't have made it this far. And having Mark close by helped Betty, because her grandson was the only part of Harley she had left.

Even though it was dark, in her mind's eye Sara could

see every inch of the property. This home, this land was where she and Harley had planned to live, raise a family, and grow old together. Sara's heart was in this place as much as her husband's had been, and in the time they'd lived here, so many good memories had been made. But then this very land they'd loved so much had taken her husband's life. Would she be able to continue forcing herself to look at the trees lining their property without letting that horrible day override the sweet memories they'd made in such a short period of time?

Sara was thankful she'd been able to lease out part of their land to a neighboring Amish man who farmed for a living. The income from that, as well as money they had saved in the bank, was helping her get by. In addition, both Sara's parents and Harley's had given some money to help out.

My year of mourning is almost up, and I'll need to make my decision soon about whether I should stay here or move back to Indiana, Sara told herself after she'd pulled the covers aside and crawled into bed. *In the meantime, I need to find an additional way to support myself and Mark, because my savings won't last forever, and I can't rely on my in-laws' or parents' help indefinitely. I need to ask God for His guidance and strength each day.*

❧

Grandma and Elaine had retired to their rooms a few hours ago, but Elaine was still standing at her window, looking toward the heavens and asking God for answers about what the future might hold. The stars seemed to be twinkling more brightly, perhaps just for her. *Lord, help me to be strong for Grandma. Help me not to lose hope and to understand why, when things seemed to be going so well, everything suddenly fell apart.* Elaine's body was tired, yet her mind whirled with a multitude of questions.

Finally, Elaine willed herself toward the bed, knowing she needed to get off her aching feet. Pulling back the covers, she slipped into the linens that still smelled like fresh air. Grandma always hung the sheets outside after washing them, and they held their fragrance for several days. Elaine loved to bury her nose into the pillowcase and breathe deeply of its freshness. It was almost like falling asleep outdoors.

She tucked the quilt, lovingly made by her grandmother, under her chin, while wiggling her toes to get the cramps out. What she wouldn't do right now for her friend Leah to give her a good foot massage. Leah practiced reflexology and was quite good at it. Reflexology dealt with a lot more than massaging feet, but right now, Elaine would have settled for just that.

She reflected on how Leah and Priscilla had been happy with the daffodil bulbs she'd given them. Even before Elaine had suggested it, both friends had said the flowers would be planted in memory of Grandpa Schrock, an affectionate name they had called him by all these years.

Elaine closed her eyes, and even with both doors tightly shut, she heard Grandma's muffled crying from the room across the hall. As Elaine drifted fitfully to sleep, her last words of prayer were for Grandma to find the strength to go on.

❦

Elaine sat straight up in bed and glanced at the clock on her dresser. It was nearly midnight, and she'd only been asleep a few hours. A noise seemed to be coming from the kitchen. She tipped her head and listened, trying to make out what it was.

Then Elaine caught a whiff of something cooking.

But that was impossible; Grandma had gone to bed hours ago.

Pushing her covers aside, Elaine crawled out of bed and put her robe and slippers on. Opening her bedroom door, she padded down the hall toward the kitchen.

When she stepped into the room, she was surprised to see Grandma standing in front of the stove, flipping pancakes with an oversized spatula.

"Grandma, what are you doing out of bed, and why are you making pancakes at this time of night?" Elaine asked, joining her at the stove.

Grandma turned to look at Elaine. "I'm sorry, dear. Did I wake you?"

"Well, I. . ."

Grandma placed one hand on her stomach and gave it a pat. "I'm *hungerich*, and I had a craving for *pannekuche*. Would you like some too?"

Elaine shook her head. "I'm not hungry, and after the long day we've had, you should be tired too."

"I couldn't sleep, and I was thirsty." Grandma's mouth twisted grimly. "My bed seems empty without my dear husband to share it."

Elaine wanted to say that she understood, but having never been married, she couldn't fully comprehend the scope of what Grandma must be feeling right now. "Would it help if you slept in one of the guest rooms upstairs?" she suggested.

Grandma shook her head vigorously. "I am not leaving the bedroom your grandpa and I shared for so many years." She sighed and turned off the propane-operated stove. "It'll take me awhile to get used to sleeping alone, but I'll manage somehow."

Grandma placed the pancakes on a plate, grabbed the syrup bottle from the cupboard, and sat at the table.

"Even in my loss, I can give thanks for all that the Lord provides." She bowed her head and closed her eyes. When she opened them again, Elaine took a seat beside her.

"Are you sure you're not hungerich?" Grandma asked, taking a drink of water from the glass she'd placed on the table. "I'd be happy to share some of these pannekuche with you."

"No. I'll just sit here and watch you eat," Elaine replied. She guessed it was good that Grandma was eating now, as she hadn't had much to eat at the meal after Grandpa's graveside service, and neither had Elaine.

"As you like." Grandma poured syrup over the pancakes and took her first bite. "Your grandpa loved pure maple syrup. He liked buttermilk pancakes the best, but I think he would have eaten any kind that was set before him." Grandma chuckled. "As much as that man liked to eat, it was amazing that he didn't have a problem with his weight."

"I guess it was because he always worked so hard," Elaine commented.

"Jah, and before he retired from farming, he labored in the fields, so it was no wonder he had such a hearty appetite."

Grandma went on to talk about how she and Grandpa had met at a young people's singing many years ago—a story Elaine had heard several times. But she listened patiently, knowing it did Grandma good to reminisce like this, and it would no doubt help the healing process. Truthfully, Elaine never tired of hearing it. She was comforted by hearing about how things had been when Grandpa and Grandma were young.

When the grandfather clock in the living room struck one, Elaine suggested that they both head back to bed.

Grandma yawned. "I guess you're right; I am awfully

tired. Danki for sitting here so patiently while I rambled on and on about the past."

Elaine placed her hand over Grandma's. "It's all right. You needed to talk, and I hope you'll share things about Grandpa with me whenever you want, because I enjoy hearing them."

Tears welled in Grandma's eyes. "We who grieve will never forget the ones we've lost, but we can be thankful for the years we had with your *grossdaadi*, for he filled our lives with love and laughter and gave me a sense of joy beyond compare." She squeezed Elaine's fingers. "And if I'm not mistaken, someday soon you'll find that same kind of love, laughter, and joy with Jonah Miller."

"I hope so," Elaine said in a near whisper. Truth was, she wasn't sure Jonah would be willing to wait until she felt ready for marriage. And if he wasn't, she wouldn't blame him for that.

CHAPTER 3

*W*hen Elaine entered the kitchen the following morning, she found a stack of Grandma's good dishes sitting on the table, and Grandma was at the sink, washing glasses.

"*Guder mariye*, Grandma."

"Good morning."

"Why do you have the good dishes out?" Elaine questioned.

"Have you forgotten that we have a group of tourists coming here on Friday?"

"Well, no, but. . ."

"Thought I would get a jump on the dishes while I have some time to clean them. That way, they'll be ready for our guests. Then I'll take them out to the dining-room table." Grandma turned and offered Elaine a weak smile. Dark circles rimmed her pale blue eyes, and Elaine was sure she hadn't slept well, if at all, last night.

"Oh Grandma, I think it's too soon for that. I had planned on calling the tour group director this morning and canceling our Friday-night dinner."

Grandma shook her head determinedly. "We made a commitment, Elaine, and we need to stick to it. Besides, we could sure use the money."

Elaine couldn't argue with that, but she wasn't up to cooking a big meal for fifty people, and she didn't think Grandma was either. "Maybe we can reschedule it for another time," Elaine suggested, moving closer to the sink.

"No, we can't." Grandma reached for another glass to wash, carefully immersing it in the soapy water. "The people who'll be coming are from out of town, not to mention that they've paid for their meal in advance."

Elaine sighed deeply, picking up the dish towel to dry what Grandma had washed. "We can refund their money, Grandma, and I'm sure once I explain the circumstances to the tour director, she'll understand."

"We need the money," Grandma repeated.

"There will be other tour groups, and we're not going to starve." Elaine's frustration mounted. Didn't Grandma realize that neither of them was up to hosting a big dinner right now? Not only would they have the meal to prepare, but while the tourists were eating, Elaine and Grandma would be expected to say a few words and answer any questions they were asked about the Amish way of life. They'd both be exhausted by the end of the evening.

"I know you're worried that I'm not up to this," Grandma said, "but keeping busy will help me not to think so much about missing your grossdaadi. I think it would be good for you too. Maybe we'll both get a good night's sleep after entertaining the group."

"Okay, we'll do the dinner," Elaine finally conceded. "Guess I'd better head over to Rockome Garden Foods and pick up a few things that we still need for the dinner."

～

Soon after Elaine left, Edna carried her good dishes out to the room where she and Elaine hosted their dinners. She wouldn't set the table today, but wanted to have everything here and ready to put in place on Friday morning. As Edna covered the stack of dinnerware with one of the embroidered cloth napkins to keep the dishes free of dust, she thought about what else she could do before Friday's gathering.

As she glanced around the spacious room, a lump formed in her throat. With the help of several men in their district, Lloyd had built this extra-large dining room to accommodate up to one hundred people. In addition to being used for their sit-down dinners, the add-on had served them whenever it was their turn to host one of their biweekly church services. It was also used on days when Edna would invite a group of women into her home for a quilting party or some other function.

She moved over to the large window, looking out at the field Lloyd had rented to one of their neighbors after he'd retired from farming. It had been planted in alfalfa and was already growing nicely. When Lloyd used to work the fields, Edna enjoyed going out to see how he was doing or bringing him water and a snack to eat. He'd always been appreciative and hadn't seemed to mind the interruption. Lloyd used to tell Edna he was glad for the break and that it was a good opportunity for them to visit awhile.

Edna's gaze went to their giant oak tree. A swing Lloyd had put up for Elaine many years ago still hung from a lower branch. It had provided hours of fun for their granddaughter through the years. Even though Elaine was twenty-two years old, she still took time to enjoy that swing and gleefully giggled as she swung back and forth.

Pushing her thoughts aside lest she give in to threatening tears, Edna left the room and headed back to the kitchen. Although difficult to face, she was glad there were so many reminders of Lloyd all around, for each one held a special memory. Memories of him would help keep her going.

Edna was just getting ready to take a stack of napkins

and a box of silverware to set by the dishes when she heard a horse and buggy coming up the lane.

Peeking out the kitchen window, she watched as the driver parked his rig near the barn. When the young Amish man got out of the buggy and secured his horse to the hitching rack, Edna realized that it was Jonah Miller. No doubt he had come here to see Elaine. Too bad he'd just missed her.

"If you're looking for my granddaughter, she's not here right now," Edna said after she'd answered Jonah's knock.

"Came by to check on both of you," Jonah replied with a grin.

Such a nice-looking, thoughtful young man, Edna mused. *He reminds me of Lloyd at that age. Not just in looks, but in his kindness for others. I'm so glad Elaine is being courted by him.*

She opened the door wider and asked him to come in. "I'm sorry, Jonah. Where are my manners? Good morning to you, and would you like a cup of coffee? I made it fresh this morning." Edna's face heated, for she felt a bit rattled right now.

"Some coffee sounds good." He removed his straw hat, placing it on the wall peg near the back door. "So where's Elaine off to this morning?" he asked, taking a seat at the kitchen table.

"She went over to Rockome Garden Foods," Edna replied, filling a cup with coffee and handing it to Jonah. "There are a few things we need for the group of tourists who'll be coming here Friday evening."

Jonah quirked an eyebrow. "You're hosting a dinner so soon?"

She gave a brief nod.

"Couldn't you have rescheduled it for a better time?

31

I'm sure you and Elaine are both emotionally drained."

"I'll admit, we're tired physically and mentally, but we'll be fine," she said, pouring herself some coffee. "Like I told my granddaughter, it helps to keep busy, and we don't want to disappoint the people who have paid in advance to have dinner in an Amish home. For some who live out of town, this might be the only chance they'll have to visit our Amish community."

Jonah blew on his coffee and took a sip. "I see what you mean. Keeping busy in stressful situations has worked for me on more than one occasion. When you're good and tired, it helps you fall asleep quickly too."

"Were you referring to situations in your work as a buggy maker or to more personal matters?" Edna asked.

"Both." Jonah went on to tell Edna how stressful it had been for him when he'd first moved to Arthur and didn't know anyone but his sister. "Then I made friends with Harley Stutzman and of course, Elaine, and every-thing changed." He smiled. "Just being with her makes me feel calm and relaxed."

"I understand. My granddaughter has a sweet spirit and a special way about her that is calming." Edna handed Jonah a plate of brownies someone had brought by when offering condolences. "Whenever I was with Lloyd, I felt a sense of peace." She sighed deeply. "I'm grateful for all the wonderful years we had together."

Jonah nodded and took one of the brownies. "I look forward to having a relationship like yours and Lloyd's with my future wife someday. And I hope to be blessed with many good memories, like I'm sure you have, and my parents do too."

Edna was tempted to ask if Jonah planned to ask Elaine to marry him, but thought better of it. If they were meant to be together, it would happen at the right time without her interference. Of course, she was hoping Jonah would eventually pop the question, and was almost certain that Elaine would say yes. She'd noticed the way they looked at each other whenever they thought no one was watching.

"Is there anything you'd like me to do for you before I go?" Jonah asked after he'd eaten a brownie and finished his coffee.

Edna shook her head. "I can't think of anything at the moment, but danki for asking."

Jonah rose from his chair. "Think I'll stop by Rockome Garden Foods and see if I can catch Elaine there before I head back to the buggy shop."

"You're welcome to wait for her here if you want, but I'm not sure how long she will be."

"That's okay. Think I'll just drop by the store. There are a few things I could pick up there anyway, and then I'll need to head back to my shop and get some work done, or else I'll end up getting behind on my orders."

"All right then. It was nice seeing you, Jonah."

"Same here. And don't forget, Edna, if you ever need anything, just let me know. Even though I'm busy at work, I'll always make time for you and Elaine."

❧

Arcola, Illinois

Elaine had only been browsing the shelves at Rockome Garden Foods a few minutes when she spotted her friend Priscilla talking to one of the clerks. Elaine waited until they were finished, then walked over and asked, *"Wie geht's?"*

Priscilla, looking quite surprised, replied, "I'm fine. How are you?"

Elaine shrugged. "Doing okay, I guess. What brings you here today?"

"I'm delivering some of our homemade strawberry jam," Priscilla replied. "We have more canned goods than we need for our small store, and the owner here said they could use some jam. Why are you here?"

"Grandma and I have a group of tourists coming to our house Friday evening, and I'm picking up a few things we're out of. Maybe I should get some of that jam too, because I think we're nearly out."

Priscilla's brows furrowed as she put her hand on Elaine's shoulder. "Are you sure you're up to that? I mean, with your grandpa dying, I figured you would put all dinners on hold for a while."

"I wanted to." Elaine sighed heavily. "But Grandma insisted on hosting this meal. I think she wants to keep busy so she won't have time to think about how much she misses Grandpa. She also reminded me that we need the money."

"If you're struggling financially, others in the community will help out," Priscilla said.

"I'm sure they would, but Grandma's an independent woman, and she won't accept money from others as long as we can provide for ourselves."

"I understand." Priscilla spoke in an encouraging tone while giving Elaine's arm a tender squeeze. "If you and Edna need help preparing for the dinner, or even cooking and serving the meal, let me know. I'm not doing anything Friday afternoon or evening, so it wouldn't be a problem at all."

"Danki for the kind offer, but I think we can manage." Elaine's throat tightened. Like Grandma, she wanted to be independent, although she still wasn't sure either of them was up to hosting another dinner so soon. All it took was one sympathetic look from her friend and she felt like she could break down in tears. *I wonder what Grandma would say if Priscilla did come to help. She'd probably tell her that we can do the dinner on our own. Maybe it's best if I don't press the issue and just see how the meal goes.*

"Well, guess I'd better get what I came here for and head back home." Elaine moved over to the cooler to select some cheese. "I don't want to leave Grandma alone for too long. She's likely to do more than she should while I'm gone."

The sounds of screeching tires and a shrill horn interrupted their conversation.

Elaine and Priscilla rushed to the window to see what had happened. "Oh no," Elaine gasped. "It looks like a car hit someone's buggy! I hope no one is seriously hurt."

CHAPTER 4

*J*onah whistled as he headed toward Rockome Gardens with his horse, Sassy, pulling his buggy. The Amish museum and other facilities, including their restaurant, would open next week, but Rockome Garden Foods, where they sold baked goods, bulk foods, various kinds of cheese, candy, and several other items, was open to the public all year.

Jonah was fascinated by Rockome Gardens and its history. He had visited the museum not long after he'd moved to Illinois and learned that the 208 acres of land had once been used for farming. It had been purchased by Arthur and Elizabeth Martin, who had a dream of creating the largest flower garden in Douglas County. They used seven acres of the farm to plant flowers, create rock formations, and build their summer cottage. Work began in 1937, but it was slowed by the Great Depression and the start of World War II. The Martins continued to expand, planting more flowers and creating additional rock formations. In 1952, they gave Rockome Gardens to the Mennonite Board of Missions and Charities of Elkhart, Indiana, and it was used as a retirement village for missionaries. A few years later, it was sold to Elvan and Irene Yoder, who opened it to the public, adding buggy rides, tours of an Amish home, and a small gift shop. Other attractions, such as a tree house, lookout tower, antique museum, and ice-cream shop were added. Whenever the Yoders traveled, they returned to Rockome with new ideas for rock formations and other attractions. In 2005, the Yoders sold the property to a group of investors. It was sold two more times, and then in 2011, Steve and Bev Maher took over. The couple had visited the gardens many times and realized it was in need of restoration.

Jonah smiled as the gardens came into view. Each of the rock formations was truly unique. This was a place where families could come to relax and find inspiration. He'd hoped to bring Elaine here, maybe sometime this summer, because she liked the gardens too.

As he neared Rockome Garden Foods, Jonah caught his breath. An Amish buggy was flipped over on its side, and the car that had hit the buggy was parked nearby. His heart pounded. A group of people had gathered around, and one of them was Elaine, who was crouched on the ground next to Priscilla. His nerves calmed, seeing that Elaine and her friend seemed to be okay. But someone was injured, and he wondered who it was they were assisting.

Jonah halted Sassy and leaped from the buggy, but his hands didn't want to cooperate as he secured the horse's reins. He'd seen one too many buggy accidents. Some were minor, while others involved fatalities. Once he'd managed to tie Sassy to the hitching rack, Jonah sprinted to the scene of the accident, where he discovered Sara Stutzman's mother-in-law, Betty, lying on the ground in front of Elaine and Priscilla. She was conscious but gritting her teeth.

"What happened? Is she seriously injured?" Jonah asked, kneeling beside Elaine.

"We're not sure how it happened, but Betty's buggy was hit." Elaine motioned to the car, then back to Betty. "Her leg appears to be broken, and she could have some internal injuries, but we won't know for sure until she's been seen by a doctor."

37

"Did someone call for help?" Jonah questioned.

"Jah. The paramedics should be here soon," Priscilla interjected.

"I'll check around the scene and make sure all of Betty's things are picked up and taken back to her place." Jonah stood and looked toward the road. "What happened to Betty's horse? I don't see it anywhere."

"We don't know yet if her horse was injured, but a passerby stopped and said he saw the mare running into a field down the road," Elaine replied. "The man offered to go after the horse, and hopefully he'll be able to bring her back without a problem."

"Looks like that might be him coming now." Jonah pointed. "At the pace they're moving, it doesn't look like the horse is seriously injured."

"That's a relief." Priscilla looked toward the stranger leading Betty's horse.

"Betty's family needs to be notified," Elaine said. "We could call and leave a message, but they might not check the answering machine in the phone shanty for several hours."

"You're right," Jonah agreed. "I'll drive over to the Stutzmans' right now and let them know about Betty. I'll tie the mare to the back of my buggy and take her with me."

❧

Arthur

"Wie geht's?" Leah called when she rode her bicycle into the Schrocks' yard and saw Edna hanging laundry on the line.

"I'm keeping busy," Edna replied. "That's the best cure for depression, I'm told."

Leah wondered who had given Edna that advice, but

she didn't ask. Instead, after parking her bike, she said, "Would you like some help with those wet clothes?"

Edna shook her head. "I can manage. Besides, I'm almost done. It's nice to have your company though."

Edna is so independent, Leah thought. *It's no wonder Elaine is like that. She probably learned from her grandma's example.*

"Where's your granddaughter? Is she busy inside?" Leah asked, clasping her hands behind her back so she wouldn't be tempted to grab a few towels and hang them on the line.

"Oh, Nancy went shopping today. We need a few things for the dinner we'll be hosting this Friday."

Leah tipped her head. "Nancy? Did you say Nancy went shopping?"

Edna's face reddened. "I—I meant Elaine. Guess I must have been thinking about my son's wife, Nancy. Even after all these years, I still miss her and Milton. Elaine lost out on so much, growing up without her parents." She sighed deeply and pushed an errant strand of silver-gray hair back under her covering. "There are times when Elaine reminds me of her mother, and during her childhood, I slipped a time or two and called her Nancy. I haven't done it much lately though." Edna readjusted the loosened clothespin that held up one side of an oversized bath towel.

Leah slipped her arm around Edna's waist. "Elaine was fortunate to have you and Lloyd, and I'm sure she knows it."

Edna nodded. "It's been a blessing to raise our only grandchild. I pray every day that Elaine will find the same happiness with Jonah that I had with my dear husband."

Leah's mouth opened slightly. "Has Jonah asked Elaine to marry him?"

"Well, no, not yet, but I'm sure it's just a matter of time." Edna reached into the basket and clipped another towel to the line. "It's obvious that they're very much in love. I can see it every time they look at each other."

"I've noticed that too. And they seem to have a lot in common," Leah agreed. "They both enjoy flowers, and Jonah admires the unusual rocks Elaine has found and painted, like that one she made to look like a bear. I think he mentioned to Elaine that he plans to take her to Rockome Gardens sometime. They sure have a lot of rocks to look at."

"Jah." Edna gestured to the now-empty laundry basket. "Since that chore is done and I'm feeling the need for a little break, should we go up to the house and have a cup of coffee?"

"None for me, thanks," Leah said. "It's never been my cup of tea." She snickered. "You may remember how I used to invite Priscilla and Elaine over to my house for tea parties when we were girls."

Edna smiled. "Oh, that's right. Instead of coffee, let's share a pot of tea while we wait for Elaine to come home."

Leah smiled. "That sounds nice."

"We can have some of that moist and delicious banana bread someone gave us the other day too," Edna said as they headed toward the house. She yawned noisily and covered her mouth. "Sorry about that. I didn't get much sleep last night and got up for some water and decided to make pannekuche."

"You made pancakes for breakfast this morning?" Leah asked.

"Not for breakfast. It was sometime during the night, but I can't remember what time it was. I was hungerich and decided to make myself something to eat." Edna smiled briefly, but her expression sobered. "Lloyd loved pancakes. Elaine didn't eat with me, but she sat and listened while I shared some memories, and then we both went back to bed."

"Oh, I see." Leah couldn't help but notice that even though Edna was trying to put on a brave front, she looked exhausted and seemed kind of forgetful. No doubt the stress and pain of losing her husband was the cause.

When they entered the kitchen, Leah went to the cupboard and got out two cups for their tea. She turned just in time to grab hold of Edna, who all of a sudden had turned pale and seemed unsteady on her feet.

"Dear me," Edna said, holding her head. "I must have stood up too quickly when I put the clothes basket down. Either that or I'm feeling a bit woozy because I've gone too long without something to eat. It's been awhile since Elaine and I had breakfast."

"Let me take care of making the tea and cutting the banana bread," Leah said as she guided Edna to a kitchen chair. "You've been through a lot this past week, and it's okay to rely on others. After all, that's what friends are for."

Rather than pushing herself to keep busy, Edna ought to take time to rest and allow herself to grieve, Leah thought. Once again, she didn't voice her concerns, figuring Edna might not appreciate it. She would, however, keep Edna and Elaine in her prayers and stop by whenever she could to help out.

∽

"We're going to see your Grandma Stutzman today," Sara said, lifting her son up to the buggy seat. Betty had invited them over for lunch, and Sara looked forward to the visit. Spending time with her in-laws made her feel closer to Harley—at least the memory of him. Betty always had humorous stories to tell about things Harley had said or done when he was a boy. Just the familiarity of being at the Stutzmans' place, where Sara and Harley had visited so many times, gave her comfort.

Riding down the lane before getting to the main road, Sara glanced in the direction of the small grove of trees on the far side of their property. Quickly, she turned away. She couldn't avoid seeing that area every time she went to and from her home. Hopefully, instead of the constant reminder that her husband's life had ended there, someday happy memories would override the bad ones and remind her of the joys they'd treasured among their once-cherished woods. Harley and Sara had enjoyed Sunday picnics there, and during the week, it was a resting place where they had many times shared lunch during warmer weather. Sara had delighted in looking up at the leaf-covered branches while relaxing on a blanket beside Harley. The steady currents from the gentle breeze made the leaves move in a beautiful, hypnotic dance as Harley and Sara talked about their future. Sometimes they'd enjoyed simply relaxing in the shade's coolness before getting back to work again. They had even flown kites one spring day, and Sara would never forget the fun they'd had.

They'd enjoyed bringing Mark to their special woodland spot as well. The baby seemed to love the fresh air, and while nestled on a blanket, cushioned by the soft grass underneath, he would kick his little legs and giggle. Like a store-bought mobile, the wafting leaves above kept him content. It never took Mark long to fall into a relaxing sleep.

"Someday, perhaps, I'll be able to smile again when I see those woods of ours," Sara said out loud, as if her husband sat right next to her. But for now, it was a constant reminder of how her life had changed in a split second of time.

Mark's sleepy blue eyes closed soon after Sara pulled onto Route 133, and he slouched in his seat. She smiled. Either her son was very tired, or the rocking motion of the buggy had put him to sleep.

As Sara guided her horse down the road, she thought about stopping to see how Edna and Elaine were doing. But she'd left the house a little later than planned and didn't want to be late for lunch. Besides, Mark was napping, and Sara wanted her precious boy to rest. She could stop by the Schrocks' either on the way home or sometime later in the week.

When Sara pulled onto the graveled driveway leading to her in-laws' house, she saw Harley's eighteen-year-old brother, Andy, coming out of the phone shanty. Sara waved but waited until she'd pulled her horse and buggy up to the hitching rack near the barn before speaking. Andy had followed her up the driveway, and he held the horse while Sara got out of the buggy.

"Harley's friend Jonah was here a few minutes ago, delivering some bad news." His forehead creased with wrinkles. "My *mamm*'s buggy got hit in front of Rockome Garden Foods, and she's been taken to the hospital. I called my *daed* at work and let him know right away."

Sara's fingers touched her parted lips as she drew in a sharp breath. "I'm sorry to hear about Betty. Was she seriously hurt?"

"I–I'm not sure. Jonah said Elaine Schrock and Priscilla Herschberger were there when the accident happened, and they thought Mom's left leg might be broken. Jonah also mentioned that she was pretty banged up. We won't know till we get to see Mom, and since Dad's on his way home now, I called one of our drivers to take us to the hospital in the next half hour or so." Andy gulped in a quick breath before slowly shaking his head. "I can't believe this happened. We aren't over losing Harley, and now Mom is hurt. What more could go wrong?"

"I know, it's hard," Sara agreed, "but at least your mamm's life was spared."

"Jah, and I'm thankful for that."

"I'll have to go home and get some things, but I'll be back in time to greet the children when they get home from school today," Sara offered.

"Try not to scare 'em with the news about Mom," Andy said. "Don't think they need to know a lot till we have all the facts."

"I understand, and don't worry about anything here. I'll take care of everyone until you and your daed return home." Harley's siblings had taken his death pretty hard, and if they thought they might lose their mother, they'd really be upset.

"By the way," Andy added, "Jonah brought Mom's horse back with him. It broke away when the buggy was hit, but the mare seems to be okay. Said he stopped by your place, but somehow you must have missed each other."

"I wonder how that happened," Sara pondered. "I took the main road here."

"Oh, I remember now." Andy scratched the side of his head. "Jonah did mention that he'd taken the back road. Guess he thought it'd be better, since he had Mom's horse tied to the back of his buggy, and there'd be less traffic and all."

Dear Lord, Sara prayed as she lifted her sleeping son from the buggy, *I hope and pray that Betty's injuries aren't serious. This family has already had to deal with one tragedy, and we sure don't need another.*

CHAPTER 5

When Elaine got home, she found Grandma and Leah sitting on the porch, drinking tea.

"It seemed like you were gone a long time," Grandma said. "Did you make more than one stop?"

"No, I just went to Rockome Garden Foods." Elaine set the paper sack she held on the wicker table and took a seat beside Leah. "I was visiting with Priscilla there when we heard a loud crash and looked out. A buggy had been hit by a car in front of the store."

"Ach, no!" Grandma's face paled. "Was it someone we know?"

"I'm afraid so. Betty Stutzman was driving the buggy, and we stayed with her until the ambulance arrived."

"Was she badly hurt?" Leah's thoughtful expression revealed her concern.

Elaine bit her lip. "It appeared that her leg was broken, and I heard one of the paramedics say that he thought she might have some cracked ribs, as well as some possible internal injuries."

"I hope they don't lose her." Grandma stared across the yard as she got the wicker rocking chair moving rhythmically back and forth. Was she thinking about Grandpa? Grandma's face looked pale, and from the droop of her shoulders, Elaine thought she appeared to be tired—even more so than she had earlier this morning.

"I'm sure they'll take good care of her at the hospital," Elaine reassured her.

"Betty and her family have been through. . .losing their son. I hope she'll. . .be okay, because. . ." Grandma teared up as she fumbled for words to express how she felt.

Elaine reached over and gently touched Grandma's arm. "You look *mied*. Why don't you go inside and try to take a nap?"

"That's a good idea," Leah put in. "You do look as if you could use some rest."

Grandma slowly rose to her feet. "All right then, I'll take the items you got at the store and put them away. Then I'm going to my room to lie down awhile. Please let me know when it's time to fix supper so I can help."

As Grandma took the paper sack and shuffled into the house, Elaine glanced curiously at Leah and said, "If she sleeps that long, I'll be surprised. It's not even lunchtime yet."

"Maybe she's *verhuddelt* about what time it is. She does seem a bit confused today."

"In what way?" Elaine asked.

"At times while we were visiting, Edna had a hard time focusing and remembering things."

"That makes sense, don't you think? I mean, it's only been a few days since Grandpa died. Since then, I don't think either of us has had much sleep. And with the funeral being just yesterday, well. . ." Elaine paused, looking out over the yard where she had played as a child.

"I realize that, but there was something else too. Your grandma became quite wobbly when we came into the kitchen. I grabbed hold of her before she lost her balance."

"What?" Elaine eyed Leah with newfound concern. "I wonder what caused that."

"I'm not sure. Edna said she thought it was because

she stood up too quickly after putting the clothes basket down."

"I guess that could have caused her to be light-headed. I've done that myself sometimes, standing up too quickly, and then the blood leaves my head." Elaine twisted her head-covering ties around her finger. "Of course, it could be because she hasn't had enough sleep or even just from being under too much stress. Grandma is emotionally and physically drained, and so am I."

"That's understandable, but she bent to set the empty basket down before we went to the kitchen," Leah explained. "Her wooziness didn't occur until after we'd gone in there to brew some tea. Edna also mentioned not having anything to eat since early this morning, so I'm wondering if her blood sugar was low. If so, that may have been the cause."

Elaine sighed deeply. "I'm so worried about Grandma."

"I am too, which is why I think it's way too soon for you and Edna to be hosting a sit-down dinner this Friday night." Leah tapped her fingers on the arm of her chair.

"She told you about that?"

Leah nodded. "Said she needed to keep busy."

"We both do." Elaine clenched her hands tightly together in her lap, watching as a bumblebee flew lazily across the porch. She didn't like where this conversation was going and figured she was probably in for a lecture.

"I understand that to a point," Leah said, "but you need to rest and take time to heal emotionally. Pushing yourself to keep going and doing is not the answer, Elaine. And it's fairly obvious, even to you, that your grandma needs to rest."

"I appreciate your concern, but Grandma's insistent

on us doing this dinner, and no matter how I feel about it, I won't go against her wishes."

❧

"Where's Mom? I didn't see her buggy parked outside, and it's not in the buggy shed either. Do you know why she isn't here?" twelve-year-old Paul asked Sara when he and his sisters arrived home from school that afternoon.

Sara removed a tray of ginger cookies from the oven and turned to face the children. "Your mamm is at the hospital."

Paul's mouth dropped open. "What? How come?"

"Her buggy was hit by a car this morning."

Marla, age seven, let out a sharp scream. "Oh no! Is our mamm gonna die?" Tears pooled in the little girl's blue eyes and splashed onto her cheeks.

"No, she'll be fine once her injuries are taken care of." Sara gathered the child into her arms. "She broke her leg and has some other sore places, so she'll have to stay in the hospital overnight, but her injuries aren't life-threatening."

"That's *baremlich*." Carolyn, who was nine, frowned deeply.

"You're right, it is terrible," her brother agreed.

"Guess I'll have to stay home from school tomorrow so I can take care of things while Mom is gone," Carolyn said.

"That won't be necessary," Sara assured the child. "I went home after lunch today and got a few things so Mark and I can stay here overnight. In fact," she added, trying to sound as cheerful as possible, "we'll stay for as long as we're needed."

"I'm glad you're stayin', but where's little Mark?"

Carolyn glanced around, as though she expected to see him appear.

"He's taking a nap in the other room." Sara placed several cookies on a plate and set it on the table. "Would anyone like some *kichlin* and milk?"

The children nodded eagerly and hurried to wash their hands before taking seats at the table.

"Are Timothy and Andy out in the barn?" Paul asked.

"Timothy is, but Andy's at the hospital with your daed. He said he'd be home later this evening, but your daed plans to spend the night at the hospital with your mamm."

Sara decided to join the children at the table, knowing they would probably have more questions about their mother. She was glad she'd thought to check the Stutzmans' answering machine earlier and had listened to Andy's message. If there was one thing Sara knew, she wouldn't be moving back to Indiana anytime soon, because Betty and her family needed her now.

❧

"Let's go, boy! Now quit your dallying!" Jonah called to his horse as he headed down the road toward the Schrocks' house. He was anxious to see Elaine this evening, and of course, Sassy chose this time to go into his plodding mode. There were moments like this when Jonah wished he'd bought a different horse when he arrived in Arthur. Since the last horse he'd owned, when he lived in Pennsylvania, had belonged to Meredith's husband, Jonah had felt the need to return it to Luke when he came home, recovered from amnesia.

"What's the matter with you, Sassy?" Jonah snapped the reins. "You'll get fat and lazy if you don't do a little running once in a while. Guess I shoulda named you

Poky instead of Sassy, because you're sure poking along today."

The horse picked up speed, and Jonah smiled. "That's better, ol' boy." Even though he'd seen Elaine at Rockome Garden Foods, he hadn't been able to visit with her due to the accident. He had left right away to let Sara know. Unfortunately, she hadn't been home. He'd wasted no time in getting to Herschel's to notify Betty's family and return her horse, but he'd promised Elaine he would stop by her house this evening to visit awhile and let her know how Betty was doing. Only trouble was, he hadn't heard anything about Betty's condition, so he planned to stop by the Stutzmans' place on his way to Elaine's and see what he could find out.

Redirecting his thoughts, Jonah smiled as he passed a sign along the side of the road. It read: YOU'RE A STRANGER ONLY ONCE. He had seen that sign when he'd first come to Arthur, and it had made him feel as welcomed then as it did now. Of course, the folks in this community had welcomed him too, and that made his transition much easier. Moving from Pennsylvania and starting over here had been a good thing for Jonah, especially after he'd met and fallen in love with Elaine. If only he felt free to ask her to marry him.

Just try to have patience, Jonah told himself. *I'll know when the time is right to propose to Elaine, and hopefully she'll say yes when I do.*

A short time later, the Stutzmans' place came into view, so Jonah guided his horse onto the path leading to their house. When he secured Sassy to the hitching rack, he noticed another buggy parked nearby and figured it must belong to Herschel or one of his boys.

Taking the steps two at a time, Jonah stepped onto the Stutzmans' porch and knocked on the door. He was surprised when Sara answered his knock.

"Afternoon," Jonah said. "Is Herschel here? I was wondering if there's any news on how Betty is doing."

"Herschel's at the hospital with Betty," Sara replied, her brown eyes downcast. "She has a broken leg, some fractured ribs, and several bruises and contusions, so they're keeping her overnight."

"I'm sorry to hear that," Jonah said, "but at least her injuries aren't life threatening. It could have been so much worse."

Sara nodded and lifted a slender arm as she swatted at a bothersome fly. "I wonder how the English woman who ran into Betty's buggy is fairing."

"From what I saw, she wasn't hurt, just shook up pretty bad."

"That's understandable. Do you know how or why she hit the buggy?" Sara questioned.

"When the police came, I heard the woman say she'd started to pass the buggy and didn't realize it was turning into Rockome Garden Food's parking lot." Jonah frowned. "It seems like there are so many accidents involving our horses and buggies. Makes me wish there were no cars on the road."

"I've thought that many times myself, but I guess it's just wishful thinking. I can't imagine that the Englishers would ever give up their cars in favor of driving a horse-pulled carriage, or that we would decide to give up our horses and start driving cars."

"I think you're right about that, Sara," Jonah agreed. "So are you here to take care of the kinner?"

"Jah. Mark and I will be staying until Betty's well enough to take over running her household again. Oh, and before I forget," Sara added, "I heard you stopped by my place before bringing Betty's horse home. I appreciate you doing that, and I'm sorry I missed you."

"It's okay." Jonah smiled. "I took a back road because Betty's mare was tied to the back of my buggy. Didn't want traffic to spook the horse any more than she was. After being in that accident earlier, the poor animal was scared enough."

"That was good thinking." Sara paused a moment. "Anyway, I'm here for however long Harley's family needs me."

"I'm sure your help will be appreciated."

Although Sara was a small-boned woman, not more than five feet tall, she had a determined spirit as well as a generous heart. Jonah didn't doubt for a minute that she would help in whatever way she could. He studied Sara for a moment, noting that her brown eyes were a shade darker than her hair. She was a good-looking woman, for sure, and Harley had often said he was a lucky man. But Jonah was lucky too, having fallen in love with Elaine, who was every bit as pretty as Sara.

"Helping each other out is what families are supposed to do," Sara said. "Betty and Herschel have helped me plenty since Harley died, and of course several others in our community have done that as well."

People helping people, Jonah thought. *That's what the Bible teaches.* Right now, though, assisting Elaine and her grandma was uppermost in his mind, because whether they wanted it or not, help from him and others in their community was what they both needed right now.

☙

After Jonah left the Stutzmans' and was on his way to Elaine's, he thought more about Sara. She was only twenty-four and already a widow. On top of that, she had a little boy to care for. Sara was fortunate to have her husband's family close by. Harley had been gone ten months already, but his family was still healing. From what Jonah had heard, they'd been a big help to Sara and her little boy. Now she would be helping them while Betty recuperated. It was good they had each other to lean on. Jonah would continue to be available if she needed anything too.

He switched his thoughts back to Elaine, hoping that by next year at this time, they might be married and living in the house he'd purchased not long ago. Jonah was anxious to get started on a few minor improvements, but other than repainting some of the rooms, the house didn't need a whole lot done to it. The place was actually in move-in condition. He also wanted to sand the living-room floor and finish it with a new coat of varnish. His goal was to get that and the painting completed before he and Elaine got married, but Jonah was confident that he had plenty of time.

The lane leading up to his home was edged by bushes that turned to a brilliant red in the fall. Those needed a bit of trimming, but he'd decided to wait on that until early in the new year. Knowing there would be little red berries on the bushes over the winter, Jonah didn't want to take a natural food source away from the birds. The property had a small barn that someday he hoped to enlarge, giving him more space for his buggy business. A pond behind the house was stocked with plenty of fish.

Jonah's mind wandered to the future. He pictured children sitting next to him as he taught them to fish and swim during the hot days of summer. On chilly winter evenings, he envisioned sitting around the bonfire at the far end of the pond, roasting hot dogs and marshmallows after ice skating with his wife and children. The house Jonah purchased had four large bedrooms on the second floor and two downstairs. Jonah smiled thinking of the children who would one day fill those upstairs rooms. He couldn't wait to become a father and give his children a loving home, just like his parents had given him. Elaine would be a good mother. Even though she'd lost her parents at a tender age, because of Elaine's grandparents, she understood what it was like to be loved and raised in a secure environment.

Jonah's thoughts did a reverse, and he wondered how his parents were doing back in Pennsylvania. He even reflected on his folks' border collie, Herbie. Jonah missed having a dog around, and soon after he and Elaine got married, he planned for them to get a dog. For now, though, Jonah just needed to be there for Elaine and Edna, helping them in any way he could.

CHAPTER 6

*L*eah had just come up from the basement of her parents' home, where she gave reflexology treatments, when her mother called from the kitchen, asking for help getting supper on the table.

"Okay, Mom, I'll be there as soon as I wash my hands," Leah responded. Ten minutes ago, she'd seen her last patient for the day, Susan Diener, an elderly woman from their church district. After Susan had left, Leah had put away her massage lotion and repositioned the recliner people sat in while she worked on their feet. As she always did after the final appointment, she checked her schedule to see who would be coming for the next treatment session and made sure the basement area was ready and in order. It was Friday, so there would be no more patients until next week.

Leah had learned reflexology from her maternal grandmother, who'd since passed away, and Leah saw her ability as a gift to help others through this unique method of healing. At least, that's what her grandmother had always called it. Reflexology wasn't a replacement for a doctor's care, but by massaging and pressing certain reflex zones on people's feet, she'd seen recoveries from various ailments.

When Leah finished up in the bathroom, she went straight to the kitchen to see what she could do to help out. "What do you need me to do?" she asked her mother, who was busy stirring a pan of gravy on the stove.

"You can make a tossed green salad and then set the table," Mom answered. Her brown eyes appeared even darker than usual in the dimness of the room.

"No problem." Leah first turned on the gas lamp that hung over the table. Then she took out the salad ingredients from the refrigerator, placing them on the counter next to the sink.

"How'd things go with Susan?" Mom asked after she'd turned down the stove and started mashing the potatoes.

"Fairly well. She's only had a few treatments, but already her sinus issues seem to have improved."

Mom looked over her shoulder and smiled. "That's good to hear, Leah."

After Leah washed the head of lettuce and started tearing its leaves into a bowl, she glanced at the perpetual calendar sitting on the windowsill. Elaine and Edna would be busy getting last-minute things done before their dinner guests arrived. Closing her eyes, she lifted a prayer on their behalf.

∽

Upon entering his sister's cozy, two-story house, Jonah sniffed the air. "Is that baked ham I smell?"

Jean, who'd been setting the dining-room table, blinked her dark eyes rapidly and smiled at him. "Jah, and I chose ham because I know how much you like it, dear brother."

He stepped up beside Jean and gave her a hug. "I'm blessed to have such a thoughtful sister."

"And I feel blessed to have her as my *fraa*," Jean's husband, Nathan, proclaimed when he entered the room with their three children. Rebecca, the oldest, who had recently turned four, ran over to Jonah and clutched his hand. "Horsey ride?" she asked in their traditional

Pennsylvania-Dutch language.

"Jah, sure." Jonah got down on his hands and knees and told the cute little dark-haired girl to climb onto his back. The next thing Jonah knew, two-year-old Stephen gave a whoop and climbed on too.

"Giddyup, horsey, let's go for a ride!" Rebecca hollered, gripping Jonah's shoulders.

Putting one hand in front of the other, Jonah made his way around the dining room, avoiding the table; then he headed down the hallway, made a U-turn, and came back again. The children giggled and shouted commands for their horsey to go as fast as he could. It was fun hearing his niece and nephew giggle, but Jonah hoped his knees wouldn't give out.

By the time they'd made it back to the dining room, Jonah was ready for the game to end, and equally relieved when Jean said it was time to eat supper.

"Come on, children, give your uncle a rest." Jean winked at Jonah and smiled. "I'm sure Uncle Jonah had a tiring day."

Jonah had a great sister, and they'd always looked out for each other. Truth was, he'd do just about anything for his twin.

After Nathan put their six-month-old son, Zeke, into his playpen, the rest of them gathered at the table, with Stephen in his high chair. After silent prayer, Jean passed the ham and baked potatoes, followed by a bowl of fruit salad, some rolls, and a dish of creamed peas.

Jonah took a bite of ham and smacked his lips. "Sure wish I had someone in my house who could cook as well as you do, Jean."

"Danki, Jonah." She smiled and blotted her lips on a napkin. "Our mamm taught me well, and if you'd hung around the kitchen a bit more when we were kinner, you could probably cook as well as I do."

Jonah grunted. "I doubt it, but I get by well enough, and I don't go hungry, so guess I can't really complain."

"Maybe you oughta find a good fraa," Nathan said, reaching over to place more peas on the tray of Stephen's high chair. Jonah was surprised when the boy ate them, and eagerly too. When he was growing up, he'd always hated peas. Green beans too, for that matter.

"Did ya hear what I said about finding a good wife?" Nathan asked, bumping Jonah's arm with his elbow.

"Jah, I heard, and I've been thinkin' on it."

"So you haven't asked her yet, huh?" This question came from Jean.

"Asked who?" Jonah grabbed his glass of water and took a drink. He didn't want to talk about this right now, but his sister probably wouldn't give up until he answered.

Jean squinted her brown eyes at him. "I was talking about Elaine. She's the one you've been courting, right?"

Jonah gave a nod.

"Well, when are you going to ask her to marry you?" Jean persisted.

"Whenever I feel the time is right." Jonah grabbed a roll and slathered it with strawberry jam. "With the recent passing of Elaine's grossdaadi, now is not a good time."

∽

"What's for supper? What's for supper? Pretty bird. . . pretty bird. . . What's for supper?"

Elaine grimaced, rolling her eyes. "I hope that silly parakeet isn't going to carry on like that all evening while the tourists are here." She didn't know why she felt so edgy tonight. Maybe it was just her fatigue.

"Millie's excited because she knows we're cooking supper." Grandma glanced across the room at her parakeet's cage. "If she gets too noisy, I'll have to cover her cage."

"That's a good idea," Elaine agreed. "Maybe we should cover it before our guests arrive. Better yet, why don't you take her to your bedroom where she'll be out of sight?"

"She might really get to squawking if she's all by herself; I may just cover the cage." Grandma drank a second glass of water, even though just moments ago she'd emptied her first. "Just remind me though. I've been kind of forgetful lately. And I don't know what's making me so thirsty. Guess I must have eaten something salty today."

Elaine couldn't deny that Grandma had been forgetful. Even before Grandpa's death, Grandma had seemed a bit absentminded at times. Elaine figured it was part of growing older, although she herself had times when she couldn't remember where she'd put something. Just the other day, she'd gone upstairs to retrieve an item, but by the time she got to the top step, she'd forgotten what she went up there for. The thing that concerned Elaine the most about Grandma were the symptoms Leah had observed the other day. When Elaine had asked Grandma about the dizziness she'd felt, Grandma made light of the situation, saying she'd gotten up too quickly after setting her laundry basket down, but felt better once she'd had something to eat.

"How would it be if I called next week and made you a doctor's appointment?" Elaine asked, reaching for the basket to fill it with the rolls she'd made earlier.

The wrinkles in Grandma's forehead deepened. "Whatever for? Is it because I'm thirsty and said I must have eaten something salty earlier today?"

"No, of course not. I'm worried about that woozy spell you had the other day, and I think it would be a good idea if you saw the doctor, just in case."

Grandma set aside the pickles she'd been slicing. "In case what?"

"In case your light-headedness was caused by something more than just bending down and standing up too quickly."

Grandma frowned and poured herself more water. "I don't want to go to the doctor. They poke and prod too much. Maybe I should see Leah and get my feet worked on."

Elaine lifted her shoulders with hands palms up. "If you see the doctor first and he doesn't find anything beyond the scope of Leah's abilities, then I'm in agreement with you letting her work on your feet."

Grandma folded her arms in a stubborn pose. "I'll think about it." Then she quickly unfolded her arms and gestured to the kitchen window. "Right now, we need to greet our guests, because the tour bus has pulled in."

CHAPTER 7

After Sharon Sullivan, the tour guide, had introduced Edna and Elaine to the people who'd come for dinner, Edna smiled and said, "I hope you're all *hungerich*, because there's enough food here for everyone to have seconds and maybe even thirds."

"What does *hungerich* mean?" a young woman who wore her hair in a ponytail questioned.

"Oops!" Edna felt her cheeks warm, embarrassed by her slip of the tongue. "*Hungerich* is the Pennsylvania-Dutch word for *hungry*, which is what I really meant to say." She glanced at Elaine to see her reaction, but she had just placed bowls of mashed potatoes on both tables and made no comment.

Edna quickly followed with the gravy, and then she set a bowl of creamed corn beside it. When everything had been put on both tables—potatoes, gravy, corn, fried chicken, roast beef, bread, and pickles, she returned to the kitchen to get some butter and jam. Edna didn't know why she felt so rattled this evening, but her hands were damp with perspiration, and her stomach did little flip-flops, like it used to when she'd first started hosting dinners for tour groups and was unsure of herself. She'd been doing this for a good many years now, so there was no reason to feel apprehensive or jittery. Maybe it was too soon to be doing this. It would be a week tomorrow since Lloyd had died. Maybe Edna was wrong in thinking she needed to stay busy in order to deal with her loss. Perhaps she shouldn't have worried about trying to fulfill her obligation to the tour group. Well, it was too late for speculations. The people were here now, and she'd make it through the evening somehow.

"That's strange," Edna muttered when she discovered there was no butter on the counter. She was sure she'd taken two sticks of butter from the refrigerator earlier and put them on butter dishes, along with knives. *Maybe Elaine took it into the other room and I didn't see it there.*

Edna opened the refrigerator and removed the strawberry jam Elaine had bought the other day. After she'd divided the jam into two dishes, she took them to the dining room and placed one on each table. Scanning the length of both tables, she saw no sign of the butter, which meant that Elaine had not brought them in. *That's so odd. I wonder what happened to them.*

Feeling even more flustered, Edna headed back to the kitchen and opened the refrigerator again, thinking she might have just thought she had taken the butter out earlier.

"What are you looking for, Grandma?"

Edna jumped. She hadn't realized Elaine had come into the room. "I'm searching for the *budder*. I was sure I had set the dishes on the kitchen counter, but now they are nowhere to be found."

"I haven't seen the butter," Elaine said. "They are probably still in the refrigerator."

"No, they're not." Edna shook her head vigorously. "Come see for yourself if you don't believe me."

"It isn't that I don't believe you, Grandma." Elaine moved across the room. "I just can't think of anywhere else the butter would be."

Edna moved aside and let Elaine look over the contents of the refrigerator. A few seconds later, Elaine stepped back and said, "You're right, there's no butter in there. Do you remember taking them out of the refrigerator?"

"I—I thought I did." At the moment, Edna wasn't sure about anything. To make matters worse, she was beginning to feel woozy, like she had the other day.

Elaine clasped Edna's arm. "You look pale, Grandma. Are you feeling *grank*?"

"Well, I. . ." Edna grabbed the back of a chair for support, fearful that she might topple over. "I don't think I'm sick, but I do feel a bit light-headed."

"Sit down and put your head between your knees," Elaine instructed, helping Edna into a chair. "Are you feeling the way you did when Leah was here the other day?"

Edna lowered her head. "Jah, but I felt better after I'd had something to eat."

"I'll fix you a plate of food right now and see if that helps. If not, then it might be best if you go to your room and lie down."

"I'm not going to bed and leave you here to wait on all those people by yourself."

"I'm sure I can manage."

"You might make it through, but then you'd be more exhausted then I am right now. I'm sure that once I've had something to eat, I'll be fine," Edna insisted.

"As you wish." Elaine took a plate from the cupboard and dished up some potatoes, corn, and gravy that had been keeping warm on the stove. Then she took a piece of chicken from the oven and added that to the plate. "Here you go, Grandma." She set the food on the table in front of Edna, along with a knife and fork.

Edna offered a brief silent prayer and quickly ate a piece of chicken. "Yum. This tastes as good as it looks. I hope our guests are enjoying their meal."

"I'm sure they are, Grandma, but right now, I am

more worried about you."

Edna ate a few bites of potatoes and flapped her hand. "I'm fine. Feeling better already, but I would like a glass of water."

"I'll get it." Elaine opened the cupboard where the glasses were kept, but instead of removing a glass and turning on the water, she lifted out the butter dishes and held them toward Edna. "It looks as though you may have accidentally put these in the cupboard when you took down the glasses to set the table for our guests."

Edna gasped and covered her mouth. "Ach, could I really have done something so *dumm*?"

"It wasn't dumb," Elaine said, shaking her head. "You've been a little absentminded since Grandpa died, but that's perfectly understandable." She started toward the other room with the butter, calling over her shoulder, "I'll take care of things in there while you finish what's on your plate."

Edna didn't argue. Her stomach seemed to appreciate the food, as did the rest of her body. In fact, with each bite she took, she felt her strength returning. *It's a simple matter, really. Just don't go too long without eating.*

❧

Elaine hurried into the other room. After she'd placed the butter dishes on the tables, she checked on the vegetable bowls and meat platters to see if any were empty.

"Yuk! What did I just bite into?" A freckle-faced boy crinkled his nose and spit something out of his mouth. "What was that in my mashed potatoes?"

Elaine hurried over to the table, perspiration dripping down the back of her neck. She knew one thing: her bed would never feel better than when she crawled under those covers tonight. *We shouldn't have hosted this dinner.*

It would have been better to have a nice quiet Friday evening, just me and Grandma.

As Elaine looked at what the boy held in his hand, she let out a breath of relief. "I'm sorry about that," she said, "but I think it's just a seasoned chicken cube that must have gotten into the potatoes by mistake. You didn't break a tooth on it, did you?"

He shook his head. "Naw, I'm fine. Just freaked me out when I bit into it."

Elaine said a silent prayer. *Please help us get through the rest of this evening without any more mishaps.*

Seeing that the gravy was the only item that seemed to be getting low, Elaine paused to answer a few questions from an elderly woman, and then she picked up the gravy bowls and went back to the kitchen.

"Are you doing okay, Grandma? Do you need something more to eat?" she asked, noting that Grandma's plate was empty.

"No, I'm fine." Grandma wiped her hands on a napkin. "I feel much better now." She gestured to the chair beside her. "Why don't you have something to eat, and I'll go check on our visitors?"

Elaine shook her head. "That's okay. I'm not hungry right now." Usually she and Grandma waited until their guests had gone home to eat their supper. But at least one of them needed to get back in the other room to make sure the food was being passed around for a second time and then to bring in the pies for dessert. "Why don't you stay here and relax?" she suggested. "I'll take care of everything else that needs to be done." Elaine kept the mashed potato incident to herself, not wanting to upset Grandma further.

Grandma gave a stubborn shake of her head. "We always work together as a team."

"I know, but if you need to rest, I can manage by

myself this time." Even though Grandma had said she was feeling better, she still looked pale, and Grandma's droopy eyelids betrayed her exhaustion.

"I won't hear of it." Grandma pushed away from the table and put her dishes in the sink. "Is it time to take the pies in yet?"

"Not quite. I need to make sure everyone has all the meat and vegetables they want, and then I'll clear away the dishes."

"That will go quicker if we both do it." Walking slowly, Grandma left the kitchen. Elaine followed.

While their guests finished eating, Elaine and Grandma answered more questions about the Amish way of life, and then they excused themselves to clear away the dishes and bring in the desserts.

"I'll carry the sour-cream peach pies I made, and you can take the strawberry-rhubarb ones that you baked," Grandma told Elaine.

Just inside the kitchen, Elaine paused. "Actually, Grandma, you made chocolate–peanut butter pies this morning."

"Now that I think of it, I had wanted to make the peach pies, but since there are no ripe peaches on our trees yet, I changed my mind and made chocolate–peanut butter instead. Of course, I could have used some of our frozen peaches." Grandma nudged Elaine's arm. "Well, don't dawdle now. You'd better get busy."

"Okay," Elaine replied, feeling suddenly like she was a young girl again and Grandma was completely in charge. Grandma had never been bossy, but she'd always let Elaine know that she was the one to make the final decision on things. Out of love and respect, Elaine had never questioned Grandma's authority.

They'd just stepped into the other room with the pies

when Elaine heard a shrill screech, followed by, "Pretty bird. . .pretty bird. . . Where's the pie? Where's the pie?"

"Why, there must be a parrot somewhere in the house," the elderly woman who'd asked a question before said.

"Millie's my grandma's parakeet," Elaine explained.

Grandma's once pale face colored to a bright pink. "Oh dear, I must have forgotten to cover Millie's cage before everyone got here." She placed one of the chocolate–peanut butter pies on the first table and was approaching the second table when she tripped on one of their throw rugs and the pie fell on the floor. "Oh no!" she gasped, tears of obvious embarrassment running down her cheeks. "How clumsy of me. I–I'd better get something to clean up this mess." She hurried back to the kitchen, walking faster than she had all evening.

Elaine quickly followed. "It's okay, Grandma. I'll clean up in the other room. Why don't you stay in the kitchen and rest awhile longer?"

"I don't need to rest." Grandma shook her head determinedly. "I feel like such a *dappich naar*, tripping like that."

"You're not a clumsy fool. An accident like that could have happened to anyone." Elaine motioned to a chair at the table. "Please sit and relax. After I've cleaned up the floor, I'll bring in that extra pie we baked earlier today."

Grandma sighed heavily and sank into a chair. "Whatever you say. I do feel like I need to sit awhile."

Elaine grabbed a large spatula and a serving tray to put the remains of the pie on, as well as a bucket and mop to clean the floor. Then she rushed back to the dining room.

"Let me help you with that," Sharon, the tour guide, said when Elaine knelt on the floor.

"My grandmother isn't quite herself tonight, and she

feels terrible about this," Elaine explained as the two of them began to clean up the pie. "You see, my grandfather died just a week ago, and—"

Sharon's eyes widened. "Oh dear, I hadn't heard. Why didn't you call and cancel this dinner?"

"I suggested that to Grandma, but she insisted on carrying through. And since she'd already scheduled it with you, Grandma didn't think it would be right to back out at the last minute."

"I would have made some other arrangements for this group, and I won't schedule any more dinners here for at least a month, or until you let me know that you're ready," Sharon was quick to say. "You and Edna need time to grieve, and I'm so very sorry for your loss."

"Thank you." Elaine blinked against tears threatening to spill over. She wished she had tried harder to talk Grandma out of hosting this meal or at the very least taken Priscilla and Leah up on their offer to help. The way Grandma had been acting this evening was proof that she wasn't ready to entertain yet.

I wonder if Leah's concerns about Grandma are founded, Elaine thought as she headed back to the kitchen with the remains of the chocolate–peanut butter pie. *She does seem quite forgetful, not to mention how pale and woozy she got earlier. I think when I see Leah at church this Sunday, I'll ask her to have a talk with Grandma about going to the doctor.* Grandma put a lot of faith in Leah's foot doctoring, so she might be more willing to listen to her than Elaine. At least Elaine hoped that would be the case, because if Grandma refused to see their doctor, then Elaine might ask if he would be willing to make a house call. One thing was for certain, she wanted to make sure Grandma was okay.

Back in the kitchen, Elaine found Grandma standing in front of the sink, staring out the window. "Are you all right?" Elaine questioned, dropping the pie mess into the garbage can.

"I was just thinking about your grandpa. If he were still here, he'd probably be in the other room right now, entertaining our guests with a few songs he liked to play on his mouth harp."

"You're right about that." The tourists had always enjoyed listening to Grandpa's music. "Well, guess I'd better take that other pie out to our guests now," she said, removing the third chocolate–peanut butter pie from the refrigerator. "If you'd rather stay here, Grandma, I think I can manage on my own for the rest of the evening."

Grandma shook her head. "I won't hear of it. But before I go back in, I'm going to get out a bowl of fresh fruit for anyone who doesn't want pie."

Just then, one of their guests walked into the kitchen with an empty cup. "Would there be any coffee or tea to go with our pie?" She set her cup down on the table.

Elaine gave a nod. "Yes, of course. I'll bring it right in."

Returning to their guests, Elaine placed the coffee-pot and pie on the table. "While you finish eating your dessert, perhaps some of you have more questions you'd like to ask."

"I do," said a middle-aged woman who'd introduced herself earlier as a schoolteacher from North Carolina.

"What is it you would like to know?" Elaine asked as she cut the pie.

"I heard that Amish children only attend school until the eighth grade. Is that true?"

Elaine nodded. "After they graduate, the young men learn a trade, and in addition to learning how to run a household, the girls will often find jobs outside the home. Sometimes if a family member has their own business, a young girl or boy might help in the store."

Just then, Grandma walked into the room, and Millie flew in right behind her. "Where's the pie? Where's the pie?" the bird shrieked.

This caused a round of laughter from some of the tourists and a few screams from others, while some of the people ducked their heads.

Oh no, now what? Elaine cringed. "Grandma, I thought you had covered her cage."

"Dear me!" Grandma exclaimed, red-faced and looking quite flustered. "I think I must have opened the cage door by mistake." Grandma stood in the archway with her arm extended, which Millie usually landed on immediately, but not so this evening. The parakeet flew this way and that, while Elaine and a few others ran around the room chasing her. Elaine could not believe what was happening. Not only did she feel like a fool, trying to catch the crazy bird, but most of the people laughed, as though they were enjoying the show. Some were rude, however, and took pictures, even though they'd been told that it wasn't permitted. Elaine couldn't really blame them though. How often did a person get photos of a desperate Amish lady chasing after a bird? This was entertainment the tourists hadn't expected. Elaine hoped she wouldn't end up on the front page of their local newspaper. She could read the headline now: *Parakeet Invades Amish Dinner.*

CHAPTER 8

*J*onah tried to concentrate on the song they were singing, but he couldn't help watching Elaine. She sat between her friends Leah and Priscilla on a backless wooden bench in Thomas Diener's barn, where church was being held. Although she sang along with the others, Elaine's heart didn't seem to be in it this morning. Jonah could tell by the slump of her shoulders and her droopy eyes that she was struggling to stay awake. He glanced at the chairs that had been provided for some of the older women, and noticed that Elaine's grandmother also looked tired.

I wonder how things went with the dinner they hosted Friday night, Jonah thought as he shifted on his bench, trying to find a more comfortable position. He'd planned to go over to the Schrocks' on Saturday to check on Elaine and Edna, but he'd gotten busy in the buggy shop and let time slip away. By the time Jonah was done for the day and had taken a shower and eaten supper, it was almost nine o'clock—too late to be making a call on anyone, he'd decided. Hopefully after church let out, he would have a chance to speak with Elaine. He'd been concerned when he'd heard that Elaine and Edna would be hosting a dinner. Jonah didn't understand why they were so determined to do it so soon after Lloyd's death. Elaine and her grandma hadn't had time to grieve properly. Hosting a big meal must have been a drain on the women, and if they weren't careful, one or both of them would end up getting sick.

⁂

During the noon meal after church was over, Elaine took a seat beside Leah. "I need to ask a favor of you," she said, leaning close to her friend.

"What is it?" Leah asked.

"Things didn't go well during our dinner for the tourists the other night, and in addition to forgetting several things, Grandma had another dizzy spell."

Leah's forehead wrinkled. "I'm sorry to hear that. What happened?"

Elaine gave her friend a recap of the events, then said, "I was so glad when the evening finally came to an end."

"I think your grandma ought to see the doctor."

"So do I, and I suggested that to her, but she wouldn't agree to it." Elaine touched Leah's arm. "Grandma's been coming to you for foot treatments for some time, and she has confidence in you, so I was hoping you might have a talk with her about this."

"When she got dizzy last week, I did suggest that she see the doctor, but I can try again if you like."

"I would appreciate it. I'm worried about Grandma."

"Why don't you bring Edna over to our place tomorrow morning around ten for a foot treatment? I'll talk to her then."

"That sounds good, Leah. We'll be there on time."

Just then, Susan Diener, whose home they were at, stopped by. "Leah," she said, "I just wanted to tell you that I haven't had any trouble with my sinuses since you worked on my feet last Friday."

"I'm glad to hear that." Leah smiled at the elderly woman, who then moved on down the table to talk with some of the other women.

Elaine hoped Grandma would have equally good results when she went to see Leah for a foot treatment. Maybe while her feet were getting massaged, Grandma would be more receptive to the idea of seeing the doctor.

For the first time all day, Elaine relaxed a bit. This was the first time since last autumn that anyone had been able to have the after-church meal outside. The Dieners' spacious backyard featured two large maple trees to sit under. The leaves were just emerging and offered little shade, but no one seemed to notice in this mild April weather. There was plenty of room in the yard for all the tables and benches to be set up as well.

Elaine smiled to herself. She could imagine Grandpa Schrock sitting among the men, as he'd done so many times over the years. Several conversations were going on at one time, each carrying a sense of excitement in the voices as they discussed various topics with friends. How Grandpa would have enjoyed being here today and taking part in the discussions.

"Are you listening to me?" Leah patted Elaine's hand gently.

Elaine shook her thoughts aside. "What was that?"

"I said, while I'm working on your grandma's feet in the basement, it might be best if you wait upstairs with my mamm. I don't want Edna to think we're ganging up on her. She may be more willing to listen to me if you're not there."

Elaine nodded, but she wasn't sure that her absence when Leah talked to Grandma would make any difference. She hadn't been around the last time Leah expressed her concerns to Grandma. Maybe this time, since Grandma had gotten dizzy again, things would be different.

⌘

Elaine had just finished eating and was heading over to see if Grandma was ready to go home when Jonah stepped up to her. "I was wondering how things are going and if there's anything I can do for you."

"You can pray for Grandma. Things didn't go well during the dinner we hosted."

"What happened?"

"For one thing, Grandma had a dizzy spell."

"Is she all right?" Jonah's expression revealed his concern.

"I'm not sure, and I'm hoping she'll agree to see the doctor."

"That would probably be a good idea. Did anything else happen at the dinner?" he questioned.

"It was a total disaster. Grandma dropped one of our pies, and that crazy parakeet, Millie, got out of her cage and created quite a stir with the tourists. I've always enjoyed helping Grandma with our dinners, but I was actually relieved when the people left." Elaine paused to massage the back of her neck. "Anyway, I'll be taking Grandma to see Leah in the morning for a foot treatment."

Jonah's forehead creased. "I have nothing against Leah's reflexology practice, but she's not able to do blood tests and some other things that the doctor would want to do. And, as I'm sure you'd agree, Leah's treatments are not a cure-all for every illness."

"I realize that." Elaine didn't know why, but Jonah's comment made her defenses rise. "The only reason I'm taking Grandma to see Leah is in the hope that while Leah works on Grandma's feet, she can talk her into seeing the doctor."

"Do you think Edna will listen to Leah?"

"I hope so, because I wasn't able to convince her." Elaine's lips compressed. "When Grandpa was alive, he could talk Grandma into almost anything. I remember once when he wanted the three of us to go camping. Grandma didn't take to the idea, because she wasn't comfortable with sleeping in a tent."

"So what happened?" Jonah asked.

"Grandpa said if Grandma went camping, then he'd wash and dry the dishes for a whole week after we got home." Elaine smiled. "That was all it took. Grandma went camping."

"Did she enjoy it?"

"For the most part, but when it came time to crawl into that little tent for the night, she let it be known that she wasn't happy about it." Elaine's smile disappeared. "If Grandpa was here now, he'd figure out some way to get Grandma to see the doctor."

"Please let me know if there's anything I can do for you or Edna. I'll drop everything to come and help if you need me." Jonah's tender brown eyes remained fixed on her face.

"Danki." While Elaine appreciated Jonah's offer, he had a thriving business to run, and the thought of asking him for help made her feel guilty.

∽

"I don't see why you felt it necessary to come with me today," Grandma said to Elaine as they headed to Leah's on Monday morning. "I've been to her house for foot treatments many times, and you never went along unless you were getting one too."

Elaine gripped her horse's reins a little tighter. How could she explain her concerns without Grandma getting upset? She couldn't admit that she'd talked to

Leah yesterday and planned the whole thing. Nor did she intend to mention that she didn't want Grandma taking the horse and buggy out alone until her physical issues had been resolved. Were these spells due to stress because Grandma missed Grandpa so much, or were they caused by some illness or other medical condition? If anything happened to Grandma, Elaine didn't know what she would do. More than anything, she longed for things to be as they were before, but that was just wishful thinking.

In an effort to relieve some of her own stress, Elaine tried to focus on the fruit trees growing in a nearby orchard, with some of their colorful blossoms opening while other blossoms were drifting away. The white blossoms looked like snow as they flew off the trees and floated in tiny swirls across the road in front of them.

"Did you hear what I said?" Grandma asked, lightly bumping Elaine's arm.

"Jah, I heard. Just thinking about how to respond, is all."

"It seems rather simple to me." Grandma's brows furrowed. "I just want to know why you felt it necessary to accompany me today."

"Well," Elaine began hesitantly, "I know how tired you've been, and I thought you might not feel up to driving the horse by yourself."

Grandma folded her arms and huffed. "I may be old and tired, but I'm not too feeble to handle a horse and buggy."

"Okay." Elaine paused, searching for the right words. "I also thought it would be nice for me to visit with Leah's mamm while you have your foot treatment. Dianna and I haven't had a chance to talk since Grandpa's funeral, and I wanted to personally thank her for helping out during the funeral dinner."

"She was very helpful," Grandma agreed, "just as so many others from our community were that day. I'm thankful for the kindness of our Amish friends and neighbors."

Elaine nodded as she clicked her tongue and gave her horse, Daisy, the freedom to trot. The mare seemed eager to go, and Elaine was equally anxious to get to Leah's. She hoped and prayed that everything would go well once they got there.

∽

"It's good to see you," Leah said when Edna and Elaine entered her parents' house. "How are you today?"

"We're both fine, but I'll probably be better once I've had a foot bath—I mean massage," Edna quickly corrected. Her cheeks colored and she fanned her face with both hands. "My, my, it's sure a warm day. Soon it'll be hot and humid."

Leah glanced at Elaine and gave her a brief smile. Then, taking Edna's arm, she said, "Why don't we head down to the basement now? Or if you'd rather not have to deal with the stairs, we can do the treatment up here in the living room."

"I've never had a problem going up and down stairs, and I'm sure I'll be just fine with them now," Edna huffed.

"Okay." Leah looked at Elaine again. "My mamm's outside in her garden. You may have seen her there when you pulled in."

Elaine shook her head. "Actually, I didn't, but I was focused on the front door. I'll go out and see if I can find Dianna now."

"Elaine wouldn't let me drive over here by myself

this morning," Edna complained as Leah led the way to the basement. "She was afraid I might get woozy again, but I feel fine today." She moved across the room where the recliner sat and grunted as she lowered herself into it. "Elaine said she wanted to visit with your mamm, but I think she only came along because she's being overprotective."

"I know that Elaine is concerned, but then, shouldn't we appreciate it when someone we love cares about us?" Leah asked.

"Um. . .what was that?"

"I said, Elaine's concerned, and shouldn't we appreciate it when someone we love cares about us?" Leah repeated.

"You're right." Edna removed her shoes and stockings and reclined the chair, giving Leah better access to her feet.

As Leah started pressure-pointing the balls of Edna's feet, she found several sore spots that caused her patient to flinch. One area in particular, on the inside of the foot, signaled that there was a problem with Edna's pancreas. "That's really tender there, isn't it?"

Edna nodded. "I'll say. It feels like I've been walking barefoot and stepped on a sharp rock."

"I believe it's sore because there's a problem with your pancreas," Leah explained.

"What does that mean?"

"Well, I'm not a doctor, so I can't give you a diagnosis, but if you want my opinion, I think you should see your doctor so he can run some tests." Leah pulled her hands away from Edna's feet. "It's possible that you might have either diabetes or low blood sugar."

"Isn't there something you can do about that?" Edna asked with a hopeful expression.

"I might be able to help some, but not until you've had blood work done and know exactly what you're dealing with. If it is your blood sugar, the doctor will have special instructions for you and perhaps prescribe medicine to take."

Edna sighed. "Oh, all right; I'll see if I can get in to see the doctor sometime this week."

"Good. I'm glad you're willing to go." Leah handed Edna her socks and shoes. She hoped Edna kept her word, because she was truly worried about her. Not just because there might be a problem with her pancreas, but because of her lack of concentration and failing memory.

CHAPTER 9

*W*hen Edna returned home after her doctor's appointment on Thursday, she was so tired she could barely put one foot in front of the other. Elaine had hired a driver to take them since her horse had thrown a shoe. After a long wait, they were finally taken into the examining room, and then more waiting, until the doctor came in. Edna had never liked waiting, not even when she was a girl. After Dr. Larkens had examined Edna, he'd asked her so many questions it made her head hurt. Then he'd given her the paperwork needed to get some blood work. Since the lab work could only be done following an overnight fast, Edna would have to wait until tomorrow morning to go to the lab. That meant hiring their driver again.

Edna looked at the calendar on the kitchen wall and frowned. They had no more dinners scheduled for the rest of April, and just one so far for May. Now that the weather was warming up, she hoped more tourists would come to the area and book a dinner in her home. With today's doctor's appointment, and now lab work to get done, she could use some extra money to pay the bills. "The Lord will provide," she murmured.

"What was that, Grandma?" Elaine asked, entering the kitchen.

Edna turned and smiled at Elaine. "What was what?"

"What were you saying when I came into the room?"

"Just that. . . Oh, never mind, it wasn't important." No

way was Edna going to admit that she'd forgotten what she'd said. It had bothered her today when Elaine told the doctor that she was concerned because Edna seemed forgetful lately.

I don't know why she even mentioned that, Edna thought. *What's forgetting a few little things got to do with the wooziness I've felt a few times?*

"Are you hungry, Grandma?" Elaine asked, moving toward the refrigerator. "It's almost noon and I can make some ham-and-cheese sandwiches, if that appeals."

"That'll be fine," Edna replied. "No *moschdept* for me, though. It makes my teeth burn."

"You mean mustard burns your tongue?"

Edna's cheeks warmed. "Jah, that's right." She was relieved when Elaine didn't make an issue out of her having said the wrong word.

"No problem. I don't particularly like mustard on my sandwich either." Elaine took the ham, cheese, and a jar of mayonnaise from the refrigerator. Then she placed them on the counter near the sink.

Wanting to help, Edna got out the bread and a knife. "I'll make the sandwiches while you set the table."

Elaine shrugged. "Whatever you want to do is fine with me."

While Edna put the sandwiches together, Elaine set the table and poured them each a glass of iced tea with a slice of lemon. When the sandwiches were done, they took seats at the table and bowed their heads for silent prayer.

As Edna thanked God for the food, she thought about Lloyd and how, whenever he'd finished praying, he would rustle his napkin so that she and Elaine would know he was done. Oh, how she missed that sound. Even more, she missed him sitting at the head of their table.

It was hard to think of her dear husband never coming back, but somehow she had to press on. Elaine needed her, and as much as she hated to admit it, she needed Elaine too.

❧

Heavenly Father, Elaine prayed, *I thank You for this meal and for the hands that prepared it. Lord, You know how much I love my grandma and how worried I am about her. I pray the outcome of her blood tests will let the doctor know what's wrong, and if it should turn out to be something serious, then please give us the grace to deal with it.*

Upon hearing a rustling noise, Elaine opened her eyes. When she looked over at Grandma, she noticed that her hand was on a napkin near the place where Grandpa used to sit. A lump formed in Elaine's throat. Hearing that familiar sound had almost been her undoing, but she held herself together in order to be strong for Grandma's sake. *Jah, Grandma, I miss him too.*

Except for the muffled crying Elaine heard coming from behind Grandma's closed door each night, she hadn't witnessed Grandma openly grieving much. Elaine figured it was because Grandma was trying to put on a brave front for her sake. Maybe keeping busy and attempting to be strong for each other was what they both needed in order to deal with their grief and move forward.

Grandma pointed to her plate. "Shall we eat?"

Elaine nodded and picked up her sandwich. She really wasn't that hungry, but Grandma needed to eat, so she would do the same.

"Will you be going with me tomorrow for the blood tests?" Grandma asked, reaching for her glass of iced tea.

"I thought I would. When we're done, maybe we can

stop somewhere for breakfast, since you'll have been fasting and will need to eat."

Grandma picked up her glass and took a drink. "Don't like it much when I prick my finger with a sewing needle, so I'm not looking forward to getting my arm stuck."

"I understand, but the blood draw is the only way to monitor your blood sugar in the morning, and I'm sure the doctor will be checking for other things as well."

Grandma frowned while fingering the edge of her plate. "Sure hope there's nothing seriously wrong. As much as I'd like to join your grossdaadi in heaven, I don't like the idea of leaving you alone."

"I wouldn't like that either," Elaine said sincerely. "But let's not put the buggy before the horse. We need to wait till the tests are all in and we've talked to the doctor again next week. Now, why don't we change our topic of conversation to something cool and tasty?"

Grandma quirked an eyebrow. "Like what?"

"Well, we have some lemon sherbet in the freezer that we can have after lunch, if that appeals."

"That sounds good, but first there's something I need to say."

"Oh, what's that?"

Grandma looked directly at Elaine. "I think you need to think about the future, not just today."

"What do you mean?"

"Maybe you should marry Jonah right away, so you won't be alone after I'm gone."

Elaine nearly choked on the cold tea she was drinking. "For goodness' sakes, Grandma, I can't get married right now. I need to be here to take care of you. Besides, Jonah hasn't even asked me to marry him, and even if he did—"

Their conversation was interrupted by a knock on

the door. "I'll see who it is," Elaine said, rising from the table.

When she opened the back door, she was surprised to see Jonah on the porch. She hadn't heard his horse and buggy pull in. She hoped he hadn't heard through the open kitchen window what Grandma had said to her. "Hello, Jonah. I—I didn't expect to see you today," Elaine stammered. "I figured you'd be hard at work in your buggy shop."

"I was, but I needed some bread at the bakery down the road, so figured it'd be a chance to drop by and see how things went at Edna's appointment this morning." Jonah smiled, and when he removed his straw hat, his curly dark hair stood straight up.

Elaine resisted the temptation to laugh, or worse yet, to reach out and flatten his hair in place. Instead, she asked him to come in. He either hadn't heard what Grandma had said or chose not to mention it.

When Jonah entered the house, he hung his hat over a wall peg and smoothed the top of his head. Elaine was glad, because she figured her outspoken grandma surely would have said something about Jonah's unruly hair if he went into the kitchen with it sticking up like that.

"Well Jonah, now isn't this a coincidence?" Grandma grinned at Jonah. "We were just talking about you."

Oh no, Elaine groaned inwardly. *Please, Grandma, don't tell Jonah what was said.*

Jonah smiled. "Is that a fact? And what, might I ask, were you saying?"

"Oh, nothing much," Elaine was quick to say. She motioned to the sandwich makings on the counter. "Have you had lunch yet? I'd be happy to make you a sandwich."

"Sure, that'd be great. I'll head to the bathroom and wash up."

As soon as Jonah left the room, Elaine whispered to Grandma, "Please don't say anything to Jonah about marrying me, okay?"

Grandma shook her head. "I would never do that."

"That's good. Let's just keep the conversation on anything other than that topic."

"No problem."

Hoping Grandma kept her word, Elaine set about making a sandwich for Jonah. By the time he returned, it was ready and sitting on the table.

"Would you like iced tea or something else to drink?" Elaine asked after Jonah took his seat.

"Iced tea is fine, since that's what you're having," he replied.

Elaine poured Jonah a glass and then sat quietly while he said his silent prayer. "The ham-and-cheese sandwich has only mayonnaise on it, but I can get the mustard if you want some of that," she said once he'd lifted his head.

"No, that's okay. This is just how I like it."

"How about some potato chips?" Grandma asked. "I think we still have some in the pantry."

"The sandwich and tea are plenty for me," he responded. "Fact is, it's more than I expected to have for lunch today."

"If you had a wife, she'd make sure you were fed properly." Grandma glanced briefly at Elaine; then, looking away, she grabbed her iced tea and took a drink.

"This is sure nice spring weather we're having, isn't it?" Elaine asked Jonah, attempting to change the subject.

He nodded. "Always did like spring. It's not too hot and not too cold. Perfect weather for fishing and taking buggy rides."

They finished their meal with a bit of light

conversation. Then Jonah turned to Elaine's grandma and said, "Did you see the doctor today?"

"Jah. He said he won't know why I've been feeling a bit puny lately until he gets the results of my blood tests." Grandma frowned. "I can't eat any breakfast in the morning because I'll be getting my blood drawn at the lab."

"We'll return to the doctor's next week," Elaine put in. "He should have the results of her blood work by then."

"It's good that you went. Please keep me posted when you know something definite." Jonah scooted his chair away from the table. "Danki for the lunch, but I probably should be on my way, unless there's something you need me to do first."

"How about doing the dishes?" Grandma asked in a teasing tone. "Since you're a bachelor, I'm sure you've learned how to wash them quite well."

A trickle of perspiration ran down Elaine's forehead. She hoped, once again, that Grandma wasn't on the verge of bringing up the topic of marriage.

"I'm sure Grandma's only kidding," Elaine was quick to say. "I'm perfectly capable of doing the dishes, and I'm sure you have better things to do with your time."

Jonah grinned and winked at Grandma. "I do know how to wash and dry the dishes, and maybe I'll prove that to you the next time I'm invited here for a meal. I hope you both have a good rest of the day," he added, moving toward the door.

Grandma leaned toward Elaine and whispered, "Aren't you going to see him out?"

"Certainly." Elaine followed Jonah to the door and handed him his hat. "Danki for stopping by, Jonah."

"No problem." He opened the door, but paused and turned to face her. "Say, I was wondering if you'd like to go for a buggy ride with me tomorrow evening. There's supposed to be a full moon, and I thought it would be a chance for us to spend a little time together."

"That sounds like fun, but with Grandma not feeling well, I'd better stay close to home in case she needs me."

"I'll be fine," Grandma called from the kitchen in a bubbly voice. "You two need to get out and enjoy this beautiful weather, and Elaine, I insist that you go for that ride."

Feeling that she had little choice in the matter, Elaine smiled at Jonah and said, "Unless something comes up to prevent it, I'll see you tomorrow night." Truth was, it would be nice to spend some time alone with Jonah, and hopefully it would lift her spirits.

CHAPTER 10

*I*f you don't need me for anything else right now, I think I'll get supper started," Sara told her mother-in-law.

"No, I'm fine," Betty said, leaning against the pillows Sara had placed under her head after she'd reclined on the sofa. Sara had also put an extra pillow under her broken leg. "I only wish I didn't have to lay here staring at the ceiling while you do all the work. I feel so *nixnutzich* right now."

"You're not worthless. I'm glad I can be here to help out." Sara patted her mother-in-law's arm affectionately. "I believe I'll get started on supper now. If you need anything, just holler."

"Carolyn can set the table," Betty called as Sara started for the kitchen. "And if the older boys aren't doing anything, they can mash potatoes or do whatever else you need."

"I'll keep that in mind," Sara said before disappearing into the other room. While she had planned on asking for Carolyn's help, it would be better if the boys stayed out of the kitchen. She remembered all too well how whenever Harley had helped get a meal on, he'd ended up either burning something or making a mess that Sara later had to clean up. *Even with the messes, I'd give anything to have Harley here right now, helping me in the kitchen.*

❧

"Let's go, boy!" Jonah snapped the reins. "You're bein' a slowpoke again."

Ignoring Jonah's command, his temperamental horse just plodded.

Jonah grimaced. At this rate, he'd never get to Elaine's for their buggy ride. It had been too long since he and Elaine had spent some quality time alone, and he looked forward to a relaxing Friday evening, just the two of them. He wouldn't keep her out long, because she'd be worried about her grandmother.

Sure hope everything's gonna be okay with Edna, Jonah thought. *She and Elaine have been through enough.* Jonah hoped that someday he and Elaine would be as blessed as his parents. Mom and Dad had been through some rough times over the years, but nothing had kept them down or driven them apart. They worked together, prayed together, had fun together. There was no doubt in Jonah's mind— his folks made a great team.

Jonah had only seen his parents once since he left Pennsylvania and hoped they would come visit him and Jean soon. Dad's buggy business was even busier than Jonah's, so it was hard for him to set work aside and travel.

Maybe Mom and Dad will come here for Jean's and my birthday in July, Jonah thought. *That would sure be nice.*

As Edna's place came into view, Jonah guided his horse and buggy up the driveway. Just as he was securing Sassy to the hitching rack, a sleek-looking black cat streaked out of the barn and darted under the buggy. Sassy spooked and nearly pulled the reins from Jonah's hand. He didn't recognize the cat as one of Edna's and figured it was either a stray or had come from one of the neighboring farms. *Probably went into the barn to steal some of Patches' food,* he mused. *Or maybe the cat was looking for mice.*

Jonah secured Sassy to the rack and sprinted up to the house.

❦

"Jonah's here," Grandma said as she and Elaine stood at the sink doing the last of the supper dishes. "I just saw a horse and buggy come into the yard. I'll bet he's anxious to take you for a buggy ride."

"I heard the *clippety-clop* of his horse's hooves too." Elaine finished drying the plate she held and went to the back door.

"How are things going?" Jonah asked when he stepped onto the porch. "Is your *grossmudder* doing okay?"

"She's still quite tired, but at least she didn't have any dizzy spells today. But then, I made sure she took it easy and ate regular meals, with a few healthy snacks in between."

Jonah smiled. "That's good to hear. I'm sure you're anxious to get the results of her blood tests."

"Jah." Elaine opened the door wider. "Would you like to come in while I finish drying the dishes? There are just a few left to do."

"No problem. I don't mind waiting." Jonah removed his straw hat and smoothed the top of his hair. "I wanted to come in and say hi to Edna anyway."

Elaine smiled. She was glad Jonah was so considerate and thoughtful. In many ways, he reminded Elaine of her grandfather—a hard worker who was always conscious of others and their needs.

Elaine led the way to the kitchen, where Grandma stood at the sink, washing the last of the dishes.

"*Guder owed*, Edna," Jonah said.

Grandma glanced over her shoulder and smiled. "Good evening, Jonah. How are you?"

"I'm doin' well. How about yourself?"

"Can't complain, although I'd be doing much better

if Lloyd was still here."

"I'm sure you must miss him," Jonah said. "I didn't know Lloyd as well as you and Elaine of course, but from the first time I met him, I knew he was a good man."

Tears welled in Elaine's eyes. Knowing she needed to get her mind on something else, lest she start blubbering, she picked up the dish towel to dry the remaining dishes.

"Would you like a cup of coffee, or maybe some tea?" Grandma asked. "Lloyd used to enjoy having tea around this time every night, because coffee kept him awake."

Jonah glanced at the clock. "If it's not too late when Elaine and I get back from our buggy ride, I'll have a cup of tea."

"We should probably go now," Elaine said, placing the last of the dishes she'd dried into the cupboard. "I don't want to leave Grandma alone too long, so it's best if we're not out real late." Truth was, Elaine felt apprehensive about leaving Grandma alone at all, but if she didn't go on the ride with Jonah, Grandma would insist.

"That's fine," Jonah said. "We can go whenever you're ready."

"Just give me a minute to get my shawl and outer bonnet." Elaine hung up the dish towel and hurried from the room. When she returned, she was surprised to see Jonah sitting at the table, alone.

"Where'd my grandma go?" Elaine asked.

"Said she was tired and went to her room."

"I'd better go check on her." Elaine started in that direction but paused. "Maybe it would be best if we didn't go for a ride tonight."

Jonah dropped his gaze to the floor. He was obviously disappointed.

"Well, maybe it would be okay," Elaine said, quickly changing her mind. "Let me just go check on Grandma first."

∽

While Elaine left the kitchen, Jonah remained in his chair. Elaine was concerned about Edna, but he wondered if she was being overly protective. Still, if Edna wasn't feeling well, they probably should put off the buggy ride until a better time.

"Grandma's resting, but she's not asleep," Elaine said when she returned. "I asked again if she'd prefer that I stay home with her this evening, but she insisted on us going for a buggy ride."

Jonah rose from his seat. "Okay, if you're sure, then I guess we'd better get going."

When they left the house and started across the yard, Jonah's horse snorted and stamped his hooves impatiently. "We'll be heading out soon, Sassy, so don't be so impatient," Jonah called before helping Elaine into his buggy. "That horse of mine is either raring to go or doesn't want to go at all. Here lately, he wants to move at a snail's pace."

Elaine smiled. "Sometimes I feel that way myself. There are days when it's an effort just to get out of bed."

"Makes sense that you'd feel that way when you have so much to do and are worried about your grandma besides." Jonah untied Sassy and had barely taken his place in the driver's seat when the horse started backing up. Any other time he would have had to coax the animal to back away from the hitch rack. "Talk about unpredictable!" Jonah chuckled and shook his head.

After Jonah guided the horse and buggy down the driveway and out onto the road, Sassy fell into a nice, easy trot. He glanced over at Elaine and smiled, noticing her peaceful expression, which he hoped meant she was beginning to relax. A romantic ride on a nice evening such as this could be good therapy for both of them.

Going past a small wetland area not far down the road, Jonah's ears perked up when the sound of nature's chorus greeted him. "Just listen to those peepers," he said, pulling back on the reins to slow Sassy. "That sounds like music to my ears every time I hear it this time of the year."

"I know what you mean," Elaine agreed. "Grandpa used to say that when the tree frogs started singing, it meant winter was over." Her voice cracked. "I wish he was still with us. Things could be much easier on my grandma. He was so good to her, and every day I miss him."

Jonah reached for her hand. "It's hard losing a loved one."

"Jah."

Feeling the need to talk about something a little lighter, Jonah said, "The other evening, when I was in the backyard picking up some twigs, I heard the peepers out behind my house by the pond. I've been opening my window every night since, 'cause that sound is like a lullaby singing me to sleep."

Elaine giggled, which was a confirmation to Jonah that she was having a good time. For Jonah, this evening would be another memorable time. He thought Elaine was one of the sweetest women he'd ever known. The fact that she was staying true to her responsibilities to take care of Edna was proof of Elaine's caring attitude, and he respected her for it. *What a great girl I have chosen. She's just right for me.*

They approached a row of sugar maples growing near the edge of the road. In autumn, the trees would be all aglow in their brilliant colors of gold, orange, and red. This area had become a popular spot for picture taking by many tourists who visited Douglas County. Jonah couldn't blame them. They were his favorite trees as well.

Although fading in the distance, Jonah could still hear the peepers behind them. That, plus the steady *clip-clop* of Sassy's hooves, was enough to put anyone into a peaceful state of mind.

"Have you done any rock painting lately?" Jonah asked, breaking the silence.

"No, I haven't had much time for that since Grandpa died." Elaine sighed. "I miss it though. It's a relaxing hobby, and it's always fun to see what kind of rocks I can find that look similar to some animal."

"Speaking of rocks, I thought it might be fun if we went over to Rockome Gardens some Saturday afternoon. We could make a day of it."

She smiled. "That sounds nice, Jonah, but I wouldn't be comfortable leaving Grandma that long."

"She could come with us."

Elaine shook her head. "Grandma gets tired when she does a lot of walking. Maybe we could go some other time, once Grandma's doing better."

"Okay, I guess that would work."

Elaine touched Jonah's arm. "How are things going with your house? Are you getting it fixed up the way you'd wanted?"

Jonah nodded. "There are still some things I'd like to have done, and I'm trying to do a little something to each of the rooms every chance I get. It's slow going at times, because making and repairing buggies can be pretty demanding. Finding a few hours to work on my house gets a little difficult." He leaned in close to Elaine and smiled. "If you get some time in the future, I could use your thoughts on the type of cabinets to put in the kitchen. I'm not too sure what would look presentable or would accommodate someone using the space."

"Maybe I could do that sometime when Grandma has company. That way she won't feel like I've left her alone. Owning a home is a lot of responsibility, but I'm sure it's rewarding."

"Jah." *It would be even more rewarding if you agreed to marry me.* Jonah resisted the temptation to pull his buggy to the side of the road, take Elaine into his arms, and ask her to marry him right then. *"Patience is a virtue,"* his mother had reminded him many times over the years. Mom was right, but that didn't make it any easier to deal with impatience—especially when it came to his desire to marry Elaine. *I'll give her a few months, until Edna's doing better physically and has gotten over Lloyd's death sufficiently so she can be by herself.* Jonah's jaw clenched. *It wouldn't be fair to expect Elaine to leave her grandmother all alone in that big house if she marries me and moves to my place. The only logical thing is to suggest that Edna come live with us too.*

As Jonah's horse picked up speed, he made a decision. When he felt the time was right to propose marriage, he would make sure Elaine knew that he intended to provide for her grandmother and that Edna was welcome to live with them.

CHAPTER 11

ow, don't look so *naerfich*, dear one," Grandma said as she and Elaine entered the clinic on Thursday of the following week. "I'm sure everything's going to be fine."

"I'm not really nervous—just anxious to get the results of your blood test." Elaine took a seat in the waiting room. *Does my apprehension show that much?* she wondered.

Grandma sat down next to Elaine and picked up a gardening magazine. She began thumbing through it as though she hadn't a care in the world. Was she putting on a brave front for Elaine's benefit, or was this Grandma's way of dealing with her own trepidation?

Guess I'm having enough anxious thoughts for both of us. I hope we don't have to wait too long to see the doctor today. Elaine twisted the handles on her purse while glancing at the stack of magazines on the table in front of them. *No point in trying to read a magazine. I wouldn't be able to focus on any of the articles, interesting or not.*

Elaine was tempted to get up and start pacing but didn't want to draw attention to herself. Instead, she sat rigidly in her chair, picking at a bothersome hangnail. She couldn't help wondering how a little thing like that could be so sore. Fortunately, she didn't have to think about it long, for the nurse came out and asked them to follow her into the examining room.

Grandma took the magazine she'd been reading with her. Elaine figured Grandma may have thought they'd have to wait awhile for the doctor, or perhaps she'd found an interesting article she wanted to finish reading.

Once they were seated in the examining room and Grandma's vitals had been taken, Grandma continued to look at the magazine while Elaine's thoughts wandered. She looked around the room at all the charts on the walls. Some showed the heart and different valves and arteries leading in and out of the chambers. Other charts listed symptoms of certain health issues.

Elaine was glad she could be here for Grandma today and remembered back to a time when she'd had the flu and Grandma had sat up with her most of the night, doing all she could to bring down the fever and settle her upset stomach.

Elaine's thoughts switched to her first day of school, when Grandpa had given her a ride with his horse and buggy. He'd told Grandma that he didn't want Elaine walking to school by herself, and until she found a friend to walk with, he'd see that she got there safely each morning. Grandma and Grandpa had both taken an interest in the things Elaine had learned throughout her eight years of attending the Amish one-room schoolhouse—helping with her homework and listening intently as she shared some of the things she'd learned in class. Along with all the other parents, Elaine's grandparents had always attended Elaine's school programs. Just seeing their smiling faces as they sat on a bench in the schoolhouse had given Elaine a sense of joy. She'd never once felt like she didn't belong.

Grandma rustled the magazine, drawing Elaine's attention back to her. "What are you doing?" she asked when Grandma began tearing out a page.

Grandma smiled. "I found a recipe that sounds really good, and I'd like to try it sometime."

"But someone else may want to try that recipe too." Elaine pulled a pen and notebook from her purse. "If you want, I'll write it down for you."

"I guess that would be the best thing to do. I don't know why I didn't think of it myself." Grandma handed the magazine to Elaine.

Elaine had just finished copying the recipe when Dr. Larkens entered the room.

"Good morning, ladies. I'm sorry to keep you waiting."

"Oh, that's all right." Grandma smiled up at him. "It didn't seem like we were waiting that long, and we know how busy you are."

He pulled up a chair in front of Grandma and motioned to the lab report he held. "All the results from your blood tests are back, Edna, and it appears that your symptoms are caused by high blood sugar."

"Does that mean my grandmother has diabetes?" Elaine asked before Grandma could offer any kind of response.

The doctor nodded. "It's Type 2 diabetes, and from the results of her tests, in addition to her symptoms, I'm guessing she's had it for a while."

"What should I do about it?" Grandma asked, calmly laying her magazine down.

"Most people can usually manage their diabetes with meal planning, physical activity, and, if needed, medications," he responded. "In your case, I want to begin by prescribing an oral form of insulin, and if that doesn't bring your blood sugar down, you may eventually need insulin shots."

Grandma's eyebrows shot straight up. "I don't like needles, and I'm sure I could never give myself an injection. If Lloyd was here, he could do it, because he always doctored our horses." She shook her head vigorously. "But no, not me. I just couldn't do it."

"It's okay, Grandma." Elaine reached over and clasped Grandma's hand. "Should it become necessary for you to take insulin shots, I'll do it for you." *I won't like it, but I'll do whatever I have to do,* she mentally added.

"Elaine, if it comes to that, my nurse, Annie, will give you the proper instructions." Dr. Larkens looked back at Grandma. "Edna, you'll also need a kit to test your blood sugar every day, and Annie will show Elaine how to use that as well."

Grandma groaned. "I'll take the pill, eat right, and exercise. I'd do anything to avoid getting an insulin shot."

Elaine took the prescription the doctor had written, as well as a list of foods Grandma should and shouldn't eat, and put them in her purse. They would stop at the pharmacy for her medicine before heading home. She hoped Grandma would do everything the doctor suggested, because even though she'd volunteered to give Grandma her insulin shots, just the idea of it made her feel nervous.

❦

"I'll walk over to the pharmacy to get your prescription," Elaine told Edna after she'd pulled her horse and buggy up to one of several hitching racks in downtown Arthur. Typical of late April, the weather had been pleasant and comfortably dry. No doubt humid weather would be coming soon. But for now, the sun shone brightly in a clear azure sky, and a pleasant breeze had come up from the south. It was a near-perfect day.

"I can go with you." Grandma opened her mouth wide and yawned, then quickly covered it with her hand. "That way I can tell the pharmacist what I need."

"He will know what you need as soon as I show

him this." Elaine reached into her purse and took out the prescription. "You look tired, Grandma, so it might be best if you stay here and rest." While that was true, the real reason Elaine didn't want Grandma to go into the pharmacy was because she'd be tempted to buy something sweet. In addition to prescriptions and other medical-related products, the pharmacy on Vine Street had an old-fashioned soda fountain where a person could sit and enjoy a tasty cold treat. Grandma had never been able to resist the root beer floats that were sold there.

Grandma frowned, making Elaine wonder if she might insist on getting out of the buggy, but to her relief, she finally nodded and said, "I am kind of tired. Maybe I'll just sit here and close my eyes for a bit."

"I shouldn't be gone long, so try to relax." Elaine patted Grandma's arm gently, then climbed out of the buggy and headed down the street.

When she entered the pharmacy a short time later, Elaine went straight to the drop-off area and turned in Grandma's prescription, since it might take awhile for it to be filled. After she was told that it would be about fifteen minutes, she headed toward the discount aisle, where things were usually marked down. On her way, she passed the candy and gum aisle. Normally, Elaine would have bought some candy, but knowing Grandma shouldn't have any, she thought better of it.

I'm going to have to think twice before I bring sugary treats into our home anymore. Since Grandma had always enjoyed sweets, it would be hard for her to give up some of the things she liked to eat. Elaine didn't like the idea of giving up sweet things either, but if it would help Grandma, she would do whatever it took to keep her from being tempted. *It's probably best for me too,* she told herself, *since diabetes can be hereditary.*

Elaine looked at a few of the discounted items but didn't see anything that interested her. She was about to head back to the prescription area and wait for her name to be called when she noticed Priscilla standing in the checkout line at the other end of the store. Elaine hurried to catch up with her and got there just as Priscilla finished paying for her purchases.

"I'm glad I ran into you today," Elaine said to her friend. "I thought you might like to know that we got the results of Grandma's blood work today."

"How did it go?" Priscilla asked.

Looking for a better place to talk, Elaine led the way to the greeting-cards aisle, since no one else was there at the moment.

"Grandma has Type 2 diabetes." Elaine cringed at the thought of what may lay ahead for Grandma—and her as Grandma's caregiver. "That's why she hasn't been feeling well lately."

"I'm sorry to hear that." Priscilla's tone was as sincere as her expression. "Can it be controlled by altering her diet, or will she have to be on insulin?"

"The doctor said Grandma will have to change her eating habits and exercise, but he also gave us a prescription for medicine, which she'll have to take every day." Elaine sighed deeply. "I hope Grandma does everything she's supposed to, because if her diabetes worsens, she may have to take insulin shots. Unfortunately, I'll be the one giving them to her, and just the thought of that makes me *naerfich.*"

"Try not to worry about it." Priscilla gave Elaine's shoulder a tender squeeze. "I'm sure with you there to remind Edna to eat right and take her medicine, everything will be fine."

〜

Edna had been in a deep sleep, but the nap hadn't lasted long. The sound of her own snoring suddenly woke her. Waiting for Elaine, she grew more restless. It was getting stuffy inside the buggy, and she could really use something to drink. Whatever breeze had been moving through the open buggy door when they'd first arrived was suddenly at a standstill. *Think I'll get out and walk over to the pharmacy,* she decided, taking a hankie and wiping the back of her neck where perspiration had collected. One of Edna's legs was on the verge of getting a charley horse, and no matter how much she wiggled and rubbed it, her toes started cramping too.

The idea of treating herself to a frosty chocolate malt, root beer float, or dish of hand-dipped ice cream sounded pretty good to Edna. The pharmacy in Arthur had been making milk shakes, malts, and sodas in a variety of flavors for a good many years, and for as long as she and Lloyd were married, they'd made a trip into town once a week to indulge in one of the icy cold treats. Edna's mouth watered just thinking about it.

With the decision made, she grabbed her purse, stepped down from the buggy, and headed toward the pharmacy. It felt good to get the kinks out of her legs, although her dress clung tightly against the front of her legs as she walked head-on into a sudden, refreshing breeze.

She'd only gone a short distance when she spotted the Stitch and Sew, which was also on Vine Street. *Maybe I'll pop in and buy some white thread,* she decided. *It won't take long, and I'm sure I'll be done before Elaine leaves the pharmacy.*

CHAPTER 12

$\mathcal{W}$hen Elaine left the pharmacy and returned to the buggy, she was surprised to discover that Grandma wasn't there. It was much warmer than when she'd gone into the drugstore, so perhaps in order to cool off, Grandma had taken a walk. *But where can she be?* Elaine felt a sense of panic. *She didn't come into the pharmacy—I'm sure I would have seen her there.*

Elaine looked up and down the street, but there was no sign of Grandma. She figured she only had two choices: wait at the buggy and hope Grandma returned soon from wherever she'd gone, or start looking for Grandma in some of the stores. Deciding on the latter, Elaine headed back down the street.

After checking a few places along Vine Street with no success, Elaine decided to stop by the Stitch and Sew. When she entered the building, the smell of material hit her nostrils and made her sneeze. Her eyes also began to water. *It must be my allergies to chemical odors kicking in.*

Stepping up to the counter, Elaine was about to ask the clerk if she'd seen her grandmother when she spotted Grandma talking to Priscilla's mother, Iva, near the notions aisle.

"Oh, what are you doing in here?" Grandma asked when Elaine walked up to her. "I thought you'd gone to the pharmacy to get my prescription filled."

"I did go there, but when I got back to the buggy, you were gone."

"It was getting stuffy, so I went for a walk, and when I saw the Stitch and Sew, I realized that I needed some thread." Grandma gestured to Priscilla's mother. "Then when I spotted Iva, we got to talking." She stared at Elaine and pursed her lips. "Is everything okay? You look like you're about ready to cry."

"I'm all right," Elaine said when Grandma handed her a tissue. "Sometimes the smell of so much material in one place makes my eyes tear up and causes me to sneeze." She smiled at Priscilla's mother. "It's nice to see you, Iva."

"You too, Elaine."

Feeling a sneeze coming on, Elaine held the tissue up to her nose. *"Achoo!"*

"Bless you," Grandma said, patting Elaine's back.

Elaine giggled self-consciously, feeling heat creep up the back of her neck and spread quickly to her cheeks. "How are you, Iva?"

"I'm doing pretty well. By the way, Priscilla was going to the pharmacy. Did you happen to see her there?"

"As a matter of fact, I did." Elaine placed her fingers against her nose to stifle another sneeze. "We visited awhile, and then I think Priscilla said she was going over to Yoder's Lamp Shop. She's probably there now."

Iva turned toward the door. "I'd better go see if I can catch her. It was nice seeing you both, and don't hesitate to let us know if you need anything at all."

"Danki." Elaine waved as Iva went out the door, but Grandma just stood there with a peculiar expression.

"What's wrong, Grandma?" Elaine asked. "Are you pondering something?"

"I—I know I came in here for a reason, but for the life of me, I can't think of what it is."

"You said you needed some thread."

"Oh, that's right." Grandma made her way to the notions aisle and picked out her thread.

"Let's go get something cold and frosty." She pointed toward the door. "I'll have a root beer float."

"That sounds good, but remember what the doctor said. You're supposed to be careful of what you eat now that you've been diagnosed with diabetes."

Grandma's chin dropped slightly. "I'll feel deprived if I can never indulge in anything sweet."

"You can have fruit in moderation, and we'll learn to make some desserts using sugar substitutes."

Grandma sighed. "If I can't get a root beer float, then as soon as I pay for my thread, we may as well head for home, because I'm hungerich."

Elaine felt bad as she watched Grandma shuffle over to the checkout counter with slumped shoulders. With all that had happened in the last couple of weeks, it would be hard to see Grandma deprived of something as simple as enjoying ice cream. Once she got started on her insulin, and with the doctor's approval, maybe it would be okay if she cheated on her diet once in a while.

"We'll stop at the market before going home and pick up some fresh fruit," Elaine said after they'd left the store.

ॐ

Jonah had just pulled up to one of the hitching racks in Arthur when he noticed Elaine's horse and buggy parked at the other end.

"How are ya doin' there, Daisy girl?" Jonah asked the horse, walking up to her and petting her velvety soft nose.

Daisy nickered in return, stomping her foot and swishing her tail to keep the bothersome flies at bay.

"Good thing you're in the shade over here. The sun's warming things up real quick today." Jonah glanced down the street as he reached up to scratch behind Daisy's ears.

Daisy shook her mane as if in agreement, then nudged her head closer. "Ah, I see that you like your ears scratched too." Jonah smiled and watched as Daisy's head lowered and she closed her eyes. He even thought he heard the horse heave a sigh.

Jonah felt silly standing here, talking to a horse, but he was actually biding time. *Should I wait till Elaine comes back to her buggy, or would I have a better chance of seeing her if I went looking in some of the shops?* As always, Jonah was anxious to see Elaine, if only for a few minutes. But knowing he needed to get back to his shop soon, he decided to poke his head into some of the stores on his way to Yoder's Lamp Shop, where he needed to pick up a gas lamp he'd taken in for repairs a week ago.

One last scratch behind Daisy's ear and Jonah began to whistle as he headed toward Yoder's. He checked a few of the other stores as he went by but didn't see any sign of Elaine. When he reached his destination, he collided with Priscilla, who was just coming out the door.

"Sorry about that," Jonah apologized, propping the door open with his foot. "Sure hope you're not hurt. I should have been watching where I was going."

Priscilla's face flushed as she quickly shook her head. "You just startled me, is all. I didn't expect anyone would be coming in the door at the same time I was going out."

"Me neither." Jonah stepped to one side. "Say, you haven't by any chance seen Elaine around town? I spotted her horse and buggy at one of the hitching racks, so I figured she must be here someplace."

"I met up with her at Dick's Pharmacy awhile ago,"

Priscilla replied. "She was getting a prescription filled for her grandma."

Jonah's forehead wrinkled. "Is Edna grank?"

"She saw the doctor today and got the results of her blood tests." Priscilla pursed her lips. "I should probably let her tell you this, but Edna has diabetes and needs to take insulin for it."

"Wow, that's too bad. Will she have to give herself shots?"

"Not at this time, but she will have to take a pill that will hopefully balance her blood sugar. She'll also need to be on a special diet."

"Hopefully between the medicine and eating right, she'll be okay."

Priscilla nodded. "I know Edna likes sweets, so it'll probably be hard for her to stay on the diet."

"I'm sure Elaine will see that she does," Jonah said. "Speaking of Elaine, do you know where she went after she left the pharmacy?"

"No, I don't. If her horse and buggy's still at the hitching rack, she's obviously in town somewhere."

"Guess I'll pick up my lamp and then check for her in some of the other stores. See you around, Priscilla."

❧

After Jonah left Yoder's, he stopped at several stores, but there was no sign of Elaine. Hoping he might catch her before she left town, he headed back to his horse and buggy. When he got there, Elaine's rig was gone. He was warm and sweaty and couldn't help thinking how refreshing a dip in his pond would feel. That would have to wait for some other time, because he had plenty of work waiting for him once he got home.

"Guess I should have come back here as soon as I left

the lamp shop," Jonah mumbled, placing the box with his lamp in it inside his warm buggy. He would have headed over to Edna's place to see Elaine right now, but he needed to get back to the shop and finish upholstering the seat he'd started this morning for the buggy he was making for their bishop. *Maybe I'll go see her this evening after supper,* Jonah decided. *I need to ask her something important.*

∞

When they arrived home that afternoon, after stopping for lunch, Grandma went into the house while Elaine tended to Daisy, rubbing the mare down and giving her fresh water. Following that, she took a few minutes to play with the cats. Patches, as usual, demanded the most attention, purring and rubbing against Elaine's ankles. This was the second cat she'd named Patches, and like the first one, whom her grandparents had given to her shortly after her parents died, Patches had always been a good mouser, even when she was a kitten.

"Oh, I know what you want." Elaine knelt on the barn floor and smiled when Patches rolled over on her back with all four paws in the air. "Does that feel good?" Elaine rubbed the cat's belly and laughed when Boots, one of their other cats, got into the act, batting at Patches' tail. Patches jumped up, and the two felines ran off. "That's okay," she murmured. "I need to quit lollygagging and go into the house."

As Elaine rose to her feet, she realized how nice it had been to take a bit of time and enjoy something as simple as petting the cat. As busy as she was, she needed to take time once in a while to do little things like that.

When Elaine entered the kitchen, she was surprised to see several things cooking on the stove, and from the wonderful aroma, something was baking in the oven.

Grandma was busily setting out the good dinnerware they used when hosting tourist guests.

"Oh, I'm glad you came in." Grandma turned to smile at Elaine. "I didn't realize it was so late, and there's so much to do before the tour group arrives."

"Oh no, Grandma, I think you're confused about—"

"Elaine, could you please check on the potatoes?" Grandma gestured to the stove. "I don't want anything to boil over while I'm in the other room, setting the table. Oh, and the cake I have in the oven needs to be tested to see how close it is to being done."

Elaine couldn't believe Grandma thought they were hosting a dinner. *Could she have booked it without telling me?* She hurried over to the desk in the kitchen to check the reservation book, but nothing was scheduled.

"We aren't hosting a dinner tonight, Grandma," Elaine explained. "The tour director said she would give us at least a month before she called to schedule another one."

Grandma's face blanched. "What?"

Elaine repeated herself and added with emphasis, "There are no tourists coming here this evening."

Grandma blinked rapidly. "Oh, how silly of me. Don't know why I thought that." She motioned to the food on the stove. "Looks like we'll have plenty to eat for our supper tonight, with lots of leftovers for tomorrow. And oh, won't it be nice to have a piece of that chocolate cake for dessert?"

"Sorry, Grandma," Elaine said, slowly shaking her head, "but that cake in the oven will have to go to someone else, because it's not going to stay here to tempt you."

CHAPTER 13

Jonah had just finished a tuna sandwich when a knock on the door startled him. Setting his empty plate on the kitchen counter, he went to answer it. Jonah hadn't heard a horse and buggy pull into the yard, or he would have looked out the window to see who it was.

When Jonah opened the door, he was surprised to see his twin sister, Jean, standing on the porch.

"From the look of shock on your face, I'm guessing you're surprised to see me," Jean said, smiling up at him.

He nodded. "It's suppertime. Figured you'd be home fixing your family's meal."

"We've already had our supper, and my thoughtful husband not only offered to watch the kinner while I went for a bike ride, but he also volunteered to do the dishes."

"Well, that was sure nice of him." Jonah opened the door wider. "Come in. I'll fix you a cup of tea."

"I'd like that."

Once Jean was seated at the kitchen table, Jonah poured them both tea and took the chair across from her.

"What's new with you?" she asked.

"I finished upholstering the seat on a new buggy for our bishop today."

"That's interesting, but I was thinking more along the lines of what's new with you and Elaine."

He folded his arms. "Oh, that."

"Jah, that." She winked at him. "Have you gotten up the nerve to ask her to marry you yet?"

Jonah's face heated. After hearing about Edna's diagnosis, he'd made a decision. Did his sister know what he was planning to do this evening when he went to see Elaine? Well, he wouldn't tell her now—not until he'd proposed and Elaine had said yes. Then Jean would be the first to know.

⌒

"Carolyn and Marla, you two need to help Sara with the dishes," Sara's father-in-law, Herschel, said after the family had finished eating supper on Thursday evening.

"That's okay; I can manage," Sara was quick to say. Truth was, she'd been dealing with the energetic children all afternoon and needed some time by herself. She'd never met two little girls who got on her nerves as much as her two young sisters-in-law, and it seemed that she had so little patience these days. Caring for Mark didn't bother her so much, because he had no siblings and wasn't looking to pick on a little brother or sister. But since coming here to take care of Betty and oversee the children, Sara's ability to cope seemed to diminish a little more each day.

"All right then," Herschel said, "Carolyn and Marla can keep little Mark occupied in the living room while you're in here getting the dishes done." He smiled at his wife. "Isn't it nice to have Sara here to manage things for us?"

Betty gave an agreeable nod. "I appreciate everything you've done, Sara, but I'll be glad when my leg is healed. Then I'll be able to resume my household duties and take care of my kinner again. It's hard to sit around all the time and watch you do most of the work, Sara."

"I don't mind, really," Sara responded, filling the sink with soapy water. "Now why don't you go into the other room and rest your leg? When I'm finished with the dishes, I'll bring in some coffee for the adults and milk for the kinner, along with some peanut butter cookies I made earlier today."

"Kichlin! Yum!" Marla exclaimed.

Sara couldn't help but smile. She remembered how much she had enjoyed the treat of cookies and milk when she was girl. For that matter, she still enjoyed eating them.

As Betty rose from her chair, Herschel handed the crutches to her. Then he removed his and Betty's dishes from the table and took them to the sink. "Now I want all of you kinner to clear away your *schissele* and then scoot on outa here and let Sara have some peace and quiet. Ya hear?"

All heads bobbed, and the children quickly did as their father said.

An hour later, after Sara had cleaned up the kitchen and finished doing the dishes, she set out the coffee, milk, and cookies. Then she took a seat at the table to rest a minute, because a sense of exhaustion had settled over her like a heavy blanket of fog. Of course, feeling this way was nothing new; she'd felt weary ever since her husband died. The tiredness Sara felt now was different though; it was the kind of fatigue that stayed with her no matter how many hours of sleep she got every night. It often came on in the afternoon, and sometimes her muscles felt weak. The other day, when she was dealing with a senseless squabble between Carolyn and Marla about who would get to feed the cats, Sara's lips had felt sort of tingly, and her limbs became weak and shaky. Figuring it was caused from the stress of it all, Sara had shooed the children outside, fixed herself a cup of chamomile tea, and gone to the room where little Mark was napping. There, she'd taken a seat on the bed and tried to relax. *"Too much stress can make your body react in strange ways,"* she remembered her mother saying.

I wonder how much longer I can continue taking care of Betty and her family, feeling the way that I do. Truth was, Sara felt like she needed someone to take care of her right now.

Sara drew in a deep breath and closed her eyes. *Heavenly Father, please give me the strength I need for each new day, and help me to be a blessing to Betty, Herschel, and their children.*

ᢙᢠ

Elaine had just turned out the gas lamp that hung over the kitchen table when she heard the whinny of a horse. Going to the window, she glanced out and saw Jonah getting down from his buggy. She hurried to the back door, anxious as always to see him. She didn't have to wait long, for Jonah was already sprinting across the lawn toward the house. Elaine smiled, watching Patches get out of his way. By the time Jonah stepped onto the porch, Elaine had opened the door.

"Good evening, Jonah," she said, smiling up at him. "It's nice to see you."

"Same here." Jonah shifted from one foot to the other and raked his fingers through the ends of his thick, curly hair. "I ran into Priscilla today at Yoder's Lamp Shop. She told me about Edna having diabetes."

Elaine nodded. "It was a surprise to both me and Grandma—especially when the doctor said her diabetes is so bad that she needs to be on insulin. Now, in addition to her taking the medicine, we'll have to start cooking differently, since her intake of sweets will need to be limited. By the way, I have a cake here that Grandma baked today, and I don't want it to tempt her. Would you like to take it home?"

"That'd be great, but I'm sure sorry to hear about her diagnosis. If she does everything the doctor says, hopefully her diabetes won't get any worse."

"That's what I'm hoping for too." Elaine was on the verge of telling Jonah about Grandma cooking a big meal for tourists who weren't coming but changed her mind. If Grandma's forgetfulness was a symptom of her diabetes, then Elaine needed to inform the doctor about it rather than telling Jonah. Besides, she was embarrassed for Grandma.

"It's a nice evening. Would you like to sit out here and talk, or would you rather go inside?" she asked, motioning to the wicker chairs on the porch.

"Out here's fine with me," Jonah replied. "That way we can talk in private."

Elaine couldn't imagine what he might have to say that couldn't be said in front of Grandma, but she nodded and took a seat.

After Jonah seated himself in the chair beside Elaine, he looked over at her and smiled. "I was going to wait awhile longer to ask you this question, but I've decided not to wait any longer."

"Wait for what, Jonah?" she questioned.

"I'm in love with you, Elaine, and if you'll have me, I'd like you to be my wife."

Elaine's heart hammered so hard, she wondered if Jonah could hear it pounding in her chest. She had been hoping for this day and would have answered yes immediately if things had been different. But not now. It just wasn't possible for them to get married anytime soon.

As Jonah watched her with an anxious expression, Elaine turned her head toward the setting sun. As she gazed at the sky, it took on a beauty of its own. Various shades of orange and pink blended with the fading blue.

Farther back, the sky looked almost purple, which added to what should have been the most romantic and memorable evening of Elaine's life. Jonah's proposal was supposed to be her dream come true, but now, even on this ideal evening with nature flawlessly cooperating, things were different. Her heart screamed, *I love you too, and nothing would make me happier than to be your wife!* If only she felt free to say those words.

Jonah reached over and touched her arm. "Your silence makes me wonder if you have no desire to marry me."

Tears sprang to Elaine's eyes as she looked back at Jonah. "It—it's not that. I do care for you, Jonah, but. . ." Her words trailed off, and she dropped her gaze, staring down at her shoes. *Why now, Jonah?*

Elaine had imagined what the first time would be like when she declared to Jonah how much she loved him. But now her mouth went dry, and the words seemed to stick in her throat. Common sense made Elaine hold her tongue, but it was the hardest thing she'd ever had to do.

"Do you care about me enough to become my wife?" he asked.

"I—I can't, Jonah."

"How come?"

"Grandma's ill, and she needs me. Not to mention that both of us are still trying to come to grips with Grandpa's death. There's no way I can leave her now."

"I'm not asking you to leave her, Elaine." Jonah lifted his hand from Elaine's arm and took hold of her hand. "I was thinking that Edna could move in with us. My home is big enough for the three of us, and if she wants an area all to herself, I could add on to the house so she would have her own *daadihaus*."

"I don't think Grandma would be happy moving from her own place here, or living in a grandparent house somewhere else. This has been my grandma's home for a good many years, and she enjoys doing the dinners here for tourists." Elaine blinked as Jonah's face became a blur through her tears. "I can't take that away from her, Jonah. She's going through a difficult time getting used to Grandpa being gone, and now finding out that she has diabetes. . . Well, it just wouldn't be fair to expect her to deal with yet another change." Elaine looked toward the horizon again, noticing that the sun had faded. The moment had passed, just like her hopes and dreams.

Jonah sat quietly with his head down, as though studying something on the porch floor. Elaine figured he was trying to process everything. After several minutes, he lifted his head and turned in his seat to face her. "I understand all that you've said, and as anxious as I am to make you my wife, maybe it would be best if we wait awhile longer to get married."

"Danki for understanding, Jonah."

"When you feel the time is right, will you please let me know?" he asked, swiping at a pesky mosquito that had picked a poor time to buzz past his ear.

She smiled and nodded. "Jah, I surely will."

CHAPTER 14

*I*t had been a month since Elaine rejected Jonah's marriage proposal. *Well, maybe not rejected, exactly,* Jonah told himself as he entered his shop on the last Thursday of May. Elaine had just put her decision on hold for a while, which to him was somewhat reassuring, and better than Elaine saying no to his proposal. He wondered, though, how long it would be before she felt ready to make a commitment to him. Would it be a year from now, when her grandmother's time of mourning was up, or would Elaine feel ready for marriage sooner? While Jonah waited, he would continue to fix up his place, and maybe it would be more than ready by the time Elaine agreed to marry him. Keeping busy always helped time pass quickly, and there were certainly several projects at home, as well as in his shop, to keep Jonah busy.

The waiting wouldn't be easy though. Jonah could still picture that night when he'd proposed marriage, with the sunset glowing on Elaine's beautiful face. Jonah couldn't take his eyes off her as he watched for a clue, anticipating the answer he'd hoped to hear. Everything about that moment would have been perfect if she'd only said yes. Afterward, like a craving that couldn't be satisfied, Elaine's image was all he could think about, for she'd never looked more radiant.

Aside from seeing Elaine at their biweekly church services, Jonah hadn't spent much time with her, and he truly missed that. Just being near Elaine stirred his heart.

It was pure agony standing around after services, talking with the other men and trying to seem interested in what they were saying. On one occasion, Jonah had only heard about half of the conversations going on around him when he'd caught a glimpse of Elaine walking with her grandma to their buggy. Jonah had excused himself and hurried in that direction, but then he got waylaid when one of his friends stopped to ask him a question. By the time Jonah got away, Elaine's horse and buggy were heading down the road toward home. He'd planned to go over there that evening, but Jean had invited him to her place for supper, and Jonah felt obligated to go.

Jonah had hoped that one day soon he could take Elaine to Rockome Gardens. Now he wasn't sure he would bring the subject up again. He doubted that she would leave Edna alone for that long.

Jonah paused at his workbench and drew in a deep breath. *What if Elaine never feels ready to leave her grandma? What if Edna isn't willing to leave her home and move in with us?*

Jonah's thoughts were halted when Adam Beachy entered his shop. Jonah didn't know the Amish man very well, but from what he'd heard, Adam was in his late twenties and preferred to keep to himself as much as possible.

"Guder mariye. What can I do for you, Adam?" Jonah asked.

"Mornin'," Adam mumbled, barely making eye contact with Jonah. "I came to see about getting a new buggy. My old one's seen better days."

"I have several orders ahead of you. How soon do you need it?"

Adam shrugged and lifted his straw hat, swishing his fingers through the sides of his thick blond hair. "There's no real rush, I guess, but I was hoping to have it before my sister and her family come to visit me."

"When will that be?" Jonah questioned.

"They live in Indiana and will be here for Christmas."

"It shouldn't be a problem to get it done before then. Starting today, Herschel Stutzman's son Timothy will be helping me in the shop. Once I get him trained, I'll be able to get more done." Jonah glanced at the battery-operated clock on the far wall. "In fact, Timothy ought to be here most any time."

Adam's pale eyebrows lifted. "So the boy wants to learn the buggy-making trade, huh?"

Jonah nodded. "He's sixteen, and now that he's done with school, his folks want him to learn a trade that will always be in demand—at least among us Amish folks. Since I need help here in the shop, I'm hoping it'll work out well for both of us." He reached for an order blank and took a seat at the desk. "Now, if you'll tell me what specifics you'd like in your new buggy, I'll write it all down."

"I'd like a dark gray color for the seat upholstery." Adam leaned on one corner of the desk. Then he went on to tell Jonah all the other things he wanted, including his need for the new buggy to be large enough to carry six people. "I want the buggy to accommodate my sister, her husband, and their three girls, even though they don't come here often," he explained.

"Okay, that shouldn't be a problem."

Jonah had just finished writing up Adam's order and taken his deposit of half down on the new buggy when Timothy showed up. "Sorry I'm late," the lanky teenager said. "One of our frisky goats got out of its pen, and I had to help my *bruder* Paul get him put back in."

"That's okay," Jonah said. "Things happen sometimes."

"Danki for understanding." The boy's worried expression quickly disappeared, and he moved across the room to hang his straw hat on one of the wall pegs.

Jonah had made a carbon copy of the buggy order, so he handed that to Adam. "I'll give you a call as soon as the buggy is ready, but feel free to drop by anytime to see how things are progressing. That way, if there's anything you want to add or change, there'll be time for me to do it. I'll probably get started on it in the next few weeks."

"All right then. I'll be in touch." With a brief "Goodbye," Adam headed out the door.

That fellow never smiled once while he was here, Jonah mused. *I wonder what soured fruit he had for breakfast. No wonder he's not married. Guess he's destined to be a bachelor.*

⁓

"Ouch, that hurts!" Sara winced when Leah pressed a certain area on her left foot. She'd come here for a treatment this morning because her feet were sore from standing so much, not to mention running after Betty's children and doing what seemed like an abundance of chores every day.

"You're not feeling well, are you?" Leah asked, continuing to massage and probe Sara's foot. "I can tell by how you're reacting to some of the pressure points I've touched so far."

"I'm not sick." Sara sighed. "Just tired and feeling quite stressed."

"That's understandable. It can't be easy for you taking care of Betty, her children, and little Mark and, on top of that, doing all the household chores."

"I don't mind, really, but it has taken a toll. Besides the fatigue, my limbs sometimes feel kind of tingly." Sara squeezed her eyes shut and clenched her fingers when Leah hit another tender spot. "It's most likely my nerves, and it's probably terrible of me to say this, but I'll be glad once Betty is back on her feet, and Mark and I can return home where it's quiet."

"How much longer till Betty's cast comes off?" Leah asked.

"Another week or so, but then she'll need physical therapy."

"Maybe once that happens you can go back to your own place and just go over to help out at Betty's during the day."

"Guess I'll have to wait and see how it goes."

"In the meantime, it might be good if you tried to get more rest." Leah reached for her bottle of massage lotion and put some on Sara's other foot. "And if possible, you may want to come back here more often for treatments, at least until you're feeling better."

"That might be a good idea." Sara smiled. "I appreciate your mamm keeping an eye on Mark while I'm down here in the basement with you. Betty's not up to watching him yet, and I sure couldn't ask Carolyn or Marla. Neither one of them is responsible enough to take care of an active toddler."

"I'm sure Mom doesn't mind spending time with your boy," Leah said. "She loves kinner and has a special way with them too."

As Leah continued to work on Sara's feet, the pain subsided, and she found herself beginning to relax. It felt good to do something for herself for a change, and hopefully after the treatment, she would have a bit more energy and be able to cope better with things.

∽

As Elaine left the phone shanty and started walking toward the house, she paused to pick a few flowers. "So pretty." Elaine smiled, inhaling their fragrance.

Millie seemed to be enjoying the moment. The

weather was nice, so Elaine had decided to bring the parakeet's cage outside on the porch. Of course, the little bird had been jabbering ever since. "Purdy, purdy, purdy," Millie repeated several times.

"Jah, you silly bird, the flowers are pretty." Elaine thought the colorful irises would make a nice bouquet to put on the table, and it might help lift Grandma's spirits. After learning that she had diabetes, Grandma had become negative, complaining about having to give up her favorite desserts. Even though Elaine had found some sugar-free recipes in a diabetic cookbook she'd bought at the health food store, Grandma said they didn't taste as good as desserts made with real sugar.

Hoping Leah could convince Grandma that she needed to follow the diet her doctor had suggested, Elaine had scheduled several more reflexology appointments for Grandma. In fact, Grandma had seen Leah yesterday, but apparently it hadn't helped much, because everything she'd talked about on the way home was negative. Was her attitude because of her diabetes, or did she miss Grandpa so much that she couldn't focus on anything positive?

Maybe Grandma needs something to look forward to, Elaine thought. Well, the phone message Elaine had found on their answering machine might put some sparkle back in Grandma's eyes. It was from Sharon Sullivan, asking if Grandma was ready to host another dinner for a group of tourists Friday evening. It had been over a month since the last one, so maybe it was time to try again.

Elaine had talked with their doctor's nurse about Grandma and been told that depression could be the cause of Grandma's memory issues, which was logical, given that she was still grieving for Grandpa and now had diabetes to worry about.

Elaine frowned, thinking back on the dinner they'd

hosted soon after Grandpa's death. After everything that happened that evening, it had been obvious to her that Grandma wasn't up to cooking a big meal or serving guests. She'd had some time to rest though, and since Grandma was taking her medicine and watching what she ate, maybe things would go better with this dinner. Elaine hoped so, because if Grandma kept making mistakes and forgetting things, they might have to give up the dinners and find some other way to supplement their income. But what could it be?

CHAPTER 15

O h, Grandma, what are you doing with that?" Elaine asked, watching in surprise as Grandma poured sugar into one of their saltshakers.

"I'm filling the saltshakers to set on the tables," Grandma replied.

"But you've got *zucker* not *salse*."

Grandma set the bag of sugar on the counter and stared at it with a peculiar expression. "Ach, my! You're right about that. I think I may need to clean my glasses." Grandma went to the sink and turned on the water. After she'd rinsed off her glasses and dried them with a soft towel, she put them back on. "There, that's better. I can see everything more clearly now."

"That's good," Elaine said, smiling with relief. Grandma had been so forgetful lately, and Elaine was worried that she may have confused the sugar for salt. Apparently it was just that she hadn't seen the label clearly.

While Grandma poured the sugar back into the bag, Elaine glanced out the window, wondering what the noise was that had caught her attention. A woodpecker was making quite a racket as it worked to get insects out of the old maple tree in their yard. This particular tree had been struck by lightning last year, which ended up scorching the leaves. In the spring when no new growth emerged, it became evident that the tree had not survived. It had become quite the meeting place for woodpeckers though. Even from inside the house, Elaine could hear the bird as it chiseled its way around the tree, leaving holes at each place it searched.

Seeing the bird gave Elaine an idea. The next time she went to town, she would check at the hardware store about purchasing a few bird feeders. Grandma would probably enjoy watching all the birds in their yard, and it might help her mind stay active, trying to identify each one. Elaine would find a good spot for the feeders so she and Grandma could see them while they were either porch-sitting or seated in the kitchen near the window. Actually, observing the birds' antics would be fun for both of them.

Elaine thought more about the dead tree. It would probably be good to find someone to cut it down. Otherwise the tree would eventually become brittle, and as much as the birds enjoyed looking for insects inside the bark, Elaine wanted to make sure the tree was no threat to the house. She would add it to her ever-growing to-do list. But like Grandpa had told her one time, *"It's better to have a full in-bin instead of an empty one."*

Elaine smirked. Right now an empty bin would be just fine.

Physically, Grandma seemed to be feeling a little better since she'd been eating right and taking her medicine, but her emotions were up and down. One minute she'd be laughing and talking about the future, and the next minute she seemed sullen and almost out of touch with what was going on. Elaine felt sure it was part of the grieving process, but she would let the doctor know if things didn't improve. In the meantime, she'd keep reminding Grandma to take her medicine, exercise, and eat the right foods.

"Shall we get busy cooking for our guests now?"

Grandma asked. "It won't be long and the evening will be upon us."

⚬∕∕⚬

Jonah had been working in the buggy shop with his apprentice all morning and was getting ready to take a break when the boy asked him a question.

"Say, Jonah, I've been meaning to ask. How long have ya been makin' buggies?"

"I started working in my daed's buggy shop when I graduated eighth grade." Jonah chuckled. "But sometimes it seems like forever."

"What makes ya say that?" Timothy asked, looking curiously at Jonah.

Jonah shrugged. "Guess it's because I've had an interest in buggies since I was a boy. When I was a little guy, my daed made me a wooden buggy that I could sit inside and pretend I was driving a horse. I had more interest in thinking up things to do with that little buggy than I did in pretending there was a horse at the front of it." Jonah rubbed his chin thoughtfully, thinking back on those carefree days, when all he had to worry about was doing the few chores his dad had assigned him and finding new things to do with his wooden buggy. One day, he'd removed all the dark blue material Dad had used on the buggy seat and replaced it with one of Mom's good tablecloths. Mom had been none too pleased about that.

"Are you enjoying the work here?" Jonah asked, pulling his thoughts back to the present.

Timothy nodded enthusiastically. "It's interesting to see how a buggy is put together, and I'm anxious to learn all I can."

"Think you might want to own your own buggy shop someday?"

The boy shook his head. "There's a lot of stress that comes with ownin' your own business. I've seen how frustrated my daed gets sometimes when things don't go right in his leather shop. Even my brothers Andy and Paul, who work with Dad, have mentioned how Dad gets upset about certain things."

"There can be some stressful times when you have a business," Jonah agreed, "but if you like something well enough and you want to be your own boss, then the stressful things don't bother you quite so much. Of course, being your own boss is not all stress, and I do have to remember to treat all of my customers right and get their orders done in a timely manner. Another advantage of having my own business is that I can take a long lunch or run errands whenever I need to."

Timothy scratched the side of his head. "Think I'll just be happy workin' for you right now and not think too hard about the future."

Jonah smiled. "That's probably a good idea." *I'd better take Timothy's advice,* he thought. *I need to quit worrying about my future with Elaine and leave it in God's hands. When the time is right for Elaine to accept my marriage proposal, it'll happen. I just need to be patient and keep offering her support as she helps Edna deal with Lloyd's death and her health issues.*

❧

As the six o'clock hour approached, Elaine checked everything twice to be sure they were ready for the tour group that would be arriving soon. Both tables had been set with their best dishes, and the food they'd be serving was keeping warm on the stove. Elaine had even checked the door on Millie's cage to be sure it was latched. She'd also covered Millie's cage so the bird would think it was nighttime and wouldn't chatter away, like she often did. Elaine did not want the noisy little parakeet to swoop into the dining room, creating a stir, as she had done during the last dinner they'd hosted. What an embarrassment that had been for both her and Grandma.

An hour ago, Elaine had made a light supper for the two of them so that Grandma could take her medicine. That would be better than waiting to eat until after the tourists all left. By then Grandma could become weak and shaky.

"Is my head covering on straight?" Grandma asked, stepping out of the kitchen and joining Elaine in the dining room.

Elaine smiled and nodded. "Jah, Grandma. You look just fine."

"That's good, because the last time these people came, I don't think I left a very good impression."

Elaine's eyebrows squeezed together. "No, Grandma, it won't be the same people we served dinner to several weeks ago. It'll be a new group of tourists coming here this evening."

Grandma pulled back slightly but then gave a quick nod. "Of course. How silly of me. I don't know what I was thinking."

Elaine didn't know what Grandma had been thinking either, but she chose not to make an issue of it. Perhaps it had just been a slip of the tongue. Maybe Grandma hadn't really thought the people coming tonight were the same ones who'd been there before. At least, Elaine hoped that was the case.

"Oh, look, they're here," Grandma said, motioning out the window to a van.

As Elaine went to the door to greet their guests, she

sent up a silent prayer. *Dear Lord, please help everything to go well this evening.*

⌇

"It's so good to see you again," a tall, dark-haired woman said when she entered the house and gave Edna a hug. "I couldn't believe it when Sharon, our tour guide, told us your name and said you'd been hosting tourist dinners for several years."

Confusion settled over Edna like a heavy quilt on the bed. She had absolutely no idea who this woman was and found it to be quite unsettling. If she were a previous dinner guest, she probably would have said so, not acted surprised that Edna was hosting meals for tourists. *Think, Edna. Think. Have I ever met this woman before, and if so, where? Maybe she has me confused with someone else.*

"Sorry, but I'm not sure. . . Have we met before?" Edna asked, looking beyond this lady as the rest of the tour group lined up to come in. She felt uneasy, making people wait while she tried to figure out who the woman standing in front of her actually was.

"I'm Cindy Hawthorne." She gestured to the older, gray-haired woman beside her. "I've been visiting my friend Dawn, who lives in Chicago, and she signed us up for this tour, not realizing that I used to live in Arthur."

Edna stared at Cindy, trying to recall her face. She felt foolish not being able to recognize someone she'd apparently known in the past.

"My husband, Rick, and I used to be your neighbors before we moved to Nevada." Cindy's dimples deepened when she smiled. "But then, that was twenty years ago, so I can understand why you might not have recognized me.

Unfortunately, time has a way of changing how people look." She touched her face, moving her fingers around. "A few wrinkles here, and several gray hairs there. Oh, and I've probably put on a couple of pounds from when you knew me too."

"Ah, yes," Edna said, relieved that she now remembered Cindy. She just hadn't recognized her at first. "And of course, I've changed a good deal since then too."

"Not that much." Cindy shook her head. "You've still got that nice smile I remember so well."

"Thank you," Edna said. "Did your husband make the trip to Chicago with you?"

Cindy shook her head. "He's working as a computer analyst and couldn't get away from work."

"Ah, I see." Of course, Edna didn't really see. She had no idea what a computer analyst did, and the truth was, she barely remembered Rick.

"So how is Lloyd?" Cindy asked. "Will I get to see him too, or is he off doing something else this evening?"

Edna swallowed hard, hoping she wouldn't give in to the tears that so often seemed near the surface. "Lloyd passed away a little over a month ago. He had a heart attack."

"I'm sorry to hear that." Cindy gave Edna another hug. "I'm sure it must be difficult for you to be without him."

"Yes, it is. I miss Lloyd so much, but I'm thankful that I have my granddaughter living with me. She's such a comfort." Edna motioned to Elaine. "This is Elaine. She came to live with Lloyd and me after her parents were killed in a buggy accident. She was just a little girl then, and it was after you'd moved, so you never got the chance to meet her."

"You mean, Milton was killed?" Cindy's eyes widened.

"Yes, Milton. You remember my son, I'm sure," Edna added.

Cindy nodded and then she looked at Elaine. "Since Rick and I lived next door to your grandparents, we knew your father when he was a boy. He was a fine young man."

Edna thought Cindy would simply shake Elaine's hand. Instead, she gave her a hug. "I wish we'd had the chance to know you, because I'm sure that any granddaughter of Edna's must be as kind and sweet as she is."

Elaine's cheeks colored. "It's nice to meet you as well."

"Well, I'd better move aside and let the others in the door," Cindy said, stepping farther into the room. "I'm sorry. I didn't mean to hold things up."

"We'll talk more later." Edna bobbed her head. "Maybe when dessert is served."

Soon everyone was inside and seated at the tables. After the tour guide introduced Edna and Elaine to everyone, the two of them headed for the kitchen to bring in the food.

"I feel so *narrisch* not remembering Cindy," Edna remarked as she removed the chicken from the oven.

"It's okay, Grandma. You're not foolish. As the woman said, it's been some time since you last saw her."

"I know, but it's just another reminder of how my memory seems to be slipping these days. Makes me wonder if I'm losing my *glicker*."

"You're not losing your marbles either." Elaine patted Edna's arm. "We all forget things sometimes, and you've been under a lot of stress since Grandpa died."

"Jah, but that's no excuse. My mind used to be sharp as a sewing needle. Guess maybe it's just old age catching up with me." Edna sighed and turned toward the door. "Well, I can't fret about that now. We have a meal to serve."

As Edna headed into the other room, a terrible thought hit her. *What if I am losing my glicker? That would be baremlich. Jah, absolutely terrible.*

CHAPTER 16

*W*hen Sara stepped into her house with Mark, she breathed a sigh of relief. It was good to be home again, with the peace and quiet of just her and her son. It wasn't that Sara didn't love her husband's family; she just wasn't used to so much commotion on a daily basis. And those petty squabbles that had gone on between her two young sisters-in-law had really grated on her nerves. She and Mark could never move into Harley's parents' home on a permanent basis. If she chose to remain in Arthur, it would be right here, in her own house.

When my sister, Marijane, and I were children, we never fussed at each other like that, Sara thought, placing Mark in his high chair before offering him a cheese-and-cracker snack. *But then, our folks would never have tolerated it if we had.*

Nevertheless, Sara couldn't help but observe that Carolyn and Marla's disagreements seemed to go unnoticed by Herschel and Betty. Could be that they were just more tolerant than some parents. Or perhaps her in-laws may have been allowing their children to work out their differences. Of course, Herschel wasn't home that much due to his business, so he probably had no idea how often the girls argued about things. And Betty may not have had the energy to deal with it.

"Well, I'm home now, and taking care of my nieces and nephews is no longer my problem," Sara said aloud.

She leaned over and kissed Mark's forehead. "All I have to worry about is taking care of you, my sweet little boy."

Mark looked up at her and grinned; then he popped a piece of cheddar cheese into his mouth and smacked his lips. "Yum. . .*gut kaes.*"

Sara smiled. "Jah, cheese is always good to eat." Watching her son, Sara's love for him swelled to overflowing. According to Betty, Mark was a mirror image of what Harley had looked like when he was that age. Sara had to admit that Mark certainly took after his daddy, with the same deep blue eyes and dark hair. He even had a dimple in the middle of his chin—a feature Sara had thought was so cute about her husband when they'd first met, before he'd started growing his beard.

The love Sara felt for Mark couldn't be measured, for there was nothing she cherished more on this earth. Even with the bumps along the way that everyone encountered in life, Sara would do all that was humanly possible to make sure Mark grew into a fine man like his father had been.

Taking a seat near Mark's high chair, Sara let her head rest on the table. She felt so tired this morning that she could almost fall asleep right now. Hopefully after Mark's snack he would go down for a nap, and then maybe she could rest awhile too. After spending the last eight weeks at her in-laws', it felt wonderful to finally be home, where everything was familiar. There were so many things she wanted to do once she caught up on her rest however.

Earlier, Sara had looked around and seen all the dust she wanted to tackle. It was so thick, she could actually write her name on some pieces of furniture. Sara didn't know how a house could get so dusty when no one was around, but somehow it had. She didn't mind though. She was anxious to start doing her own household chores and get back into a routine of some sort.

Sighing, and unable to keep her eyes open any longer, Sara let them close and soon succumbed to sleep.

❧

"*Mammi!* Mammi!" *Bang! Bang! Bang!*

Sara's head came up and her eyes shot open. Poor little Mark, tears rolling down his flushed cheeks, pounded his fists on the high-chair tray with a look of desperation. How long had she been sleeping, with her poor little guy crying like this? Sara certainly didn't enjoy upsetting her son and figured from the appearance of his aggravated red face that it must have been long enough to frustrate him.

"Mamma's sorry." Sara rose to her feet, and after lifting her son from his chair, she patted his back, soothing him the best that she could. Glancing at the clock on the far wall, she grimaced, realizing that she'd been asleep for thirty minutes. It was a wonder Mark hadn't woken her sooner, but either he'd remained quiet for most of that time, or she'd been in such a deep sleep that she hadn't heard him.

"Let's get you cleaned up, and then you and Mamma can take a nap," Sara murmured, holding her son tightly to her chest. Mark squeezed his arms around Sara's neck, burrowing his face into her shoulder.

Sara's limbs felt weak, and her hands tingled as she made her way to the bedroom. Hopefully after sufficient rest, she would feel better.

❧

"Where are you going, Grandma?" Elaine asked when

Edna put her black outer bonnet on and opened the back door.

"I'm gonna head into town to run a few errands," Edna replied, turning around.

"Do you have to go right now?" Elaine asked. "I need to get the rest of the clothes washed and hung on the line, but I can go with you after that's done."

Edna shook her head. "There's no need for that. I'm perfectly capable of going to town on my own."

"But I thought—"

"If you're worried about me going out alone, please don't. I'll be fine." Edna motioned to their wringer washer. "You go ahead and finish the laundry. When I get back, we can fix lunch and spend the rest of the day working in our vegetable garden."

Elaine hesitated a moment but finally nodded. "If that's what you want to do, Grandma, but I'm willing to run errands with you."

"We'll go shopping together some other time." Edna smiled and stepped out the door. She didn't want to hurt her granddaughter's feelings, but the truth was, she was eager to spend some time alone. Ever since Lloyd had passed away, and particularly after she'd been diagnosed with diabetes, Elaine had been acting like a mother hen, always reminding Edna to take her medicine, check her blood sugar, eat this and not eat that. Even though it was a bit irritating, Edna realized her granddaughter meant well.

Edna's thoughts took her back to the past. In all the time she and Lloyd had been raising Elaine, it had been them telling her what to do, but now the tables were turned. It made Edna feel almost like a child again. Well, their roles seemed to be reversing, but for a few hours today she would be free as a bird, and she planned to enjoy this time to herself. She'd been feeling better these past few weeks and hadn't had any dizzy spells or memory lapses, so she felt perfectly capable of running a few errands by herself.

⁂

Elaine hummed as she hung the last batch of clothes on the line. It was such a beautiful June morning, and she was trying not to worry about Grandma but to keep her focus on positive things. The birds chirped joyfully in the trees nearby, and she watched with interest as a robin pulled a worm from the lawn. It was amazing how God provided for the birds with insects and seeds, and how their continual singing made it seem as if they were nearly always at peace.

She glanced at the dying maple and felt sorry for the tree, knowing that next week it would be gone, for their closest neighbor had agreed to cut it down. The birds sure loved that old tree, even without its leaves. Maybe after it was gone, the stump could be left for a birdbath to sit on, or perhaps one of their feeders. Elaine and Grandma could plant some wildflowers around the bottom of the stump and finish it with some pretty-shaped rocks scattered among the flowers. That way, a section of the tree that held so many memories would still be a part of the landscape.

Maybe I'll even get a bit of painting done, making some of the rocks I've found look like different animals. Elaine sighed. She surely did miss painting. It was so relaxing, not to mention fun. Right now, she could use a good dose of that. It would be better than any medicine she could take.

Elaine thought of the words of Matthew 6:26: *"Behold the fowls of the air: for they sow not, neither do they reap, nor gather into barns; yet your heavenly Father feedeth them. Are ye not much better than they?"* It was a timely reminder that, despite any hardships she or Grandma might face in the future, God would take care of them.

Elaine's thoughts switched gears as she reflected on the fact that Jonah hadn't come around much lately. Was he avoiding her, or had his visits lessened because he was too busy in his shop? "But if he is staying away on purpose, what could be the reason?" she wondered aloud. *I hope because I haven't given Jonah an answer about marrying him yet, he doesn't think I'm not interested.* Elaine remembered, not too long ago, when she'd seen Jonah watching her after church one Sunday. But Grandma had been in a hurry to get home, so unfortunately, Elaine hadn't been able to talk with him.

Elaine loved Jonah and was eager to become his wife, but she couldn't say yes until she was sure that Grandma would be willing to move to Jonah's house with her. "If only I could tell him how much I love him," Elaine grumbled out loud. But the right time never seemed to happen. Elaine knew it was more than that, but it was easier not to admit how the words stuck in her throat every time she tried to tell Jonah the way she truly felt about him.

Anyway, I couldn't move and leave Grandma here by herself, she thought. *I'd be worried every minute, wondering if she was taking her medicine and eating the right foods. If only Grandma wasn't so determined to keep hosting the tourist dinners, I might be more apt to ask her to move. But is it too soon for another major change in Grandma's life? Or am I justifying things because I'm afraid to make a change?*

Elaine picked up a towel and pinned it to the line. *No, I can't take the tourist dinners away from Grandma. She enjoys doing them. Besides, I'm not sure Grandma would be willing to move from this place, and I can't expect Jonah to sell his home, which is close to the buggy shop—especially since he purchased his house not long ago and has been fixing it up for our future together.* She frowned. *Do we still have a future together? Maybe it would be best if I didn't marry Jonah. He deserves to have a wife and family, and as much as it hurts to even think about it, I'm not sure I'll ever be able to give him that.*

❦

Things went well for Edna as she made her purchases in several stores, and she'd even run into her long-ago friend, Cindy, who'd been shopping in one of the stores. Edna invited Cindy to come over in a few days so they could get caught up on each other's lives, but when Cindy said she'd be going home later today, the women said goodbye and parted ways.

Edna's morning had been fun, but when she entered the Stitch and Sew and glanced at the clock, she realized it was way past noon and she should have been home already, eating lunch. She'd planned to bring a snack along, in case she got hungry. But she'd been in such a hurry to leave, she had forgotten about packing a snack.

Maybe I'll go across the street to the Country Cheese and More and get something to eat, she told herself. *Then I'll come back here and finish my shopping before heading home.*

Edna left the store and made her way across the street. When she entered the store, she spotted Leah and her mother, Dianna, sitting at one of the tables. They smiled and waved her over.

"Is Elaine with you?" Leah asked.

Edna shook her head. "She's at home doing the laundry, and I came into town to do some shopping. It's taken me a little longer than I thought, so I decided to come over here and get some lunch."

"Why don't you join us?" Dianna suggested. "We've

just barely started on our sandwiches, and it'll give us a chance to visit."

"I'd like that." As Edna started for the counter to place her order, a feeling of wooziness came over her. *I probably feel this way because I need to eat,* she told herself.

After she'd ordered a sandwich and some iced tea, Edna took a seat across from Leah. Then she reached into her purse to get her medicine, which she was supposed to take before her meal. "Oh, oh," she muttered, rifling through her purse.

"Is something wrong?" Dianna asked.

"I can't find my medicine." Edna's hands trembled and perspiration beaded on her forehead. "I—I must have forgotten to put it in my purse before I left home this morning."

"Are you feeling all right?" Leah asked. "You look pale, and. . ."

Leah's face blurred, and her words faded. A wave of dizziness descended on Edna, and she spiraled into darkness.

CHAPTER 17

*E*laine glanced at the kitchen clock and frowned. It was an hour past lunchtime and Grandma should have been here by now. *What in the world could be keeping her?* she worried, pacing the floor. *I wonder if she stopped somewhere to eat lunch.*

Elaine looked at the shelf where Grandma kept her medicine and gasped. There sat the bottle. *Oh dear,* Elaine fretted as she reached for the medicine. *Grandma forgot to take it with her this morning.*

If I knew all of the places Grandma was planning to shop, I'd go looking for her right now. Elaine went to the door, hoping to see Grandma pull in. *But I might not find her, and what if Grandma came home while I was out searching for her?*

Elaine drew in a deep breath and tried to relax, realizing that fretting about this was getting her nowhere. What she needed to do was stay right here and hope that Grandma was okay and would be home soon.

Taking a seat at the table, Elaine bowed her head. *Heavenly Father, I'm worried about Grandma because she's been gone so long and didn't take her medicine. Please be with her, wherever she is, and bring her safely home.*

Elaine heard a car pull into the yard, and her eyes snapped open. Thinking it might be someone who had seen the sign at the end of their driveway advertising the dinners they hosted, Elaine hurried to the door. When she opened it, she was surprised to see Leah get out of her driver's car. She only lived a few miles away and always came over by horse and buggy or on her bicycle.

Leah hurried to the house and approached Elaine with a worried expression. "I came to tell you that your grandma's in the hospital."

Elaine's heart pounded and her mouth went dry. "Wh–what happened?"

"Mom and I were at Country Cheese and More, having lunch, and your grandma came in. She ordered something to eat and sat down at our table. A few seconds later, she blacked out."

Elaine covered her mouth to stifle a gasp. "I just discovered a few minutes ago that she forgot to take her medicine along when she left home this morning, so I'm sure her blood sugar was probably out of whack."

"We called 911, and the paramedics came soon after," Leah explained. "As soon as they put her in the ambulance, I called our driver to bring me here. I knew you'd want to get to the hospital right away."

"I certainly do. Danki, Leah, for coming to tell me. I'll get my purse and be right with you."

❧

Sara had been avoiding the picnic area where she and Harley used to relax under the trees at the back of their property, but this afternoon she'd felt the need to go there. She had felt better after sleeping awhile and soon after started doing housework. Mark played contently after his nap and seemed well rested, but eventually he lost interest in amusing himself. Sara was more than ready to get some fresh air and figured Mark was too. So she packed a picnic lunch, set her work aside, and decided to take a break. After being at Betty and Herschel's, she needed a little downtime with her son.

As they sat together on the blanket she'd brought along, eating the last of their peanut butter and jelly sandwiches, Sara felt her body relax for the first time in many weeks. It did her heart good to see her little boy's contented expression. She hoped he was enjoying this time with her as much as she was with him. Being in this area, near where Harley had been killed, didn't bother Sara as much as she'd expected it to. In fact, she felt a sense of peace. Although she didn't understand the reason her husband had been taken from them, she'd finally come to terms with his death, accepting it as God's will. *For His ways are not our ways,* she reminded herself.

When they'd finished eating and Sara had washed Mark's face and hands with some wet paper towels she'd packed, she decided that it might be nice to take a walk. "Should we go walking awhile?" Sara asked Mark in their traditional Pennsylvania-Dutch language.

He bobbed his head.

Sara clasped the boy's hand as they strolled along their property line, stopping every once in a while to listen to the birds, look up at the lofty trees, and pick a few wildflowers. June was such a beautiful month. Adult birds were busy feeding their young, crickets had begun chirping, and the tiger lilies bordering her land were just beginning to bloom.

After a while, Mark stopped walking and said he wanted Sara to pick him up. So she lifted him into her arms and headed back to the blanket. She'd no more than laid him down when his eyes closed and he fell asleep.

The warm sun shining down on them made Sara feel sleepy too, so she curled up on the blanket beside her precious little boy and closed her eyes. Lying there, she felt the gentle breeze as it blew across her face. That, along with the sweet melodies the birds sang, made her relax even more. Sara opened her eyes and watched as a flock of quacking ducks flew over. She glanced at her son and could tell by his even breathing that he was sleeping soundly.

Sara smiled and closed her eyes once more. The last thing she remembered before falling asleep was an image of her husband's face the final time they'd come here together.

ↄ∕ↄ

"Can you hear me? Can you open your eyes?" From a faraway distance, Edna heard a stranger's voice.

Where am I? she wondered, trying hard to open her eyes. People were talking. A child cried. A strange beeping noise kept going in the background. *Nothing seems familiar to me. I don't think I'm at home in my bed.*

Slowly, Edna's eyes opened. She blinked at the middle-aged woman dressed in white, standing beside her bed. "Who are you?" she murmured through parched lips.

The woman offered Edna a drink of water. "I'm a nurse. Do you know where you are?"

"I–I'm not sure." Edna moistened her lips after drinking some water. It helped to quench her thirst.

"You're in the hospital."

Edna's head ached, and she reached up to touch the lump on her forehead. "Wh–what happened to me? Why am I here?"

"Some of your friends followed the ambulance to the hospital," the nurse explained. "They said you passed out, and they alerted us to the fact that you're diabetic."

"Oh, yes, I am." Edna remembered going into the restaurant and ordering something to eat, but that was all.

"I'm going to leave you for a few minutes," the nurse said, touching Edna's hand. "The doctor will be in to see you soon, and your granddaughter will come once she gets here and has finished filling out the necessary paperwork."

"Okay." Edna took another sip of water and closed her eyes, trying to remember the events that led up to her being taken to the hospital. It was frustrating not to be able to recall the details of passing out, much less to be brought to the hospital and not know it until now. *I must have bumped my head when I fainted,* she told herself, touching the knot on her head. *That must be why I can't remember much of anything right now.*

✌

"Sara, wake up!"

Sara's eyes opened suddenly, and she sat up with a start. *Harley?* She'd been dreaming about her husband, and then she'd heard his voice. That must have been part of the dream, she realized, rubbing her eyes as she became more fully awake. It had been such a nice dream until she'd heard his alarming voice.

Remembering that she'd lain down beside her sleeping son, Sara glanced at the spot where he lay. "Ach, Mark! Where are you?" she cried, seeing that her little boy was gone.

Sara looked this way and that. Mark was nowhere to be seen. Fear enveloped her, and she shivered involuntarily. Had he woken up and wandered off, or. . .God forbid, had someone come along and taken her child? She couldn't believe that she'd fallen into such a deep sleep and hadn't heard her son wake up.

Heart pounding and perspiration rolling down her forehead, Sara scrambled to her feet and cupped her hands around her mouth. "Mark, where are you? Please, answer me, Mark!"

No reply. As if life was normal, the only sounds were

the wind whispering gently through the tops of the trees and several birds calling to their mates. But for Sara, life was far from normal.

She called her son's name over and over, running up and down the length of the property line as she did so. There was still no sign of the boy. To add to her mounting fear, thunder rumbled loudly in the distance, and the sky turned darker toward the west. "Help me, Lord," Sara prayed aloud, her panic mounting as she headed toward the house, hoping her little boy had gone there. "Please help me find my son. I lost Harley; I can't lose Mark too."

CHAPTER 18

"Come on, Sassy, I know you can go faster than that," Jonah called to his temperamental horse. He was heading over to see Elaine this afternoon and was anxious to get there. They hadn't visited in a while, and he wanted to see how she and Edna were doing. Despite the fact that marrying Elaine was all he'd been thinking about, Jonah wouldn't bring up the topic and had come to accept the fact that Elaine might not be ready until next year perhaps. Well, Jonah was a patient man, and he would wait for as long as necessary. After all, what other choice did he have?

As Jonah continued on down the road, he noticed the sky was darkening in the distance. Then he heard a far-off rumble of thunder. Jonah liked listening to thunderstorms, especially the gentler ones. When he was a boy, he'd enjoyed lying on the floor upstairs in his room and listening to the pouring rain pelt down on the tin roof of their home in Ohio. He remembered a few wicked storms, where the lightning was actually pink, and the air felt like it was charged with electricity. Constant lightning with claps of thunder, one right after the other, caused him to hide under the covers back then. Those kinds of storms, Jonah could do without.

This afternoon, Jonah could smell rain in the air, but fortunately, this approaching storm didn't sound violent, and hopefully he would arrive at Edna's place before the skies opened up.

Jonah's thoughts came to a halt when he caught sight of a young Amish boy chasing a butterfly in a field near the road. The child looked like Sara Stutzman's little boy. But if that were the case, where was Sara, and why would Mark be out here by himself?

Jonah guided his horse to the side of the road, secured him to a tree, and sprinted into the field, calling the boy's name. He hadn't seen any lightning yet. Only the sound of thunder in the distance, and for that, Jonah was grateful. He felt confident time was on his side.

When the butterfly landed on the stem of a wildflower, the child stopped chasing it. Then, turning to Jonah with a grin, he pointed and said, *"Die fleddermaus."*

Jonah nodded and said in Pennsylvania-Dutch, "Jah, Mark, that's a butterfly, but where is your mamm?"

"Schlaeferich," Mark replied, grinning up at him.

Jonah frowned. If the boy thought his mom was a sleepyhead, was Sara at home in bed? Could she be sick, and had Mark been wandering around her place unattended? Jonah hoped not. While Sara had been at her in-laws, taking care of Betty after she'd broken her leg, he'd heard that Betty was better now, so Sara had gone home. And this field bordered Sara's place, so if Mark had meandered off by himself, he easily could have ended up here. With no hesitation, Jonah decided to get Mark home right away, especially in light of the approaching storm. The wind had started to pick up, and dark clouds nearly blocked out the sun.

"Kumme," Jonah said, urging the boy to come to him. "Come now, I need to take you home."

When Mark didn't resist, Jonah bent down and picked him up. He was almost to his buggy when he heard Sara screaming in the distance, calling her son's name.

"That sounds like your mamm." Jonah smiled as little

Mark pointed in the direction of Sara's voice.

"He's here, in the field!" Jonah shouted. "Stay where you are, and I'll bring him to you."

⤲

Sara's heart pounded as she stood near the edge of her property. Had she imagined it, or had someone shouted that he'd found Mark in a field and was bringing him home?

With heart pounding and legs trembling, she waited. *Dear Lord, please let it be that I heard someone,* she prayed as a few drops of rain mixed with her tears.

Several minutes went by, and then she heard the distinctive sound of a horse and buggy approaching. When it drew within sight, she knew immediately that it belonged to Jonah, and she could see inside the buggy that Mark was with him.

"Oh, thank the Lord," Sara cried as the buggy pulled up alongside of her. Happy tears welled in her eyes as Jonah handed Sara her son. "Where did you find him?" she asked, clinging tightly to Mark. It felt so good to have her son back where he belonged, held in the safety of her arms.

"In the field on the other side of the wooded area that borders your property," Jonah replied. "He was chasing a fleddermaus. When I asked where his mamm was, he said you were a sleepyhead, so I was worried that you might be sick in bed."

Sara shook her head, pointing. "I took Mark for a picnic out there by the trees, and after we'd eaten and taken a short walk, he fell asleep on the blanket. I foolishly laid down beside him and went to sleep." She paused and kissed her son's head. "When I woke up, he was gone. I was so afraid. I called Mark's name over and over, with no response, and of course I prayed and asked God to help me find my son. Danki, Jonah, for bringing my precious boy back to me." Sara grabbed Jonah's hand and squeezed his fingers; she was ever so grateful.

"No thanks is needed." Jonah smiled. "I'm sure God must have directed me to head down this road on my way to see Elaine at just the right time so your prayers would be answered.

"Come on," he suggested. "Hop in the buggy and I'll take you and Mark back to your house before the rain really lets loose."

Sara nodded in agreement, appreciative of his offer.

Because they had a little time yet to beat the storm, Jonah asked Sara where her picnic things were so she could take them home. As they headed to the grove of trees to retrieve the blanket and picnic basket, she was tempted to tell Jonah about hearing Harley's voice in a dream, telling her to wake up, but she didn't say anything, thinking he might not understand. Truth was, she didn't understand it either, but was thankful that it happened. If she hadn't woken up when she had, there was no telling what might have happened to Mark. Of course, Jonah most likely still would have found him, but from now on, Sara would try to keep a closer watch on her boy and make sure she never fell asleep unless they were inside the house with the doors closed and locked.

∽

Elaine sat beside Grandma's hospital bed, thanking God that she was all right. They'd given her the insulin she needed and gotten her blood sugar stabilized, but they wanted to keep Grandma overnight for observation, since she'd hit her head on the floor when she'd passed out. Outside the window, Elaine could see a downpour from a thunderstorm. *What if Grandma had been trying to get home in the buggy during this storm?* Elaine thought. She was thankful that Grandma was safe at the hospital, although she wished Grandma had remembered to take her medicine and hadn't gotten ill to begin with.

"How are you feeling?" Elaine asked, taking Grandma's hand.

"Other than feeling foolish for passing out at the restaurant this morning, I'm fine." Grandma offered Elaine a weak smile.

"What about your head? Does it hurt?"

Grandma reached up and touched her head. "Jah, just a bit. I don't see why I can't go home with you right now. Didn't you say Leah and her driver are still in the waiting room?"

"They are, but the doctor wants to keep you overnight, just to make sure your blood sugar remains stable and there are no problems from your head injury. There may be a few more tests to run as well."

Grandma wrinkled her nose. "I don't like all the prodding and poking they've already done to me."

Elaine gently patted Grandma's arm. "I know, but I'm sure you'll be able to come home tomorrow morning."

"I hope so, because I don't like hospitals one bit. Your grandpa didn't like them either."

"I understand, but this is where you need to be right now." Elaine sat quietly with Grandma until a nurse came in to take vitals.

"I think I'd better tell Leah and her driver they can go now," Elaine said, rising from her chair. She was relieved when Leah had said that her brother had gone and taken Grandma's horse and buggy back to their house.

"You should go with them," Grandma said. "There's nothing you can do here but sit and hold my hand."

"Which is exactly what I want to do."

"But really, there's no need—"

Grandma's words were cut off by the nurse placing a thermometer under her tongue.

"I'll be back soon," Elaine called over her shoulder as she hurried from the room. No way was she going home until she knew the results of all Grandma's tests.

CHAPTER 19

*W*hen Jonah headed back down the road in the direction of Elaine and Edna's place, he thought about Sara and her grief at losing her husband. It was a shame little Mark would never know his father. Life could sure be hard sometimes. But Jonah knew firsthand that when faced with adversity, with the strength, help, and guidance of the Lord, a person had to pick themselves up and move on, rather than giving in to grief and despair. It appeared that Sara had done that, although Jonah was sure it hadn't been easy. Probably the support she'd received from her husband's parents had a lot to do with her being able to cope. He wondered once more why she hadn't moved back to Indiana to be close to her own parents. *Must be a good reason,* he rationalized. *Besides, it's really none of my business.*

Jonah held on tight as a car sped past, spraying water on his horse and buggy. "It's okay, boy," Jonah said softly to Sassy, trying to calm him down after the inconsiderate driver flew farther down the road.

Sassy nickered as if he understood.

"What's wrong with that guy, driving like there's no tomorrow?" Jonah shook his head, muttering under his breath. "If he's not careful, he's likely to hurt someone, and it could be himself or some innocent victim." How people could drive like that, when it was raining so hard, was beyond Jonah's comprehension. Didn't that fellow have a family or worry about hurting someone else's family? Families were important, which was why Jonah was thankful he lived near his twin sister. If anything were to happen to Jonah's parents, his sister, or anyone in her family, he didn't know what he would do.

Jonah really wished his folks would move to Arthur so they'd all be in the same area. Now that he'd gotten busier with his buggy business, it would be nice if he and Dad could be partners again. Jonah had always worked well with Dad, and if things had turned out differently for Jonah back in Pennsylvania, they would most likely still be working together in Dad's buggy shop.

Maybe I can talk Dad into moving, Jonah thought as he turned his horse and buggy up the Schrocks' driveway. He hadn't spoken to his parents in a while and decided he needed to call them soon. *In the meantime, I'll keep training Timothy and be thankful for the help he's giving me.*

Jonah guided Sassy up to the hitching rack and secured him. Then he sprinted through the wet grass, which he noticed was getting a bit too long, and stepped onto the porch, making a mental note to see about cutting the grass for Edna. The rain had lingered, falling steadily after the initial storm had passed, but Jonah was grateful to have gotten Sara and Mark home before it really cut loose.

As Jonah waited, a siren wailed in the distance; then the sound grew louder as the rescue vehicle raced down the road. Jonah couldn't help wondering if the car that had passed him moments ago might have been in an accident. Of course, with the slick roads, it could have been some other vehicle in an accident.

Quickly, Jonah offered up a prayer. *Thank You, Lord, for being with me and Sassy and for getting us here safely. Please be with the driver of the rescue vehicle, and also with whoever was involved in an accident.*

After several knocks on the door, with no response,

Jonah determined that Elaine and Edna must not be home. Since he had a pen and tablet in his pocket, he wrote a quick note and placed it inside the screen door, letting them know that he would be back sometime tomorrow, at which time he would cut the grass. Hopefully the lawn would have a chance to dry out by then.

Whistling, Jonah hurried back to his horse and buggy and headed for home, where his own chores awaited.

❧

Sara gently stroked her son's silky head as she sat in the living room, rocking him to sleep. She was ever so thankful that Jonah had come along when he did. What if Mark had gotten out in the road? He could have been hit by a car, especially with that storm making visibility difficult for drivers. *Heavenly Father, You were surely watching over my boy,* she prayed. *Thank You.*

"Mama will never be so careless again," Sara murmured as Mark's eyelids grew heavy and he closed his eyes.

The sound of the rain gently falling against the window was soothing. Once she was sure that Mark was sleeping soundly, Sara rose to her feet and carried him down the hall toward his room. *Maybe I should move Mark's crib into my room,* she thought. *Think I'd feel better if he slept closer to me.*

First, Sara entered her room and placed Mark in the middle of the bed. Then she rolled the crib across the hall and into her room. Once she had it in place against the wall adjacent to her bed, she picked up her son and laid him in the crib. "Sleep well, precious boy," Sara whispered, covering him with a sheet.

The rain was coming straight down, so she could lower the top window a little, allowing some fresh air to drift in and clear the stuffiness in the room.

Sara yawned, and after she'd changed into her nightgown and brushed her hair, she stretched out on the bed. The sound of rain made her feel relaxed and sleepy. Not only did she love hearing rain, but Sara liked the smell of it, and how clean everything looked afterward. Even though it was only eight o'clock, she was exhausted and more than ready for bed. She'd left their supper dishes soaking in the sink, but they could wait until morning. Right now, all she wanted to do was sleep. Tomorrow was another day, and maybe when she awoke she would have more energy.

Sara's last thought before falling to sleep was a prayer that Jonah had arrived safely at the Schrocks'.

❧

Elaine's frustration mounted as she sat beside Grandma's hospital bed waiting for all the test results. *What in the world could be taking so long? It's getting late, and if we don't hear something soon, we probably won't know anything until tomorrow morning.*

She glanced at Grandma, sleeping peacefully after she'd been given something for the pain in her head. The doctor had determined that there was no concussion, so there wasn't any danger in Grandma going to sleep now. Several tests had been run before Elaine had gotten to the hospital, and more were done while she'd gone to the hospital cafeteria to eat supper. What Elaine couldn't figure out was what the other tests were about. They knew Grandma had diabetes, her blood sugar had been stabilized, and her head injury wasn't serious, so what else could there be?

She stood and began to pace the floor. Waiting had never come easily for her, and especially now, when she was worried about Grandma and wanted to take her home. When they'd said Grandma should be kept overnight, Elaine had decided that she would stay at the hospital and sleep in the reclining chair beside Grandma's bed. Leah had offered to stay with her, but Elaine had insisted she would be fine by herself. As she became more frustrated, however, she wished she'd agreed to let Leah stay. She could have used the company, not to mention some moral support.

Elaine jumped when the door to Grandma's room opened and a middle-age doctor with thinning blond hair stepped in. "I'm glad you're still here. I'd like to speak to you, if I may," he said, glancing briefly at Grandma, then back at Elaine.

"Yes, of course. My grandma's sleeping right now. Should I wake her?" Elaine questioned.

He shook his head. "There's no one in the waiting room right now. Let's go in there so we can talk privately."

Elaine didn't like the sound of that. Seeing the doctor's furrowed brows, she feared he might have bad news, but she nodded and said, "The waiting room will be fine." She followed the doctor down the hall.

Once they were seated in the waiting room, he cleared his throat and got right to the point. "When you first got here, you were asked some basic questions about your grandmother's health history. Is that correct?"

Elaine nodded.

"Well, besides needing to know that, we tested Edna's cognitive skills."

"Why did you feel that was necessary?" Elaine asked, feeling a bit agitated. Did they, like some other people she'd met, think Grandma was uneducated because the Amish only go through eight years of schooling?

"Because when one of the nurses asked your grandma some questions during her initial examination, she gave many unclear answers."

Elaine leaned slightly forward in her chair. "What do you mean?"

"She couldn't remember certain things. Things that were important. Answers to questions that most people would know right away. Edna also kept asking some of the nurses the same question about why she was here."

"Grandma was probably confused and scared. She doesn't care much for hospitals."

He shook his head. "We thought it was more than that, so we did a few more tests."

"What other tests?" Elaine clutched her arms to her chest.

"For one thing, we did some reasoning and perceptive tests, where Edna was asked several questions, for which she either had no answers or the ones she gave didn't make sense."

Elaine opened her mouth to say something more, but the doctor rushed on. "We also did some blood work, and after your grandmother gave us her written permission, we did advanced brain imaging."

Elaine sat in stunned silence as the doctor gave her the worst possible news. Grandma was in the early stages of dementia, and there was no cure for the disease.

"Dementia is a progressive illness, and each person experiences it in their own way," the doctor said. "Your grandmother's ability to remember, understand, communicate, and reason will decline as time goes on. It will probably be gradual at first, but in some cases, a person may lose their memory very quickly. Now, if you are caring for someone with dementia, there is a lot you can do in the early stages to help that person maintain their independence and be able to cope for as long as possible. I will go over all of that with you before Edna is released from the hospital tomorrow, as well as a list of things to watch for as she progresses to the middle and final stages of the disease."

He paused for a few minutes, as though knowing Elaine had a lot to digest. "And I think it would be good if you would attend a support group we have here at the hospital for caregivers of patients with dementia," he added, lightly touching her arm.

Speechless, Elaine slumped in her chair. Diabetes they could deal with, but this? No, the news the doctor had just given her was impossible to accept. If there was no cure for dementia, then Grandma would need Elaine more than ever. They faced some tough decisions.

Elaine gripped the arms of her chair. *Oh Lord, what am I going to do? How will I ever tell Grandma this horrible news?*

A still, small voice seemed to say, *"Trust Me. I will see you through."*

CHAPTER 20

$\mathcal{I}$t's good to be home," Grandma said, smiling at Elaine as they settled themselves on the sofa the following day. "No more poking and prodding, with doctors and nurses asking me a bunch of silly questions when they wouldn't answer any of mine. Now we can get busy working in the garden and planning the menu for the dinner we'll be hosting tonight."

"No, Grandma, that's not tonight," Elaine corrected. "Our next big dinner isn't scheduled until two weeks from this Friday."

Grandma blinked rapidly and tapped her fingers against her chin. "Are you sure? I was certain it was tonight."

"No, Grandma. I can show you our appointment book if you like."

Grandma shook her head. "That's okay. I believe you."

Elaine drew in a deep breath and released it slowly. She hadn't told Grandma what the doctor had said about dementia and wanted to put it off as long as she could. Grandma would be terribly upset by this news. Then again, maybe she wouldn't believe Elaine at all.

Instead of me telling the doctor last night that I would explain things to Grandma, it might have been best if I'd asked him to give Grandma the devastating news, Elaine thought. *But then, Grandma may have become upset with him and gone into denial. Or maybe I should ask Leah to help me tell Grandma. Well, however it's done, I'm not ready just yet.*

Elaine leaned her head against the back of the sofa and rubbed her temples, reflecting on everything the doctor had told her last night before she'd returned to Grandma's room. Some of the common signs of dementia included memory loss, impaired judgment, faulty reasoning, disorientation of time and place, and even the loss of some motor skills or balance problems. As much as Elaine hated to admit it, Grandma had already experienced several of those things. Some she'd noticed before Grandpa's passing, such as repeatedly asking the same questions, having difficulty paying bills, and forgetting people's names.

Elaine closed her eyes, fearful that if she didn't, the tears that had gathered might splash onto her cheeks. *So some of the symptoms Grandma's been having lately may not be related to her diabetes at all. Now we are dealing with two different diseases, both with similar symptoms that could overlap, such as loss of balance.*

"Elaine, are you listening, or have you fallen asleep?"

Grandma's question brought Elaine's eyes open, and she blinked several times. "No, I'm not sleeping. What was it you were saying?"

"I asked if you wanted to get started on the garden right away, or should we wait till after supper to do it?"

"Supper's several hours away, Grandma," Elaine reminded. "Maybe we should eat lunch first, and then if you're feeling up to it, we can work in the garden awhile. Otherwise, the weeding can wait until another day."

Grandma shook her head with a determined expression. "It can't wait. The weeds will choke out the garden if we don't get 'em pulled today. Especially after that rain we had yesterday." She rose from her seat. "And I'm feeling perfectly fine, so there's no reason not to do it right away. The weeds will pull easy since the ground is still damp."

"You're right," Elaine admitted. "All right then, I'll

make our lunch now while you rest here in the living room."

"I'm not tired," Grandma argued. "When they weren't poking me with needles at the hospital, I slept."

Elaine could see by the fixed set of Grandma's jaw that she was not going to stay here and rest. "Okay. I'll make a tossed green salad, and you can fix some iced tea. How's that sound?"

"Sounds good." Grandma headed straight for the kitchen. Based on what the doctor had said, Elaine figured the symptoms of dementia would probably come and go until Grandma moved into the next phase of the disease, at which time her memory loss would worsen. He'd also said the changes could occur quickly or slowly over time. Elaine hoped in Grandma's case that her memory loss and other symptoms came slowly, for she wanted as much time with her as possible. Once Grandma no longer recognized Elaine, it would be unbearable, but she couldn't allow herself to dwell on that. One day at a time. That was the only way to deal with something like this.

Following Grandma into the other room, Elaine's gaze came to rest on the note she'd found tucked inside the screen door when they'd returned from the hospital this morning. It was from Jonah, saying he was sorry he'd missed her and that he would be by again sometime today.

Oh, how she dreaded having to tell Jonah that she couldn't marry him, but there was no point in putting off the inevitable. Jonah needed the freedom to plan for his future—a future that didn't include her. As much as it hurt, Elaine had concluded that it must not be God's will for her and Jonah to marry.

❧

Elaine and Grandma had just finished eating lunch when

Grandma yawned and said, *"Ich bin mied wie en hund."*

Elaine chuckled, despite her dark mood. "Well, if you're tired as a dog, maybe you ought to take a nap. I'll wash and dry the dishes."

"What about the garden? I thought we were going to do some weeding."

"We can do it after you wake up, Grandma. Getting some much-needed rest is more important than weeding."

Grandma yawned again, covering her mouth with her hand. "You're probably right. I'll have more energy to work in the garden after I've rested a bit."

Elaine watched with pity as Grandma ambled out of the room. If only she could do something to make Grandma better.

She couldn't solve Grandma's problem by bemoaning her fate, so Elaine poured dishwashing liquid into the sink and filled it with warm water. Methodically, she washed and rinsed each dish while staring out the kitchen window. A robin landed in the grass and quickly sought out a worm, while one of the barn cats chased an unsuspecting mouse. For the worm and the mouse, their lives were over, but the cat and the bird had been fed, so some good had come from the insect's and rodent's deaths.

"But what good comes from people dying?" Elaine murmured aloud, spiraling deeper into depression. Eventually, Grandma's body would shut down from the dementia, but worse yet, by then she wouldn't know who she was or that she'd ever had a granddaughter who loved her so much.

Tears trickled down Elaine's cheeks and splashed in the soapy water. Crying wouldn't change the situation, but she desperately needed the emotional release, so she let the tears fall.

Sniffling her way through the chore, Elaine managed

to finish washing, drying, and putting away the dishes. Then, deciding that she needed to work off her frustration, she went to the utility room and grabbed a pair of gardening gloves and a small shovel. Then she stepped out the back door, closing it quietly so as not to wake Grandma.

As Elaine worked silently in the garden, she tried to keep her focus on the weeds and not the situation with Grandma. It was difficult, with the doctor's words still playing over and over in her head. If only there was some way they could stop the dementia in its tracks, or at least keep it from becoming any worse.

May Your will be done, Elaine prayed. *But if it's Your will for Grandma to get better, then please show us the way. And help me to know when and how I should tell her about the doctor's diagnosis.*

❧

Elaine had been attacking the weeds for nearly an hour when Leah and Priscilla rode into the yard on their bikes.

"I'm glad you're home," Leah called. "We're anxious to find out how Edna's doing."

Elaine swallowed hard. Did she dare tell Priscilla and Leah what the doctor had said? She really needed to unburden her soul and talk to someone about this. And who better than her two best friends?

"You look *umgerennt*," Leah said as she and Priscilla parked their bikes and approached Elaine. "Weren't you able to bring Edna home this morning, like you said when you called and left me a message last night?"

"I did call our driver, and we brought Grandma home. She's inside taking a nap." Elaine groaned, rubbing the bridge of her nose. "And you're right. I'm upset."

Priscilla touched Elaine's arm. "What's wrong? Is your grandma's diabetes worse than you thought?"

Elaine shook her head. "Grandma has something else, and it's much worse than diabetes."

Leah's eyes widened. "What is it, Elaine?"

"Grandma has dementia." Elaine's voice faltered, and she gulped on the sob rising in her throat.

Immediately, Elaine's two special friends gathered her into their arms, and they wept bitterly. Elaine was certain that Priscilla and Leah understood and even felt her pain.

anki for that delicious meal," Jonah said, patting his stomach as he pushed away from the table and stood. He'd been invited to his sister's house for supper again and had enjoyed some of Jean's crispy fried chicken, creamy mashed potatoes, a tasty fruit salad, and steamed peas, fresh from her garden.

"You're welcome, but don't rush off," Jean said. "I made strawberry-rhubarb pie for dessert."

Jean's husband, Nathan, smacked his lips. "That sounds *wunderbaar*."

"It does sound wonderful," Jonah agreed, giving his stomach another pat. "But as full as my belly is, I'm not sure I could eat any pie right now. Guess that's what I get for takin' two helpings of chicken and potatoes." He looked over at Jean's daughter, Rebecca, and grinned. "If I'm not careful, your mamm's good cooking is gonna fatten me up," he said in Pennsylvania-Dutch.

The little girl snickered and poked Jonah's stomach. "You're not *fett*, Uncle Jonah."

"Jah, well, I could end up being fat if I keep eating like I did tonight." Jonah smiled at Jean. "I want to stop over and see Elaine this evening, so if you don't mind, I think I'd better get going. If I hang around here till my stomach's ready for pie, it'll be too late to make a call on Elaine, not to mention mowing her lawn, as I'd planned."

"No problem," Jean said. "I'll put a few pieces of pie in

a plastic container, and you can take it along to share with Elaine and her grandma."

"None for Edna," Jonah said with a shake of his head. "She has diabetes, remember?"

Jean touched her flushed cheeks. "Oh, that's right, I'd forgotten about that. How would it be if I send some fresh strawberries for Edna?"

"I'll bet she'd like that," Jonah said.

While Jean put the pieces of pie and a container of berries into a box for Jonah, he took a seat at the table again and visited with Nathan, while Rebecca and her little brother, Stephen, scampered into the living room to play. Baby Zeke snuggled contently in his father's arms.

Jonah couldn't help feeling a bit envious, watching Nathan and his son. It made him wish, once again, that he and Elaine were already married and had at least one child of their own. Hopefully, one day soon, she would accept his marriage proposal.

"From the way the weather's been lately, looks like we're in for a nice summer," Nathan said, pulling Jonah's thoughts aside.

"Jah," Jonah agreed. "Seems like everyone's crops and gardens are doing real well."

"How's that new apprentice of yours workin' out in the buggy shop?" Nathan questioned, patting little Zeke's back.

"Real well. Timothy's a quick learner and seems eager to please. Not only that, but so far, he's never questioned anything I've said or asked him to do."

"That's good to hear. Glad things are working out."

"How's it going with your job at the bulk foods store?" Jonah asked.

"Pretty well. Seems like everyone came shopping

there today. We were busy from the time we first opened till right before closing."

"It's always good to be busy." Jonah rubbed his chin, wishing he had the beard of a married man, like Nathan.

"Here you go, Brother." Jean placed a small cardboard box on the table. "Tell Elaine and Edna I said hello."

"I sure will." Jonah stood and tousled little Zeke's hair, which was dark and curly, just like his and Jean's. He gave Jean a hug, shook hands with Nathan, and picked up the box. "I'm going to the living room to say goodbye to the kinner, and then I'll be on my way."

❧

Elaine had just finished the supper dishes and decided to sit outside on the porch awhile to enjoy the fresh evening air. Grandma had already gone to bed, saying she was tired and couldn't keep her eyes open any longer.

Grandma needs all the rest she can get, Elaine thought, taking a seat on the porch swing. Trying to sleep in the chair beside Grandma's hospital bed last night hadn't given Elaine much quality rest either. She hoped she would sleep better tonight in her own bed, but with so much on her mind, she wasn't sure that was even possible. Between concern over Grandma and the dread she felt about telling Jonah she couldn't marry him, Elaine was a ball of nerves.

Oh Grandpa, I wish you were still here to help us during this difficult time. You were so smart and patient; I'm sure you would know just what to do.

But the reality was, Grandpa wasn't here, and a lot of responsibility rested on Elaine's shoulders. She'd made a promise to Grandpa that she would take care of Grandma, and that's exactly what she planned to do, no matter how exhausting or difficult it might prove to be.

I have Leah and Priscilla to lean on, Elaine reminded herself. The three of them had been there for one another since they were young girls, and they'd never let each other down. While her friends couldn't make her problems go away, Elaine felt certain that they would offer her support and help in any way they could. Like today, when they'd mowed the lawn for her. Leah had gone around picking up small branches that had fallen from the trees, while Priscilla did the mowing.

Elaine lifted her gaze toward the sky, which was just beginning to darken. *Please guide and direct me through this, Lord,* she prayed. *And help Grandma to deal with all the challenges she'll be faced with as her memory worsens. Give us what we need for each day, and show me what to do about our financial situation.*

She watched as the first fireflies came up out of the grass and began lighting up the trees. Smiling, Elaine continued to gaze as some of the insects soared high above the trees. It was almost as if they'd become part of the twinkling stars overhead. She was tempted to get a jar and catch a few, like she'd done when she was a child. Grandpa had shown her how to cut holes in the lid to give the bugs some air once they'd been caught. He'd also told her to put a few blades of grass inside the jar so the lightning bugs, as they were sometimes called, would have something to crawl onto. What fun it had been, taking the jar of fireflies up to her room when it was time for bed. After Grandma and Grandpa kissed her good night, Elaine would lie in bed for a long time, watching the lightning bugs blink rapidly, until they put her to sleep. The next day, as Grandpa had also taught her, she released the bugs back into the air.

Elaine put that happy memory aside and thought

about her current situation. She and Grandma couldn't keep hosting dinners for tourists once Grandma's memory had severely declined. However, they would do it for as long as possible, which would not only help financially, but hopefully give Grandma a purpose in life and keep her focused on something positive.

Elaine smiled when Patches, who'd been lying at the edge of the porch, meowed as if understanding the anguish Elaine had been facing since Grandma took ill.

Elaine's musings halted when a horse and buggy turned up the lane. She recognized Jonah's horse, Sassy, plodding along at a snail's pace.

Tempted to rush out to meet Jonah, Elaine remained on the porch swing, waiting for him to join her. Patches lay watching, and her tail swished back and forth.

After Jonah secured his horse, he stepped onto the porch, carrying a small box.

"Guder owed," he said, smiling at Elaine as he took a seat beside her. "Did you get the note I left for you yesterday?"

She nodded but was barely able to tell him good evening because her throat felt so swollen. Just the sight of him caused her to feel so many regrets.

"I came from Jean's place, and since I was too full to eat dessert, she sent over two slices of strawberry-rhubarb pie for us and some fresh strawberries for your grandma. Thought maybe we could enjoy them together after I mow your lawn."

Elaine's forehead wrinkled as she pointed to the yard full of fireflies. "I think it's getting too dark for that, Jonah. Besides, Priscilla took care of mowing it when she and Leah were here earlier today. Leah got all the sticks in the yard cleaned up too. With all that rain we had, a lot of twigs and leaves had come down from the trees."

"That was nice of them. Guess I should have come by sooner, but I was kept busy all day in the shop, and then after promising Jean I'd come for supper, the day got away from me."

"It's not a problem." Elaine looked at the box of goodies. "A piece of pie sounds good. I haven't eaten many sweets since Grandma was diagnosed with diabetes."

"Guess that must be kinda hard for both of you."

She nodded. "It's harder on Grandma than it is me. She's always enjoyed eating most anything that's sweet. Should I take the box inside and put the pie on some plates for us?"

"Jah, that'd be great. Think now I have room for dessert."

Jonah remained on the porch while Elaine went to the kitchen, where she placed the berries for Grandma on the counter and made some tea. As she was putting the slices of pie on the plates, Grandma walked into the kitchen. "Ach, my, that looks so good!" She rubbed her hands together, smiling eagerly. "I'm more than ready for dessert."

Elaine jumped at the sound of Grandma's voice. "You startled me! I thought you had gone to bed."

"Thought I was tired, but I couldn't sleep." Grandma stared hungrily at the pie. "I heard you moving around in the kitchen and decided to come see what you were up to."

Elaine felt bad having to disappoint Grandma, but she needed to be reminded that she shouldn't eat such things. "Jonah's out on the porch, Grandma," she said. "He brought the pie for him and me, and his sister sent fresh strawberries for you." She motioned to the container.

"Oh, I see." Grandma didn't argue, but took the bowl of berries and ambled out of the kitchen with her head down. She was clearly disappointed.

"Are you all right, Grandma?" Elaine called after her.

"I'll be fine. Just want to find a good book to read while I'm eating these berries."

"Okay then. I'm heading out to the porch to be with Jonah. If you need anything, just give a holler." Elaine went out the back door, closing it behind her so Grandma wouldn't hear her conversation with Jonah. She dreaded telling him what was on her mind, but it had to be said before she lost her nerve.

"Here you go." Elaine handed Jonah the plate, then placed the tray with two cups of tea on the small table between their chairs.

They sat in silence for a while as they ate. "The pie was delicious," Elaine said after she'd finished eating. "Your sister's a good cook."

"Jah, Jean's always been an excellent baker. Our mamm taught her well."

Elaine handed Jonah his cup of tea. It was all she could do not to burst into tears as she reflected on all the other times she and Jonah had sat on this porch together. *A year ago, who would have thought things would be so different now?*

"Is something wrong?" he questioned. "You look umgerennt."

"I am upset," she admitted.

"What's wrong? Are you still worried about your grandma's health?"

"Jah, and things are even worse now."

"In what way?"

"Yesterday, Grandma went shopping by herself, and she forgot to take her medicine along. Since she was gone longer than she'd planned, she decided to get some lunch while she was in town."

Jonah sat quietly as Elaine told him how Grandma had blacked out and been taken to the hospital and kept overnight.

"I'm sorry to hear that," he said. "Is she doing better now?"

"They managed to get her blood sugar stabilized with the proper dose of medicine, but since she'd hit her head, the doctor wanted her to be kept overnight for observation and more tests." Elaine paused, struggling not to break down. "At the hospital last night, one of the doctors took me aside and gave me some very distressing news."

"What was it?"

"Grandma has dementia."

Jonah's head jerked back. "What made them reach that conclusion?"

"They ran several tests, including an oral cognitive." Elaine's fingers curled around her cup of tea. "The results helped them determine that she has dementia."

"But a loss of memory can be typical for a person her age," Jonah said. "Some folks much younger than Edna become forgetful. Even I forget certain things—especially when I get busy or am under too much stress. That's pretty normal, don't you think?"

"It's more than that, Jonah," Elaine explained. "The results of Grandma's tests showed that she does have dementia, and sorry to say, it's only going to get worse in the years ahead."

Jonah sat several seconds, head down, as though studying something on the porch floor. Slowly raising his head, he reached for Elaine's hand and gave her fingers a gentle squeeze. "I know how upset you must be by this news, but I want you to know that I'll be here to help you through it."

Elaine moistened her lips with the tip of her tongue, barely able to make eye contact with Jonah. "I appreciate that, but Grandma's my responsibility, and—"

"And you're going to need all the support you can get."

Elaine couldn't argue with that, but it wasn't going to come from Jonah. She had to make him understand. "I'm not free to marry you, Jonah."

"Why not?"

"I just told you. I need to take care of Grandma."

"I can help you with that."

"You have enough to do with your buggy business."

"My business is important, but I would still take time to help out where Edna's concerned."

Elaine shook her head forcefully. Apparently, Jonah did not understand. "If we were to get married, I'd want to be a full-time wife, and since I'll be acting as grandma's caregiver, for what could be several more years, I need to concentrate fully on that."

Jonah slipped his fingers under Elaine's chin and tilted her face so she was looking directly into his eyes. "I'm in love with you, Elaine."

She swallowed hard and lowered her gaze, unable to look at him. "It's not meant for us to be together, Jonah. You need to move on with your life because there is no future for us. Oh, and please don't say anything about this to Grandma. I haven't told her yet that she has dementia." Before Jonah could offer a response, Elaine rushed into the house. Leaning her full weight on the back of the door, she let the tears flow. It was all she could do not to run back outside and tell Jonah she'd changed her mind and would marry him, despite all the hardships they would endure. But as Elaine grappled with her emotions, she heard Jonah's horse and buggy pull away. Jonah was hurt, but the decision she'd made was final. For Jonah's sake, as well as Grandma's, it had to be.

CHAPTER 22

Two weeks had passed since Elaine told Jonah she couldn't marry him, but to Jonah the pain was as intense as the moment she'd given him her reasons. Thinking about it gave Jonah a headache and made it difficult to concentrate on his work.

There has to be something I can say or do to make Elaine change her mind, he thought, reaching for a piece of upholstery that would cover the seat of the buggy he was working on. *Maybe after some time goes by, Elaine will reconsider. She's most likely overwhelmed by all that happened with Edna.*

Jonah stopped for a minute, hearing a squirrel chattering in the elm tree outside his shop. "I wonder what's got that critter so worked up," he muttered, walking to the open door.

"Could be most anything, I guess," Timothy called from across the room. "I can hear him carrying on clean over here."

Jonah stood by the doorway and watched as the squirrel clung to the side of the tree, repeatedly shaking its tail. Then Jonah saw another movement, on a branch higher up. It was partially concealed by all the leaves, but he could see there was a hawk sitting quietly, watching the squirrel as if it was just waiting for the right opportunity to have a meal. The squirrel kept climbing, closer and closer to the hawk. Jonah thought if the squirrel moved any closer to the bird of prey, it would be a goner. At one point, the bushy-tailed critter got on the same branch as the hawk, and they sat watching each other. The whole time, the squirrel never relented and seemed to bark out warnings of the hawk's trespassing. Soon after that, a bunch of crows flew in, giving the hawk a piece of their minds. The crows' scolding, plus the squirrel's chattering, went on for several minutes. Quick as a wink, the squirrel hopped to another branch. The hawk flew away, with the crows following close behind.

That's one lucky squirrel, Jonah thought, watching the tree limbs bob as the squirrel jumped from branch to branch. *Guess even God's creatures have their own frustrations, same as me.*

Jonah hadn't told anyone, not even Jean, that Elaine wouldn't marry him. Since he was hopeful that he could get Elaine to change her mind, he'd decided not to say anything about it, unless he was put on the spot.

He needed to think about something else before he gave in to self-pity, so Jonah decided to check for mail. "I'll be right back," he called to Timothy, who was busy sanding some wood for another buggy. A week ago, Jonah had started on Adam Beachy's new rig, and it was progressing nicely.

The boy gave a nod. "Okay. I'll just keep workin' on this while you're gone."

As Jonah headed down the driveway to the mailbox, he thought about how grateful he was that he'd hired Timothy as his apprentice. There was little doubt that the boy would keep working while he was gone. At the age of sixteen, Timothy was already a responsible young man.

When Jonah opened the mailbox, he was pleased to find a letter from his folks. Grabbing it, along with the rest of his mail, he stepped into the phone shanty and took a seat. This would be a good place to read Mom and

Dad's letter in quiet and without any interruptions. Jonah needed to relax a bit before he went back to work, so he settled into the fold-up chair and kept the door open to let in some fresh air.

Tearing open the letter, Jonah was pleased to learn that Mom and Dad were both doing well and were anxious to come for a visit soon. It seemed like forever since he'd last seen his folks, and it would sure be good to see them again. Jean would be pleased with this news too, and he figured she'd probably gotten a letter from their folks as well.

As Jonah read on, he was surprised to learn that Luke and Meredith were expecting another baby. He was happy for them of course, but it made him long all the more for a wife and children. As much as Jonah hated to admit it, maybe that was not meant to be.

℘

That morning when Elaine went out to the phone shanty to check for messages, she discovered one from Priscilla, suggesting that she, Elaine, and Leah get together soon for a girl's day out. Priscilla said she figured Elaine probably needed some time away to do something just for fun, and that her mother had agreed to stay with Elaine's grandma while they were gone.

Elaine stared at the answering machine. *Should I take Priscilla up on that offer? It would be nice to spend some time with my two best friends. We haven't done anything together for quite some time.*

With no further hesitation, Elaine picked up the phone and dialed Priscilla's number. When she left the phone shanty a few minutes later, there was a new spring to her step. She looked forward to spending a few hours with her friends and felt confident that Grandma would be in good company with Priscilla's mother, Iva.

❧

"It's good to see you," Sara said when Jean Mast stopped by shortly before noon. "It's been awhile since we've had a visit. Can you stay for lunch?"

"That would be nice. Nathan's mamm volunteered to watch the kinner for me today so I could run some errands, and since she said I could take all day if I needed to, I have plenty of time to stay for lunch." Jean smiled and bent to ruffle Mark's hair. He'd been sitting on the throw rug in front of the kitchen sink, playing with some of Sara's pots and pans while she was making sandwiches. "He's sure growing, and such nice thick hair."

"It's like his *daadi's*," Sara said.

Jean smiled. "Is there anything I can do to help with lunch?"

"The sandwiches are almost finished, but you can pour some iced tea for us if you don't mind." Sara gestured to the refrigerator. "I made sun tea yesterday and it should be nice and cold."

"No problem. I'll get the tea and glasses."

While Sara put the finishing touches on the roast beef sandwiches and Jean poured the tea, Sara told her how she'd fallen asleep a few weeks ago and Mark had wandered off. "I was ever so grateful that your brother spotted Mark in the field near my property," she said. "It was right before a storm hit, and I'm thankful that no harm came to my boy."

"I heard about that from Jonah." Jean placed their glasses on the table. "You must have been really scared when you woke up and discovered that Mark had wandered off."

"I really was. Thankfully, God was watching over my

boy. And when I saw him with Jonah, I knew that my prayers had been answered. Jonah got us back to the house in the nick of time, before the rain let loose." Sara picked Mark up and put him in the high chair. "I was surprised that Mark took to Jonah right away. Even though my little guy doesn't know Jonah very well, he didn't cry or seem to be afraid at all."

"Jonah has a way with children," Jean said, taking a seat at the table. "All three of my kinner adore their uncle Jonah."

"If he's as kind and gentle with them as he was with Mark, I can understand why."

"Jonah will make a good daed someday," Jean commented. "He plans to marry Elaine, and I hope it will be soon, because I want my brother to be happy, and I'm anxious to become an aunt."

"When will they be getting married?" Sara had known Jonah and Elaine were courting but hadn't heard there was a wedding in their future. Of course, she should have assumed that would be the case. Couples who'd been courting awhile usually ended up getting married.

"It probably won't be until Elaine is sure her grandma can live on her own," Jean replied. "Edna was recently diagnosed with diabetes, so between that and losing Lloyd, I'm sure it's been quite an adjustment."

Sara nodded in understanding. "I've never had a serious illness, but losing Harley and facing all the responsibilities of raising our son, plus everything there is to do around here, has been a difficult adjustment for me. Some days I think I can do it. Other days, I don't know how I will manage."

"I understand. After I lost my first husband, Silas, I felt as if my whole world had fallen apart. With two small kinner to raise, I was sure I'd never make it. But then

Nathan came along, and my life took on new meaning. He's such a kind, loving man, and a wonderful stepfather to my two older children. I'm grateful that God has given me a second chance at love." Jean touched Sara's arm. "Perhaps someday you'll have the opportunity to fall in love and marry again too."

"I doubt that, because I'm not looking for love. Besides, my heart belonged to Harley, and no one will ever take his place."

"I felt the same way about Silas. But eventually I came to realize that I could love again. Even though I will never forget what Silas and I had, my love for Nathan is strong."

Sara smiled. "I'll keep an open mind and trust God with the future. In the meantime though, I think we ought to pray so we can eat. *Heavenly Father,* she silently prayed, *thank You for good friends like Jean, and if it's Your will for me to ever marry again, please give me wisdom in choosing the right man.*

CHAPTER 23

*E*laine took a sip of iced tea as she opened the book she'd picked up at the library the other day. She'd received some information from the doctor on dementia, but this book was more detailed and provided a lot of information about the disease, as well as things that caregivers could do. Elaine felt better knowing all the facts. Understanding the disease was important, but so was knowing what she could do to help Grandma through the agonizing process that lay ahead. Elaine would have to be strong. She was committed to taking care of Grandma the best way she could, and since that meant making some sacrifices, she wouldn't have a lot of free time to spend with her friends.

But I don't have to worry about that today, she thought with anticipation. *Grandma is still doing well enough for me to leave her awhile. Besides, Priscilla's mamm will be with Grandma while I go to lunch and do some shopping with Leah and Priscilla, and I'm sure we'll all enjoy the day.*

Elaine's thoughts turned to Jonah. He had dropped by again yesterday to see how she and Grandma were doing. Elaine appreciated that but hoped he wouldn't come over on a regular basis. It was difficult seeing him and knowing they couldn't get married. She was also concerned that if they saw each other too often, Jonah might try to pressure her into accepting his proposal. She couldn't marry him now, and she wouldn't ask him to wait.

If it becomes necessary, I may ask him not to come around anymore, Elaine decided. Oh, how she dreaded having to tell him that. She would miss Jonah so much.

Elaine had cried herself to sleep so many nights recently, and it had only made her more miserable, knowing her dreams of a life with Jonah were no longer possible. She was exhausted, holding her emotions in throughout the day and then letting them loose after she'd gone to bed. Crying was good; Grandma had often said that when Elaine was a girl, but Elaine couldn't allow herself to give in to tears too often, for it would do no good. She needed to pull herself together and take one day at a time.

A squirrel chattered from a tree nearby, as if to scold Elaine. "I know. . .I know," she said. "I need to perk up."

It was a beautiful morning—the kind of day that made a person feel energetic. Elaine had always been appreciative of the simple things, but life's challenges had overwhelmed her, and she wondered if she'd ever be truly happy again.

She glanced over at the stump where the old maple tree once stood. The yard looked almost bare without it, even though a few other trees stood nearby. It just added to the emptiness that consumed Elaine. She truly needed to be with her friends today, and maybe, if only for a little while, some of that emptiness she felt would be replaced.

"What are you doing out here?" Grandma asked a bit harshly, stepping out the back door. "I thought you were going to clean Millie's cage."

"I did that yesterday, Grandma." Taken aback, Elaine quickly closed her book. It wasn't like Grandma to speak to her in such a severe tone. Elaine took a deep breath, allowing her heartbeat to slow to a normal rate again. "I've been sitting out here waiting for Leah and Priscilla to arrive."

"Oh, are they coming to visit?" Grandma's tone softened as she took a seat beside Elaine, folding her hands in her lap.

Elaine had told Grandma during breakfast that her friends would be coming by to pick her up shortly before noon, but apparently she'd forgotten about that. "I'm going out to lunch with Priscilla and Leah," Elaine said patiently. "Priscilla's mamm will stay here with you to visit."

Grandma smiled. "Oh, that'll be nice. I haven't seen Iva Herschberger for a long time."

"We just saw her on Sunday, Grandma," Elaine reminded. It had only been three days, yet Grandma couldn't remember? *Is she one of those dementia patients I read about in the book who goes downhill quickly? Oh, I hope not.*

Grandma looked out into the yard and pointed. "Would you look at those pretty birds drinking from the birdbath? I wish Millie could join them." She sighed. "But then, I guess if we brought her cage out here and let her out, she'd probably fly away and we might never get her back."

"You're right," Elaine agreed. "Even if we bring her cage outdoors for some fresh air, we must never open the latch on her door."

"When Iva gets here, I'll see if I can get Millie to talk for her." Grandma snickered. "I like it when she says, 'Pretty bird. . .pretty bird.'"

"It's fun to listen to your parakeet mimic the things she hears." Elaine was glad Grandma had a pet. The little bird gave her such pleasure and, quite often, a good laugh.

"Millie can be quite the chatterbox sometimes."

Grandma yawned and covered her mouth as she leaned back in her chair. "I don't know why I feel so tired today. Guess maybe I didn't get enough sleep last night."

"Would you like a glass of iced tea?" Elaine asked, pleased that she and Grandma were having a nice conversation and that Grandma seemed to be thinking more clearly right now. These were the moments Elaine would always cherish.

"No thank you, dear. I'm not thirsty just now, but you go ahead and enjoy yours." Grandma pointed to Elaine's glass of iced tea on the small table between them. It was a piece of outdoor furniture Grandpa had made several years ago, and except for a few water stains, the table was still in good shape. Some folks might try to get rid of those stains, but Elaine saw them as memories from the days when Grandpa was still with them. He'd enjoyed relaxing on the porch after a hard day's work, and the three of them had spent many an evening out here together, drinking iced tea and having dessert.

Elaine reached for her glass and took a drink. She'd just placed it back on the table when she spotted Priscilla's horse and buggy coming up the driveway.

"Looks like your friends are here," Grandma said, rising to her feet. "Should we walk out to the hitching rack to meet them?"

"We can," Elaine responded, "but it might be better if we wait here on the porch."

Grandma tipped her head and looked at Elaine curiously while rubbing the tiny mole on the left side of her nose. "How come?"

"Some horses can get a bit spooky while they're being tied to the rack. At least that's how mine is sometimes."

"My horse is never spooky," Grandma said. "Misty is

gentle as a sweet little lamb."

It was true. While Misty was calm, Grandpa's horse, Dusty, acted up sometimes. When Grandpa was alive, he'd always been able to handle the gelding. Since they didn't use his horse for pulling a buggy anymore, Elaine thought they ought to sell him. She hadn't mentioned that to Grandma though, knowing she probably wasn't ready to part with Grandpa's horse. Grandma often went out to the barn to talk to Dusty and had even told Elaine that being near Grandpa's horse made her feel closer to him. Elaine wasn't about to take that pleasure from her—not yet, at least. Besides, Grandma needed as much familiarity around her as possible right now.

❧

Knowing his folks would be arriving early next week, Jonah decided to take some time away from the buggy shop and shop for groceries as well as a few cleaning supplies. He'd left Timothy in the buggy shop to work by himself, knowing he'd only be gone a couple of hours. Sassy must have wanted to make a trip to town too, for he seemed to be quite frisky this morning, trotting down the road without Jonah having to flick the reins or holler at him to get moving.

Jonah couldn't blame his horse for feeling energetic. It looked to be a glorious day, one that could win first place if there was a weather contest. He'd been up early, and standing in the door of his buggy shop, he'd watched the sun slowly rise. Jonah wasn't sure what the temperature had been, but after exhaling a few times, he thought he could actually see his breath. Of course, that was probably his imagination, since it was still summer. Today was so cool and crisp though, that it felt like fall.

Jonah looked up at the bluest of skies and breathed

deeply, filling his lungs with fresh, clean air. On a day like today, he didn't feel weighed down by the humidity. There was not a cloud in the sky, which made being outdoors pure pleasure.

As far as I'm concerned, this kind of weather could stick around for the rest of summer, Jonah mused. *Bet it'll be a good night for stargazing too.*

When Jonah guided his horse and buggy to the hitching rack outside the bulk foods store, he spotted his friend Melvin Gingerich getting out of his buggy.

"How's it going?" Melvin called, lifting his hand in a friendly wave.

"Fair enough, I guess." Jonah stepped down from his buggy and secured his horse. "How are things with you, Melvin?"

"With weather like this, I can't complain. My crops are doing well, and oh, you may not have heard, but Sharon Otto and I will be getting married this fall, so I have much to be thankful for."

"Glad to hear it." Jonah gave Melvin's shoulder a squeeze.

"How are things going with you and Elaine?" Melvin questioned. "Will you two be setting a wedding date soon?"

Jonah shook his head. "Afraid not. Elaine hasn't agreed to marry me. At least, not yet," he quickly added.

"How come? I thought you two were getting along well."

"We were, but Elaine's grandmother isn't well, so Elaine doesn't want to commit to marriage right now." Jonah's forehead wrinkled. "I told her I'm willing to help out, but she refused my offer."

"That's ridiculous. You'd think she'd want your support."

"That's what I thought too, but apparently Elaine thinks taking care of Edna is something she has to do alone, and she doesn't want to burden me with it."

"What's wrong with Edna?" Melvin asked.

"For one thing, she has diabetes."

"That can usually be controlled with medication, exercise, and eating right."

"I know, but there's more." Jonah paused, wondering if he should be telling Melvin this. But he really needed someone to share his burden with, and who better than his good friend? "You see, Elaine found out recently that her grandma has dementia."

"You mean, Edna's losing her memory?" Melvin's forehead creased.

Jonah gave a slow nod. "I'm afraid so."

"That's baremlich."

"I agree; it's terrible, and short of a miracle, Edna's condition will deteriorate."

Melvin rubbed his chin, wearing a thoughtful expression. "That's a pretty heavy burden for Elaine to carry by herself. She really needs someone to share in Edna's care."

"I know that, and I'd like it to be me, but if I can't convince Elaine, then there's little I can do. I'm not sure Elaine has told Edna about her condition yet either, so please don't mention this to anyone."

"The only one I'll talk to about this is the Lord, and I'll surely keep you and Elaine in my prayers." Melvin's dark eyes revealed his concern as he placed his hand on Jonah's shoulder and gave it an encouraging squeeze. "Maybe something will happen that'll open Elaine's eyes, and then she'll realize just how much she needs you."

"That would truly be an answer to prayer," Jonah agreed. "Jah, a God-given answer to the prayers I've been sending up ever since Elaine turned down my marriage proposal."

"Well, don't give up," Melvin said sincerely. "With God all things are possible."

CHAPTER 24

ou're not eating much today," Priscilla said, gently bumping Elaine's arm.

Elaine looked at her half-eaten salad and sighed. "Guess I'm just not all that hungry right now."

"You're worried about your grandma, aren't you?" Leah questioned from across their table at Yoder's restaurant.

Elaine nodded slowly. "I'm trying not to worry, but I can't help feeling apprehensive when I'm not with her. What if she doesn't take her medicine? What if she doesn't eat what she's supposed to?"

"My mamm's there with her," Priscilla said. "I'm sure she'll remind Edna of those things."

"That's right," Leah agreed. "So just try to relax and have a good time. After all, it's not very often that the three of us can get together for lunch like this anymore."

"And don't forget, we're going shopping afterward." Priscilla flashed Elaine a cheery smile. "I wish we could have more days like this. I know we're getting older, but I still miss how things used to be with the three of us."

"That would be nice." Elaine took a drink of water. "But we all have responsibilities, and life is full of changes. I've certainly been reminded of that recently."

Leah reached for the bottle of ketchup and poured some on her french fries. "It's true, but we should still take time out to be together. Even if it's just to sit on the porch and talk, it's good for all of us." She grinned and pointed at her plate. "These fries are sure good. Would you like to try some, Elaine? Maybe they'll pique your appetite."

"No thanks."

"Maybe we should set one night a week aside so we can get together and talk," Leah suggested.

Priscilla bobbed her head. "I agree with that."

"We'll have to see how it goes." Her friends meant well, but she had a feeling that in the not-too-distant future times like today would be few and far between. She shivered as a blast of cold air from the air-conditioning vent above her blew down across her shoulders. She almost asked the waitress if the air-conditioning could be turned off, but maybe she was the only one who minded the chill. While it was nice to be indoors away from the summer heat, especially on days when it was unbearable, too much time spent in a room with air-conditioning sometimes made her throat feel sore. Hopefully that wouldn't be the case today.

✧

"I appreciate you coming over to clean my house, but I didn't expect you to bring lunch for me too," Jonah told his sister when she entered the buggy shop with a basket of food.

Jean smiled and set the basket on the counter. "What else is a little sister for if not to help her older bruder?"

He chuckled. "I'm not that much older. According to Mom, I was born just ten minutes before you." He gave Jean a hug. "Are you excited about our folks coming to see us next week?"

"Definitely. It's been too long since we've seen them, and I'm sure they'll be surprised to see how much my kinner have grown."

"You've got that right," Jonah agreed. "Every time I see 'em it seems like they've grown another inch or two."

She swatted his arm playfully. "You're such a kidder."

"Can you join me for lunch?" Jonah asked. "Timothy left early today because he had a dental appointment. And since there are no customers right now, it's a good chance for us to talk."

"Sure I can, but I don't want to sit too long or your house will never get cleaned."

Jean took a seat at the metal table near the window. Jonah followed with the wicker basket. After their silent prayer, she opened the basket and handed Jonah a sandwich.

"Danki," Jonah said, thankful for his sister's thoughtfulness. "Ham and cheese is one of my favorites."

"There's a thermos of coffee, some peanut butter cookies, and a few apples in there too." Jean gestured to the basket.

Jonah thumped his stomach. "If I'm not careful, you're gonna fatten me up."

She smiled. "It would take a lot more than one of my lunches to make you fat, Jonah. You work hard out here in the shop, and once I go back up to your house to finish cleaning, you'll probably burn off most of the calories you're about to take in."

"That could be." Truth was, Jonah had never had a problem with his weight, and at twenty-four, he wasn't worried about his metabolism slowing down.

They ate in companionable silence, until Jean posed a question. "Have you seen Elaine lately?"

"Not since last Sunday at church," Jonah replied.

"Why do you ask?"

Jean tilted her head. "I thought since you two are courting that you'd see her as often as possible."

Jonah swallowed the last bite of his sandwich and washed it down with some coffee. "To be honest, Elaine and I aren't courting anymore."

Jean's eyebrows lifted, and her mouth formed an O. "You're kidding, right?"

"No, unfortunately I'm not. Elaine broke things off with me." It was hard admitting this to Jean, especially when Jonah had been hoping that Elaine would change her mind. But now, with his sister's question about him seeing Elaine, he figured he may as well tell her the truth.

"But why would she do that?" Jean questioned. "I thought you two would be planning a wedding soon."

"That's what I'd hoped for." Jonah groaned. "But with her grandma ill, Elaine thinks it would be a burden on me if we got married and she was caring for Edna. I think Elaine also believes that under those circumstances, she couldn't be the kind of wife I need."

"She's not thinking straight." Jean placed her hand on Jonah's arm, giving it a supporting pat. "I'll bet Elaine changes her mind when she realizes how difficult it will be to take care of Edna on her own. Besides, from what I can tell, Elaine loves you, Jonah. I'm sure if you just wait patiently, she will agree to marry you. In the meantime, you ought to keep going over there, offering your support and letting her know that you're there for her."

Jonah nodded. "You're right, Jean. Think I'll go on over there tonight."

❧

"Your garden is doing so nicely," Iva said as Edna sat beside her on the porch swing. "Have you had much trouble with bugs this year?"

"I—I don't think so." Edna glanced briefly at Iva, then turned her attention to a big black beetle that had found its way to the porch.

A few seconds later, Patches leaped onto the porch, spotted the bug, and nudged it with her nose. That was clearly a bad idea, for the beetle latched right onto the cat's nose and hung on with its pinchers. Screeching, Patches leaped into the air, then tumbled off the porch, landing on her back in the flower bed.

"Oh dear!" Iva gasped. "That poor cat!"

Edna chuckled. "Patches seems to be all right; she just had an encounter with a very determined beetle."

By this time, the creature had let go of the cat's nose and disappeared among the foliage of a miniature rose-bush. Patches got up, shook her head a couple of times, and hissed all the way to the barn.

"Sometimes I forget how silly Elaine's *katze* can be," Edna said.

"I know what you mean," Iva agreed. "The other day one of our cats ran up a tree and sat there meowing for most of the day."

"Did it ever come down?" Edna asked.

"Oh jah, but not till Daniel got the buggy out of the shed so we could get ready to go to the bulk foods store." Iva laughed, flapping her hand. "That crazy cat leaped out of the tree and landed in the back of the buggy. Guess it wanted to take a ride to town with us."

Edna smiled and got the swing moving faster. It felt good to sit here, laughing and chatting. She hadn't found much to laugh about since Lloyd died. "You know, cats aren't the only pets that do silly things," she said. Then she went on to tell about some of the silly words her parakeet often repeated, and how whenever she let Millie out of her cage, she would fly around the house and sometimes land on Edna's head.

"My mamm used to raise canaries when I was a girl," Iva said. "They sang beautifully, but I think it would have been more fun if they'd mimicked some of the things our family said."

Edna sat quietly for a bit, thinking about how Lloyd had been able to get Millie to say so many different words. She squeezed her eyes shut, hoping she wouldn't give in to the tears she felt pushing against her eyelids. *It feels a lot better to laugh than cry,* she thought.

"Are you all right?" Iva asked.

Edna quickly opened her eyes. "Oh, I'm fine. Just thinking, is all."

Several minutes went by. Iva touched Edna's arm. "I was sorry to hear about the physical problems you've been having."

"Oh, you mean my diabetes?"

Iva gave a nod. "That, as well as your dementia diagnosis."

Edna blinked several times, sitting straight in her chair. "Wh–who told you that?"

"Priscilla. She said Elaine told her about your memory loss."

Edna's spine went rigid, and she halted the porch swing abruptly. "I may be a bit forgetful at times, but I don't have dementia! If I did, don't you think the doctor or Elaine would have told me about it?"

Iva's face blanched. "Perhaps I've spoken out of turn. I just thought—"

"Well, you thought wrong! If I had dementia, I'm sure I would know it, and I can't understand why Elaine would tell anyone such a horrible thing. I'm certainly going to ask her about it when she gets home." With her hands shaking and her mouth suddenly dry, Edna got up from the swing and tromped into the house. She knew Iva had brought lunch, but right now, Edna didn't think she could eat a thing!

CHAPTER 25

$\mathcal{E}$dna felt bad leaving Iva on the porch by herself, but she couldn't face the look of pity on her friend's face. All Edna wanted was to be left alone so she could think and try to sort things out.

She took a seat in her rocking chair, staring at the clock Lloyd had given her when they'd first gotten married. What Iva had said was such a shock. If it was true, then why hadn't Elaine or someone at the hospital told her?

A knot formed in Edna's stomach as she thought about a woman in their church district, Lizzie Bontrager, who'd died a few years ago after suffering through the agony of dementia. The poor woman had ended up not knowing anyone, even her own family members.

She folded her arms and held them tightly against her chest. *Is that what's going to happen to me?* Just the thought made Edna feel sick to her stomach. How could she ever forget her dear husband or all the years of raising Elaine? Would the memories from her own childhood be gone? Her parents, her friends, and everyone in their community—would she forget them all? And what about this farm, the animals, and all the simple joys she'd known over the years? Was it really possible that the chapters of her life could be completely erased by this terrible disease, as though they had never been there at all?

Edna got the rocking chair moving faster, her fear

of the unknown changing to anger. This was not going to happen to her—not if she could help it. She'd keep herself busy and her mind alert so the disease wouldn't get the best of her. *I will not allow it to rob me of a life's worth of memories!*

☙

"Where's Grandma?" Elaine asked when she returned home with Priscilla, after they'd taken Leah to her home. Iva was sitting on the porch by herself.

Iva's cheeks turned pink. "She's inside. I'm afraid I said something to upset her."

"What'd you say, Mom?" Priscilla asked, joining them on the porch.

"I said something I shouldn't have, but I didn't realize it was a mistake until it was too late."

"Too late for what?" Elaine moved closer to the chair were Iva sat. "What was it that you said?"

"I told Edna that I was sorry to hear that she'd been diagnosed with dementia." Iva stared down at the floor. "It didn't take me long to realize that she hadn't been told."

"Ach, no!" Elaine covered her mouth with both hands. She'd been fearful that something like this might happen and blamed herself for not telling Grandma the truth right away. "I was planning to tell her but was waiting for the right time."

"Is there ever a 'right' time to tell someone they have serious memory issues?" Priscilla interjected.

Elaine's chin quivered as she slowly shook her head. "No, I suppose not, but I didn't think Grandma was ready to hear such distressing news yet."

"I—I wouldn't have said anything, but I thought Edna already knew." Iva's voice cracked. "I'm very sorry about this. I just had no idea." She folded her hands as though she was praying.

"It's okay. How could you have known? What's done is done." Elaine drew in a shaky breath. "Guess I'd better go inside and speak to Grandma about this now."

Priscilla nodded. "We understand, and we should be going anyway—unless you'd like us to stay."

"I appreciate your offer," Elaine said, "but this is something I should handle by myself." Elaine wondered, though, how much longer she'd be able to cope with situations concerning Grandma on her own.

"Please let us know if there's anything we can do to help," Iva said, standing up and gathering the basket she'd brought with lunch for her and Grandma. "We were having such a nice visit until—"

"Don't think any more about it." Elaine patted Iva's arm. "It really is my fault for not telling Grandma right up front, and I will let you know if I need anything." She opened the door and hurried inside.

Grandma was in the living room, sitting in the rocking chair, staring at the clock on the far side of the room.

Elaine knelt on the floor in front of Grandma and clasped her hands. "I–I'm so sorry for not telling you about your illness, Grandma." Tears welled in her eyes, and she nearly choked on the sob rising in her throat. "I didn't think you were ready to hear it just yet."

"I could never be ready to hear something like that." Grandma slowly shook her head, sniffing, as though trying to hold back tears. "I believe I had the right to know, and I shouldn't have heard it from Iva Herschberger." She paused a moment, as if to gain control of her emotions. "Now I know why I haven't been able to remember some things. I thought it was just ordinary forgetfulness, but I. . .I guess I was wrong."

Elaine rubbed her fingers gently over Grandma's

hand. It nearly broke her heart to see Grandma's pained expression.

"The one thing that saddens me the most is knowing that one of these days I won't be able to remember much of anything. I still can hardly believe it." Tears trickled down Grandma's cheeks as she rose from her chair.

Elaine wrapped her arms around Grandma and held her tight. "Oh Grandma, there was no easy way I could tell you. I just couldn't seem to find the right words." She was repeating herself, but she wanted to make sure Grandma understood how truly sorry she was.

Elaine felt even worse when Grandma started rubbing her back, just like she'd done when Elaine was a child and needed to be comforted. "I promise I'll be here for you, Grandma, and we'll fight this together for as long as we possibly can."

✍

Sara winced as Leah probed several sore spots on her left foot. "I don't understand why my feet are always so sore," she complained.

"Some people's feet are more tender than others," Leah said. "And of course, when there's inflammation anywhere in the body, it's usually indicated by the sensitive areas of certain meridian zones on a person's feet."

"Does that mean there's inflammation somewhere in my body?" Sara questioned.

Leah nodded, continuing to rub the places on Sara's feet that were the most painful.

"Do you know what's wrong with me—why my arms and legs sometimes feel numb or tingly?"

"I can't be sure," Leah responded. "But as I've mentioned before, I think it would be a good idea for you to see your doctor."

"Doctors are expensive, and I'd much rather come here to see you and just make a donation." Sara wiggled her toes. "Besides, I always feel better after I've had a foot treatment."

Leah smiled. "I'm glad to hear that, but there are some things reflexology can't help, so you need to use good judgment in deciding when to see a doctor and when to visit me."

"I understand, and if my problem gets worse, I'll make an appointment with the doctor."

∽

Hoping his mission this evening would be successful, Jonah directed his horse and buggy up the lane leading to Edna and Elaine's house. After tying Sassy to the hitching rack, he started for the house, but had only made it halfway there when a sleek black cat darted out of the barn and ran in front of Jonah. *Sure am glad I'm not a superstitious man,* he thought, sidestepping the cat as it zipped this way and that, in hot pursuit of a little gray mouse. *Otherwise, I might think something bad is about to happen.*

Jonah's hands grew sweaty as he stepped onto the porch and knocked on the door. He didn't know why he felt so nervous; it wasn't like he'd never come to call on Elaine before. A few seconds went by, and then Elaine, wearing an apron decorated with splotches of flour, answered the door.

"Jonah, I—I didn't expect to see you this evening," she stammered, brushing at the front of her apron. "I was just making some biscuits to go with the stew I'm preparing for supper."

Jonah couldn't help noticing that the rims of Elaine's eyes looked red, and so did her cheeks, indicating that she may have been crying earlier. "Is everything all right?"

he asked, feeling concern.

She nodded.

"I came over to see how you were doing, and I. . ." Jonah paused, groping for the right words to say what was on his mind. "I was wondering if you've changed your mind about us."

Elaine stepped out to the porch. "No, Jonah, I'm not able to marry you. My obligation is to Grandma right now."

"I realize that, but I really want to help, and I'm going to keep coming over until you accept that fact." It was all Jonah could do not to reach up and wipe away the tiny streak of flour clinging to Elaine's cheek.

Elaine lowered her gaze. "We really don't need any help right now, and I'd feel better if you'd just move on with your life."

"But I don't want to move on, Elaine. I want to be with you." Frustration welled in Jonah's chest. "The only way I'll ever give up on us is if the day comes that you stop loving me."

She lifted her gaze to meet his. "That day has already come, Jonah."

He jerked his head, feeling as though he'd been slapped. "What are you saying, Elaine?"

She looked him straight in the eye and said, "After thinking about it these last few weeks, I have come to the conclusion that what I felt for you before was never love; it was infatuation."

"I don't believe you," he said with a shake of his head. "You're just saying that because you're too proud and stubborn to let me help with your grandma's care."

"That's not true. I just don't love you, Jonah, and I'm not sure I ever did. Now please go home, and don't stop over here anymore. What we had is over." Elaine's lips quivered slightly, but she held his steady gaze.

Jonah stared into Elaine's beautiful blue eyes, and still her expression did not waver. On most things, Jonah was pretty easygoing, accepting people's decisions without question. Not this. But even though arguing the point was what he really wanted to do, he held back. Emotions that had taken him a long time to bury came rising to the surface again. Jonah felt just as bad as, if not worse than, when his plans back in Pennsylvania with Meredith had been crushed. Could he handle another rejection?

Staring across the yard, Jonah noticed the black cat he'd seen earlier gripping a dead mouse between its teeth and disappearing slowly into the barn. *Superstitions, huh?* he thought, feeling as if his world had just been turned upside down. Looking back at Elaine, Jonah said. "Tell me the truth, Elaine. Is that the way you really feel?"

She nodded.

Jonah could see by the set of Elaine's jaw that her mind was made up. Suddenly, he realized that even if he stayed here all night, he wouldn't get Elaine to change her mind or say she loved him. "Then I guess I have no other choice but to accept your decision."

With shoulders slumped and head down, Jonah turned and stepped off the porch, feeling like a rambunctious horse had just kicked him in the stomach. Never in a million years had he expected Elaine to say she didn't love him or that what she'd felt before was just infatuation. Of course, looking back on it, she'd never really said she did love him—just things like she enjoyed his company and she cared for him. *Have I been fooling myself all this time?* he wondered. *Maybe our relationship was one-sided, and I was just too blind to see it.*

CHAPTER 26

$\mathcal{E}$laine woke up the following morning with a sore throat. "Oh, great," she said, grimacing as she swallowed. *Could my throat hurt from all the talking I did yesterday with Leah and Priscilla?*

She sat up and swung her legs over the side of the bed. She swallowed again, just to make sure. She might expect to have a sore throat during the winter months, but not in July. Maybe it was from sitting under the air-conditioning vent at the restaurant during lunch.

"I sure don't need this right now," she grumbled, ambling across the room to her closet. This evening, Elaine and Grandma would be hosting another sit-down dinner, and there was still a lot that needed to be done before their guests arrived.

Elaine hoped Grandma was feeling up to it. After yesterday's discovery that she had dementia, Grandma might not want to host any more dinners.

What had made things worse was that after Elaine had apologized for not telling the truth right away, Grandma had tried to reassure her. Elaine felt helpless but reminded herself once again that Grandma wouldn't have to go through this alone.

Swallowing again while rubbing her throat, Elaine was convinced her glands weren't swollen. *I can't let a little thing like a sore throat keep me from doing what needs to be done.*

For so early in the morning, it was already warm, in

sharp contrast to yesterday's cooler temperatures. That's how July could be on the plains as weather systems moved through.

Elaine hurried to get dressed and then went to the kitchen to start breakfast. She found Grandma mixing a batch of pancake batter. A slight breeze from the shady side of the house drifted through the open kitchen window.

"Don't go to any trouble for me this morning, Grandma," Elaine said. "My throat hurts, and I don't feel like eating much right now."

The wrinkles in Grandma's forehead deepened. "Are you grank? Do we need to call the doctor?"

Elaine shook her head. "I don't feel sick, and my glands aren't swollen. Think I either did too much talking yesterday, or my sore throat is from sitting under an air-conditioning vent at the restaurant where I went with Priscilla and Leah yesterday."

Grandma went to the cupboard and took down a jar of honey. "I'd better fix you a lemon-and-honey drink. That'll make your throat feel better," she said, after taking a lemon from the refrigerator.

Once the lemon had been squeezed and the juice poured into a glass, Grandma added a spoonful of honey and stirred it well. Then she handed the glass to Elaine. "We have to get you better so you don't miss too much school. Sure don't want you falling behind on your studies or ending up with a lot of homework to do in order to catch up." Grandma touched Elaine's forehead with her cold hands. "I don't think you have a fever, but it might be best if you skip school today and go back to bed."

Elaine drank the lemon/honey mixture and grimaced; not from the taste of it, but because of what Grandma had just said. "Grandma, I've been out of school for several years now, so you don't have to worry about me missing school or having any homework to do."

Grandma's eyebrows squished together as she stared at Elaine for several seconds. Then a light seemed to dawn, and she snickered, giving a quick nod. "Well, of course you're not still in school. Silly me. Guess it was just wishful thinking."

As Grandma resumed making pancakes, Elaine placed her empty glass in the sink and stared out the window. If only she could turn back the hands of time, she'd go back to when she was a little girl. Her life had been carefree, and Grandma's memory had been just fine. Was this what she could expect in the days ahead—Grandma acting okay one minute and living in the past the next?

Elaine closed her eyes. *Dear Lord, please give me the wisdom and strength I need in order to care for Grandma.*

❧

Jonah reached for the thermos of coffee he'd brought to his shop that morning and opened the lid. Overnight, a warm front had moved in, and he hadn't slept well. It was going to take more than one cup of coffee to get through the day, much less get the house ready for his folks' arrival in a few days. Jonah wished the cooler weather had lasted a bit longer, but it wasn't the temperature that had given him a restless night. Thoughts of Elaine and her announcement that she didn't love him had kept him awake. He'd tossed and turned for hours, trying to come to grips with everything. He still couldn't believe she didn't love him. All these months they'd been courting, and even though she'd never actually said the words, she'd never given any indication that she didn't love him.

Why now? he wondered. *Maybe I need to talk with one of Elaine's friends about this. I'm sure either Leah or Priscilla would know if Elaine has ever loved me or not. Think I'll stop by and see Priscilla after I'm done working today.*

"Wow, it's sure gettin' warm out there." Timothy wiped his brow as he entered the shop. "Where should I put the bolt of upholstery that just came in?"

"I don't care. Put it anywhere!" Jonah snapped.

Timothy flinched, and he silently hauled the material to the table on the other side of the room.

Jonah knew immediately that he'd spoken too harshly. "Sorry for snappin' at you, Timothy. I didn't get much sleep last night. Guess it put me in a bad mood, but then, that's no excuse." He poured coffee into his cup and took a drink. "Hopefully this will help me wake up and be more civilized."

Timothy shrugged. "That's okay. My daed isn't worth much till he's had a few cups of coffee in the morning. He doesn't snap though. Just doesn't say a lot till he's fully awake."

"Jah, well, my being tired is not a good reason for barking at you, and I'll try not to do it again."

♫

"Would you please load that up and take it over to Rockome Garden Foods at Rockome?" Priscilla's mother asked, motioning to a box filled with raspberry jam that sat on the counter in their small shop.

Priscilla nodded. "Sure, Mom. Is there anything else you want me to take over there?"

Mom shook her head. "Just the jam for today. Oh, and when you're out and about, maybe you could drop by

Edna's place and see how she's doing. I still feel terrible about blurting out that she has dementia."

"It wasn't like you did it on purpose." Priscilla gave her mother's shoulder a gentle pat.

Mom sighed. "I wish there was something I could do to help Edna deal with the terrible disease."

"I feel the same way about Elaine. It's going to be difficult for her too."

"We can pray for them and be there to help out whenever possible."

"You're right about that." Priscilla picked up the box. "Guess I'd better get going. I'd like to be home before it gets too hot. This weather isn't good for me or my horse. See you later, Mom."

*

"Mammi! Mammi!"

Feeling as though she'd been drugged, Sara groaned and forced her eyes open. Mark stood at the side of her bed, red-faced, with tears running down his cheeks.

"Oh, my poor baby." Sara rolled out of bed and scooped Mark into her arms. Feeling a bit light-headed, she sank back to the bed and cuddled him close. She glanced at the clock on her nightstand and grimaced when she saw that it was nine o'clock. She couldn't believe she'd slept so long, even after a restless night. It had been so warm in her room that she'd lain awake for several hours before finally dozing off. Apparently, she'd been sleeping so hard that she hadn't heard Mark climb out of his crib and walk to the side of her bed, tugging on the quilt as he continued to fuss. She wondered how long he'd been calling to her.

When Sara stood up again, her head felt fuzzy and the room seemed to tilt at an odd angle.

I wonder if I'm coming down with something. Maybe it's just the stuffy heat in this room making me feel so off-kilter.

Going to the window, Sara opened it to let in some fresh air. After taking in several deep breaths, she felt a bit better, so she took Mark by the hand and headed down the hall to the kitchen.

Moving slowly so as not to upset her equilibrium, Sara managed to scramble some eggs for breakfast. When they finished eating, she ran water in the sink to wash their dishes. By the time she had them washed, dried, and put away in the cupboard, Sara had little strength left in her arms.

Something is terribly wrong, she thought, taking a seat at the table while Mark sat on the floor, playing with a few pots and pans. *Maybe I overdid it yesterday when I was cleaning house.*

Sara sat with her head down, massaging her temples, until she heard the *clip-clop* of horse hooves coming up her driveway. She groaned. "Now is not a good time for company."

Rising to her feet, Sara peered out the kitchen window, watching her friend Jean climb out of her buggy and secure her horse at the hitching rack near the barn. Then Jean went around and helped her three children out of the buggy.

Mark would be excited to have someone to play with this morning, but Sara wasn't sure she could take all the activity. Well, she couldn't be impolite and tell them not to come in, so she forced herself to go to the door.

"Guder mariye," Jean said cheerfully when she and her children entered the house. "We've been out doing some shopping, plus I wanted to show you the progress I've made on the quilt I've been making for our upcoming charity event."

Sara knew how much Jean liked to quilt. Her current project was going to be auctioned off to benefit a local family in need.

"Morning," Sara said, forcing a smile. "I'm interested in seeing the quilt, but first, why don't we have a cup of tea?"

"That sounds nice. The kinner can play while we visit awhile."

Another wave of dizziness came over Sara, and she grabbed the back of her chair to steady herself.

"Are you all right?" Jean took hold of Sara's arm and guided her into a seat.

"I had trouble sleeping last night, and when I finally dozed off, I slept later than I'd planned," Sara explained. "I think I'm still kind of drowsy and a bit light-headed."

Jean eyed Sara curiously. "This isn't the first time you've felt like this. I really think you ought to see a doctor, at least to rule out any kind of problem."

"Maybe another foot treatment with Leah will help. In fact, I'll make an appointment with her right away."

"That's up to you, but please don't put off seeing the doctor."

Sara nodded slowly. Until she saw some money coming in from the aprons she'd been making for one of the gift shops in town, she really couldn't afford to see the doctor. Still, she had to be well in order to care for Mark, so if another treatment with Leah didn't help, she would call the doctor.

∽

Jonah was about to tell Timothy they were done for the day when Priscilla entered the buggy shop.

"What can I do for you?" Jonah asked, pleased to see her, since he'd planned to ask her about Elaine.

"I'm on my way to Rockome Garden Foods and

discovered that there's a problem with one of my buggy wheels," she replied. "It's kind of wobbly, and I'm worried that it might fall off."

"Want me to go take a look at it?" Timothy offered, rolling up his shirtsleeves.

Jonah nodded. This would give him a few minutes to talk to Priscilla privately, which was exactly what he needed.

As soon as Timothy went out the door, Jonah turned to Priscilla and said, "I'll see what I can do about your wheel in a minute, but first, there's something I'd like to discuss with you. In fact, I was planning to stop by your place later today to talk about it."

She tipped her head back to look up at him, and he noticed that her cheeks were flushed, probably from the warm weather. "Oh, what's that? Is something wrong?"

He cleared his throat a few times, feeling suddenly unsure of himself. "Uh. . .well, it's about Elaine."

"What about her?"

"She says she doesn't love me and that what she felt for me before was just infatuation." Jonah paused and moistened his parched lips with the tip of his tongue. "Do you think that's true, Priscilla, or did Elaine only say that so I'd quit coming around?"

Priscilla's gaze dropped to the floor. "Well, I can't speak for Elaine, and it's really not my place to give my opinion."

"But you have an opinion, right?" he prompted.

She lifted her shoulders in a brief shrug but continued to stare at the floor.

Jonah took a step closer to Priscilla. "Please tell me what you think. Does Elaine love me or not?"

CHAPTER 27

*P*riscilla, did you hear what I asked?"

"Jah, Jonah, I heard," Priscilla murmured, refusing to look into his eyes.

"Does Elaine love me or not?"

Perspiration beaded on Priscilla's forehead, and not just from the heat. She didn't like being put on the spot, but Jonah was expecting an answer. It made her feel like a go-between, and the truth was, she couldn't be sure how Elaine really felt about Jonah.

"I think that question should be answered by Elaine," Priscilla said, forcing herself to look at Jonah again.

A muscle on the side of his neck twitched. "She already has, but now I'm asking you."

"I've always thought Elaine loved you, but maybe I was wrong. No one but Elaine really knows how she feels."

"Would you ask her how she feels about me? And also find out if I've said or done something to cause her to pull away?"

Priscilla clutched the folds of her apron, feeling like a helpless fly trapped in a spider's web.

"Please, Priscilla. I really need to know."

Jonah's pleading tone and his look of desperation made Priscilla reconsider. "Okay, I'll speak to Elaine."

Jonah's face relaxed a bit. "Danki, Priscilla. I'm grateful." He motioned to the door with his head. "Guess I'd better take a look at that buggy wheel now."

∽

As Edna moved around her kitchen, preparing food for tonight's tourist dinner, she couldn't stop thinking about the book she'd found earlier today, tucked inside one of the drawers inside the desk in their kitchen. Elaine had been reading that book yesterday while she sat on the porch, waiting for her friends. It was about the various types and symptoms of dementia. What a rude awakening it had been for Edna when she read a few pages of information about the different stages of the disease and what could be expected in the months ahead. From the little she'd read, dementia was incurable, and there wasn't much that could be done to stop the loss of her memory. Oh, there were some medicines she could try, but they all had side effects and offered no promise of a cure. *Well, I won't be taking any of those,* she determined.

Edna had slammed the book shut, unwilling to accept her plight and praying that none of the things she'd read about would happen to her.

Maybe it was an old book and by now there are new treatments, she consoled herself. But even as the thought flitted through her mind, Edna knew her future looked bleak. *Wish it was me who'd died instead of Lloyd. At least he had a healthy mind and would have been here for Elaine.*

While Edna stirred the filling for her special sour-cream peach pie, she continued to fret. She wasn't about to forget her dear husband or any of the wonderful memories they'd made together. How could she forget about raising their son, Milton, and the joy of seeing him and his wife get married and later become happy new parents? And what about Elaine? There was no way Edna would let some disease keep her from remembering who her granddaughter was. Elaine had brought new meaning to her and Lloyd's existence after the tragic accident that took their son and his wife. Surely those were memories that would never slip away.

Edna placed the crust into the pie pan, added the peach filling, and placed it into the oven. Leaning against the counter, she thought about the last time she'd talked with her older sister, Margaret. How long had it been since she'd seen Margaret or their younger brothers, Irvin and Caleb? As Edna recalled, it had been a few years, but that was because they lived in some other state. Her brothers had farms to tend, and even though Edna's sister still taught sewing classes, she was in her eighties and didn't travel much anymore. All these things made it difficult to visit, but they'd managed to keep in touch through letters and phone calls.

Maybe I should call and tell them about this terrible disease. No, I'm going to wait. What if it's all a mistake?

Edna hadn't told Elaine that she'd seen the book on dementia, and she thought it might be better not to mention it. Elaine had probably checked the book out from the library, looking for information that might enlighten her as to what to expect if Edna's memory loss worsened.

If it's true, then I wish there was something I could do to spare my granddaughter this experience, Edna thought with regret. *It's not fair to expect Elaine to take care of me and put her own life on hold. Like other young women her age, she should be allowed the freedom of getting married and raising a family, instead of caring for an old woman who will one day not even know who she is.*

With conflicting thoughts swirling through her head,

Edna left the kitchen and went out the back door. She wandered around the yard for a while, until she became bored.

Returning to the kitchen, she stared vacantly out the window, barely noticing the birds flitting back and forth to their feeders. *Maybe the doctor who told Elaine I have dementia was mistaken. The tests could have been wrong. Oh, I just need to stop worrying about this.*

"How's it going in here?" Elaine asked, stepping into the kitchen from the dining room, where she'd gone to set the tables for their dinner guests.

Edna watched as Elaine glanced around the room, sniffing the air. "It smells like something is burning."

Edna turned and looked at the stove, suddenly remembering her pie. When she opened the oven door and smoke poured out, she gasped. "Ach, my peach pie is burned. It's burned to a crisp!"

"Burned. Burned," Millie screeched from her cage across the room.

Elaine grabbed a pot holder and quickly removed the pie, placing it on a cooling rack. Then she opened the kitchen window to let out the smoke.

Edna stood nearby, slowly shaking her head. "I'm sorry about this. Guess I got preoccupied and forgot to set the timer."

"It's all right, Grandma." Elaine slipped her arm around Edna's waist. "I'll put another pie together, and it should be done in plenty of time. Remember, we also have two coconut cream pies to serve to our guests this evening, and there will only be twenty people this time."

Edna's throat constricted. Forgetting to check on her pie was just one more reminder of how forgetful she'd become. All these years, cooking and baking had been second nature to her. She'd made countless meals without giving it much thought. Ruining the peach pie might be a small thing, but it made her wonder with dread what else she might forget. Next time she baked a pie, she'd be sure to set the timer and stay right here in the kitchen until it was done.

∽

Elaine felt bad as she watched Grandma staring at the burned pie. *Will something like this be a regular occurrence? How much longer will we be able to keep doing dinners for tourists? If we have to give it up, then I'll need to think of something else Grandma can do so she won't become bored. And of course, I'll have to look for some other way to make extra money—something I can do from home.*

A knock sounded on the back door, halting Elaine's musings. "I'll get it," she said, but Grandma gave no reply, just moved away from the pie and walked over to Millie's cage.

When Elaine opened the door, she found Priscilla on the porch. "How's your grandma?" Priscilla whispered. "Is she still upset about what my mamm blurted out yesterday?"

Elaine stepped onto the porch and shut the door. "Grandma took it hard, and I still feel guilty for not telling her myself, but she seems to have forgiven me."

"Mom feels badly about it too." Priscilla motioned to the chairs. "Do you have time to sit awhile? I'd like to ask you something."

Elaine glanced toward the house, massaging her throat. "I can sit a few minutes, but I need to get back inside soon and bake a pie because we're hosting another dinner tonight." She decided not to mention the pie Grandma had burned. After all, most people had burned something in their kitchen at one time or another.

"How come you're rubbing your throat? Does it hurt?" Priscilla asked, taking a seat.

"A little, but it was worse when I first woke up. I think it may be from yesterday, when I sat under that air-conditioning vent at the restaurant." Elaine took the chair next to Priscilla.

"I felt a little chilled from the AC as well, but at least I didn't wake up with a sore throat." Priscilla paused, crossing her leg and bouncing it up and down. "Um. . .I saw Jonah earlier today."

"Oh?"

"I stopped by his buggy shop so he could take a look at my wobbly buggy wheel."

"Is everything okay?"

"It is now, since he fixed it." Another pause. Leaning closer to Elaine, Priscilla said, "Jonah wanted me to ask you a question."

"What's that?"

"He said you told him that you're not in love with him, and he wants to know if it's true or not."

Elaine squeezed her hands tightly together in her lap. "So he sent you here to ask me?"

"Jah. Is it true?"

Elaine bit the side of her cheek. She'd lied to Jonah; did she dare lie to Priscilla too?

Priscilla touched Elaine's arm. "You've told me before that you care for Jonah, and I thought you were looking forward to him asking you to be his wife. Have you changed your mind about that?"

"I do care about Jonah," Elaine murmured, "but not in the way I once did. When you speak to Jonah again, would you please tell him that?"

"Are you sure? I mean—"

"I'm very sure. This is the way it's meant to be,

Priscilla." Elaine rose from her seat. "I appreciate you stopping by, but I need to get back inside now. I'll see you at church on Sunday." She turned and slipped into the house, feeling even guiltier for lying to Priscilla, while trying to convince herself that breaking up with Jonah had really been the best thing to do.

∽

After Jean left with her children, Sara, feeling somewhat better, decided to see Leah for a reflexology treatment. She'd tried calling first but had gotten Leah's voice mail. If Leah was at home today, Sara hoped she wouldn't be too busy to see her.

As Sara headed to Leah's with her horse and buggy, she began to feel a bit woozy again. Perspiration beaded on her forehead and dripped onto her face. Reaching for the bottle of water she'd placed on the seat between her and Mark, she took a drink and offered him one as well.

By the time Sara arrived at her destination, she felt even worse, and the heat of the day had become almost unbearable. After taking another drink of water, Sara secured her horse and took Mark out of the buggy. When she knocked on the door, Leah's mother, Dianna, greeted her on the porch.

"Is Leah here?" Sara asked. "I was hoping to get a foot treatment today."

"Jah, she is at home, but unfortunately, she's not feeling well right now. When Leah got up this morning, she complained of a sore throat, so I suggested that she go back to bed." Dianna sighed. "I think sometimes my daughter tries to do too much and then she ends up wearing herself out. Her immune system is probably weak, and I'll bet she got the sore throat from being around someone who came to her for a treatment."

"I'm sorry to hear that." Sara lifted one hand to wipe the perspiration from her forehead, while clutching Mark's hand with her other.

"You look flushed. Why don't you and Mark come inside for a cold drink?" Dianna suggested.

Sara shook her head. "Danki for the offer, but I have some water in the buggy, and I'm not feeling the best right now, so I think we need to go home."

"You could be coming down with whatever bug might be going around."

"Maybe, so I'd best be going home."

Dianna reached out and tousled Mark's hair. "Take care, Sara, and I hope this little guy doesn't get sick too. Oh, and let us know if there's anything we can do for you."

"Danki, I will."

As Sara headed for home, Mark became fussy, and she noticed that his face was flushed. She hoped it was just from the heat and that he wasn't coming down with something. As eager as Sara was to get home, she didn't want to push Lilly to go any faster than necessary, so she kept the horse at a slow, steady pace. She'd have to rub the horse down once she got there, and she dreaded it. She wished she could take Mark up to the house, curl up on the bed beside him, and take a long nap.

By the time they'd made it home, Mark had cried himself to sleep. After securing Lilly to the hitching rack, Sara took her boy inside and tucked him safely in his crib. Then she went back outside to take care of her horse.

As Sara began brushing Lilly, her arms started to tingle, and they didn't seem to want to work. Her shoulders tightened as she breathed slowly in and out. *What's happening here?* she asked herself. *Could I be having a stroke?*

CHAPTER 28

On Saturday morning when Sara woke up, she felt some better. *Guess all I needed was a good night's sleep,* she thought as she fixed breakfast for Mark. It didn't make sense how one day she could feel so bad, and the next day she felt better.

"*Melke!*" Mark hollered, smacking his palms on the tray of his high chair.

"Okay, little man, Mama will get you some more milk, but can you say please?" Sara asked in Pennsylvania-Dutch.

Mark extended his hands. "*Sei so gut.*"

Sara smiled. "That's better, Son."

After she poured milk into Mark's sippy cup, she took a seat at the table and bowed her head. *Heavenly Father, I thank You for the food You've provided for us and for the blessings You give every day. Thank You for helping me to feel better, and please give me the strength I need for this day. Amen.*

As Sara began eating her toast and eggs, she thought about her visit with Jean the other day, and how, just before Jean went home, she'd invited Sara and Mark to join her family at Yoder's restaurant this evening. It had been awhile since Sara had gone out to eat and would be a nice change from having to cook supper. Mark would no doubt enjoy being with Jean's children. It was good for him to be around kids close to his age—especially since it seemed unlikely he'd ever have any siblings.

Is it God's will that I should marry again someday? Sara wondered. *How will I know if the right man comes along? One thing's for sure. He'd have to love Mark as if he were his own son.*

∽

Elaine stood at the kitchen sink washing the breakfast dishes. The room was quite warm, so she'd opened the window, hoping for a breeze, but there was none. From what she'd read in yesterday's newspaper, a round of thunderstorms was predicted for later today that would push the humid air eastward, bringing in more comfortable temperatures like they'd had earlier in the week.

Yesterday had been a stifling day, and even with the battery-operated fans, the dining room, where they'd hosted their dinner last night, had been much too warm. Most of the tourists didn't complain, except for one of the teenagers in the group. The girl acted rather spoiled, fanning her face with a napkin and making rude remarks about the lack of air-conditioning, asking how the Amish could stand the heat. Sometimes, Elaine had actually wondered that too, but just like the pioneer women from long ago, the Amish were used to it, and better acclimated to the heat than those having the comfort of an air conditioner at the touch of a button.

Elaine had been pleased at how well Grandma had done throughout most of the evening, until someone asked her what kind of pie they'd been served. With a blank expression, Grandma looked at Elaine and said, "What kind of pies did we make?"

Elaine could still picture Grandma's red face when she'd replied, "Sour-cream peach and coconut cream."

How many times had Grandma made those pies and served them to their guests, without ever forgetting their names?

This morning when Elaine had looked for some honey to put on her toast, she'd finally discovered it under the sink where all their kitchen cleaning supplies were kept. Grandma must have put it there, since she was the last one to use the honey. There was no doubt Grandma's memory was failing, and it seemed to be happening fast.

Think I'll go to the health food store and look for something that might help Grandma's memory. Surely there has to be a remedy that would at least slow the progression of her illness, Elaine decided.

She glanced to her right, noticing the calendar on the wall. It was then that she was struck with the realization that today was Jonah's birthday. Last year, when he'd turned twenty-four, Elaine had invited Jonah over for supper and baked him a birthday cake. She had been full of dreams for the future—dreams for her and Jonah that she'd thought by now would be coming true. But those dreams had dissolved like ice cubes on a hot summer day. This year Elaine wouldn't even see Jonah on his birthday. As much as that hurt, she had to sever all ties with him. She needed to keep her focus on Grandma's care; that was the only way.

❧

After Jonah sent Timothy on an errand to pick up a few supplies, he stood in front of the window of his shop, watching for his folks to arrive. Mom had said they were hiring a driver to bring them to Arthur and should arrive sometime this afternoon. They would stay at Jonah's house for the week they'd be here, since he had more room than Jean. Tonight, Jean had made plans for them all to go to Yoder's restaurant to celebrate her and Jonah's birthday. It would be great to have their parents here for the occasion, although Jonah had mixed emotions. Last year Elaine fixed him a nice birthday supper and even baked him a cake. But much to his disappointment, she wouldn't be helping him celebrate his birthday this year.

It's not fair, he fumed inwardly. *Some men meet the woman of their dreams, get married, and raise a family, but not me. Seems like the women I fall in love with are always out of reach. Maybe I'm just unlucky at love. It took me a long time to get over Meredith, and now I have to do it all over again with Elaine.*

Jonah's thoughts halted when he saw a silver van coming up his driveway. It must be his folks. He hurried outside as his parents stepped down from the van.

"It's just wonderful to see you," Mom said, giving Jonah a big hug. Her hair was the same light brown color as when Jonah had left home, only now he noticed a few gray hairs mixed in too. Jonah's mother was a tiny woman, with a narrow waist and flat stomach. Even at the age of fifty-seven, she almost looked like a teenage girl.

Jonah hugged Dad. "It's sure good to see you both. How was your trip?"

"It went well; no problems at all." Dad smiled and lifted the straw hat from his head, revealing dark, curly hair with a few streaks of gray. "We stopped by Jean's place for a few minutes before coming here, and we're sure glad to be able to spend some time with both of you. Happy birthday, Son." He gave Jonah's back a few thumps.

"Danki. Jean and I are getting the best present ever, having you and Mom here to celebrate our special day with us. We've both been lookin' forward to your visit." Jonah motioned to the van. "Does your driver need a place to stay? I've got plenty of room in my house if he'd like to stay here."

Mom shook her head. "Al has a cousin in Arcola, so he'll be at his place till we're ready to go home. Before we got out of the van, he said he wanted to get going, since he heard there's supposed to be a storm moving in later this afternoon or evening."

"He's right about that, but after the storm blows over, the weather's supposed to be more comfortable." Jonah moved toward the back of the van and opened the hatch. "Now, let's get your suitcases hauled into the house. Once you two are settled, we can sit and visit awhile."

"Don't feel that you have to entertain us if you're busy in the buggy shop," Mom said. "We can unpack our suitcases and fend for ourselves until it's time to meet Jean and her family for supper."

Jonah pulled out his pocket watch to check the time. "I'm just about done with the work I planned to do today, so as soon as my helper gets back, I'll close up the shop."

"I'm anxious to see your new place of business," Dad commented as their driver pulled out and they began walking toward the house.

"It's not as big as the shop you have in Lancaster County," Jonah said, "but it's working out okay."

"How about your helper?" Mom asked as they entered the house. "Is he working out for you too?"

Jonah nodded. "Timothy still has a ways to go, but he's a hard worker and eager to learn. How's your helper doing, Dad?"

"Aaron already knew the buggy business when he came to me, and we work well together, so I'm sure things will be fine there while I'm gone." Dad thumped Jonah's back. "I still miss working with you though."

"I miss that too," Jonah said, "but it would have

been too hard for me to stay in Pennsylvania after Luke returned to Meredith and their son."

"We understand." Mom slipped her hand through the crook of Jonah's arm. "I'm glad you've found someone else, and your daed and I are anxious to meet her."

"That's right," Dad agreed. "Will Elaine be joining us for supper this evening?"

"Elaine won't be there, Dad. We aren't seeing each other anymore," Jonah muttered.

"What?" Mom's eyebrows lifted as she removed her hand from the inside of Jonah's arm. "But I thought you were on the verge of marrying her."

Jonah's shoulders slumped, and he held his elbows tightly against his sides. "I thought so too, but I was wrong. Elaine broke things off with me."

"Why would she do that?" Mom asked. "I thought you two were in love."

"I do love Elaine, but I guess the feeling was never mutual." Jonah touched the base of his neck, where a muscle had knotted. "Elaine's grandma was diagnosed with dementia, and Elaine has to care for her now."

"Aren't you willing to help her with that?" Mom questioned.

"Of course I am, but Elaine seems determined to do it all on her own."

"Maybe she'll change her mind when she sees how hard it's going to be," Dad put in.

Jonah shrugged. "I was hoping for that, but the truth is, Elaine said she never really loved me, so as hard as it is, I've come to the conclusion that I may need to accept her decision."

"Maybe there's some other available woman in this area who might be better suited to you," Dad said.

Jonah shook his head. "I doubt it, but even if there

was, it's too soon for me to be thinking about that."

~~~~~

Jonah had just begun showing his dad around the buggy shop when Timothy showed up. "Did you get all the supplies I needed?" Jonah asked.

Timothy shoved his hands into his trouser pockets. "Jah, they're in the trailer behind your buggy. Should I bring everything inside?"

"That'd be good, but first I want you to meet my daed."

After Jonah made the introductions, Dad smiled at Timothy and said, "So how do you like the buggy-making business?"

"Like it just fine." Timothy grinned at Dad. "I was glad when Jonah offered me the job."

"And I'll bet Jonah's happy to have you." Dad looked at Jonah and winked.

"I'll go out and give you a hand bringing in the supplies," Jonah said. "Dad, you can stay here and look around the rest of the shop if you like."

"Once we get everything hauled inside, you're free to go," Jonah told Timothy as they walked toward the buggy trailer.

"Are ya sure?" the boy questioned. "It's still kinda early yet."

"That's okay. I've decided to close the shop earlier today so I can visit with my folks before we head out to supper. After all, it's Jean's and my birthday."

"All right, that sounds good to me. Maybe I'll stop at your fishin' hole on my way home. Oh, happy birthday, and I hope you have a good birthday meal tonight."

Jonah smiled. Timothy had been bringing his fishing pole with him to work every day, and often fished in

Jonah's pond before going home.

"Better keep an eye on the sky this afternoon while you're fishing," Jonah cautioned the boy. "Just in case the storm they're predicting rolls in."

"I'll do that," Timothy said with a nod. "And if it starts rainin', I'll head straight for home."

After Jonah and Timothy made a few trips into the shop with supplies, Timothy headed for the pond. A few minutes later, Jonah caught sight of Priscilla riding in on her bike. Was she here on business, or had she spoken to Elaine?

She pulled her bike alongside of him near the empty trailer. "I came by to tell you that I talked to Elaine," she said, getting right to the point. Her grim expression told Jonah that it wasn't good news. "There's no easy way to say this, Jonah, but Elaine said she doesn't love you."

Jonah's stomach twisted. "Do you believe her?"

"I don't know, but Elaine's never lied to me."

"I see. Well then, I guess I have no choice but to accept her answer." Jonah felt like someone had punched him in the stomach. It was just as he feared—what he thought he had with Elaine was over.

"I'm really sorry, Jonah," Priscilla said sincerely. "With the way things are for her grandma right now, I think Elaine may have shut herself off from love."

Or maybe, Jonah thought with deep regret, *Elaine made her decision because she really never cared for me at all. It might be that until recently, she was just too afraid to say it.*

CHAPTER 29

*A*re you all right, Jonah?" Jean asked as they entered Yoder's restaurant with their family. "You look like you're not feeling well this evening."

"I'm okay," Jonah said. "Guess I'm just tired, is all." There was no way he would spoil the evening by talking about his woes. Besides, discussing the situation with Elaine wouldn't change a single thing. He needed to move on with his life, but it wouldn't be easy. Although Jonah was uncertain of his future, he had to trust God and wait to see what the plan was for him from here on out.

"Looks like there's quite a crowd here tonight," Dad commented, glancing around the restaurant. "The place must have good food."

"They sure do," Jonah and Jean said in unison.

Jean's husband, Nathan, chuckled. "You two may not be identical twins, but I think it's kind of funny the way you often speak at the same time, and sometimes even say the exact thing."

"We've been doing that since we were kinner." Jean giggled and nudged Jonah's arm. "Haven't we, big brother?"

Jonah chuckled. "Jah, we sure have."

The hostess came then and led them to the back of the room where two tables had been set up for eleven people. Since only eight were in their group, Jonah didn't know why there were three extra seats. He was about to ask when Jean spoke up.

"I invited your friend Melvin to join us this evening, and also Sara and little Mark, since Sara's my best friend," Jean explained. "They should all be here soon, I expect."

"The more, the merrier." Jonah helped Jean and Nathan situate their children on booster seats before taking a chair himself. Try as he might, he couldn't help but wonder what Elaine was doing tonight.

"Hallich gebottsdaag," Jonah's four-year-old niece, Rebecca, said, grinning over at Jonah from where she sat in a booster seat.

Jonah smiled, reaching over to tweak the little girl's nose. "Danki, Becca." It was amazing how the simple smile of a child could lift one's spirits.

A waitress came to take their beverage orders, and just as Jonah asked for a glass of lemonade, his friend Melvin showed up.

"Sorry I'm late." Melvin seated himself in the chair on the other side of Jonah. "There seems to be a lot of traffic on the road this evening."

"Not a problem," Jonah replied. "We're still waiting for Sara and her son, Mark, so we wouldn't have ordered our food without you."

"I appreciate that, and oh, by the way, Hallich gebottsdaag, Jonah. You too, Jean." Melvin handed Jonah a paper sack. "Here's a little something for your birthday, my friend."

"You didn't have to get me anything."

"I know, but I wanted to." Melvin bumped Jonah's arm. "Go ahead, open it. I'm hopin' you'll like what's inside."

"Okay, but first let me introduce you to my mom and dad, Raymond and Sarah Miller."

After Melvin shook hands with Jonah's folks and had told them a little about himself, they got to talking as if they'd known each other for a good many years. Then Melvin looked over at Jonah and said, "I think your little niece is anxious for you to open the gift I brought ya."

Jean laughed. "That's right. Rebecca's been sitting there quietly, staring at it, since you first arrived."

"Do you want to see what's in the sack?" Jonah asked Rebecca after seeing the anxious look on her face.

"Jah, open it, please." With an eager expression, she clapped her hands.

"Naw. Think I'll wait till after we eat." Jonah winked at Rebecca. "Just kidding." When he opened the sack and withdrew an ornate pen with a buggy carved on the wooden base, he grinned. "Wow, this is sure nice. Danki, Melvin."

"You're welcome."

"Where'd ya find something like this?" Jonah asked.

"Had it special-ordered. If you turn the pen over, you'll see that the name of your buggy shop is engraved there. Thought if you liked it well enough, you might want to order more of the pens to give out to your customers."

"That's a good idea." Jonah bobbed his head. "I never thought of doing something like that."

"Can I take a look at that?" Dad asked, peering over at Jonah.

Jonah handed the pen to his dad, and after Dad studied it for a bit, he passed it around the table so the rest of the family could see.

"Think I might have to get some of those made up to hand out to my buggy-shop customers too," Dad said. "I really haven't done much advertising in that way; just mostly through word of mouth."

"Sometimes word of mouth is the best form of advertising," Nathan put in. "But then, handing out the pens to customers could also be beneficial. It's useful to them and good advertising."

"Oh good. Sara and Mark made it," Jean said, motioning toward the front of the restaurant. "Now we can all order our meals."

∽

When Sara entered the restaurant, holding tightly to Mark's hand, she struggled with her balance. Pausing to take in a deep breath, Sara started walking again toward the tables where Jean and her family sat. She didn't know why, but she felt out of place tonight. It wasn't that she didn't want to spend time with Jean. She just would rather have gotten together with Jean on her own—maybe gone out to lunch or had Jean over to her house for a meal. They would have had a better chance to visit that way.

A few days ago, Sara and Jean had gotten together, but Sara couldn't count that as much of a visit. She hadn't been feeling well, and Jean had ended up entertaining Mark, along with her own children, while Sara rested. She hoped she and Jean could get together again, maybe sometime next week, after Jean's parents went home.

"I'm glad you and Mark could join us," Jean said as Sara and Mark neared the table. She quickly introduced Sara to her and Jonah's parents, noting her mother had the same first name as Sara, only spelled differently.

"It's nice to meet you." Sara shook hands with them both and placed Mark in a booster seat. She sat in the chair between him and Jonah.

"Have you met Jonah's friend Melvin?" Jean asked.

Sara nodded and smiled at Melvin. "I heard you and Sharon are getting married this fall."

Melvin grinned. "Jah, and we're gettin' pretty excited about it."

"Are you okay, Sara?" Jean touched Sara's arm. "Your face is pasty white and you appear to be shaken."

"I had a little problem with my horse on the way to the restaurant," Sara replied, "but it was nothing serious, and I'll be okay once my nerves settle down."

"Was it due to all the traffic?" Melvin questioned. "It was pretty bad for me tonight."

Sara shook her head. "Lilly kept tossing her head, and at one point I lost my grip on the reins. I guess my horse figured that meant she had the freedom to gallop." Sara shivered, remembering how hard she'd had to pull on the reins in order to get Lilly to slow to a trot. It made her wish she had the strength of a man. For some reason, her hands and arms seemed to have less strength these days.

"I'm glad you and Mark are okay," Jonah said. "And it's nice that you both could join us tonight."

"Der gaul laafe," little Mark exclaimed, his eyes shining brightly.

"Jah, the horse ran, didn't he?" Sara smiled, while the others chuckled at the boy's innocent remark. She tried to remember how wonderful it was to see everything through a child's eyes.

Sara relaxed a bit. Just those few kind words from Jonah made her glad she'd come to the restaurant to join them this evening. Jean was fortunate to have a brother who cared about people the way Jonah did. She still felt grateful that he'd found Mark when he did. The day they'd had their picnic by the woods could have ended tragically if her little boy had gotten out on the road. God was surely watching out for them, just as He had been this evening when she'd had trouble with her horse. She just needed to relax more and put her trust in Him.

A huge clap of thunder sounded, and the lights in the restaurant flickered. Sara nearly jumped out of her seat, and she grabbed Mark's little hand, thinking he must be frightened too. But her brave little boy seemed not to notice the storm brewing outside as he played with his spoon. Sara glanced out the closest window and shuddered. The rain was coming down in sheets, and soon it became a torrential downpour.

"I hope this storm passes by the time we leave here," Sara said. "It'll only spook Lilly if it's still storming like this on the way home."

"Don't worry," Jonah reassured her. "I'm sure that none of us are in a hurry to go. If the storm continues for a while, we can just sit here enjoying ourselves and hang out till the storm passes by."

"My guess is that it'll be over quickly," Melvin put in as another crash of thunder boomed from above.

Sara was glad to be with everyone instead of being home alone with Mark. It made the storm less menacing. She glanced around and noticed that everyone else in the restaurant seemed to be paying little attention to what was going on outside. She decided to try to forget about the storm and concentrate on having a nice evening.

Remembering that she'd brought a gift for Jean and had tucked it in her tote bag, Sara wished she'd thought to bring something for Jonah as well. After all, today was his birthday too.

Maybe it's just as well that I didn't, she decided. *It*

might have seemed out of place for me to give him a gift since Jonah is courting another woman.

A new thought leaped into Sara's head. *If Elaine and Jonah are courting, then why isn't she here tonight? I guess it wouldn't be polite to ask.*

Several minutes went by, and when Sara next glanced out the window, the rain had stopped. That was a relief. At least she wouldn't have to drive home in the midst of a storm this evening.

CHAPTER 30

Two months later

*E*dna stepped outside with a basket of laundry and shivered, wondering why it felt so chilly this morning. During breakfast, Elaine had said something about it being the first day of autumn, but Edna didn't know what had happened to summer. Had it really gone by that quickly, as each day blended into another?

Sighing, Edna set the basket on the ground under the clothesline. She was about to hang one of the towels when she heard a horse whinny from the barn. She ignored it at first, but the whinnying continued, so she decided to check on things.

When Edna entered the barn, she walked to the back and discovered that the door to the stall where Lloyd's horse, Dusty, was stabled hung open. She gasped, seeing that his horse was gone.

Panicked, Edna dashed outside, calling for Dusty and looking all around. When she saw no sign of the horse in their yard or the field bordering her home, she headed down the driveway, hoping Dusty hadn't gotten out on the road.

Making sure to stay on the shoulder of the road, Edna walked for a distance, until she spotted a horse in a field to her right. It had to be Dusty. Its coat was a deep brown.

Several times she hollered for Dusty to come, but he merely kept eating with his head down.

Now, why is Dusty ignoring me? Edna fumed. *He's*

always come to me before, whenever I've called. Of course, I usually have a lump of sugar for him. Guess I should have gotten a piece before I came looking for Lloyd's horse.

Disgusted, Edna tromped up the driveway toward the house next to the field and knocked on the door. Several minutes passed before a middle-aged English woman, whom Edna didn't recognize, opened the door. "May I help you?"

Edna nodded. "My husband's horse, Dusty, got out, and he's in your field."

The woman stepped out of the house to take a look. She peered at Edna strangely over the top of her metal-framed glasses. "Sorry, but that horse belongs to my son, and his name is Chester, not Dusty."

Edna pursed her lips and stared at the horse. He sure looked like Dusty. Despite what the woman said, Edna was certain that was Lloyd's horse in the field.

"I'll go home and get my husband," Edna said determinedly. "He'll come and tell you that Dusty's his horse." She whirled around and started back down the driveway, but when she reached the road, Edna couldn't remember which direction she'd come from, or even how to get home. *Do I turn right or left?* she wondered, feeling a sense of panic.

❧

Having just finished washing another batch of clothes, Elaine piled them in the laundry basket. She'd help Grandma hang them on the line and then do some baking for the dinner they'd be hosting tomorrow evening.

As she took the clothes from the wringer washing machine, Elaine reflected on how Grandma had been these past two months. Some days were good, and others were bad.

Elaine had purchased a natural remedy from the health food store that was supposed to help with memory problems. Grandma usually forgot to take it, even when Elaine set it out with her other breakfast pills. Sometimes Grandma became argumentative, stating that she didn't need any pills and wasn't going to take them, no matter what Elaine said.

At times, Grandma wandered around the house as though looking for something, but when Elaine asked about it, Grandma would say she couldn't remember what it was. All of these things concerned Elaine deeply, because in addition to Grandma's forgetfulness and mood swings, her diabetes seemed to be getting worse. It was getting harder to monitor her numbers because Grandma snuck food she shouldn't eat and sometimes refused to take her insulin pills.

The doctor had recently put Grandma on insulin shots, but she wouldn't always allow Elaine to give them to her. On a few occasions, Grandma had phased out all of a sudden, until her insulin kicked in, and the struggle of getting her stabilized was hard on Elaine. It was difficult to know when she might have another spell, and Elaine simply couldn't be with Grandma every minute of the day. Leah, Priscilla, and a few other women from their community came by each week to help with things, but most of the responsibility for Grandma's care fell on Elaine's shoulders.

Oh Lord, I need Your help and guidance, because I'm getting so tired. Please show me the best way to take care of Grandma.

A few weeks ago, Elaine and Grandma had gone to a quilting bee, and when refreshments were offered, Grandma helped herself to several cookies and a hefty piece of pie. Elaine scolded her for it, but Grandma got snippy and said she was not a little girl and didn't need anyone telling her what to do.

Grandma had also begun losing things. To make matters worse, she'd get huffy and accuse Elaine of taking missing items, or moving them to some other place. Just yesterday, Grandma had let Millie out of her cage and accidentally left the back door open when she went outside to sit on the porch. Of course, Millie took the opportunity and flew right out. Grandma got upset and accused Elaine of leaving the door open and letting Millie out on purpose because she didn't like the parakeet.

Sadly, Elaine had later found the remains of the bird near the barn. She figured it had fallen prey to one of their cats. She'd buried poor Millie but hadn't said anything to Grandma about it, not wanting to upset her more than she was. Grandma had asked about the bird several times but seemed to accept the fact that Millie flew away and might never come back.

Grandma's personality change was the hardest thing for Elaine to deal with. Before, Grandma had always been so easygoing, rarely saying a harsh word to anyone, especially Elaine. But Elaine kept reminding herself that it was the disease making Grandma this way and that she wasn't being mean on purpose. That didn't make it any easier to deal with though. Some nights, after a difficult day of trying to reason with Grandma, Elaine would fall into bed in a state of exhaustion, but often, sleep wouldn't come. She'd sometimes lay there for hours before her mind and body relaxed enough so that she could finally doze off.

Knowing she needed to get busy and think of something else, Elaine took the clothes outside to be hung on the line. Glancing over at her swing, Elaine wished she had time for a little fun, or even just a few minutes to clear her head. Unfortunately, that would have to wait.

As Elaine approached the clothesline, she was surprised to see the basket Grandma had taken out awhile ago sitting on the ground with most of the towels still inside.

Elaine's brows furrowed. Grandma was nowhere in sight.

"Where are you, Grandma?" she called.

No response.

She called Grandma's name once more, but still, no reply.

Grandma hadn't gone back inside, for she would have come through the back door and into the utility room, and Elaine would have seen her right away.

Maybe she went to the barn. Elaine hurried inside and looked throughout the barn, but Grandma wasn't there.

A sense of panic welled in Elaine's chest, and she wasn't sure what to do. She hated to even consider it, but one section of the book on dementia talked about a person wandering away from home in a state of confusion. *Could Grandma have become confused and wandered away from our property? Should I get my bike and go looking for her, or wait here, hoping Grandma comes back from wherever she went?*

෧෮

Mark had spent the night at his grandparents' house, and they wouldn't bring him home until after supper. Deciding to take advantage of this free time, Sara went to do a few chores in the barn. Cobwebs were everywhere, and her horse's stall was a mess.

Sara hadn't had any more dizzy spells lately, and thankfully, she felt a bit stronger than she had this summer. She figured that was probably because she'd been seeing Leah for weekly foot treatments, which she would continue doing whenever possible. In addition to the benefits she experienced from reflexology, Sara enjoyed every opportunity to visit with Leah. While Jean was still Sara's best friend, Sara and Leah were quickly establishing a strong relationship too.

Think I'll begin by cleaning the cobwebs. Sara got a broom and knocked down all the webs around the windows. Then she moved on to take care of those in less obvious places. It was dark in the back of the barn, so she lit a gas lantern. As the area became illuminated, more cobwebs came into view. *How did I let things get so bad?* The barn had never looked this way when Harley was alive. He'd kept it nearly as clean as Sara kept the house.

All of Harley's tools were in the barn, just as he'd left them, neatly hanging on the wall or placed on a shelf. Sara wondered if she should continue to keep them. Harley had taken good care of his tools, and any other equipment that he used. Her husband had always said, *"If you take good care of your things, they'll last a long time."*

At times like this, Sara missed Harley so much: not just for the things he did around the place, but for his companionship and the love they shared. It would be hard to get rid of the items she remembered him using, but then, didn't everyone go through this when they lost their spouse?

Sara remembered Harley saying something else to her one evening as they were getting ready for bed: *"If anything ever happens to me, please move on with your life and do whatever is necessary in order to make things easier for you and Mark."*

Sara didn't like having that kind of conversation, but Harley had always been the practical one who liked to be prepared. She'd felt so loved by her husband, and now, even in death, she could almost hear him encouraging her to do what needed to be done.

It did no good to dwell on the past or wish for things that could never be, but thinking about the man she'd loved so dearly caused tears to fill her eyes, making everything look fuzzy.

"Just keep working," she said aloud. "If I work hard enough, I won't have time to think about all that I've lost."

Swiping the broom toward yet another cobweb, Sara missed, and hit the lantern instead. It fell on a bale of straw and quickly ignited. As the flame grew, she stood staring at it, disbelieving that it had happened.

"Oh no!" Sara gasped, coming to her senses. "I need to put the fire out before it burns out of control!"

CHAPTER 31

Sara's eyes stung and her lungs felt like they were going to burst as she battled the flames with her garden hose. It did little good. The fire was burning out of control.

A loud whinny from the back of the barn reminded Sara that Lilly was still in her stall.

"Ach, I need to get her outside before anything happens to her!"

Sara skirted around the flames and by the grace of God made her way to Lilly's stall. Releasing the latch, she swung the stall gate open and slapped the horse's rear. "Go on, girl!" she shouted. "Get out of the barn!"

Lilly didn't hesitate as she raced out of her stall. Sara followed, barely able to breathe or stay on her feet. Suddenly, she halted and looked back at Harley's tools. *Should I try to save some of his things?* For a split second, Sara almost turned around. But the heat from the fire had grown more intense, and she only had seconds to save herself. The barn could not be saved. Thank the Lord, her son was safe with his grandparents and Lilly was unharmed and out of the barn. Did anything else really matter?

Gasping for breath, Sara prayed for the strength to make it safely outside.

∽

"Giddyup there, Sassy," Jonah called to his horse, shaking the reins. As he quite often did, the lazy horse was poking along. Jonah was anxious to get home from his dental appointment, since work orders had been piling up again. If he knew for sure that business would continue to grow as it was and if he had a bit more money saved up, he'd be tempted to hire on another man. Of course, unless he could find someone with experience in buggy making, he'd have to train him, like he was doing with Timothy, and he really didn't have time for that. So Jonah would continue to do his best and hope that business remained steady, but not more than he and Timothy could handle.

It would be so nice if he could convince his folks to move to Arthur. Then he and his dad could work together again. But Dad seemed pretty set on staying in Pennsylvania.

Jonah couldn't believe how well things had gone at the dentist's today. Once the hygienist had cleaned Jonah's teeth and he'd seen the dentist, Jonah nearly fell out of the chair when the dentist said, "All is well; you have no cavities. I'll see you next year, Jonah."

Not only was he enjoying that good news, but he was glad it was the first day of autumn. Something in the air when he took a deep breath made Jonah glad to be alive. The rich, earthy scent that only fall could bring was one he welcomed every year.

Jonah looked up at the sky and couldn't believe its color. Like the blush of a ripened blueberry, it was so beautifully clear. On a day like today, he had to admit it would have been easy just to keep on riding, letting his horse take him wherever he wanted to go.

Jonah remembered how pretty it was in Pennsylvania, but he was glad to be here, where there were fewer people and not as many tourists. Illinois was already in his blood. Some folks living in the area still farmed for a living; some grew wheat and oats, and others planted corn and clover. Jonah loved seeing the farms and knew how important they were for one's existence. But as times had changed, many people began using other skills to make their way in life, like Jonah had chosen to do with his buggy shop. Some of the men created fine cabinetry and beautiful oak furniture. Still other Amish men and women had jobs in various businesses around the Arthur area.

As Jonah went a bit farther, he took another deep breath. His nose twitched, and he sniffed again. Was that the odor of smoke? It wasn't the aroma of burning leaves or someone's barbecue; it smelled like a building was on fire. As Jonah rounded the next bend, smoke and flames colored the horizon. He realized with alarm that they were coming from Sara Stutzman's place. Immediately, he turned into her lane, urging Sassy to hurry up the driveway.

Sassy didn't want to move at first, but the normally lazy horse must have sensed the urgency in Jonah's voice, because he trotted quickly up the driveway leading to Sara's house.

When Jonah spotted Sara lying on the ground, several feet from the barn, he hopped out of the buggy, haphazardly secured Sassy to the fence post, and dashed across the yard.

"Sara!" he yelled. "Sara!"

She lay unresponsive, and that worried him even more. Jonah dropped to his knees beside her and felt relief when he discovered that she was breathing. He couldn't see any evidence of burns on Sara's body; just a few streaks of ash across her forehead and cheeks. If she had been in the barn, which Jonah suspected, then she may have breathed in a lot of smoke, as the structure was now burning out of control.

Jonah could feel the heat from the fire and thought it best to move back away from the sparks that were floating through the air. Gently he picked Sara up and laid her on the cool, thick grass a safe distance away.

Seeing water seeping out of a hose a few feet away, Jonah wet his hanky and wiped Sara's face, tenderly removing the smudges. "Can you hear me, Sara?"

A few seconds passed, and then Sara opened her eyes. "Jonah?" she croaked after a series of coughs.

"Jah, it's me. What happened here? How'd your barn catch on fire?"

"I was doing some cleaning and accidentally knocked a gas lamp over. Before I knew it, the whole barn was in flames."

Sara tried to sit up, but Jonah told her to lie still a bit longer. "Is anyone in the barn right now?" he asked.

"No. I got Lilly out, and then. . ." Another round of spasmodic coughing came from Sara's mouth. "My barn is surely lost, and all of Harley's tools are in there."

Jonah could see that Sara was visibly shaken and needed comforting, so he gathered her into his arms, gently patting her back. "It's okay, Sara. The barn can be replaced, and so can any items that were inside. I'm glad you don't seem to be seriously hurt, but I think you oughta see a doctor. If you inhaled a lot of smoke, it could harm your lungs."

Sara shook her head. "I—I don't think I took in that much smoke, and I'd rather not go to the hospital. What I really need most is just to be with my son."

With deep concern, Jonah glanced around. "Where is Mark? Is he in the house?" He hoped the little boy wasn't running around the yard someplace or, God forbid, had somehow gotten into the barn.

"No, no. My boy's okay. He spent last night with my in-laws, so he's safe. I just need to be with him right now." Tears streamed down Sara's face, and she gulped on a sob.

Sighing with relief that Mark was safe, Jonah nodded in understanding. "I hear sirens coming this way. Someone must have seen the smoke and called the fire department." He helped Sara to her feet and held on to her, since she seemed a bit wobbly. "Are you okay to go into the house and wash up and change your clothes?" he asked.

"Jah, I'm all right," she reassured him.

"Okay. While you're doing that, I'll talk to the firemen, and afterwards take you over to Herschel and Betty's place to get your boy."

❧

As Elaine pedaled her bike quickly along, she spotted Grandma plodding along the shoulder of the road, away from their home. *Where in the world is she going, and why did she leave the yard without telling me?*

Elaine sped up until she was alongside of Grandma. She stopped the bike right in front of her, halting Grandma in her tracks.

Grandma blinked and touched her fingers to her lips. "Nancy, I'm so glad to see you. Can you help me find my way home? I think I'm lost."

"It's me, Grandma. . .Elaine. Mama is. . .well, she's not here anymore." Elaine figured it would be best if she didn't mention that her mother was dead. No point in confusing or upsetting Grandma any more than she was.

Grandma tipped her head, staring intently at Elaine. After a few seconds, a slow smile spread across her face. "You're my *grossdochder*, aren't you?"

"That's right, Grandma. I'm your granddaughter. What are you doing out here on the road by yourself? I've been worried about you."

Grandma's cheeks flushed a bight pink. "I went looking for Dusty because he wasn't in his stall. Thought I saw him in someone's field, but the lady there said the horse was her grandson's." Her forehead creased. "That horse was brown, and it sure looked like Dusty."

Elaine got off her bike, set the kickstand, and gave Grandma a hug, realizing that she needed a little reassurance right now. "We sold Dusty a few weeks ago. Remember?"

Grandma squinted while rubbing the bridge of her nose. "Why would we sell your grossdaadi's *gaul*?"

"Because we have no need for three horses now that Grandpa's gone."

"Gone? Where did he go?" Grandma glanced around as though looking for answers. She was clearly quite confused.

Oh great, Elaine thought. *Grandma must think Grandpa is still alive.*

Undecided as to what else she should say, Elaine patted Grandma's arm tenderly, hoping to reassure her that everything was okay. "We need to go home now. I'll ride my bike slowly, and you can follow me there."

Grandma looked uncertain at first, but finally nodded. "That's good, because I need to talk to Lloyd about his horse. He'll be upset knowing Dusty got out of the barn."

Elaine hoped by the time they got home, Grandma might remember that Grandpa had died. She didn't want to shock her with that news.

Climbing back on her bike, Elaine noticed some smoke in the distance. *I hope that's just from someone burning something and that no one's house has caught fire.*

While Elaine pedaled slowly toward home, glancing back every few seconds to see if Grandma was following, she made a decision. Tomorrow she would call the doctor and ask why Grandma's memory was failing so fast. According to that book on dementia, Grandma was losing her memory quicker than she should be and heading toward the more advanced stages of the disease. Elaine wished with all her heart that there was something she could do to slow the progression. She could hardly stand seeing her grandma like this.

CHAPTER 32

The following day after Jonah finished working, he decided to drop by Sara's and see how she was doing. He took a quick shower, put on clean clothes, and headed outside to get his horse and buggy ready. Hopefully Sassy, having rested all day, would move a little faster this time.

Going down the road, Jonah remembered another time when he'd come to someone else's rescue. Memories took him back to Pennsylvania, when he'd first arrived in Bird-in-Hand. He'd just gotten settled in at Mom and Dad's house when he'd learned about the tragedy concerning Meredith's husband, Luke. Jonah had decided to visit Meredith and offer his condolences. It was good that he got there when he did, because shortly after his arrival, Meredith collapsed and could have gone into labor and lost her baby if she hadn't gotten to the hospital in time.

Was it divine intervention that Jonah had come to Sara's aid when her barn caught fire? *Maybe it's my responsibility to rescue people in distress by showing up at just the right time,* Jonah decided, pulling his thoughts back to the present.

Jonah was halfway to Sara's when he saw Elaine's friend Leah riding her bike. She must have seen him too, for they both waved at the same time.

Jonah was tempted to stop and ask Leah how Elaine was doing, but decided against it. He wanted to get to Sara's before she started cooking her supper. Besides, he'd talked to Leah's dad, Alton, the other day when he'd stopped by the buggy shop. Elaine's name had come up when Alton mentioned that Leah and her mother had been helping Elaine do some canning a few weeks ago. Alton said that Edna wasn't doing well and if things didn't improve, she and Elaine might not do the sit-down dinners for tourists anymore. Jonah had also learned that with her grandmother's approval, Elaine had sold her grandfather's horse and was renting acreage on her grandparents' property to one of their neighbors, so if they quit doing the dinners, they would at least have enough money to live on. But would it be enough?

Jonah wished he was free to help out, but Elaine had made it clear that she didn't want that.

"Did she ever really feel anything for me?" Jonah muttered as he continued on down the road. "Or was I always just a passing fancy for her?"

Sassy's ears perked up and he neighed as if in response.

"Was that a yes or a no?" Jonah asked with a snicker. At least he wouldn't be showing up at Sara's house with a sour expression.

Jonah thought about how he'd been one of the witnesses at Melvin and Sharon's wedding last week. Seeing their smiling faces after they'd said their vows had made Jonah wish all the more that he too was happily married.

∽

Sara wasn't sure what to fix for supper this evening. Nothing appealed, and she'd worked hard cleaning house most of the day, so she had no energy for cooking. Of course, some of her fatigue could be related to the ordeal she'd gone through yesterday when the barn caught fire. She still couldn't believe it was gone or that she'd been so careless when she was attacking all those cobwebs. Each time Sara glanced out the window, it made her sick to see what little was left of Harley's barn. What would he think of her being so careless?

I should have been watching what I was doing, Sara berated herself as she sat on the living-room floor next to her son while he played with some of his toys. She was glad Mark was young and wouldn't remember any of this as he got older.

Sara thought about Jonah and how thankful she was that he'd come along when he did. In addition to talking with the firemen after they'd arrived, he'd helped Sara calm down and reassured her that if she decided to rebuild the barn, he would come to help out. Jonah had also made sure that Sara's horse was put out in the field. After the fire was extinguished, Sara was checked over by the paramedics, who had followed in an ambulance behind the fire trucks. Once it was determined that Sara was okay, Jonah had taken her over to Herschel and Betty's, where she and Mark had spent the night.

Turning her attention back to Mark, Sara realized that she couldn't sit here all evening; she needed to feed him something. Maybe she would make them sandwiches for supper. That wouldn't be much trouble.

Since Mark seemed content to play with his toys, Sara made her way to the kitchen. She'd just opened the bread box and taken out a loaf of bread when she looked out the window and saw a horse and buggy pull in. Pleased to see that it was Jonah, Sara set the loaf of bread on the counter and opened the back door.

When Jonah stepped onto the porch, he smiled and

said, "I came by to see how you're doing. That was quite an ordeal you went through yesterday."

She nodded, appreciating his concern. "It was, and I'm thankful you were there to help me through it."

"Are you doing okay?" Jonah moved closer to Sara.

"I'm fine now. Still coughing a bit from the smoke I inhaled, but otherwise doing okay. However, I fear all of Harley's tools have been lost."

"You can worry about that later." Much to Sara's surprise, Jonah slipped his arm around her shoulder and gave it a gentle squeeze. "I can even come over once the area has cooled and see what things might be salvageable."

"You would do that for me after all you've already done?" she asked in disbelief.

"Sure, why not?" A blush of pink spread across Jonah's cheeks. "That's what friends are for, right?"

Sara nodded in agreement.

He shifted his weight from one foot to the other, as though nervous about something. "Um. . .I know it's short notice, Sara, but if you haven't started supper yet, I thought maybe you and Mark would like to go out someplace to eat."

"I haven't started supper and going out does sound nice, but I'm worried that with us being seen together at a restaurant, it might cause some people to talk."

"Talk about what?"

"Well, it might not seem right for you to be seen with me when you're courting Elaine."

"That won't be an issue, because Elaine and I broke up a few months ago," Jonah said. "With the way information travels around here, I thought you would have heard by now."

"No, I hadn't heard." No wonder Elaine hadn't been

at Jonah and Jean's birthday dinner. Sara wondered if Jonah had broken things off with Elaine, or if it was the other way around. Even though she was curious, she wouldn't ask, because it just wouldn't be polite. If Jonah wanted her to know the details, he would share them with her.

"So, how about it, Sara? Will you and Mark go out to supper with me?"

Barely giving it a second thought, Sara nodded. She looked forward to spending the evening with Jonah.

"I'm glad you were free to have supper with me," Elam Gingerich said as he and Priscilla took seats at Yoder's restaurant.

"It was nice of you to invite me." Priscilla had known Elam since they were children and had attended the same school together. Her family worshipped in a different church district than his, but they'd spent time together during several young people's gatherings. Priscilla had known for some time that Elam was interested in her, but he was kind of shy and hadn't made his intentions known until last week, when he'd invited her to have supper with him tonight. Elam was twenty-five and had never had a serious girlfriend that Priscilla knew of. He had medium-brown hair, hazel eyes, an average nose, and ears that were a bit larger than most. But Elam wasn't ugly; there was actually a handsomeness about him, and Priscilla found his quiet way and genuine smile appealing.

Elam worked part-time at his parents' bulk foods store and also helped an English man in their area who was a roofer. Elam seemed to be highly motivated and had joined the church last year, so Priscilla figured he was secure in his faith and had no plans to leave his Amish heritage. He would probably make someone a good husband. But if Elam decided to pursue a serious relationship with her, could she see him as more than a friend?

"Did ya hear what our waitress said?" Elam's question pulled Priscilla's thoughts aside.

"Oh, sorry, I didn't realize you'd come to our table," Priscilla stammered, feeling foolish as she looked at Barbara Yoder, their Amish waitress.

Barbara smiled. "Would you like something to drink besides water?"

"I'd like a glass of iced tea," Priscilla responded.

"And I'll have a root beer, please," Elam added.

"I'll get those now and be back to take your order." Barbara smiled and walked away.

"Sure is nice weather we've been having," Priscilla commented after several minutes of awkward silence.

Elam glanced out the window. "Jah, and I'm glad for it, 'cause my boss has a couple of roofing jobs that need to be done next week, and we sure don't need any rain."

"Do you enjoy roofing more than working in your folks' store?" Priscilla asked.

He nodded. " 'Course when the weather's bad and we can't roof, it's nice to have a second job to fall back on."

Barbara returned with their drinks and asked what they'd like to eat. Elam ordered a burger and fries, and Priscilla said she'd like some fried chicken, mashed potatoes, and a small garden salad.

While they waited for their food, they talked about some of the things they'd read in the paper lately, like the accident that had taken place in the town of Sullivan, not too far away.

"At least that collision didn't involve a horse and buggy." Elam drew in a deep breath and exhaled quickly. "As bad as it was, if one of our people had been in a buggy and gotten hit by that truck, they probably would have been killed."

Priscilla was about to comment when she glanced toward the door and saw Jonah enter the restaurant with Sara and her son, Mark. Priscilla was so surprised to see them together that she choked on the iced tea she'd just sipped.

"You okay?" Elam asked, leaning toward her with a look of concern.

Priscilla nodded, blotting her lips with a napkin. "I'm fine. Guess I must have swallowed the wrong way." She watched with curiosity as the hostess seated Jonah, Sara, and Mark on the opposite side of the room. Had they seen her? Should she go over and talk to them? Maybe not. It might be best just to keep her focus on Elam and pretend she hadn't seen Jonah with Sara and her little boy.

 ༄

"How come you're frying so much chicken?" Edna asked, peering over Elaine's shoulder as she stood at the stove. "There's just the two of us, and we can't eat that much chicken for supper tonight."

"This isn't just for us, Grandma," Elaine said. "We're hosting another dinner tonight for a small group of tourists."

Edna rubbed her forehead as she pondered this information. "Really? Did I know about that?"

"The tour director set things up with us a few weeks ago. Do you remember?"

Edna continued to rub her forehead. It was upsetting

not to be able to recall something like this. "I can't say that I do, but if it's true, then we need to get busy, because there's a lot yet to be done."

"Not so much." Elaine motioned to the hefty-size kettle on the back burner. "The potatoes are cooked, mashed, and keeping warm on the stove, and the salad is in the refrigerator."

Still puzzled, Edna squinted. "Oh, really? I don't remember making those."

"Actually, you didn't. I made them while you were napping earlier this afternoon."

Edna slid one finger down the side of her nose, stopping at the tiny mole. "That's right; I was kind of sleepy." She smiled at Elaine, removing her finger. "Danki for doing all of that, Nancy. You've always been a hard worker. My son picked well when he married you."

"No, Grandma, I'm not Nancy. I'm your granddaughter, Elaine."

Edna's cheeks warmed. "Of course. How silly of me to say such a thing. You look so much like your mamm; it's easy to get you mixed up sometimes."

Elaine nodded as she continued to fry the chicken.

Edna turned and moved slowly across the room. "Think I'll go to the dining room and make sure the tables have been set." *Sure wish I didn't feel so confused. Makes me feel like I'm losing my glicker.*

∽

Things went okay during the first half of the dinner, but when it was time to serve dessert, Grandma started talking to Elaine like she was a child, saying things like, "If you can't be a little faster serving that pie, I'll send you to bed without any dessert."

Elaine merely smiled and tried to shrug it off,

hoping none of their guests had heard what Grandma said. But when Grandma started talking about Grandpa and said someone had stolen his horse, Elaine became concerned.

"Grandma, could I speak to you in the kitchen for a minute?"

"Whatever you want to talk about can be said right here with my friends." Grandma turned and smiled at their guests.

Feeling a sense of panic, Elaine gave Grandma's arm a little tug and whispered, "Would you please come with me for just a minute? It's important that I talk to you alone."

"Well, okay, if you must, but we can't be gone too long." Grandma followed Elaine into the kitchen and pulled out a chair at the table. "What did you want to talk to me about, Nancy?"

"I'm not Nancy, I'm Elaine, and—"

"Are you jealous because I have friends here and you don't?"

"No, it's not that. You look tired, Grandma, and I think it might be better if you went to your room now and rested, while I serve dessert to our guests."

"Well, if that's the way you feel about it, then fine!" Glaring at Elaine, Grandma stood up and then tromped out of the room.

It nearly broke Elaine's heart to see Grandma responding to her in such a negative, almost hostile, way. She wasn't acting like the grandmother she'd always known.

Breathing deeply as she tried to calm her racing heart, Elaine returned to the dining room.

"Is there a problem?" the tour guide asked as Elaine approached the table.

"No, everything's under control." Elaine placed two pies on the first table and was about to set the other ones on the opposite table when she heard Grandma loudly mumbling while stomping around in her room. *This will be the last dinner Grandma and I host,* Elaine thought regrettably. *Tonight has been too difficult for us.*

CHAPTER 33

The following day, Priscilla decided to stop and see Elaine. Rather than taking the time to hitch Tinker to her buggy, she rode over on her bike. Along the way, she rehearsed what she was going to say.

Last night at the restaurant, Priscilla had chosen not to speak with Jonah or Sara. They'd seemed to be preoccupied and didn't appear to notice her, so she had simply concentrated on visiting with Elam.

Jonah couldn't be in love with Sara; it hasn't been that long since he was courting Elaine, and I know he was crazy about her, Priscilla told herself as she pedaled along, keeping her bicycle on the shoulder of the road. The more she thought about it, the more concerned she became. *If Jonah and Sara are courting, will Elaine be upset?* Jonah had been good friends with Sara's husband, so maybe he and Sara were just friends too. But if Jonah was courting Sara, there was nothing she could do about it, so it did no good to fret.

Priscilla turned up the Schrocks' driveway. After she'd parked her bike, she hurried up to the house. She was about to knock on the door when Elaine stepped out, quickly shutting the door behind her.

"I'm glad you're here; I need some moral support right now."

"Oh, what's wrong?" Seeing the stress lines on Elaine's face had Priscilla concerned.

Elaine signaled to the chairs on the porch. "Let's take a seat."

Noting that Elaine wasn't wearing a sweater, Priscilla suggested they go inside. "It's chilly this morning."

Elaine shook her head. "I'd rather talk with you here. Grandma's in the kitchen, and I don't want her to hear our conversation."

"Okay, but maybe you should get a sweater."

"No, I'm fine." Elaine took a seat, and Priscilla did the same.

Priscilla couldn't help but notice the dark circles beneath her friend's eyes. *I'll bet she hasn't slept well in weeks.*

Tears sprang to Elaine's eyes, and she clasped Priscilla's hand. "Grandma's getting worse, Priscilla. Much worse than I expected, and it's happening so quickly."

Priscilla sat quietly as Elaine told how her grandma thought she'd seen her husband's horse and that she often believed Elaine was her mother, Nancy. "And you should have seen how Grandma acted during the dinner we hosted last night." Elaine shook her head as more tears came. "I can barely cope with things anymore, Priscilla. It's overwhelming."

"Have you spoken to her doctor about this?" Priscilla questioned.

"Not directly, but I called his office and talked with the nurse."

"What'd she say?"

"Just that some dementia patients' memory loss is gradual and can take place over several years. But with some who have advanced dementia, like Grandma apparently does, their memory goes quickly. Trouble is, I already knew all of that." Elaine paused and blew her nose on the tissue Priscilla had just given her. "To make all this worse, since Grandpa died, Grandma seems to have lost her zest for living. At first she was a fighter and said she'd go down kicking. Now it makes me wonder if she's just given up on life."

"Have you tried giving her that remedy you found at the health food store?"

"I have, but she usually won't take it. It's hard to get her to cooperate when it's time for her insulin shots too." Elaine's chin quivered. "It's difficult to take care of her when she doesn't cooperate. And it's even more so when she gets upset with me and says harsh things."

Priscilla gave an understanding nod while gently patting her friend's hand. "I feel so bad for what you're going through, but I'm sure you must know that your grandma would never treat you that way intentionally."

Elaine sniffed. "I—I know, but it still hurts."

"I'm sure it does, and I wish there was more I could do to ease your burden."

"You, Leah, and so many others have helped out as often as you can, and I appreciate it so much. But you have busy lives of your own, and I don't expect someone to be here all of the time." Elaine sighed, leaning back in her chair. "Besides, even if you could be here on a regular basis, it wouldn't make any difference in how things are going with Grandma right now. No one but God can stop or even slow this horrible illness that is taking the grandma I've always known from me."

"It's a terrible disease, and sometimes it can be harder on family members than on the patient when their loved one becomes like a stranger to them."

"You're right, Priscilla, but I can only imagine the struggle going on inside Grandma's head with all this." Elaine paused and swiped at the tears that had fallen onto her cheeks. "Just talking to you about this has been helpful. Danki for listening."

"Oh, you're welcome. It's the least I can do for a

special friend like you."

"You and Leah are such good friends, and I don't know what I'd do without your love and support." Elaine sniffled. "Something else happened the other day too. On Thursday, Grandma's parakeet got out, and later on, I found her remains over by the barn. I haven't the heart to tell Grandma that one of the cats probably got her pet bird. Even though I took Millie's cage out of the house and put it in the back of the barn, I don't think Grandma realizes that the bird is gone. If she does, she hasn't said anything about it."

"Oh, that's such a shame." Priscilla blinked against her own tears. *I'm definitely not going to tell Elaine about seeing Jonah and Sara at the restaurant last night. She has enough to deal with right now.*

"After all that happened at the dinner we hosted last night, I've made a difficult decision." Elaine shivered, crossing her arms in front of her chest.

"What's that?"

"There will be no more sit-down dinners for tourists in this house. In fact, after everyone left, I spoke with the tour guide and explained my decision."

"How'd she respond to that?"

"Said she understood, but was sorry to lose our business. She also stated that if things should ever change, and I decide to start doing the dinners again, to let her know." Elaine stared out across the yard. "It's not likely that I'll ever host dinners for tourists again. Those days are behind us now."

"If you want to keep doing them, I'd be happy to come over and help out," Priscilla offered.

"Danki for your willingness, but I don't want to invite strangers into our house for dinners anymore, never knowing what Grandma might say or do."

"How will you support yourselves?" Priscilla questioned. She wished again that there was more she could do for her dear friend.

"We have the rent money from the land we're leasing, and there's still some money left in our bank account." Elaine shifted in her chair. "I could take in some sewing or maybe try selling some of my rock paintings at one of the gift stores in town. I'm going to take one day at a time and keep trusting the Lord to provide for our needs."

Priscilla nodded. "And remember the words of Psalm 125:1: 'They that trust in the Lord shall be as mount Zion, which cannot be removed, but abideth for ever.'" She gave Elaine's arm a reassuring squeeze. "Please don't forget to ask for help whenever you have a need."

More tears fell as Priscilla stood and gave Elaine a hug.

❧

Jonah stepped out of his house and paused a minute before heading to the shop. His mind was full of scattered thoughts as he reflected on the enjoyable evening he'd had with Sara and Mark. It had been fun, being with Sara, and that little boy of hers had just about stolen Jonah's heart. Jonah looked forward to spending more time with them.

What would it be like to have a son like Mark and be able to pass on to the child the same values as my parents taught me? Jonah was beginning to think his desire for a wife and children was just a dream—a dream that had twice been broken.

Lifting the apple he'd taken from the house, he took a bite. Some of the juice sprayed out and dribbled down his chin. Apples always tasted best this time of year. Jonah munched on it while his thoughts kept spinning. Some of the leaves in his yard were slowly turning, with just a hint of color, but for the most part they were still green. Birds had begun flying in larger groups as they started migrating. Acorns were falling, and the apple harvest was in full swing. Soon the trees would be bare, and then the upcoming holidays would swoop in.

Jonah reflected on how Jean had told him the other day that Mom and Dad might be making another trip to Illinois to be with them for Thanksgiving. At first, Jonah and Jean, along with her family, had talked about going to Pennsylvania, but Mom and Dad said they thought it would be easier for them to come to Illinois, since it was only the two of them. Jean had already begun planning a festive dinner with all the trimmings.

Jonah wished Dad was here right now so he could talk to him about Sara. Jonah wasn't sure how he really felt about her, or if he was ready to establish another relationship, especially so soon. The last two had ended up emotionally draining, so maybe it was best just to remain friends with Sara. Although he had to admit, he did have a good time, and little Mark took to him so easily. Jonah loved kids. Even when he was out and about and saw children he didn't know, as soon as he made eye contact, the child would smile at him.

The subject of the holidays didn't come up last evening, but I guess I could ask Sara if she and Mark would like to join us for Thanksgiving this year. But then, she might be planning to go to Indiana to spend the holiday with her parents.

Jonah didn't know why he was thinking about all of this right now. Thanksgiving was still a ways off. Not only that, but there was work to be done in his shop, so he'd better quit thinking and get busy.

∾

As Sara sat at her sewing machine, making another apron

to sell, she thought about last night and how much she'd enjoyed being with Jonah. He reminded her of Harley—not in the way he looked, but with his caring attitude and gentle spirit. Jonah had been so attentive to Mark during the evening and kept the boy occupied when he'd become restless, waiting for his meal. When Jonah brought them home afterward, Mark had fallen asleep, so Jonah carried him inside for Sara. Before he left, Jonah had told Sara that he'd had a good time and hoped they could go out for supper again sometime soon.

Does Jonah want to court me? she wondered. *Is he over Elaine, and could he possibly be interested in beginning a relationship with me?*

Sara looked out the living-room window and focused on the swirling leaves. The wind had picked up, and the few leaves that had fallen from the trees in her yard were being carried away on the breeze. It wouldn't be long before Thanksgiving would be upon them.

Sara's thoughts turned to Harley again and how much he'd loved this time of the year. He had enjoyed seeing the leaves turn color, and after a heavy frost, Harley had mentioned how much he liked those see-your-breath-in-the-air mornings. Many times, when their chores were done early, he'd say, "Let's go for a ride, Sara." They'd hop in the buggy and drive through the farmlands, enjoying the stunning colors of autumn. Fields would be turning a rich golden tan, with hay cut for a second time. The mums were brilliant colors, blooming by fence posts and throughout flower beds in many backyards. Sara enjoyed fall days too, with less humidity and crystal-clear skies.

She closed her eyes, not wanting to let go of the past. Was it only a year and a half ago that Harley had died? Sometimes it seemed like just yesterday. Other times, memories of Harley felt like such a long time ago.

Sara had never known any man who loved the holiday season like her husband did. Harley became almost child-like when the first white flakes of snow started falling. He loved the smell of wood burning in their fireplace, and many times during a snowy afternoon, they'd get out one of their board games, make a batch of buttery popcorn, and relax in front of a cozy fire. She missed those times so much.

Sara would stay home for Thanksgiving this year but had been considering going to see her parents for Christmas. But traveling that far with a two-year-old might prove to be stressful, so she'd invited her folks to come here. Mom and Dad had agreed, and Sara looked forward to their coming. She couldn't help wondering, though, what Jonah would do for the holidays. Would he stay here in Arthur and celebrate with his sister and her family, or return to Pennsylvania to be with his parents?

If he stays, she thought, *maybe I'll get the chance to see him during that time. I'm sure Mark would enjoy it, and truth be told, so would I.*

CHAPTER 34

*D*anki for agreeing to stay with my grandma while I do some shopping today," Elaine said when Iva came over on the first Monday of October. "I'd take her with me, but she seems to be afraid of riding in the buggy lately."

"That's too bad. Where's Edna now?" Iva lowered her voice to a whisper as she took a seat at the kitchen table.

Elaine gestured toward the door leading to their dining room. "She does have some good days, and she's working on a puzzle. It was something I thought might help to stimulate her brain. Even though Grandma probably won't be able to get many of the pieces to fit, she seems content at the moment."

Iva sat quietly and then slowly shook her head. "I feel so bad for Edna—and you too, Elaine. I never expected your grandma would go downhill so quickly."

"Neither did I," Elaine admitted. "It's unbelievable."

"I have an aunt who was diagnosed with dementia, and it took several years for the disease to progress to the stage Edna appears to be in now."

"I've taken Grandma back to see the doctor several times, but he always says the same thing: she apparently has an aggressive form of dementia, and. . ." Elaine's voice trailed off as tears sprang to her eyes. She was tired of crying, and just plain tired. "I've tried everything I know of to help her, but nothing seems to make much difference. All I can do is to watch Grandma's memory fail a little more each day. My greatest fear is that soon she won't recognize me at all."

"It's a shame. I wish there was something more I could do to help you, Elaine." Iva's tone was comforting.

"You have helped, just by coming to sit with Grandma while I'm gone." Elaine looked down at her hands, red and chapped from all the work she'd been doing. "I still have some moments with Grandma when everything seems somewhat normal, and believe me, I cling to those times."

"That's what you have to do, Elaine." Iva gave Elaine's arm a tender pat. "As I've said before, please don't hesitate to call on me or any of your friends during this difficult time. You need time for yourself and deserve to get out whenever you can."

"It helps, knowing that." Sighing, Elaine rose from her seat. "Guess I'd better get going. I should be back before lunch, but if you and Grandma get hungry, there's a container of vegetable soup in the refrigerator that you can reheat."

"That's fine. Just take your time. I'm free for the rest of the day. Oh, and if it helps even a little, someone told me awhile back that, while every day may not be good, there's something good in every day."

❧

Elaine entered the bulk foods store and started down the aisle where the spices were shelved. She'd just started filling her basket when she heard voices she recognized in the next aisle over.

"Did you know that Jonah Miller might be courting Sara Stutzman?"

"I figured as much. Saw them eating a meal together at Yoder's restaurant awhile back. Of course, Sara's son was with them, but to me it looked like they were on a date."

"I've heard that he goes over to her place quite often these days."

Elaine gripped the basket she held so tightly that her fingers ached. She could hardly believe the conversation Leah and Priscilla were having, or that Jonah had begun courting someone else so soon after she'd broken up with him. *Of course,* she reasoned, *it has been a few months.* She couldn't expect Jonah to remain unattached, especially when she'd made it clear that there was no hope for the two of them to be together.

Elaine squeezed her eyes shut, trying to come to grips with all of this and remembering how difficult it had been to tell Jonah that she didn't love him. *Will Jonah end up marrying Sara?* Since Sara was a widow and her little boy needed a father, it was quite likely she would marry again. *I wonder if Sara is in love with Jonah. Could he love her too?*

Jonah deserved to be happy, but it hurt to hear that he and Sara might be courting. Elaine hoped Sara realized how fortunate she was, because as far as Elaine was concerned, there was no finer man than Jonah.

Elaine couldn't help feeling betrayed, hearing her friends talking about this. If they thought Jonah and Sara were courting, why hadn't they said something to her about it?

Placing the spices back on the shelf, Elaine turned and rushed out the door. She'd return some other time. Right now, she just wanted to go home.

∽

"You're awfully quiet," Iva said as she sat across the table from Edna, eating lunch.

Edna shrugged. "Don't have much to say, really. My husband's dead; people don't want to come here for dinners anymore, and I'm just sittin' around waiting to die, so that doesn't give me much to say."

Iva frowned. "I wish you wouldn't talk like that."

"Why not? It's the truth."

"None of us knows when we are going to die, and we need to see each day as precious." Iva handed Edna some crackers to go with the soup. "From what I understand, you and Elaine aren't doing the dinners anymore."

Edna placed both hands against her temples, trying ever so hard to recall. Had they really decided that? Could she have forgotten such a thing? "My granddaughter is precious to me, but sometimes I can't even remember her name. Do you know how frightening and frustrating that is?"

"I'm sure it must be devastating, but I'm equally certain that Elaine understands. She loves you so very much, Edna."

"I love her too." Edna broke some crackers into her bowl of soup and took a bite. "Sometimes Elaine takes things that are mine and puts 'em in strange places. The other day, she took my glasses." She blinked rapidly, pointing across the room. "I found them in the kichlin jar, of all things."

Iva looked at Edna strangely at first; then she chuckled and said, "Were they full of cookie crumbs?"

"No, there weren't any kichlin in there right then." Edna laughed too. She was glad Iva had come to visit. It was nice to relax, share a meal with a friend, and find something to laugh about. Things almost felt normal. If only they could remain so.

⁓

"Wasn't that Elaine who just went out the door?" Priscilla asked Leah.

Leah nodded. "I think it was. I wonder why she dashed out of here in such a hurry. Think I'll go outside and see if I can catch her before she leaves."

"I'll come too." Priscilla set her shopping aside and followed Leah out the door.

When they came to the area where the horses were tied, they found Elaine getting ready to leave.

"Elaine, wait up! We saw you rush out of the store. It looked like you were in a hurry, but we wanted to say hi." Priscilla put her hand on the side of Elaine's buggy.

"I was in the aisle next to where you two were talking and left the store after hearing what you said." Elaine's lips quivered slightly. She was clearly upset.

Priscilla shifted uncomfortably. "Was it about Jonah and Sara?"

"Jah. All this time has gone by, and you've never said a word to me about this. Why, Priscilla? I thought we were friends."

"We are friends, and the reason I didn't say anything is because you have enough to deal with taking care of your grandma, and I didn't want to upset you with information that might not mean a thing."

"You must have thought it did, or you wouldn't have discussed it with Leah." Elaine's shoulders drooped as she picked up the reins.

Leah reached into the buggy to touch Elaine's arm. "Please don't go yet. Like Priscilla said, we didn't want to upset you. Besides, we don't know for sure if Jonah and Sara are actually courting. They just went out for supper together, and from what I hear, Jonah's been over to Sara's a few times." Leah paused a few seconds and then continued. "You know, Sara went through a horrible experience awhile back, narrowly escaping from her burning barn, so maybe Jonah was just doing a kind deed when he took her and Mark out for supper."

"I heard about the fire. It's a shame Sara lost her barn."

"Then you probably know that Jonah was the one who saw the smoke, and when he went to investigate, he found Sara collapsed on the ground." Leah hesitated another moment. "Jonah may have been checking on Sara the other day, and then they decided to go out to eat someplace. Friends sometimes do that, you know, and Jonah was good friends with Sara's husband."

"That's right," Priscilla interjected. "He may feel a sense of obligation to Sara, and that might be all there is to it."

Elaine shrugged.

"Are you in love with Jonah? Is that why you're upset?"

"I'm upset because you kept it from me," Elaine responded, instead of answering Priscilla's question about her loving Jonah. "Friends aren't supposed to have secrets from one another. Now, if you two will excuse me, I need to go home." Before either Leah or Priscilla could respond, Elaine backed her horse up and headed down the road.

"We need to do something to make things better." Leah's tone was full of the regret she obviously felt over this misunderstanding.

"I agree, Leah, but I'm not sure what it could be."

"Well, for one thing, we need to start by apologizing to her."

Priscilla bobbed her head. "Jah, and the sooner the better."

Elaine pulled Daisy into the driveway, unhooked her from the buggy, and put her in the corral, where there was a trough full of water. She'd have to rub her down later and put her in the stall before dark. Right now, she wanted to go inside and relieve Iva. Besides, she was hungry and needed something to eat. Even though Iva had said she didn't mind staying all day, Elaine thought it would be better if she sent Iva home.

Elaine had chores she needed to get done, and after hearing the news about Jonah and Sara, she had to get her mind on something else and quit feeling sorry for herself. Working around the house had always helped before, and it kept her from dwelling on the negative when something was really bothering her, like it was now. While it was true that Elaine wanted Jonah to get on with his life, it hurt to know he'd moved on so quickly and seemed to have forgotten about her. Elaine's heart ached from letting him go. After their breakup, she figured that Jonah would be miserable from her rejection. But that didn't seem to be the case. Maybe he hadn't cared about her as much as he'd said. Well, none of that mattered now. She and Jonah were no longer together, and he really did have the right to move on with his life.

Taking a deep breath before walking in the door, Elaine heard laughter coming from the dining room. She found Iva and Grandma working on the puzzle together while carrying on what almost sounded like a normal conversation.

"Oh, you're back so soon." Iva looked up with a surprised expression when Elaine entered the room.

"Did you get all the items on the list?" Grandma

asked as she tried to make an unmatched piece fit in the puzzle.

"I didn't go shopping, after all. Decided what I had on my list could wait for another day. Maybe I'll go again tomorrow, or the day after." It was wrong to fib, but she didn't want to admit the real reason she'd left the store. Besides, looking back on it now, she had over-reacted. She should have just done her shopping rather than running out of the store. It seemed like Elaine's emotions ruled her actions these days, but that was no excuse.

Elaine remembered when the doctor at the hospital first told her about Grandma's dementia and had suggested that Elaine attend a support group. She hadn't felt it was necessary at first, and then later, when she really needed more support, she made the excuse not to go because it would mean asking someone to sit with Grandma while she was gone. Besides, Elaine didn't relish the idea of talking about her situation with strangers. She felt more comfortable discussing things with close friends, like Leah and Priscilla. *I'll bet they're upset with me right now. I need to apologize for my behavior.*

Grandma tugged on Elaine's arm. "I was hoping you'd get me that sugar-free angel food cake mix. Can't you go back to the store and get everything now? It's still early, and you know what? I'd like to go with you."

"Not today, Grandma. We'll go tomorrow." Elaine really didn't feel up to going back to the bulk foods store right now and hoped Grandma would just drop the subject.

Grandma stared at Elaine, and Elaine held her breath. *Please, Grandma, let it go for now.*

For the moment, Grandma just sat staring at the

puzzle pieces in front of her. This was one time Elaine hoped Grandma had forgotten what had been said. There were times when Grandma would get upset about something and start whining, and then she'd suddenly get distracted and forget all about what she had wanted. Maybe this was one of those times.

Elaine glanced at Iva, who appeared to be busy snapping in another piece of the puzzle. "You're free to go on home now, Iva. I can handle things from here."

"Are you sure? I can hang around longer and assist you with anything you need to have done."

"I appreciate it, but everything's fine, and now that I'm home, I can take over," Elaine assured her. "I may need to call on you again soon though, and I'm grateful that you came here today, short as the time was."

"Not a problem at all." Iva smiled as she rose from her chair. "Guess I'll be going then." She paused and placed her hand on Grandma's shoulder. "Oh, and Edna, you keep working on that puzzle, 'cause you're doing a good job. Why, I'll bet you will probably have a lot more done on it when I come by again."

Grandma grunted in reply as she studied the puzzle intently.

Elaine walked Iva to the door. "Thank you again for taking the time to be here today, Iva."

"It was no problem at all. Edna and I had a good time visiting while we worked on the puzzle." Iva gave Elaine a hug. "Remember, now, to let me know when you need me again. I really don't have anything going on that's all that pressing these days."

"I'll keep that in mind." Elaine couldn't help thinking how lucky Priscilla was that her mother was still with her. Elaine would give anything to have either one of her parents here to lean on right now.

She stood in the doorway and watched as Iva's horse and buggy went down the driveway and turned onto the main road, thanking God, once again, for people like Iva who truly cared about others and wanted to help out in their time of need.

When Elaine returned to the dining room, feeling just a bit better, she was greeted with an angry scowl.

"I want to go to the store today." Grandma's tone was defiant, and she looked at Elaine in such a cold way that it caused her to shiver. "I want that cake mix, Nancy, and I want it now!"

"We can go later on." Elaine would never win this argument, so she might as well give in. There was no point in correcting Grandma about her name either. Whenever Grandma referred to her as Nancy these days, Elaine chose to ignore it. "First, I need to eat some lunch and get a few things done around here. We'll go after that. Okay, Grandma?"

Grandma's expression softened some, and appearing to be satisfied, she gave a quick nod.

❧

While Elaine did some cleaning around the house, wiping several small blood spots off the wall, she tried not to get too frustrated. It wasn't Grandma's fault that she had to have her finger pricked to test her blood, but Elaine wished Grandma would at least wait until the bleeding stopped before she touched anything. *Grandma probably doesn't realize what she's doing,* Elaine reasoned, blowing a straggly piece of hair off her forehead while she scrubbed. She walked slowly back toward the kitchen and used her sponge to wipe another red spot off the wall.

As Elaine continued to clean, she remembered a story

that Grandma had read to her a long time ago. The tale involved a young girl who had been exploring a forest, and in order to keep from getting lost, she would drop a piece of popcorn along the path every few feet. That way, if the girl got confused, she could find her way home by following the popcorn trail.

Grandma could do something similar. Only for her, she would have specks of blood on everything she'd touched.

"That should do it," Elaine murmured after she'd finished cleaning. She collapsed into a chair at the table, then jumped back up when Grandma tromped into the kitchen.

"Can we go now?" Grandma asked, sounding kind of huffy again.

"Okay. Just let me get Daisy hitched to the buggy again."

"Let's take Misty instead. She hasn't been out for a while and could use the exercise."

Elaine was hesitant about taking Misty, but Grandma was right. It had been a few weeks since they'd used Misty to pull their buggy. The animal probably needed to stretch her legs. Elaine hoped the ride to town would be without incident and that Misty wouldn't be too full of pent-up energy.

Everything went well at first, but all of a sudden, Misty became rambunctious. It took Elaine several minutes to get the horse under control, but fortunately, Misty started behaving rather well for not having been out on the road in a while.

Grandma's contented smile told Elaine that she was enjoying the fresh air and, at least for today, had forgotten about her recent fear of riding in the buggy. Elaine had relaxed a bit too after getting Misty to settle down.

October was a beautiful month, and this afternoon was no exception. Elaine noticed how beautiful the landscape was, with the glorious colors of autumn all around. The crimson red maples and bright yellow birch with the orange of sumac mixed in would have made a lovely scene for a painting, mingling with the earth tones of freshly cut fields. Elaine had never painted anything on canvas, but if she ever found the time, she might give it a try sometime. Meanwhile, she'd been able to squeeze in a few minutes each evening after Grandma went to bed to paint more of the rocks she'd found near the creek not far from their home.

Last Monday, when their bishop's wife, Stella, had come by to visit Grandma, Elaine had been able to slip away for a short time. She'd gone to the creek and picked up several nice rocks. Visits from others in their community were the only times when Elaine could get away, as she wasn't about to leave Grandma alone, for fear of her wandering off or burning something on the stove.

"Are you warm enough, Grandma?" Elaine pulled the blanket over Grandma's legs.

"I'm fine. Quit fussing all the time. You're acting like a mother hen." Grandma frowned, but then she reached over and patted Elaine's arm.

Elaine relaxed a little, taking in a deep breath. This was one of those rare times when things seemed almost normal. If only it could last. Even Misty seemed to enjoy the crisp autumn air, having no pesky bugs to swish away with her tail.

Big puffy white clouds billowed on the horizon as they continued toward town. Elaine remembered how, a long time ago, she and Grandpa had put an old blanket on the grass and, lying there together, watched the clouds roll by. One time, Grandpa had looked over at Elaine and said, *"Someday, Lainie, I'll be sittin' on one of those beautiful clouds, watching over you and your grandma."* Did Grandpa know back then that he'd be the first to die? Was he looking down on them today from one of those puffy clouds?

Maybe it's just wishful thinking, Elaine thought. *At least I can be sure of one thing—our heavenly Father's watching over us.*

Elaine was thankful that even through the darkest of times God was only a prayer away, and He knew what they were going through and cared about all their troubles.

Riding farther along, Elaine looked into an open field and spotted a doe watching as they approached. Elaine was about to point it out to Grandma when a smaller deer shot out from the opposite side and ran right in front of Misty. How the two animals kept from colliding was beyond Elaine's reasoning, but unfortunately the horse spooked. Misty took off like a bullet, and Elaine held on to the reins with all the strength she could muster. To make matters worse, Grandma seemed to enjoy the adventure, hollering for Misty to go faster.

"It's like being in a race!" Grandma clapped her hands like an excited child. "This is fun. Go! Go faster, Misty!"

Elaine didn't have time to look at Grandma, but from her shouts of delight, it was obvious that she had no idea of the danger they were in. At this speed even the slightest bump in the road could send them crashing into a tree, someone's fence, or worse—a car.

"Whoa there, Misty! Slow down, girl!" Elaine shouted. But Grandma's exuberant horse had a mind of her own. All Elaine could do was cling tightly to the reins and hope that Misty would tire out soon.

"Sit back, Grandma, and hang on to your seat!" she instructed.

Grandma seemed oblivious to everything as she continued to clap, shout, and giggle.

Elaine should have slowed down when she first saw the doe standing by the road. Again, she could almost hear Grandpa's words when he'd told her another time: *"If a deer runs across the road, slow down, because there will most likely be another."* This doe had obviously been waiting for her fawn to catch up before going any farther. Elaine had only gotten a glimpse of the young deer before Misty went haywire.

After what seemed like forever, Misty finally slowed to a trot, snorting and shaking her mane. Elaine's arms felt as though they were coming out of their sockets as she let up on the tension of the reins. She was relieved that no cars had passed during Misty's wild romp and that they were now out of immediate danger.

The rest of the trip was uneventful, and it gave Elaine time to calm down. By the time she guided Misty to the hitching rack, Elaine was breathing normally again.

Once in the store, Elaine hurried to get everything on her list, and then she stopped to look in the aisle where the baking supplies were kept.

"There's no angel food cake mixes here," Grandma mumbled, pouting like a child as she pointed to one of the shelves. "It's your fault, Nancy. You shoulda got it for me this morning. I'll bet they had plenty of cake mixes then."

"I can make a sugar-free cake from scratch after we get home," Elaine said, hoping that would appease Grandma.

"That'll take too long." Grandma shuffled toward the checkout counter, muttering under her breath.

Elaine placed the things in her basket on the counter and waited for everything to be rung up by the cashier.

"Is that a wig you're wearing?" Grandma asked the clerk while pointing to her hair.

Elaine was about to apologize for Grandma's impolite behavior, but the clerk just smiled and said, "Yes, it is a wig. You see, I have cancer, and my treatments have caused most of my hair to fall out."

Elaine hoped that Grandma would respond properly, or better yet, just drop the subject. To her surprise, Grandma looked at the cashier with a sympathetic expression and said in a tone of sincerity, "I'm very sorry. I didn't realize that."

"I'm sorry too," Elaine put in. "And I hope you'll be better soon."

"Thank you."

After Elaine had paid for her purchases, she gathered up the packages, took hold of Grandma's arm, and led her out the door. She was relieved that this shopping trip was over.

CHAPTER 35

I hope Elaine is at home," Leah said to Priscilla as she guided her horse and buggy down the road the following day. It was another beautiful autumn morning, but there was a definite bite in the air—the kind of nip that warns of winter coming soon. "Maybe we should have called and left a message yesterday to let her know we were coming."

"Well, if she isn't home, we can visit with Edna," Priscilla responded. "I'm sure she would appreciate some company too."

"I doubt that Elaine would leave her grandma at home unless someone is there with her." Leah shivered as the cold air seeped into the buggy. "Let's hope Edna knows who we are today. Sometimes when I've dropped by, Edna didn't have a clue who I was. Elaine's even mentioned that some days her grandma thinks she's Elaine's mother, Nancy."

"That's so sad. Dementia is such a cruel disease for the person who has it, as well as for their family. I wish this had never happened and that Edna could be healthy again."

Leah shook the reins to get her horse moving faster. "I guess that won't happen till she's in heaven with Jesus. Only then will God's children be completely healed of their diseases."

❧

Elaine gathered up the living-room throw rugs and was on

her way to take them outside when she smelled something burning. *Oh no, not this again.* Had Grandma decided to bake another pie or some cookies and left them in the oven?

Elaine dropped the rugs on the floor and hurried to the kitchen. No sign of Grandma in there. She opened the oven door and was relieved to see that it was cold and nothing was inside.

When she sniffed again, she suddenly realized that the odor she'd smelled was drifting down the hall. As she headed in that direction, it became clear that something in Grandma's bedroom was burning.

Alarmed, Elaine jerked the door open. When she stepped into the room, she gasped. Grandma stood near the ironing board, staring across the room with a faraway look, as though completely out of touch with what was going on. One of her dresses lay on the ironing board, with the iron resting on top of the bodice. Smoke from the burning material drifted in front of Grandma's face, but she didn't seem to notice.

Elaine rushed over, snatched the iron up, and grimaced when she saw a nasty hole with the telltale signs of brown where the iron had scorched the material.

"Oh Grandma, just look at your dress!"

No response. Grandma kept staring across the room.

Elaine tried again, this time giving Grandma's arm a little shake and hoping to get through to her. "What happened here? Didn't you see that your dress was burning, or even smell the smoke?"

Slowly, Grandma turned to look at Elaine and blinked her eyes several times, as though coming out of a daze. "I've been thinking about Lloyd and wondering if he fed the katze this morning."

Elaine groaned inwardly, placing the iron upright on

the end of the ironing board. Today was starting off on a bad note. "Well, your *frack* is ruined now, and you should have asked me to iron it for you." Annoyed, Elaine gestured to the hole. Sometimes she felt like she was dealing with a child instead of a seventy-five-year-old woman. But then, she had to remind herself that Grandma was ill and couldn't help the things she said and did. *"Be kinder than necessary, for everyone you meet is fighting some kind of a battle,"* she'd heard Grandma say. Now it was Grandma's turn. She was fighting the battle of dementia, and Elaine needed to be as kind as possible. She touched Grandma's arm. "I'm not mad at you, Grandma. Just concerned. Next time you need to have something ironed, would you please ask me?"

Grandma pointed at the hole in her dress. "What happened to that? It's disgusting!"

"You were ironing and must have forgotten to lift the iron from your dress." Elaine talked calmly, trying to keep her patience and not upset Grandma.

"Why would I do that?" Tears welled in Grandma's eyes and dribbled down her wrinkled cheeks. "Lloyd won't like this one little bit. He always liked it when I wore that dress."

Elaine made no comment. She picked up the dress, as well as the iron, and left the room. She would need to find a better place to store the iron so that Grandma couldn't find it, because she couldn't take the chance of her burning another dress—or worse yet, catching the house on fire. From now on, she would need to keep a closer watch on Grandma.

❧

Sara hummed to herself as she buttered a piece of toast for Mark. He'd already eaten breakfast, but around ten this morning he'd said he was hungry again, so some toast with peanut butter would get him by until she fixed their noon meal. It wouldn't be a big lunch, however, because this evening Jonah would be coming to take them out for pizza. Sara looked forward to going. Not just for the taste of tangy pepperoni pizza, but because it was another opportunity to be with Jonah. The more time she spent with him, the more she found herself enjoying his company. And the more she got to know Jonah, the more he reminded her of Harley. Of course, he had been Harley's friend, so they must have had some things in common. Something seemed to be happening between Sara and Jonah—something she hadn't expected. Was it possible that after just a few short months of spending time together, she could be falling in love? Or could it be that she still missed Harley and being with Jonah filled a void in her life? And how did Jonah feel about her? Was he still in love with Elaine, or had he begun to see Sara in some other way than just Harley's widow who needed a friend? She remembered her mother saying, *"When God wants to bless you, He brings certain people into your life."* Sara certainly felt blessed to have Jonah in her life right now—even if it turned out that he was only a friend.

Sara's musings halted when Mark meandered into the room, asking for his toast. She lifted him into the high chair, placed the toast on his tray, and then filled his sippy cup with milk and gave him that too.

While Mark ate his snack, Sara busied herself at the sink, cutting vegetables for the soup they would have for lunch. She was glad Mark liked most kinds of soup and wasn't a picky eater, like some children his age. That made it easier to prepare meals they could both enjoy.

Once the veggies had been cut, Sara placed them in the kettle, added water and some beef broth, then set it on the stove to simmer. By the time the noon hour rolled around, it should be ready to eat.

The *clip-clop* of horse hooves drew Sara's attention to the window. She was pleased when Jean got out of the buggy, along with her three children. It had been a few weeks since they'd visited, and Sara was eager to find out what was new with her friend.

When Jean and the children entered the house, Sara asked if they would like to have some toast. The children eagerly agreed, and after Sara fixed their snack, she and Jean sat at the table so they could visit.

"Would you like a cup of peppermint tea?" Sara asked.

Jean nodded. "That sounds nice."

"You're welcome to have toast too, if you like."

"No thanks. I had a big breakfast."

"Will you and the kinner stay and have lunch with us?" Sara motioned to the stove, where her soup simmered in the pot. "I have more than enough soup for all of us."

"That sounds good, but not today. We were on our way to town to do some shopping, and I decided to stop in here first and see how you're doing. Maybe you and Mark can come over to our place soon, so he can play with our new beagle pup, Chubby." Jean smiled. "That little beagle loves to play with the kinner, and he seems to be full of boundless energy. I don't know who gets played out first, Chubby or Rebecca and Stephen, but they sure do have a good time together."

"Mark likes puppies too. I've even thought about getting him one but haven't done it yet, since training a pup and taking care of its needs requires a lot of work."

"That's true," Jean agreed. "But I think it's worth all the trouble. Chubby is just the right size for our kinner too. He's a miniature beagle and won't grow to be a whole lot bigger than he is right now." Jean's expression turned serious. "I've been meaning to ask. Have you had any more dizzy spells or other unusual symptoms lately?"

Sara hated to admit it, but she told Jean how, just last night, when she was heading upstairs to get ready for bed, she'd had trouble making her left leg work.

"That does not sound good. Now, when are you going to see the doctor about this, Sara?" Jean released her breath in a huff. "You could be dealing with something serious, and if that's the case, then you need to know what it is so you can handle it."

Sara nodded, and as she looked up at Jean, a lump formed in her throat, making it difficult to swallow. "You're right. Tomorrow morning I'll call the doctor's office and make an appointment."

Jean placed her hand on Sara's arm. "Promise?"

"Jah. I won't forget." Sara sat quietly for several seconds; then, gathering up her courage, she decided to ask a question that had been on her mind for some time. "I know that Jonah isn't seeing Elaine anymore, but I was wondering if you know the reason."

Looking a bit uncomfortable, Jean quietly said, "Elaine told Jonah that she doesn't love him and never did. He didn't admit that to me at first, but several weeks after they broke up, I questioned him about it, and he told me what Elaine had said."

"I see. Danki for sharing that with me." Now that Sara knew the truth about why Elaine and Jonah had broken up, she felt a little more hopeful that there might be a possibility of her and Jonah developing a serious relationship. But she couldn't understand how Elaine, after being courted by Jonah for nearly a year, could not have fallen in love with him.

❧

When Elaine stepped onto the porch to shake out a few

more throw rugs, she spotted Leah and Priscilla riding in on their bikes. She knew without asking why they were here. No doubt they wanted to talk to her about what had happened yesterday. Elaine wished she hadn't overheard their conversation, and more than that, she still wished one or both of them had told her about Jonah and Sara. She guessed it was better hearing it that way than if she'd seen Jonah with Sara in town or noticed them leaving together after church.

"Wie geht's?" Leah asked after she and Priscilla parked their bikes and joined Elaine on the porch.

"I'm doing okay, but Grandma isn't." Elaine went on to explain how Grandma had burned a hole in her dress.

"That's baremlich," Priscilla said. "I'll bet it really upset her."

Elaine shook her head. "Not really. I was the one who was upset. Grandma seemed more concerned about how Grandpa would respond, saying she'd ruined his favorite dress."

"Sounds like she's getting worse."

Elaine nodded, her shoulders sagging from the weight of the day. "When we went to the kitchen for coffee awhile ago, Grandma pointed to the coffeepot and called it a 'putalator.' I was about to correct her when she squinted and pointed again, saying this time that it was a 'purfalatore.' I can't stand to see her like this. I've done everything I know to do, but it's just not enough, and I feel like I'm at the end of my. . ." A slight sigh punctuated her unfinished sentence, and she let her head fall forward into her hands.

"I'm sorry, Elaine; I know how difficult this is for you, but remember that when you've done all you can, God will do what you can't." Leah touched Elaine's shoulder gently. "Priscilla and I came over here today, not just to check on you and Edna, but to say how sorry we are for not telling you about Sara and Jonah. You were right to be upset when you heard us talking at the store."

"That's right, and we hope you'll find it in your heart to forgive us," Priscilla put in.

Elaine had to move past her feelings of betrayal and had already come to realize that she'd overreacted. Priscilla and Leah were her best friends, and she wanted to keep it that way. "I accept your apology," she said sincerely. "I'm sorry too for responding in such a negative way. It was just such a shock to hear it like that. But to be truthful, I would have been stunned no matter how I found out."

Leah and Priscilla slipped their arms around Elaine's waist, and they shared a group hug. Then, at Elaine's suggestion, they all took a seat on the porch.

"It concerns me," Elaine said slowly, "that at the rate Grandma's memory is failing, any day now she could completely forget me, her sister, or her two brothers and never remember any of us again."

"Say, here's a thought," Leah spoke up. "Why don't you invite your Grandma's relatives here for a get-together? It will give them all the chance to spend time with her now, before her memory is completely gone."

"That's a good idea." Elaine nodded. "I don't know why I didn't think of that myself. Grandma's birthday is in three weeks, so maybe I could plan a party in her honor and invite her sister and brothers, as well as any of their families who might be able to come. Hopefully it will be a good day for everyone—especially Grandma."

CHAPTER 36

*O*blivious to the scenery as they went down the road, Sara stared blindly out the window of her driver's van, struggling not to cry. She'd just come from seeing the doctor, and the news wasn't good. It was so dreadful she could hardly believe it. After a series of tests she'd been given the week before and based on her symptoms, the doctor had determined that Sara had multiple sclerosis. She should have gone to see the doctor much sooner. No wonder she'd been having such unusual symptoms.

The doctor had explained that Sara's blurred vision, extreme fatigue, loss of balance, numbness, tingling, and weakness in her arms and legs were all symptoms of the disease. He'd also told Sara that MS was a complex illness, and it could affect people differently. A person with MS might have a single symptom and then go for months, or even years, without any other indications of the disease. For some people, however, their symptoms could be varied and become worse within months or even weeks.

For Sara, the worst part of learning all of this was in knowing that there was no cure for MS. Some medications had been developed that helped control symptoms, but all of them had side effects. Sara didn't want that. The disease alone was enough to cope with. She thought she might be better off trying a more natural approach, which would include getting plenty of rest, exercising regularly, eating a healthy, well-balanced diet, finding ways to relax, and keeping herself as cool as possible, since the symptoms of MS often worsened when a person's body temperature increased.

The worst thing Sara's doctor had told her was that some MS patients' symptoms got so bad they eventually ended up in a wheelchair. Of course, some people with the disease never reached that point, but Sara couldn't help worrying that she would be severely disabled. If she decided to stay in Arthur, her barn could be rebuilt. While the fire was an unfortunate event, her MS diagnosis was far worse. Unlike a barn that could be built again, there was nothing that would cure her body. It seemed like any chance of hope and happiness was out of Sara's reach.

As the scenery rolled by, Sara thought of the night Jonah had taken her and Mark out for pizza. It had turned out to be a wonderful, relaxing evening. She'd felt pretty good that entire day, almost normal, and for that she'd been thankful. It was one of those rare times lately when she hardly knew she had any health issues at all. Mark had enjoyed himself too, especially when Jonah surprised him with a wooden horse he had carved. Ever since then, Mark wouldn't let that toy out of his sight.

After their meal, Jonah had brought them home, and he and Sara had visited awhile. When it was time for Mark to go to bed, he wanted Jonah to tuck him in. Smiling, Sara remembered how she'd stood in the doorway watching and how the scene had tugged at her heart. Harley would never be able to do these simple little acts of love for their son. But Sara was glad Jonah was there and had taken such a liking to Mark. Watching the two of them together, she'd felt something that, until that moment, had been buried for too long. She felt hope.

Dared she even dream of living a normal life now that she'd been diagnosed with MS? There were so many things Sara wanted to do. She had yet to go through the barn to see what items could be salvaged, and several projects around the house needed work too.

Her eyes brimmed with tears, and Sara tried to hold them back. *What if I'm one of those people who will become hampered by my symptoms? I won't be able to take care of Mark if I end up in a wheelchair. Should I move back home with my folks, so they can help me raise my boy? That would be the sensible thing to do, but I need to pray about this before I make a decision.*

❧

"Have you seen my *aageglesser*?" Grandma asked, shuffling into the living room where Elaine was dusting.

"No, I haven't, Grandma. You usually put your glasses on top of your dresser when you're not wearing them. Have you looked there?"

Grandma gritted her teeth while twisting the end of her apron. "Of course I looked there. Do I look *dumm*?"

"Of course you're not dumb. I just thought—"

"Never mind. I'll just have to keep looking." Grandma turned and plodded out of the room, but not before Elaine heard her mumble, "She's always hiding my things."

It was then that Elaine noticed Grandma was wearing two different shoes. On her left foot, she wore one of her black dress shoes. On Grandma's right foot was a navy blue clog that she wore when she worked in the garden. Elaine debated about whether to say anything or just let it go. She decided on the latter for now but would make sure Grandma wore her dress shoes for her birthday party tonight.

It would be good to see Grandma's older sister, Margaret, and her two brothers, Irvin and Caleb, who all lived in Iowa, where Grandma had been born. Grandma would probably be living there still if she hadn't met Grandpa at a friend's wedding when they were teenagers. In addition to Elaine's great-aunt and great-uncles, some of their children and grandchildren would also be visiting to celebrate Grandma's birthday. Elaine hoped the festivities not only would be a fun time for all, but also would give Grandma a chance to reconnect with her family before she lost her memory of them forever.

Elaine had the house almost cleaned, and she'd made plans to cook Grandma's favorite meal—baked chicken, mashed potatoes, coleslaw, and creamed corn. For dessert she'd baked a chocolate cake for everyone else, and a sugar-free apple pie for Grandma; although she would make sure that Grandma didn't eat too big of a piece, since the pie did have some natural sugar in the apples, as well as in the apple juice concentrate that was added for flavor and sweetening.

Elaine went to the sink to get a glass of water and glanced out the window as she raised the cup to her lips. She stopped abruptly, her hand in midair. "Now when did she go outside?" Elaine watched as Grandma walked through the backyard and over toward the swing, hanging from the big maple tree in their yard. Her first thought was to go out there and bring Grandma back inside, but something compelled her to remain where she was and watch.

Grandma sat down on the swing and started moving it slowly back and forth, then a few minutes later, she got it going a little bit higher.

Seeing the contented look on Grandma's face took Elaine back in time. Grandma appeared to be so happy, and it made Elaine want to cry. How long had it been since she'd seen that peaceful expression on her beloved grandma's face? Oh, how Elaine could relate to that carefree feeling of swooping down, then up again, over and over. She could almost feel the butterflies and the tickly feeling that being on a swing could bring.

Grandma's face turned almost childlike as she continued swinging back and forth. Elaine had to restrain herself from joining her. Grandma wasn't going too high and wasn't likely to fall off, so Elaine just kept on watching.

Before Grandpa died, Elaine had gone out to that old swing many times. Sometimes, just to be outside, especially after the days they'd hosted dinners. Other times, swinging helped her think more clearly about life or make plans for her future. It didn't happen often anymore, but a few times when Grandma was napping, Elaine had gone out to that old swing just for the pure joy of it and to reclaim how it felt during those untroubled years as a young child when she'd had no real worries to drag her down. Elaine longed for that feeling again.

Everything was happening too fast. With Grandma going downhill quickly, then hearing about Jonah courting again so soon, Elaine didn't know how much more she could take. But she couldn't run away from the problems or the fact that Jonah was moving on with his life. She was the one who had prompted their breakup, and if Jonah and Sara ended up getting married, she'd have to face it, no matter how difficult it might be.

One thing at a time, Elaine told herself, upending her thoughts and hoping once more that tonight would be special for Grandma.

She closed her eyes and whispered a prayer. "Dear Lord, please help everything to go well this evening and make this one of Grandma's best birthdays ever."

~

"Look who's here, Grandma!" Elaine gestured to her great-uncles, Irvin and Caleb, who'd just entered the house.

Grandma tipped her head and stared at the men a few seconds. Then she turned and shook her finger at Elaine. "Why didn't you tell me the tourists were coming here tonight? We don't even have our dinner started yet."

"Oh no, Grandma. We're not hosting a dinner for tourists. Some of our family has come to celebrate your birthday."

Grandma stared at her brothers a bit longer, looking as though she was seeing them for the very first time. She looked over at Elaine and said, "Is today really my birthday?"

Elaine nodded. "Yes, it is, and your brothers, Irvin and Caleb, have come to help you celebrate it."

"How old am I?"

"You're seventy-six," Irvin answered, pulling his fingers through the ends of his mostly gray beard.

Grandma moved a little closer to the men, squinting as she looked first at Irvin, then at Caleb. "You sure don't look like my *brieder*."

"We are your brothers," Uncle Caleb said with a decisive nod. The poor man looked quite flustered. "It's been a few years since we've seen you, Edna, and we're all getting older, so maybe that's why you don't recognize us."

Grandma bobbed her head, but Elaine wasn't sure she'd identified the men even yet.

"Ich ab mic him busch verlore," Grandma said, moving closer to Irvin.

His bushy gray eyebrows lifted. "You got lost in the woods? When did that happen?"

Grandma shrugged in response.

"I think she may be referring to a time when she wandered off our property and couldn't find her way home," Elaine quietly explained. She didn't bother to go into all the details, figuring it was best not to discuss this right now. Maybe later, after Grandma went to bed, she would talk about the situation with Grandma's brothers and the rest of the family. For now, Elaine just wanted to try to make this day as pleasant as she could.

A short time later, Great-Aunt Margaret showed up with her daughter and son-in-law. Margaret was in her eighties and used a cane to walk, but after talking to her just a few minutes, Elaine knew her aunt was sharp as a tack.

"How are things going?" Aunt Margaret whispered, giving Elaine a hug after she'd first greeted her sister, Edna. "Are you getting by all right?"

"Some days are more difficult than others," Elaine admitted, "but Grandma and I are getting by the best we can."

Aunt Margaret clasped Elaine's hands and gave them a little squeeze. "What about that young man you've been seeing? I'll bet he's a big help to you right now."

Elaine grimaced. She disliked having to tell her aunt that she and Jonah had broken up but figured it was best just to get it said. "Jonah and I aren't seeing each other anymore. We broke up some time ago."

"Oh dear, I'm sorry to hear that. I never got the chance to meet him, but from the things Edna said in her letters, he seemed like a nice man."

"He is, but with the way things are with Grandma right now, I thought it best if Jonah and I went our separate ways." Elaine lifted her hands and let them fall to her sides. "Anyhow, I'm not sure what we felt for each other was strong enough to continue with our relationship."

"That's a shame, but I'm sure you'll find someone else when the time is right."

Elaine made no comment because there really was no point in talking about this anymore. Besides, she wanted to get Grandma's sister and brothers' things taken upstairs to their rooms so they could get settled in.

Soon other family members from Iowa arrived, including Grandma's niece, Doris, and her six-year-old twins, Mary and Melinda. Grandma said she had no memory of the girls at all, but then, she'd only seen them once, a few weeks after they were born.

After everyone greeted Grandma, they gathered in the living room, where Grandma proceeded to open her gifts. While she did that, Melinda took out a tablet and began drawing Grandma's picture.

Grandma had just opened her sister's gift, a small bird feeder, when she stopped what she was doing, looked at Melinda, and said, "Are you cooking me?"

"Cooking you?" The girl's eyes widened. "What are you talkin' about, Aunt Edna?"

Embarrassed for Grandma, Elaine quickly said, "Melinda is drawing your picture, Grandma."

Grandma glanced around, as though expecting something to happen, or maybe someone to say something. Then she grinned at Elaine and said, "I can explain more when they get here. They said they weren't ready?"

"Who else is coming, and what is it they're not ready for, Edna?" Aunt Margaret asked.

Grandma snickered. Then she leaned back against the sofa cushions and closed her eyes. "I'm tired."

Oh dear, Elaine thought. *If this is how the evening is going to be, I wish I'd never invited any of these people.*

CHAPTER 37

*B*y the time Elaine went to her room to get ready for bed, she was exhausted. Not only did they have a house full of relatives sleeping in the bedrooms upstairs, but she'd had a hard time getting Grandma settled into her room downstairs. While it had been good for Grandma to connect with her family from Iowa, Elaine had spent most of the evening reminding Grandma who everyone was or trying to make light of the strange things Grandma said. One minute she'd be talking to her sister, Margaret, about old times, and the next minute she'd confuse her with someone else.

At one point, Grandma thought she was at Aunt Margaret's house and had even complimented her sister on how nice everything was. She'd asked Aunt Margaret to show her around the place, until Elaine stepped in and said, "Maybe later."

Poor Aunt Margaret had teared up more than once. Grandma's brothers hadn't shown quite so much emotion, but it had been obvious from their furrowed brows and exchanged glances that they were concerned about their sister's declining memory.

To make the evening more tense, Grandma had taken not one, but two pieces of chocolate cake when Elaine wasn't looking, in addition to a piece of no-sugar apple pie. It was so difficult to stabilize Grandma's blood sugar when she kept sneaking sweets, and that too caused Elaine to worry about the days ahead and how she would manage Grandma's declining health on her own. At times, Elaine couldn't help wondering, *Would it really hurt if once in a while I let Grandma enjoy some sweets? Why not let her take pleasure in what little time she has left doing something as simple as eating a piece of cake?*

Elaine stood at her bedroom window staring out at the bright, full moon. She didn't know what was more difficult: watching Grandma's condition deteriorate, or seeing others react when they tried to communicate with her.

A knot formed in Elaine's stomach. *I never expected something like this would happen to my dear, sweet grandma. Growing up, I could always count on her. Now, she needs me, even if she doesn't realize it.*

Focusing again on the October moon, Elaine marveled at how it was so bright that it lit everything up, casting shadows on the ground. She glanced toward the barn and caught sight of something moving across the yard. After watching a few seconds, she realized that a raccoon was heading to the area where a bird feeder hung. She assumed the raccoon was looking for sunflower seeds that had dropped to the ground from the birds feeding all day. Slowly, it searched the grass, picking its way as it went along. What a treat it was to observe something so ordinary and simple.

Moving away from the window, Elaine removed her head covering and loosened her hair. After brushing it thoroughly, she undressed and slipped into her nightgown. Then, turning off the gas lamp, she slipped into bed. The freshly laundered sheets smelled clean and felt cool against her skin. Soon she'd be adding another blanket to the bed as cold weather swept across their state.

She closed her eyes and conjured up a mental picture

of Grandma tucking her in, just as she'd done when Elaine was a girl. "Snug as a bug in a rug," Grandma would say. *Oh, those were such special days.*

Elaine smiled, remembering fondly how it had felt to be secure and warm in her bed and to be loved that much by her grandparents. *Oh Grandpa, I miss you so much, but I'm glad you're not here to see Grandma the way she is now.* It would have been especially hard on Grandpa, seeing Grandma struggling with dementia and not being able to do anything to stop it.

Tears seeped out from under Elaine's lashes and dribbled down her cheeks. She loved Grandma so much and would do anything for her, but at times she resented the sacrifices she'd been forced to make in order to act as Grandma's caregiver. Some days, she felt depleted, physically and mentally. Guilt consumed her whenever bitterness crept in. She often had to remind herself of all the sacrifices Grandma and Grandpa had made for her over the years.

As she readjusted her covers and plumped up her pillow, Elaine's thoughts turned to Jonah. If not for Grandma's diagnosis of dementia, she and Jonah might be married by now—or at least planning a spring wedding. He would have been at Grandma's birthday party tonight too, and everything would have seemed normal and right.

At awkward moments, like tonight when Aunt Margaret had asked if Elaine was still seeing Jonah, she wondered if her decision to break things off with him had been the right thing to do. Aunt Margaret brought the subject up again later, and Elaine was surprised that her aunt thought she'd been a little hasty in making such a decision.

In hindsight, Elaine couldn't deny that it would be

comforting to have Jonah's support through all of this, but taking care of Grandma was Elaine's duty, not his. If they were married, they'd most likely have children, and that would have stretched Elaine's responsibilities even further. No, Jonah deserved to be happy with someone else, and Elaine loved him enough to make that sacrifice and give Jonah his freedom—although guilt still plagued her for lying about her feelings for him. It was wrong to be deceitful, but she simply saw no other way. If she had admitted to Jonah that she loved him, he'd probably still be coming around and may have insisted they get married so he could share in the responsibility of Grandma's care.

Maybe I should have considered it; God does intend for couples to see each other through the tough times. And when you get married, you never know what the future holds. Elaine clutched the edge of her quilt. *Lord, did I mess up? If I did, well, it's too late now. Jonah's moved on with his life, and I have responsibilities.*

But the fact that Jonah and Sara might get more serious was difficult to accept. What if they did get married? How would Elaine be able to face them at church or anywhere else she might see them? She would have to put on a happy face and pretend everything was okay and as it should be.

"I'll never get married," Elaine whispered, turning her head into the pillow as more tears came, "but I'll always love Jonah."

⟋⟍

Sara's throat constricted as she stood at the foot of Mark's crib, watching her son suck his thumb as he slept contently, with slow, even breathing. In his other hand, he clutched the wooden horse Jonah had crafted.

The moon shone into the bedroom, illuminating the

crib and Sara's precious son. He looked so angelic and peaceful. *If only the light could protect my boy. Of course, only God can do that.*

Sara had prayed often throughout this day, hoping for clear direction on whether she should move home with her folks or stay in Arthur, close to Harley's family—and to Jonah. Her parents, as well as Harley's, still had children living at home, and neither couple needed the burden of caring for her and Mark. Yet Sara didn't see how she could manage on her own if her MS symptoms increased. It was a no-win situation, and she dreaded having to tell her family.

Moving slowly across the room toward her own bed, Sara decided not to say anything just yet. She needed more time to pray about things and wrap her mind around the whole situation. Until a clear answer came, she would leave things as they were. And while waiting for God's will to be revealed to her, she would make a concentrated effort to do all the things the doctor had mentioned and hope that her symptoms improved.

∽

A pounding on her bedroom door roused Elaine from a deep sleep. It was dark in her room, and except for the moon's brightness, no other light shone in from the window. Rolling over, she fumbled for her flashlight, switched it on, and shined it at the clock on her nightstand. It was two o'clock, and that meant whoever was at her door must have an urgent need.

"I'm coming," she called, crawling out of bed and slipping into her robe.

When Elaine opened the door, she was surprised to see Grandma standing in the hall, fully dressed and holding a flashlight.

"It's time to go, and my driver's not here." Grandma's shrill voice was a bit too loud.

Elaine put her finger to her lips. "Time to go where?" she whispered, hoping Grandma's knocking hadn't wakened anyone upstairs.

"I have an appointment with the doctor, and if I don't leave now, I'm gonna be late."

Elaine shook her head. "No, Grandma. It's two o'clock in the morning, and you don't have a doctor's appointment till next week." She slipped her arm around Grandma's waist. "I'll walk you back to your room so you can get undressed and back into bed."

Grandma folded her arms and refused to budge. "I am not going to bed, and you can't make me!"

With a sigh of exasperation, Elaine motioned Grandma into her own room. The last thing she needed was for Grandma to wake everyone upstairs and perhaps create a scene.

Grandma balked at first, but then she finally relented and stepped into Elaine's bedroom. "If my driver isn't here in the next five minutes, I'm gonna hitch up my horse and buggy and go see the doctor myself."

Please, Lord, Elaine prayed. *Help me get through to her.*

Talking softly in an effort to calm Grandma, Elaine shined her flashlight on the clock near her bed. "See, there? It's only two o'clock, so it's way too early to be up. And just look out the window. It's still dark outside."

Grandma tapped her foot as she stared at the clock and then toward the window, as though trying to decide if Elaine was telling the truth. "What about the doctor? Won't he be waiting? Looks like daylight out there to me."

"No, Grandma. It's only the full moon making it look so bright. Your appointment isn't until next week, and it's in the afternoon, not the middle of the night."

Grandma stood silently for several seconds. Then she pointed to Elaine's bed. "Can I sleep here?"

At first Elaine was going to tell Grandma that she'd be more comfortable in her own bed, but she didn't want to provoke her. Besides, if Grandma slept here for the rest of the night, Elaine could keep an eye on her, and there'd be less chance of Grandma sneaking outside to the barn and buggy shed.

"Sure, you can sleep in my room." Elaine gently patted Grandma's arm. "Oh, and since you're here, there's something special I want to give you. Now, close your eyes and hold out your hands."

As Grandma sat on the edge of the bed with her eyes shut and hands extended, Elaine moved to her dresser, where she'd set the rock she had painted for Grandma yesterday morning. She had planned to give it as a birthday present, but it wasn't dry by the time Grandma had opened her other gifts. The rock was oblong and actually stood on end. Elaine had painted the rock to look like a parakeet, using the same color green that Millie had been. "Happy birthday, Grandma," she said, placing the rock in Grandma's outstretched hands.

Grandma opened her eyes and squealed, "Millie! You've come home!"

Elaine was tempted to explain that it wasn't really Millie but decided it would be better to let Grandma think whatever she wanted.

"Why don't you take off your dress so it doesn't get wrinkled, and then you can sleep in your underskirt?"

With a brief nod, Grandma did as she was told. A few minutes later, holding Millie in one hand, she was tucked under the covers in Elaine's bed. With a peaceful smile on her face, Grandma fell asleep soon after.

"Thank you, heavenly Father," Elaine whispered as she slipped under the covers on the other side of Grandma.

A frightening thought occurred to her. *What if Grandma had actually gone outside, hitched her horse to the buggy, and headed down the road? In her state of confusion, she'd surely have gotten lost.*

Elaine clutched the edge of her quilt. *I need to do something to prevent that from happening. I'm just not sure what.*

CHAPTER 38

*E*laine smiled as she watched the birds flit from feeder to feeder as though in search of the best seeds. She'd just finished filling each of the bird feeders and had left Grandma in the house, where she'd been relaxing in the living room with a magazine. Elaine wasn't sure if Grandma had actually been reading or just looking at the pictures, but at least she seemed content. So far today, she hadn't accused Elaine of taking or hiding any of her things.

Deciding to take a few extra minutes to enjoy the fresh fall air, Elaine stood in the yard and took it all in. Fallen leaves lay scattered about, and she caught sight of a squirrel taking its share of the seeds that had dropped on the ground under one of the feeders.

Suddenly, the loft doors of the barn opened. Grandma, sitting in the hay on the second story, smiled down at Elaine in the yard.

"Look at me!" Grandma called, waving her hands. "I'm a bird, high up in a nest."

Elaine's heart pounded. "Grandma, stay right there. Don't move!" She ran into the barn and hurried up the ladder to the loft. "What are you doing up here?" she asked, taking a seat beside Grandma.

"I was looking at Millie and saw that she couldn't fly, so I brought her up here to the loft."

It was then that she noticed Grandma was holding the parakeet rock Elaine had painted for her. She cringed.

Even though Grandma had never mentioned that her parakeet had flown out of the house, never to return, here she was now, convinced that the parakeet on the rock was real. If that wasn't bad enough, poor Grandma thought the bird would be able to fly. *Should I tell her that Millie got attacked by one of the cats? No, that would probably upset her too much.*

She patted Grandma's hand ever so gently. "You know, sitting up here like this brings back memories from a time long ago when I used to climb into the loft and pretend I was a bird."

Grandma sat without saying a word. Then she looked over at Elaine and grinned. "I remember when you did that. Used to scare me half to death seeing you way up so high, but your grandpa said I shouldn't worry so much and that every child had the right to pretend and explore." She chuckled. "Of course, you didn't know it, but he kept a close watch to make sure you were safe."

Elaine smiled. "And I remember how he'd sometimes climb the ladder and sit beside me. We'd watch the birds in the yard below as they flew back and forth between the trees."

They sat quietly for a while, and then Elaine managed to take the rock from Grandma and coax her back down the ladder, coming down each rung behind her. When they reached the bottom, Elaine paused to thank God for keeping Grandma safe and for giving them those few moments when Grandma could remember a special time from the past. Elaine could only hope there would be more days like this. Oh, how she longed for things to be as they once were, with her and Grandma simply enjoying each other's company, without any worries about the horrible disease that was taking Grandma from her.

⸜❧⸝

Sara fiddled with the ties on her head covering as she waited for Jonah to arrive. He'd invited her and Mark to go out for supper with him again, but Mark had the tail end of a cold, so Sara thought it would be better to fix supper here, rather than taking her son out on this chilly November evening. Besides, it would be easier to talk to Jonah here than in a restaurant, where others might hear what she had to say.

It had been two weeks since Sara received her MS diagnosis, and she'd finally made a decision. She was going to put her house up for sale and move home to live with her folks. It had been a difficult decision, but she felt it was the best thing for both her and Mark. She really had little choice. Sara had also decided not to do anything with the barn, although she had asked some of the men from her district to haul the remains of it away. Maybe whoever bought her place could build a barn of his choosing. She planned to go to her folks' for Thanksgiving, at which time she would tell them about her MS and ask if she and Mark could move in with them.

Sara went to check on the roast she had cooking in the oven. The potatoes and carrots surrounding the meat poked tender, and the thermometer showed that the roast was done. She turned down the temperature, closed the oven door, and went to the counter to slice some pickled beets. In addition to the meat and vegetables, she'd also made coleslaw, mixing mayonnaise and vinegar into the shredded cabbage, just like her mother always did. Some people preferred a sweeter-tasting coleslaw, to which a bit of sugar had been added, but she'd always liked it on the tangy side. She hoped Jonah would enjoy it that way too.

Certain that everything was ready to be put on the table once Jonah arrived, Sara went to the living room to check on Mark. She'd left him happily sitting on the floor with the wooden horse Jonah had made.

When Sara entered the room, Mark looked up at her and grinned. *"Scheme gaul,"* he said, pointing to the horse that had been painted brown with a white patch on its head.

Sara nodded. "Jah, Mark. It's a pretty horse."

Jonah had already won her son's heart. Not just with the little gifts he often brought Mark, but with the attention and quality time he gave the boy. That would be something she'd be taking from Mark if she moved back with her parents, although she was sure that Dad, busy as he was, would show Mark some attention. Still, it wouldn't be the same as time spent with Jonah, for Mark had bonded with him in a special way. *It's almost like how Mark would have been with his dad if he were still alive.* Sara reached out to touch her son's soft cheeks. Remembering how tender the scene had been when Jonah had tucked Mark into bed one night, she grieved to realize there would never be a man in Mark's life whom he could call Daadi.

❧

"Come on now, Sassy, let's get a move on it," Jonah called to his horse, snapping the reins. "I'm gettin' hungry, and I don't want to be late for supper."

Jonah had to admit it was more than appeasing his hunger that made him anxious to get to Sara's house this evening. He looked forward to visiting with Sara again and, most of all, spending time with Mark. It was hard not to spoil the little guy, but Jonah figured he could get away with it, since he wasn't the boy's father.

But I wish I was, Jonah admitted to himself as he approached Sara's driveway. *I'd give anything to have a son like Mark—to love and cherish, and to have carry on my name.* Once again, his thoughts turned to Elaine. *If only she hadn't shut me out. I really believed she was the woman for me. Could I have been that wrong?*

Pulling up to the hitching rack, Jonah stepped out of his buggy and secured his horse. *I need to quit thinking about Elaine and enjoy this evening with Sara and Mark.*

Stepping onto the porch, he knocked on the door, glancing over at the burned-out barn and wondering if Sara ever planned to see about having a new one built. It seemed odd that she'd let it go this long, but perhaps she had her reasons.

Sara answered the door, wearing a dark blue dress with matching apron and cape. She smiled, but there was no sparkle in her eyes.

"Is everything all right?" Jonah asked, feeling concern. "You look mied."

She released a ragged sigh and pushed a wayward lock of hair back under her head covering. "I guess I am a bit tired tonight."

"If having me here for supper is too much, then I can come some other time," he was quick to say.

Sara shook her head. "I'm not that tired. Besides, I made too much food for me and Mark to eat by ourselves. And Mark would be very disappointed if he didn't get to see you this evening. I told him you were coming, and he's been saying your name over and over all day." Sara laughed. "Onah. That's what he says instead of Jonah."

Jonah grinned as he walked into the house. "For a little guy who's not even three yet, even saying 'Onah' seems pretty smart to me. A lot of kinner his age don't say near as many words as Mark does already."

"That's true. He can be quite the little chatterbox at times." Sara motioned to the living room. "Mark's in there, if you'd like to keep him entertained while I put supper on the dining-room table."

"Is there anything I can do to help?" Jonah asked.

Sara shook her head once more. "I think I can manage on my own, but danki for asking."

"Okay. Call me if you need anything though."

When Jonah entered the living room, he found Mark sitting on a braided rug in the middle of the floor with some wooden blocks, which he'd placed in a large square. The wooden horse Jonah had given him was inside the square. As soon as Mark saw Jonah, he held out his hands and shouted, "Onah!"

Jonah knelt on the floor beside Mark, and the little boy crawled right into his lap. "*Der gaul is darichgange.*"

"Jah, that's right," Jonah said, laughing. "The horse ran away." Then he picked up the horse and made it prance around the wooden-block corral, smiling as Mark laughed and clapped his hands.

A short time later, Sara entered the room and announced that supper was ready. Jonah stood and, lifting Mark onto his shoulders, followed Sara into the dining room.

"Yum. . .something sure smells good in here." Jonah surveyed the food she had set on the table before placing Mark in his high chair. "Makes my mouth water just looking at all that food."

"Well, I hope it tastes as good as it looks." Sara motioned for Jonah to take his seat. Then they bowed their heads for silent prayer. When the prayer was over, Sara passed the platter of roast beef to Jonah, followed by the potatoes, carrots, and other items she'd set on the table. Then she gave Mark what she knew he would eat.

"Aren't you going to eat anything?" Jonah asked, gesturing to Sara's empty plate.

Her cheeks colored. "Oh, jah, of course."

"This is a great meal, Sara. The meat is so tender, and I like how you cooked the vegetables with the beef. That's how my mamm's always made it too."

"Danki, Jonah." Sara's cheeks darkened further.

After Sara dished up some food for herself, they ate their meal and visited. Every once in a while, Mark looked over at Jonah and said, "Onah."

Jonah had to admit it felt pretty good sitting here with Sara and Mark, enjoying some of her delicious cooking. It almost seemed as if they were a family. *But of course,* he reminded himself, *Sara's not my wife and Mark's not my son.*

"I've been wondering what you plan to do about your barn," Jonah said. "Are you going to have a barn-raising before winter sets in, or wait till spring?"

"I won't be putting up a new barn," Sara said with a shake of her head. "You may have noticed when you arrived that I had the remains of the old barn hauled away."

"What about your horse? Won't she need a warm, dry place this winter?"

"She's doing well in a three-sided lean-to, so I think she'll be fine for now."

"Oh, I see." Jonah could hardly believe that Sara wouldn't want a new barn to replace the one that had been burned or provide a warmer place for her horse, but it was her decision.

They visited about other things, and by the time they'd finished dinner and enjoyed apple pie and coffee for dessert, Jonah was full to the point of being drowsy. In an effort to keep awake, he pushed away from the table and began clearing the dishes.

"You don't have to do that." Sara shook her head. "Why don't you and Mark go back to the living room, and I'll do the dishes?"

"I wouldn't hear of it," Jonah said. "You worked hard fixing this meal, and the least I can do is help with the dishes."

"Okay, if you insist. I'll wash, and you can dry."

Sara took Mark out of his high chair, and he followed them into the kitchen. While they did the dishes, Mark sat on a throw rug nearby, playing with his wooden horse. Every once in a while, the child would call out, "Onah!"

Jonah smiled and hollered in reply, "Mark!"

"He sure has taken a liking to you," Sara said, placing a few clean plates into the dish drainer for Jonah to dry.

"The feeling's mutual." Jonah smiled. "I'm hoping we can enjoy a lot more times like this. Maybe during the holidays, if we get some good snow on the ground, I'll get out my sleigh and take you and Mark for a ride. Does that sound like fun to you, Sara?"

She lifted her hand from the soapy water and opened her mouth as if to comment, but then, almost as though she was moving in slow motion, she closed her mouth and began scrubbing the roasting pan.

"Sara, what's wrong? Did I say something I shouldn't have?" Jonah questioned.

She drew in a quick breath. "It's not that. It's just that. . .well, Mark and I won't be here for the holidays."

"Oh, I see. Are you planning to go home to spend Thanksgiving and Christmas with your family?"

Sara nodded but avoided making eye contact with

him. "The truth is, Mark and I will be moving to Indiana permanently—as soon as I can find a buyer for my house."

Jonah's mouth dropped open. "Really? I had no idea you were planning to move. Do you mind if I ask what caused you to make that decision?" Jonah felt like he'd been kicked in the stomach by an unruly horse. He would miss Sara, and the idea of never seeing little Mark again was the worst part of all.

"Why would you do that, Sara?" he asked again. "I thought you liked living here in Illinois."

Still refusing to meet his gaze, she said in a shaky voice, "I–I'm not well, Jonah. I recently found out that I have MS."

Jonah silently let what she'd said sink into his brain, while searching for the right words in response. Once he'd collected his thoughts, he looked at her and said, "I'm sorry to hear that, Sara. I didn't have an inkling that you were ill."

"Neither did I." Sara continued to scrub at the pan. "Well, I knew there might be something wrong because at certain times I've had some strange symptoms. Although some days I feel perfectly fine, at other times I'm dizzy, exhausted, or my arms and legs tingle and won't work as they should." She paused and looked down at her son. "If my disease progresses, I may not be able to take care of myself as I should, much less do everything I need to for Mark. So moving home with my parents is the only logical solution."

"I see." Jonah dried a few more dishes as he mulled things over. "You know, you really wouldn't have to move if you didn't want to, Sara."

"Jah, I do. Didn't you hear what I just said about the possibility of me not being able to take care of myself and Mark?"

He gave a slow nod. "I heard, and I understand why you feel the need to move, but. . ." Jonah swiped his tongue over his lips and swallowed a couple of times. "You could marry me and stay right here."

Sara's eyes widened. "Oh Jonah, it's nice of you to make such an offer, but I know you're not in love with me, and—"

Jonah touched his fingers gently to her lips. "I care for you and Mark, and I wouldn't have suggested that you marry me if I didn't mean it, Sara. Will you at least consider becoming my wife?"

Sara's eyes filled with tears. "I don't think something like this should be entered into lightly, Jonah. Why don't we both take some time to think and pray about the matter?"

"All right, then how about this: for the next seven days, you can pray about the matter, and then a week from today I'll come back here, and you can give me your answer. How's that sound?"

"I—I suppose that would be okay, but you need to be praying about it too."

"Jah, I sure will." Jonah glanced down at Mark, and a lump formed in his throat. *But I've already made up my mind.*

CHAPTER 39

*A*s Elaine sat in church next to Grandma the following Sunday, she was pleased to see that Grandma was singing along with everyone else. Many times during the last month, Grandma had sat through church with a blank expression. Today was obviously a good day for her, and for that Elaine felt relief. To add to her joy, just a few minutes ago, Grandma had looked over at her and smiled sweetly. It was the kind of smile Elaine remembered from her childhood, when Grandma would give Elaine a quick nod and a pleasant smile, letting her know that she was loved.

She knew Grandma still loved her, but there were days, such as yesterday, when Grandma's frustration with not being able to remember something had caused her to be irritable and out of sorts.

When Grandma got up this morning, she'd put her everyday dress on over her Sunday dress and come into the kitchen saying she was ready for church. Elaine had thought this would turn out to be a difficult day, but to her surprise, Grandma had agreeably taken off her regular dress when Elaine asked her to. She'd also helped do the breakfast dishes and waited patiently in the buggy while Elaine brought her horse out of the barn. On the trip to church, Grandma had actually carried on a fairly normal conversation with Elaine, although she had mentioned Grandpa a few times, referring to him as though he were still alive. Grandma hadn't mentioned Millie needing to fly again, but Elaine often saw her holding and talking to the rock parakeet. Apparently, Grandma truly believed that the rock was Millie. Well, if it made Grandma happy to believe that, then Elaine wouldn't tell her otherwise. It was easier just to let Grandma think whatever she wanted in that regard.

I'm thankful for the good days, Elaine thought, returning Grandma's smile. *And as for the not-so-good days, I'll just keep asking God for more patience.*

Pulling her gaze away from Grandma, Elaine glanced at the men's side of the room and caught sight of Jonah. He sat straight and tall on his bench, looking attentively at their song leader. Unexpectedly, he glanced Elaine's way, and she quickly averted his gaze, fearful that her true feelings for him might show.

Always on her guard whenever Jonah was around, Elaine had to make sure he never found out that she hadn't stopped loving him.

∽

Jonah didn't know who he was the most worried about this morning—Sara, who hadn't come to church with Mark, or Elaine, who appeared to be tired and strained. He planned to head over to Sara's house to check on her as soon as church was over, even skipping the noon meal, but he didn't know what he could do about Elaine's situation, for she'd made it clear that she didn't want his help or attention. Still, he couldn't get rid of the feeling of wanting to protect Elaine.

Even yet, Jonah had a hard time accepting the fact that Elaine had never loved him, but if she'd told one of her best friends that, it must be true. Elaine's decision was one of the reasons he'd begun courting Sara—that and his connection with Sara's son. Then three nights ago when he'd learned of Sara's illness, Jonah knew what he had to do. By marrying Sara, he'd not only gain a wife, but he'd have the son he'd always wanted. *Sara needs a husband*, Jonah reminded himself. *And if she says yes to my proposal, I'm going to be the best husband and father I can possibly be.*

∽

As soon as church was over, Jonah headed straight for his horse and buggy.

"Where are ya going?" Jean's husband, Nathan, called.

"Over to Sara Stutzman's to see why she wasn't in church today," Jonah said after Nathan caught up to him.

"Aren't you gonna stay long enough to eat?" Nathan questioned.

Jonah shook his head. "I had a big breakfast this morning, and I'm not all that hungry right now."

Nathan eyed Jonah curiously. "According to Jean, you've been seeing a lot of Sara lately."

Jonah nodded.

"Maybe it's none of my business, but are you two getting serious about each other?"

Jonah felt like telling Nathan that he was right, it was none of his business, but that would be rude. So he gave a simple one-word reply: "Jah."

Nathan blinked rapidly. "Wow, that was sure quick."

"What? My reply, or the fact that I haven't been courting Sara very long?"

"Both." Nathan drew his fingers through the ends of his beard. "You're not thinking of marrying her already, I hope."

Jonah's jaw clenched. He didn't like the way his brother-in-law was giving him the third degree. "Would there be anything wrong with it if I was?"

Nathan shrugged. "Well, no, I guess not, but as you

said, you haven't been courting her very long."

"That's true, but when a man knows what he wants, why should he have to wait?" Jonah grabbed Sassy's rope and led the horse over to his buggy.

Nathan followed. "When are you planning to ask her to marry you?"

"I already have. Just waitin' for Sara's answer." Jonah saw no purpose at this point in telling Nathan about Sara's MS. He figured Nathan might already know, since his wife was Sara's best friend. But if that was the case, why hadn't he mentioned it?

Nathan placed his hand on Jonah's arm. "Uh, listen, before you go, there's one thing more I'd like to say."

"What's that?"

"If you decide to marry Sara, you'll have Jean's and my blessing, but I think you oughta give it a little more time—maybe wait till spring to get married."

Jonah rolled his shoulders, trying to release some of the tension he felt. "I appreciate your advice, but Sara hasn't said yes yet, and if she does, then I doubt we'll wait till spring." With that, Jonah finished hitching his horse, said goodbye to Nathan, and climbed into the buggy. As he rode away, he pondered Nathan's words. Had he reacted too soon where Sara was concerned? Should he have thought it through a bit more before asking her to marry him? Well, it was too late for that. He wouldn't feel right about un-asking her now, and if she said yes to his proposal, then he would take that as a sign from God that he'd done the right thing. And if she said no, he would let her move back to Indiana with his blessing.

❧

Curling up on one end of the sofa, with her sleeping son on the other end, Sara yawned and closed her eyes. In addition to the fact that she felt more tired than usual today, Mark's cold seemed to have gotten worse than it had been earlier in the week. So Sara decided it would be best for them to stay home from church and rest. Since the doctor had said she needed plenty of rest, she felt her decision was justified.

As Sara lay there, covered with the quilt she was sharing with Mark, she thought about Jonah and his marriage proposal. There was no doubt that he'd make a good husband and father, but was she ready to marry again and start a new life with another man? Did she care enough for Jonah to become his wife? Would it be fair for him to be faced with the challenges of her illness?

I need to make a decision soon, she told herself. *Jonah will be coming by in a few days, and he'll expect an answer.*

Sara had been praying about this ever since Jonah had asked her to marry him, yet she hadn't received an answer from God. If she went home to live with her folks, she would place a burden on them. But wouldn't becoming Jonah's wife be a burden for him too?

Why can't life be simple? Why's it so hard to know what God wants me to do? she wondered. Ever since Harley's death, it seemed like she had been faced with one challenge after the next. Some days, when she didn't think she had the strength to go on, she would turn to the Bible and find comfort in God's Word. *That's what I should do right now.*

Sara slipped out from under the quilt, being careful not to disturb Mark, and tiptoed across the room to where she kept her Bible on the end table near the rocking chair. Taking a seat, she opened the Bible to the book of James and read chapter 1, verse 5 out loud. "If any of you lack wisdom, let him ask of God, that giveth to all men liberally, and upbraideth not; and it shall be given him."

She bowed her head and closed her eyes. *I'm asking You, Lord, for wisdom in deciding what to do about Jonah's proposal. If I'm supposed to say yes, then please give me a sign.*

Sara had just finished her prayer when she heard the *clip-clop* of horse hooves coming up her driveway. Figuring it was probably Harley's parents stopping by to check on her, Sara rose from her chair and went to the door. When she opened it, she was surprised to see Jonah securing his horse to the hitching rack.

"Hi, Sara. Are you okay?" Jonah asked when he joined her on the porch. "When I realized you weren't at church, I became worried about you."

Sara smiled. "It was nice of you to come by, Jonah. I'm more tired than usual today, and Mark's cold seems to have gotten worse, so I decided it would be best if we stayed home and rested today."

"That makes good sense." Jonah moved closer to Sara. "Is there anything I can do for you—maybe spend some time with Mark so you can rest?"

"It's kind of you to offer, but Mark's sleeping right now."

"Oh, I see."

Sara couldn't help but notice the look of disappointment in Jonah's dark eyes. He'd obviously been hoping to enjoy her son's company for a while, and she couldn't blame him for that. Mark was such a sweet boy, and Sara relished every moment she had with him.

"Sure is chilly out today," Jonah said when a harsh wind blew under the porch eaves. "Bet it won't be long till we see our first snowfall. Could even happen before Thanksgiving."

Sara nodded as Jonah briskly rubbed his arms. Thinking Jonah might like to get in out of the cold for a bit, she invited him inside for a cup of coffee.

"That sounds real good," Jonah said, following

Sara into the house.

She was about to suggest that they go to the kitchen for coffee, when Mark woke up. Seeing Jonah, he bounded off the sofa and darted into the utility room, where Sara and Jonah stood, shouting, "Onah! Onah!"

Jonah bent down and scooped the boy into his arms. "Hey, little buddy, it's sure good to see you."

"Don't get too close or you might catch his cold," Sara cautioned, handing Jonah a tissue.

Jonah shook his head as he wiped Mark's nose. "Aw, I'm not worried about that. I've never been one to catch many colds. Even if I did, it'd be worth it just to spend some time with this special boy."

Sara's heart nearly melted as she watched the tender way Jonah looked at Mark. And her son looked equally enchanted with Jonah as he clasped his hands around Jonah's neck and held on tight. Drowsy from just waking up, Mark laid his head on Jonah's shoulder and closed his eyes, while Jonah gently rubbed Mark's back. Suddenly, as Sara's heartbeat thudded in her chest, she felt as if she'd been given her answer.

"Jonah," she said, pausing to take in a quick breath. "I know we agreed that we'd both take a week to decide, but if you still want to marry me, then my answer is yes."

Jonah's face broke into a wide smile, and he reached for Sara's hand. "I still want to marry you, and the sooner the better."

CHAPTER 40

$\mathcal{I}$'m sorry to hear you have MS but glad you finally went to see the doctor," Leah said as she worked on Sara's feet. "Most of the symptoms you were having weren't responding to reflexology, but I think my treatments should at least help you relax."

Sara nodded. "I always feel calmer after you've worked on my feet, and according to the doctor, feeling less stressed can help decrease the symptoms of MS."

"So where is that cute little boy of yours today?" Leah questioned.

"I left him with my mother-in-law. She'll be keeping him most of the day so I can get some shopping done after I leave here."

"It's nice that Betty and Herschel live close to you and are willing to help out with Mark." Leah pressed on an area of Sara's foot that appeared to be inflamed.

Sara flinched.

"Sorry if that hurts."

"It's okay. You're just doing your job."

As Leah continued to massage and pressure-point Sara's feet, they talked about the upcoming holidays.

"Will your folks be coming here for Thanksgiving or Christmas?" Leah asked.

"I was planning to go there for both holidays, but since Jonah and I are planning to be married the first week of December, they'll probably come here for Thanksgiving and then stay on for the wedding."

Leah's eyes widened. "You're getting married?"

"Jah. I thought you might have heard." Sara gave a nervous laugh. "You know how quick news travels in our community."

"No, I hadn't heard, and I'll admit, I am a bit surprised, since he hasn't been courting you very long."

Sara's cheeks darkened with a pinkish blush. "That's true, but we've known each other for some time—since Jonah moved here and he and Harley became friends."

Leah wasn't quite sure how to respond. Sara and Jonah may have known each other for a reasonable amount of time, but most of that had been while Sara was married to Harley and Jonah was courting Elaine. While Jonah and Harley had been friends, it wouldn't have been possible for Jonah and Sara to establish a close relationship—at least not in a romantic sort of way. The fact that they hadn't been courting very long concerned Leah. She'd always felt that a long courtship was the best for most couples, in order to know if they were truly compatible. Leah would certainly never marry a man unless they'd been seriously courting for a while.

"Jonah's a wonderful man, and my son adores him," Sara went on to say.

Leah slowly nodded. "I hope you and Jonah will be happy, and I wish you all of God's best." She reached for the bottle of massage lotion and poured some into her hand. *I wonder if Elaine knows about this. If so, what does she think?*

❧

"It's nice to see you," Elaine said when Priscilla pedaled her bike into the yard on Wednesday of the following week.

Priscilla smiled. "It's good to see you too. I was out

checking some of the stores that sell our jams to see if they're running low and decided to come by here before I went home." Priscilla parked her bike and moved toward the line where Elaine was hanging clothes. "Um. . .there's something I think you need to know."

Holding a clothespin in her mouth, Elaine tipped her head. "What's that?"

"I was talking with Leah the other day, and she said Jonah's asked Sara to be his wife and they're planning to get married the first week of December."

Elaine's whole body trembled, and she let the clothespin fall to the ground. She'd suspected this could happen but hadn't thought it would be so soon. Had Jonah gotten over her so quickly?

Priscilla slipped her arm around Elaine. "Are you okay?"

"It just took me by surprise." Elaine picked up the clothespin, reached into the basket, and clipped a towel on the line. She hoped Priscilla wouldn't notice how badly her hands were shaking.

"You love him, don't you?"

"It doesn't matter how I feel about Jonah. He's made his choice, and there's nothing I can do about it."

Priscilla stepped in front of Elaine, looking directly into her eyes. "Jah, there is, Elaine. You can go to Jonah right now and tell him you love him. If you did that, I'm sure he would break things off with Sara."

Elaine shook her head vigorously. "I can't, and I won't say anything to Jonah about this. My responsibility to Grandma hasn't changed, and if Jonah's asked Sara to marry him, then he must be in love with her now." She shrugged. "Jonah deserves to be happy, and I would never think of coming between them. Besides, even if Jonah wasn't with Sara, with everything going on in my life, where would we find time for each other?"

Priscilla looked like she might say more on the subject, but she reached into the basket and picked up a towel instead. "You look tired, Elaine. Think I'll stay here awhile and help out."

"You don't need to do that. I'm fine." *But you're not fine*, Elaine's conscience told her. She wished she could just go to her room, have a good cry, and sleep the rest of the day. But she couldn't do that. Chores still waited, and in a little while, it would be time to test Grandma's blood sugar and fix them both some lunch.

"I'm sure you have plenty to do today, so I am staying to help," Priscilla insisted. "If I was in your situation, I'm sure you'd do the same thing for me."

Elaine couldn't argue with that. If either of her best friends had a need, she would do whatever she could to help out. "Okay," she said, appreciating Priscilla's offer. "You can help me finish the laundry, and after that, we'll have lunch."

Priscilla smiled. "That sounds good to me, and if you have the ingredients, I'll make some chicken noodle soup for our noon meal."

"Leah's mamm came by yesterday to sit with Grandma, and I was able to do some shopping," Elaine replied. "The cupboards and refrigerator are full, so I'm sure I have everything you'll need to make soup."

❧

"This soup is sure good," Elaine said after taking her first bite. "Don't you think so, Grandma?"

Grandma sat across the table from Elaine and Priscilla, her lips compressed as she stared at her bowl.

"Grandma, did you hear what I said?" Elaine asked, speaking a little louder.

As though coming out of a daze, Grandma looked over at Elaine and blinked. "Did you say something to me?"

"I said the soup is good and asked if you like it too."

Grandma spooned some into her mouth and smacked her lips. "It tastes pretty good, but I think it needs more salse." She picked up the saltshaker and sprinkled some into her soup. Then she pointed at Priscilla. *"Sie is en gudi Koch."*

Elaine nodded. "You're right, Grandma, she is a good cook."

Elaine glanced at Priscilla to see her reaction, but Priscilla just smiled and handed her the basket of crackers.

They ate in silence for a while. Then Priscilla asked Elaine if she'd made any special plans for Thanksgiving.

Elaine shook her head. "Not really. I'll probably fix a small turkey, along with some potatoes and a vegetable for Grandma and me. Then we'll have some no-sugar apple pie for dessert."

"You two are welcome to join my family for Thanksgiving," Priscilla offered.

"That's nice of you, but I think it would be better if we stay here and have a quiet day by ourselves." Elaine would have enjoyed spending the holiday with Priscilla's family, but it would be too stressful taking Grandma there and not knowing what she might say or do that could be embarrassing.

"Hot eier nei haus viel geld gekoscht?" Grandma asked, looking at Priscilla again.

Elaine grimaced. She had no idea why Grandma had just asked Priscilla if her new house cost a great deal of money.

"No, Edna," Priscilla said, shaking her head. "I don't have a new house. I'm still living at home with my parents."

Grandma's brows furrowed as she pursed her lips.

"Really? I thought I'd come to visit you there."

"You've been to the home of Priscilla's parents many times," Elaine said, handing the crackers to Grandma.

Grandma nodded and set the basket down. "I know, and I. . ." She stopped talking and looked absently across the room.

"What were you going to say, Edna?" Priscilla prompted.

Grandma sighed. "I forgot."

"That's okay." Priscilla gave a nod of understanding. "Sometimes we all forget things."

Grandma picked up her bowl of soup and began slurping it, like a child might do. Elaine was on the verge of telling her to eat the soup with a spoon, but hearing a horse and buggy coming up the driveway, she went to see who it was.

◌ᴖ◌

Struggling with the desire to flee, Jonah secured his horse to the hitching rack and started for Edna's house. After praying about it, he'd decided to tell Elaine about his plans to marry Sara, before she heard it from someone else. But now that he was here, he'd begun to have second thoughts. Jonah hated to admit it, but somewhere deep inside, he hoped Elaine might say that she still loved him. Of course, that wasn't likely, but as close as he and Elaine had once been, he thought she had the right to know of his plans.

As Jonah walked across the yard, he noticed a bicycle sitting near the clothesline and figured Elaine or Edna might have company. Maybe this wasn't the best time for him to be here.

Jonah was about to return to his horse when Elaine stepped out of the house. "I thought that was you, Jonah. What brings you by here today?"

Jonah shuffled his feet and cleared his throat. "Well, first of all, I've been wondering how your grandma is doing. I haven't seen her for quite a while."

"Grandma's memory is failing fast," Elaine replied, refusing to look directly at him. "Her diabetes seems to be getting worse too."

"I'm sorry to hear that." Jonah cleared his throat again. "I. . .uh. . .wanted to also tell you that I'm planning to. . ."

"Marry Sara?"

"Jah. How'd you know?"

Elaine pointed to the bicycle. "Priscilla's here, and she told me." She turned to face him directly. "I appreciate you coming by, and I wish you and Sara the best." Elaine didn't smile, but her expression was sincere.

Jonah kicked at a clump of dead grass with the toe of his boot. "Well, uh. . .guess I'd better head back to my shop. Tell Edna I'm praying for her." He started to go but turned back around. "I'm praying for you too, Elaine."

"Danki. Goodbye, Jonah." Elaine opened the door and went back into the house.

When the door clicked shut behind her, Jonah headed back to his horse and buggy, full of mixed emotions. He was relieved that Elaine didn't object to him marrying Sara. But on the other hand, he was disappointed that she hadn't challenged his decision. It was confirmation that Elaine didn't love him. *Maybe this is how it's meant to be,* he told himself. *Sara and Mark need me, and apparently Elaine does not.*

CHAPTER 41

*I*t was the week after Thanksgiving, and as Jonah sat at his kitchen table, his shoulders tightened. He remembered a March day much like this morning, when the weather had been nearly the same. Only back then his marriage to Meredith had been only hours away. A cold rain had fallen overnight, but by morning the clouds had broken up, with the promise of a clear blue sky for his wedding. So far, the weather was turning out to be the same today.

As Jonah continued to reflect on the day he and Meredith were to marry, a nervous flutter went through his stomach. What if something happened and Sara changed her mind? He'd been jilted before. Could it happen again?

"Come on, get ahold of yourself," Jonah murmured. The weather might be similar, but Jonah could think of no reason his marriage to Sara would not take place. The circumstances that led to the halt of his and Meredith's wedding were quite understandable after finding out that Luke was still alive. *So why am I worrying now?* Jonah took a deep breath to calm himself.

Jonah's parents had come for Thanksgiving, and Sara's mom and dad had done the same. They'd been staying at Sara's house and would be there until after the wedding. On Thanksgiving, Jonah and his parents had been invited to Sara's. Jonah had been relieved that from the moment the two sets of parents met, it was as if they'd known each other all their lives.

Sara had moved some of her and Mark's belongings into Jonah's place, but after the wedding, they'd get the rest of their things.

Getting up from the kitchen table, Jonah took one last look out the window. He was glad all seemed normal and no buggies were coming up his lane with distressing news. Sparkling drops of rain left over from last night's showers glistened like diamonds as the sun warmed the earth. Today was a new beginning, and it would be the start of the rest of his life with Sara and Mark. Jonah could hardly wait for that.

✑

As Sara stood beside Jonah in front of their bishop, responding to their marriage vows, joy and hope flooded her soul. Even though she'd been married once before, her heart swelled with emotion and a sense of excitement over becoming Jonah's wife.

"Can you confess, brother, that you accept our sister as your wife, and that you will not leave her until death separates you?" Bishop Levi asked Jonah.

"Yes," Jonah replied with a nod.

"And do you believe that this is from the Lord and that you have come thus far because of your faith and prayers?"

Jonah, glancing quickly at Sara, answered, "Yes."

The bishop then turned to Sara. "Can you confess, sister, that you accept our brother as your husband, and that you will not leave him until death separates you?"

Barely able to speak around the constriction in her throat, Sara nodded and said, "Yes."

"And do you believe that this is from the Lord and that you have come this far because of your faith and prayers?"

"Yes," Sara replied, struggling not to let the tears slip out.

Bishop Levi looked at Jonah again. "Because you have confessed that you want to take Sara for your wife, do you promise to remain loyal to her and care for her if she may have any adversity, sickness, or weakness, as is appropriate for a Christian husband?"

"Yes, I will."

The bishop asked Sara the same question, and she also replied, "Yes, I will."

Then Bishop Levi took Sara's right hand and placed it in Jonah's right hand, putting his hands above and beneath their hands. "May the God of Abraham, the God of Isaac, and the God of Jacob be with you together and give His blessings upon you and be merciful to you. And may you hold out until the blessed end. This all in, and through, Jesus Christ. Amen."

At this point, Bishop Levi, Jonah, and Sara went down on their knees for prayer. When they rose, the bishop said, "Go forth now in the name of the Lord. You are now man and wife."

As Sara and Jonah returned to their seats, she almost felt like she was floating. It was as if all of her burdens had suddenly been removed. Her illness would still present challenges, but with Jonah at her side, Sara was sure she could get through them.

Glancing at the women's side of the room, she smiled when she saw that Mark had fallen asleep on Grandma Stutzman's lap. How grateful she was that Harley's parents hadn't objected to her marrying Jonah. They'd given Sara their blessing, as had Sara's parents, who were also here for the wedding. Jonah's sister and his parents were here too, along with several others from Sara and Jonah's church district, including Leah. Because it was a smaller wedding than most, and since this was Sara's second marriage, she hadn't invited many people. But she didn't mind the smaller group. The people she was closest to were here, and that's what mattered.

❦

As Jonah listened to the words of testimony from one of their ministers, he reflected on the vows he and Sara had just agreed upon. He was relieved that his silly fears from this morning had been for nothing. Jonah cared deeply for Sara and would take those vows seriously as they made a new life together. He would be a loving husband to Sara and a good father to her son. Hopefully someday, if the Lord allowed, they would be blessed with more children. It would be nice for Mark to have a little brother or sister to grow up with.

In the meantime, though, Jonah would enjoy his time with Mark, setting a godly example and creating pleasant memories for their family of three. At last, Jonah's desire to be a husband and father had come true, all in the same day, and he was convinced that God had brought him and Sara together. Christmas was just around the corner, and for the first time, he would enjoy the holiday with a wife and son.

After the other ministers in attendance spoke, Bishop Levi offered a few closing remarks. Then he asked the congregation to kneel in prayer. When that was over, everyone rose and sang a closing hymn. The church service was over, and the wedding meal could begin.

❦

Elaine sat on the sofa in the living room, trying to focus on the article she'd been reading in *The Budget*, but she couldn't seem to keep her mind on it. All she could think about was that today Jonah and Sara were getting married and had probably become husband and wife by now. All those months during Elaine and Jonah's courting days, Elaine had thought she would be the woman who'd become Jonah's wife. Instead, Sara had ended up with the man Elaine loved. How ironic was that?

There's no point in having regrets or even thinking about this, Elaine reminded herself. *I'm doing what's best for Grandma, and Jonah's doing what is best for him. He obviously loves Sara and her little boy, and I need to set my regrets aside and try to be happy for them.*

She glanced at the clock, wondering if Grandma was still asleep. She'd gone to her room shortly after breakfast, saying she was tired and needed more sleep. But that was almost two hours ago. Surely she ought to be awake by now.

Elaine was about to check on Grandma when a knock sounded on the door. *That's strange,* she thought, rising from the sofa. *I didn't hear a horse and buggy pull in.*

Elaine opened the door and was surprised to see Priscilla on the porch. "What are you doing here?" she asked. "I thought you'd be at Jonah and Sara's wedding this morning."

"I decided not to go. Figured you would need me today."

Overcome with emotion, Elaine hugged Priscilla and invited her in.

"How's your grandma doing?" Priscilla asked after following Elaine to the living room.

"She's about the same. Still has a few good days, but mostly bad." Elaine frowned.

"I'm truly sorry, and I wish there was more I could do to help you through all this."

"It helps every time you or Leah drop by." Elaine motioned to the sofa. "Why don't you have a seat while I go check on Grandma? I won't be gone long. Just want to see if she's awake or needs anything."

"No problem. Should I make us some tea?"

"Jah, that'd be nice." Elaine hurried from the room, thankful for friends like Priscilla.

When Elaine entered Grandma's bedroom, her body tensed. Grandma wasn't in her bed. *That's strange. Could she have gone to the bathroom without me hearing her walk down the hall? Oh, I hope she didn't make her way outside somehow.*

Elaine was about to leave the room and investigate, but she decided to go to the window and look out first. As she started around the foot of Grandma's bed, she froze. There lay Grandma on the other side of her bed, stretched out on the floor.

Elaine dropped to her knees and reached out to touch Grandma's hand. It felt cold. Grandma's eyes were open, as if she were staring at the ceiling.

"Grandma! Can you hear me, Grandma?" Elaine shouted, vaguely hearing Priscilla's footsteps in the background, running toward the room.

No response.

Elaine's muscles jumped under her skin as she felt Grandma's wrist for a pulse. She found none. There was no movement in Grandma's chest or breath coming from her mouth. This seemed like a dream—a horrible nightmare.

Elaine's thoughts became fuzzy. She couldn't think—could barely breathe. It wasn't possible. Grandma couldn't be dead.

CHAPTER 42

$\mathscr{J}$onah stood at the side of the bed, looking down at his new bride, who'd taken sick with the flu during the night. "Is there anything I can bring you right now? Maybe some soda crackers or a cup of mint tea?" he asked, pulling the covers up to her chin.

Shivering, Sara shook her head. "I don't think I could keep it down, Jonah."

"Maybe later then." He felt her forehead and was thankful that it wasn't as hot as it had been earlier this morning.

Sara's eyes fluttered. "I'm sorry we couldn't go to Edna Schrock's funeral today."

"It's okay," Jonah replied. "I'm sure there will be plenty of people from our community to offer Elaine support."

"Now that Edna's gone, Elaine is free to marry," Sara said, her voice barely above a whisper. "Are you sorry you didn't wait for her instead of marrying me?"

Jonah reached under the covers and clasped Sara's hand. "No, Sara, I made the right decision and have no regrets about marrying you." He squeezed her fingers gently. "I'm looking forward to the days ahead and seeing what God has planned for our lives."

"Me too. And Jonah, I have no regrets about marrying you."

"Onah! Onah!" Mark hollered from across the hall.

"I'd better go see what our little guy wants, but I'll be back to check on you soon. Oh, and there's a glass of water on the nightstand for you. You need to sip it so you don't get dehydrated."

"Okay, but please keep Mark out of our bedroom. I don't want him to get sick too," Sara called as Jonah exited the room.

"I'll make sure he doesn't come in." Jonah hurried into Mark's room and lifted him from the crib. "Let's get you some breakfast, little buddy."

After Jonah had Mark settled in his high chair with a bowl of cereal, he made a pot of coffee and took a seat at the table. He too felt bad about missing Edna Schrock's funeral, but his first obligation was to Sara. He sure couldn't leave her alone when she was this sick.

Jonah had gone to Edna's viewing the other day, and it tugged at his heartstrings to see the look of despair on Elaine's face. As difficult as it had been for her to be Edna's caregiver, it would be even harder for Elaine to cope with the loss of her grandmother. It had been a rough year for Elaine, losing both of her grandparents.

Jonah wished once more that she would have allowed him to help her through it. Of course, that was out of the question now. He was a married man, and it wouldn't look right for him to go over to Elaine's by himself to help with chores or anything else she may need to have done. But Elaine's friends would be there for her, helping in whatever way they could. Eventually, Elaine would meet someone special, fall in love, and get married.

"Onah! Onah!"

Jonah jumped at the sound of Mark's voice. He looked over at the boy and laughed when he saw that Mark had turned his empty bowl upside-down and put it on top of his head.

Jonah was glad for this lighthearted moment. It

wasn't good to think too deeply about things that were out of his control.

Removing the bowl from Mark's head, Jonah cleaned Mark's face and hands with a wet paper towel. Then he lifted Mark out of the high chair, returned to his seat at the table, and held the boy in his lap while he waited for the coffee to perk.

Mark burrowed his face into Jonah's chest, and Jonah's throat constricted. The love he felt for the boy was beyond measure, and Jonah had no doubt he would love and nurture this child as if he were his own flesh and blood.

∽

Elaine's throat burned as she struggled not to break down. She, along with several others from their church district, had arrived at the cemetery a few minutes ago. It had been determined that Grandma's death was caused by a heart attack, just as Grandpa's had been. Her somber funeral had taken place inside the Otto Center earlier this morning, and afterward, the mourners had come to the cemetery to lay her body to rest.

If I'd found her sooner, could she have been saved? Elaine winced. Hadn't she thought the very same thing when Grandpa died? All the wishing for what she might have done would do her no good now. Grandma was gone, and Elaine was alone. Now she needed to find the strength to go on.

"We're here for you," Leah whispered as she and Priscilla slipped their arms around Elaine's waist.

Elaine's forehead broke out in a sweat, even though it was a chilly day. Oh, how she needed their friendship—more now than ever before. The anguish she felt over losing Grandma shook Elaine to her very core.

She shivered as Grandma's simple coffin was placed

inside the rough pine box that had been set in the opening of the grave. Elaine felt certain that Grandma was with Jesus and Grandpa now. Her dear grandmother was no longer bound by any illness, and in that, Elaine found some measure of comfort. She really wouldn't wish Grandma back with her, suffering and confused. But someday she would see her grandparents again, when it was her turn to be called to heaven. What a joyous reunion they would have—the three of them.

A group of men from their church district began to sing as the grave was filled in by the pallbearers. With each shovelful of dirt, the heavy feeling in the pit of Elaine's stomach increased. At one point, she felt as if she might faint, but the support of Priscilla and Leah kept her standing firm. As the last shovelful of dirt was placed over the coffin, she remembered the promise she'd made to Grandpa before he'd died—to take care of Grandma.

I did the best I could, Elaine thought. *I only wish I could have done more.*

Bishop Levi asked the congregation to pray the Lord's Prayer silently and concluded the graveside service. It was time to head back to Grandma's house for the funeral meal her friends and neighbors had prepared. Eating at their table wouldn't seem right without Grandma to share in the meal. Elaine would miss all the times she and Grandma had together—even on Grandma's bad days— but somehow she must learn to cope.

As all the people turned from the grave site and began walking back to their buggies, Elaine made a decision. She would try to make the best of her situation and look to God for answers concerning her future. She would claim and cling to His promises to help get her through the grieving process. And she would call upon her special friends, Priscilla and Leah, whenever she had a need. No more trying to do everything in her own strength, for she had tried that and failed. Elaine could count on her dear friends—not just for today, but in the days ahead. And someday, if the Lord willed it, she might meet someone special, fall in love, and get married. But until then, she would put her trust in the Lord.

EPILOGUE

Six months later

ow are you feeling today?" Jonah asked, stepping behind Sara as she stood at the sink, washing their breakfast dishes.

"I'm good. In fact, I feel better than I have in a long time."

"Glad to hear it."

"And remember, the doctor said there is no evidence that MS is linked to any problems with pregnancy." Sara leaned her head against Jonah's chest. "He also said that most women experience relief from many or even all of their MS symptoms during pregnancy, and I'm happy to say that I seem to be one of those women."

Jonah slipped his arms around Sara's waist and gently patted her slightly protruding stomach. They had only been married two months when Sara became pregnant. At first, Jonah had been concerned for Sara's health because of her MS, but Sara had been feeling quite well, for which he was thankful. Their child would be born in November, and Jonah could hardly wait to introduce Mark, who was now three, to his baby brother or sister. Life was good for Jonah, and he was happier than he'd been in a long time.

To add to his joy, the last time Mom and Dad came to visit, Dad had informed Jonah that he was going to sell his buggy shop in Pennsylvania and move to Illinois to be partners with Jonah. Mom and Dad were even going to buy Sara's old house. They would also see that the barn was rebuilt once they'd moved in, but other than that, not much else needed to be done. Having his parents living closer would make Jonah's life complete. Without question, he'd made the right decision when he'd moved to Arthur. At first, he'd thought his future would be with Elaine, but the Lord had other plans for Jonah, and every day he thanked God for bringing him and Sara together.

∽

As Elaine sat on the old swing Grandpa had hung for her when she was a girl, she looked up at the crystal-clear June sky and thought of all the changes that had taken place during the past year. She'd lost both of her grandparents, inherited their house, and with the help of her friends, had learned how to cope with the changes.

In addition to hosting dinners for tourists again with the help of a neighbor girl, Elaine now had a suitor, Ben Otto, who was a cousin of Melvin's wife, Sharon. Ben and his family had moved from Sullivan to Arthur a few months ago. Elaine wasn't sure what she felt for Ben was strong enough to develop into anything serious, but she enjoyed his company, and it was nice to go out to supper with him once in a while.

Hearing a bird chirp overhead, Elaine looked up and saw a bright yellow finch sitting on one of the feeders. She didn't know why, but the beautiful golden bird made her think of Grandma's parakeet, Millie. Grandma had been so upset after the bird had first disappeared. But after Elaine had given Grandma the painted parakeet rock, Grandma became convinced that Millie had come back. It was nice to know that a simple little thing like that rock could have brought Grandma happiness during her last days on earth.

Elaine still missed her grandparents, but she had

learned to take one day at a time and be content. Life was full of disappointments, but there were lots of good things too. Elaine looked forward to seeing what the future held for her, and as she continued to watch the finch, she whispered a prayer. "Heavenly Father, may Your will be done in my life. Please give me the wisdom to make good decisions in all things."

RECIPES

ELAINE'S SUGAR-FREE APPLE PIE

INGREDIENTS:

8 cups peeled and sliced Yellow Delicious apples (or other sweet variety)

1 (12 ounce) can frozen apple juice concentrate

2 tablespoons butter

1 teaspoon cinnamon

½ teaspoon nutmeg

4 tablespoons tapioca

1 (9 inch) pie shell, baked

In a saucepan, cook apples with frozen apple juice concentrate. Add butter, cinnamon, nutmeg, and tapioca. When apples are tender, pour into baked pie shell. Cool and serve with whipped topping or ice cream.

GRANDMA'S SOUR-CREAM PEACH PIE

INGREDIENTS:

1 egg, beaten
½ teaspoon salt
½ teaspoon vanilla
1 cup sour cream
¾ cup sugar
2 tablespoons flour
2½ cups sliced
    fresh peaches

1 (9 inch) pie
    shell, unbaked
Topping:
½ cup butter
⅓ cup sugar
⅓ cup flour
1 teaspoon
    cinnamon

Preheat oven to 375 degrees. In a saucepan, combine egg, salt, vanilla, sour cream, sugar, and flour; add peaches and stir. Pour into unbaked pie shell and bake for 30 minutes or until pie is slightly brown. Remove pie from oven. Combine topping ingredients and spread on top of pie. Bake for 15 minutes.

DISCUSSION QUESTIONS

1. Elaine felt that the care of her grandmother was her responsibility, so she had trouble accepting help from others at first. Have you ever been in a situation where you needed help but tried to do everything on your own? How did you feel when someone stepped in to help?

2. When Edna first learned that she had dementia, she was in denial. Have you or someone you know ever been told by a doctor that something was seriously wrong? If so, how did you deal with it?

3. Elaine told Jonah a lie when she said she didn't love him. Is there ever a time when it's okay to lie?

4. When Sara began having health issues, she put off going to the doctor, using the cost as an excuse. Have you or someone you know ever avoided going to the doctor due to lack of money? Was Sara right in neglecting her health, or should she have asked someone for the money she needed? By not going to the doctor sooner, was Sara putting her son at risk?

5. Edna knew she was losing her memory, and her biggest concern was that she wouldn't remember any of her family or friends. If you suffered from memory loss, what would you do to help remember those who are closest to you?

6. Elaine's closest friends, Leah and Priscilla, helped her deal with the sorrowful events that came her way. What are some ways we can help a friend who is going through a difficult time?

7. Jonah had been hurt by two women and was afraid to take another chance. Have you or someone you know ever been fearful of entering a new relationship because of past failures? If so, how did you or your friend deal with those fears?

8. Elaine's friends often gave her advice. When should we listen to a friend's recommendations, and when should we choose to ignore them?

9. Elaine waited too long to tell her grandma about her illness, and Grandma ended up hearing it from someone else. If you knew someone in your family had been diagnosed with a serious illness, would you tell them right away, or would it be better to keep it from them?

10. Do you think Jonah gave up too quickly on Elaine, even though she said she didn't love him? Should Jonah have tried harder to assure Elaine of his love for her and his willingness to help during her time of need?

11. Do you think Elaine was being overprotective of her grandmother? As a caregiver to a relative with dementia, how would you handle things?

12. While reading this story, what did you learn about the Amish community of Arthur, Illinois?

13. Did any passages of scripture mentioned in the book specifically speak to you? If so, in what way?

14. Does reading about the Amish influence you to simplify your life? What are some ways we can simplify?

ABOUT THE AUTHOR

New York Times bestselling and award-winning author Wanda E. Brunstetter is one of the founders of the Amish fiction genre. She has written close to 100 books translated into four languages. With over 11 million copies sold, Wanda's stories consistently earn spots on the nation's most prestigious bestseller lists and have received numerous awards.

Wanda's ancestors were part of the Anabaptist faith, and her novels are based on personal research intended to accurately portray the Amish way of life. Her books are well read and trusted by many Amish, who credit her for giving readers a deeper understanding of the people and their customs.

When Wanda visits her Amish friends, she finds herself drawn to their peaceful lifestyle, sincerity, and close family ties. Wanda enjoys photography, ventriloquism, gardening, bird-watching, beachcombing, and spending time with her family. She and her husband, Richard, have been blessed with two grown children, six grandchildren, and two great-grandchildren.

To learn more about Wanda, visit her website at www.wandabrunstetter.com.

MORE FROM WANDA!

The Amish Hawaiian Adventures

Join Mandy and Ellen on a trip of a lifetime to Hawaii in this two-novel collection. Will the discoveries these Amish girls make forever change the direction of their lives?

The Hawaiian Quilt

Before joining the Amish church and settling into family life, Mandy convinces three friends to join her on a cruise of the Hawaiian Islands. When Mandy and Ellen miss the ship after a port of call on Kauai, they get a room at a bed & breakfast where they make new friends, learn about local history, and participate in Christian church. But when it is time to fly home, Mandy feels torn between feelings for Ken Williams, a farmer on Kauai, and Gideon Eash, her boyfriend in Indiana.

The Hawaiian Discovery

Ellen Lambright thought she was going back to Hawaii only to help her best friend through multiple challenges, but she also befriends a man who has been hiding from his past. Reuben Zook works on the Williams family's organic farm, far from his past mistakes and burning regrets. The attraction is mutual, but Ellen's commitment to the Amish faith stands between them. Could a heartfelt discovery lead to forgiveness, reunion, and love? Or is Ellen's destiny waiting for her in Indiana?

Paperback / 978-1-64352-204-3 / $16.99